Wendy Roberts
was recently A
women's prison.
novel in a list w
and children's novels. She lives in the north of England.

Honesty's Daughter

Wendy Robertson

headline

First published in 2003
by HEADLINE BOOK PUBLISHING

First published in paperback in 2004
by HEADLINE BOOK PUBLISHING

10 9 8 7 6 5 4 3 2 1

ISBN 0 7472 6606 9

Typeset in Times by Avon DataSet Ltd,
Bidford-on-Avon, Warwickshire

Printed and bound in Great Britain by
Mackays of Chatham plc, Chatham, Kent

Paper and cover board used by Headline are natural, recyclable
products made from wood grown in sustainable forests.
The manufacturing processes conform to the environmental
regulations of the country of origin.

HEADLINE BOOK PUBLISHING
A division of Hodder Headline
338 Euston Road
London NW1 3BH

www.headline.co.uk
www.hodderheadline.com
www.wendyrobertson.com

For Judith Gates
in appreciation of our continuing conversation

Acknowledgements

Although Benbow Hall, and the Benbow family which lie at the heart of this story are pure fiction, this novel was inspired by Whitworth Hall, for hundreds of years the home of the Shafto family, whose ancestor Bobby Shafto is familiar to all lovers of English nursery rhyme. The Hall is now a hotel partly owned by the Gates family, to whom I am indebted for privileged access to the Hall, its extensive park and its wonderful walled garden. I would thank Peter Clark the gardener, who allowed me to share his insights into, his old photographs and his unique knowledge of the garden and the house as well as Dawn Smith, who kept me going with coffee and biscuits as I scribbled away for hours in the toasting heat of the vinery. Also artist Fiona Horner, who, like me, was inspired by the Hall. I would thank Judy Otter who offered me peace and quiet beside the Tasman Sea to complete my work on this long novel. Last, but most certainly not least I would like to thank Gillian Wales and her staff at the wonderful Bishop Auckland library for their support and assistance with the research without which this novel would never have been possible.

The Hall by Fiona Horner

Main Players

This generation
Astrid Benbow – amateur artist
Her mother Carmel Benbow – gardener

Her brothers
Michael John Benbow – soldier
Ambrose Benbow – nail-maker & flautist

Carmel's servant Melanie Tyler
Jacob Ellenberg – a friend of Rufus Benbow, Astrid's father
Jerry Carmedy – estate manager/agent at Benbow

Keziah Leeming, formerly Lomas – gypsy horse-trader
Her husband Freddy Leeming – blacksmith
Edith Leeming – Keziah's sister-in-law
Her son Jack Lomas – inventor & entrepreneur
Her daughter Honesty Lomas Leeming – acrobat

Constance Redoute – young American of substance
Her father General Richard Redoute
Their servant Aunt Beatrice

Lady Margaret Seland – an aristocrat of sorts
Her daughter Gertrude – a modern woman

The next generation
Rose Benbow, foster daughter of Astrid
Rufus, twin son of Astrid
Kenneth, twin son of Astrid

Prologue

Honesty keeps her eyes low, gazing no higher than the diamond pendant that nestles against the slightly withered skin just above the fold between her ladyship's breasts. She does not raise her eyes to the face. You never look at the faces. She was told that on her first day in this house.

'How very nice. You've done very well, Mrs McCoy. Absolutely a silk purse from a sow's ear.' Her ladyship's voice is soft, like the inside of a goose-feather pillow. 'Now, child! Turn around.'

Honesty resents being called 'child'. She's fourteen and tall for her age. Why, sometimes she's even taken for fifteen.

A dig in the ribs from the housekeeper makes her turn round so that her back is to the two women. She wishes they'd let her keep her boots on. The stone floor is so very cold on her bare feet. She can feel her ladyship's butterfly hands on her waist tugging at the hair where it falls from the new green ribbon.

'Very nice,' repeats the soft voice. 'Well done, Mrs McCoy.'

'Thank you, ma'am.'

'You may take her now.'

Honesty feels the shirring rush of skirts, smells the scent of sweet sweat and thick perfume, hears the tap of heels on the stone. Then she is alone with the housekeeper.

With unusual intimacy, Mrs McCoy links her arm through Honesty's and steers her down the corridor. They turn onto the wide main landing and make their way past the ornate door of the best guest room to a narrow door further down. The housekeeper selects a key from her ring and opens this door wide. Honesty can see a fireplace with a blazing fire, and red plush hanging from the bedposts. The room is empty.

'Now you go in there, child. Go in and sit down on the little chair.'

'What do I do? What do you want me to do?' Honesty tries very hard to keep her voice steady.

'You wait till he comes. Then you curtsy to him proper. And you do what he says. Mebbe you can do those little tricks of yours.' Mrs McCoy's voice is grim. She gives Honesty a sharp push so that she almost tumbles into the room. The key clicks in the door behind her.

She looks round. It's quite a small room with a second door in the wall opposite the bed. The room is bigger than her own cupboard space in the top attic but certainly smaller than any on this floor. Honesty knows this from doing the fires. But this room is new to her. She has never lit this fire. There is little space to spare here. Certainly not much room for cartwheels and handstands.

Beside the bed – itself not much more than a swagged couch against one wall – is a very wide padded chair. The flicker from the branch of candles on the dresser beside it deepens the shadows in its carved red velvet. Beside that stands a small chair with wooden arms. Honesty sits on the smaller chair and waits.

She sits there for what seems like a very long while. The heat from the fire seeps into her and makes her drowsy. This is really a very nice room, she thinks dreamily. So much nicer than . . . She sits bold upright as the second door opens and an old man slips inside. She gulps. He is stout and not very tall. He has a polished, clean face with twinkling eyes and a well-brushed beard. His long embroidered dressing gown is tied neatly with a silk cord and his bare white feet are thrust into velvet slippers. The air from the door brings with it the fruity, dusty smell of his cigar.

She considers for a moment whether even here she should not look this one in the face. After all there is no doubt he *is* one of them. Then she lifts her head and looks him in the eye. He smiles at her quite sweetly and puts the cigar between his teeth so that he can use two hands to shut and lock the door properly. Then he turns back to face her. 'Now, my dear,' he said. 'I'm told you are the most wonderful contortionist.'

Part One

The Edwardians

County Durham
Late August 1906

August 9 London: Boer War Commission says corruption and incompetence in the war cost over £1 million

August 15 Germany: King Edward VII spent a pleasant day with his nephew Kaiser Wilhelm II . . . In the afternoon the two monarchs drove by motor car to the spa of Homburg, which is a favourite with the King

August 25 St Petersburg: Premier Stolypin survives a bomb attack which kills thirty people, including his daughter

One

The Shooting Party

8am

Astrid Benbow peered down at the busy scene below her narrow window. The cloaked and gaitered men huddled together by the portico steps, too well schooled to take their places in the brakes before their sovereign had mounted his waiting vehicle. The still morning air fizzed with the jingle of harnesses, the guttural ejaculation of men's voices, the tinkle of women's laughter and the low growling of dogs. Human and animal breath joined together in the chill morning air before the late August sun rose to burn off the dawn mist and brighten the day. The extraordinary summer heatwave was just about over and the chill of autumn was making itself felt here in the north.

Two heavy brakes creaked on their springs a short distance from the steps; behind them lurked a wagonette piled with baskets which were still being fussed over by a grizzled man in livery. Behind the wagonette eight saddled horses skittered in the gravel, each held quiet by its own whispering groom.

Astrid had seen many such mornings here before the great doors of Seland Hall, the country home of the recently ennobled Lord Seland. As a child, she'd ridden her pony across that gravel with his daughter, Gertrude Seland who was her friend. How many misty mornings had they, straight-backed on their ponies, bumped their way through the paths and dripping woodland of Seland Park? What pleasure they'd taken in outstripping Mr Warrington the groom who was hampered by his rather inferior hack. Gertrude was not at home this weekend. It seemed she'd married a rather low South African and gone to find diamonds.

Astrid opened the window wide and peeked sideways to catch sight of her friend Constance being led down from the stable block on her tall black mare by old Mr Warrington. Constance's mount, Diamond, had spent yesterday locked in a livery carriage on the train from London but she looked in fine enough fettle today. Astrid peered closer at Constance and smiled. Oh dear. She was riding astride! She did so like to tease. American girls were often like that. This boldness, this sense of fun had attracted her to Constance from the first.

At the very front of the cavalcade the senior Seland groom started to mutter into the ear of the lead horse which was jumping about in its leather harness. The man pulled the horse's head close, snuckled into its ear with fleshy, pouting lips. It settled down, quiet again.

The chatter down below faltered for a second. Then the voices started again as, with a small dog yapping at his heels, the elegantly caped King trod lightly down the steps in his highly polished boots. His gait was graceful for someone of his bulk. Beside him fluttered Lady Seland, smart in a narrow-waisted jacket and a flowing skirt whose sleek lines had the stamp of Paris. She was wearing indoor clothes. Obviously she had not opted to go and watch the men at their easy slaughter.

Just to the left of the King, swathed in tailored outdoor clothes, was the rather stout well-dressed woman who was the King's great friend and companion. To his right was another favourite: a clever woman who knew his appetites and even after so many years could think up ways to entertain and amuse him. She too was wrapped up close against the biting northeast wind. These women would watch the kill and then join the King at his alfresco luncheon. Their devotion knew no bounds and their stout figures were evidence that, like him, they would relish the fine food wrought by Monsieur Ledon, Lady Seland's chef: delicacies which were even now laid tenderly in tissue in large baskets and being watched over in the wagonette by the butler, Mr Selby.

Behind these two favourites fluttered a covey of women, coming not to join the shoot but merely to admire the King and their own men embarking on their day. Unlike the loyal Mrs Keppel each one of them was secretly pleased that they weren't condemned to drive out to the moors to endure a chilly day's sport.

The woman at his side drew His Majesty's attention to the young American girl on the black horse at the back of the party. The whole company turned to scrutinise her, as though she were some strange species of bird. One woman fished a lorgnette from her bosom to see more clearly.

The King put up a podgy hand and Constance cantered across and spoke to him. Her back was as straight as a ramrod and her beautiful face with its very white skin was veiled lightly under her black hat.

The King spoke. All Astrid could hear from the window was the questioning tone in his voice. Now the chatter of the whole group was stilled, and Constance's clear voice travelled clearly up to Astrid on the still morning air. 'I'm just a poor unknowin' American, sir. You must forgive me.'

His voice rumbled again.

'Well, back at home, sir,' she said, 'we-all hunt bears and muskrats, and the occasional Indian. Mountain roads're too tortuous to ride woman-ways.'

Astrid smiled in admiration. Constance did not normally speak in that drawling fashion: normally it was hard to tell her from an English girl apart from an occasional dropped g. She would say 'goin', and 'blowin', and did not seem to notice it. The King knew she didn't talk like a cowboy; he'd spoken to Constance for several minutes last night, complimenting her graciously on her gown and asking about her father and the

Rocky Mountains. She'd answered him without mincing or lowering her eyes. The King beamed across at her, savouring as he always did the company of an intelligent woman. Then, as she flowed into a full explanation of her life in America, his gaze had left her and he'd asked a woman down on his right about the new German play which had just started a run in London.

Astrid had seen His Majesty do this before: ask questions of people and withdraw his attention from them before they had answered fully. He was like a fisherman with many hooks on his line.

Now down below in the courtyard there was an expectant silence. The King barked a laugh and made a great play of getting her joke. 'I swear, Miss Redoute, you're playing the American on me.' There was faint mimicry of her accent in his voice. This brought a tittering chuckle from the ladies at his side, followed by a rumble of amusement from Lord Seland and his friends. Then the King mounted the front brake with the ladies and his lordship. Some of the other men crowded into the second brake with the dogs. Mr Selby the butler and two heavily shawled maids sat primly in the wagonette among the baskets and boxes. The other men mounted horses with the help of their grooms and the party moved off slowly, those on horseback being very careful to stay behind the leading brake.

Astrid knew that Constance planned to trail the party to the moor's edge, and then leave them to complete her early morning ride away from the sound of the guns. Constance loved to ride. She'd had two fine horses shipped from America and hunted every other week during the season with friends in the Cotswolds. She hunted side-saddle, of course; to ride astride would have offended the sensibilities of the hunting fraternities. Astrid wondered briefly why her friend had taken the risk of riding astride today. To draw the King's attention, of course. In that case it had worked. She was lucky. The King was known to be frosty about people who broke protocol.

The cluster of women at the great door melted back into the house, some to complete their breakfast, some to write letters, to play games, attend to embroidery and the more urgent business of London gossip. The house was full to the seams, as it always was when the King joined any of his friends for a shooting weekend. The conversation might even touch upon the recent events in Russia that the Czar, the King's cousin, had handled so well. A severe hand was always the best way with these annoying insurrections.

Astrid, who had forsworn breakfast in her customary desire to be alone, stood at the window and watched until the shooting party and Constance, trailing on her black horse, were out of sight. She closed the window, twitched the curtain into place and turned back into a room which, though elegant and well appointed was somewhat narrow, matching her own modest status as a guest in this crowded house.

The sense of displacement that she'd felt since she and her friend had arrived at Seland Hall swept back over her. How much she regretted now that she had submitted in London to the blandishments of Lady Seland. Her ladyship had gone on so winningly about how much she missed her own dear daughter Gertrude, now unfortunately in South Africa with that dreadful man. How *much* her ladyship thought of poor dear Carmel, Astrid's mother, who had been her lifelong friend. She had written to Carmel to tell her of the invitation. They all knew how *much* the King enjoyed having young beauty around him. It brightened his eye and lightened his step. His more mature companions no longer rose so readily to his witty banter. With them he could no longer enjoy the sport of blushing rewards, and lowered eyes. Younger women found it harder to resist the gallantry, the power and the patronage fused into one jocular remark, one thick well-manicured hand laid on a bare forearm.

The King had mentioned specially how much he had enjoyed Astrid's company last time he was at Seland. And

how much, went on Lady Seland, the King would enjoy
meeting the young American daughter of an heroic general of
the civil war as well as – dare we say the words? – one of the
richest men in America. Americans were very fashionable in
London these days. So charming. Her ladyship's tone had
become a little shrill at that point. She was irritated that her
old friend's rather plain daughter should resist an invitation
that would have been jumped at by anyone else.

Astrid would indeed have resisted Lady Seland's persuasion
but she could not resist the desire to surprise her friend
Constance, who would, she knew, very much like to meet the
King of England. Her hunting forays into the Cotswolds had
provided her with many honourables, even a duke or two as
notches on her social belt. But to be with the King close by!
She would be very pleased.

Astrid, wondering now whether she should make a move to
get dressed, was pulled from her thoughts by the creak of the
bedroom door. A slender, neat girl in sombre morning uniform
glided in. Her skin was honey-coloured and her soft black hair
struggled to escape the confines of her uniform cap; the face,
lit by rather over-large dark eyes, was surprisingly finely
moulded. But there was strain in that face. Shadows under the
eyes.

The girl flinched at the sight of Astrid. 'Beg pardon, miss. I
should have lit this before you got up but there are so very
many fires today. I thought you'd be downstairs with the ladies.
They're all at breakfast.' She turned to go.

Astrid smiled and sat down in the window seat. 'Just pretend
I'm downstairs having breakfast with the ladies. Pretend I'm
not here. Do continue.'

The girl moved stiffly around the room under Astrid's
vaguely benevolent eye. She placed her workbox by the
fireplace and took out the sacking sheet to spread it carefully
over the carpet. She opened the box and laid out her tools.
Deftly she scraped out the ashes of the dead fire into a shallow

tin and set about laying the fire and polishing the surround.
She lit the fire and sat back on her heels to wait while it caught.
Then, with the neat economy of long practice, she returned
everything to her box. She stood up and caught a glimpse of
the watching Astrid in the overmantel mirror. Catching Astrid's
gaze she burst out, 'I'm real sorry I'm late with this, miss. I'm
very late this morning.'

Astrid recognised the familiar low slightly sing-song tones:
echoes from her own childhood. 'What're you called?' she
asked, her head on one side. 'I think I must know you.'

The girl stared closely at her. 'I don't think so. I never seen
you before. I'm called Honesty. That's a flower with a bright
white disc. Honesty Leeming's my name, miss. But in this
house you've to call me Peggy.'

'Why must I call you Peggy? Honesty's a much better name.
A white disc. I like that.' Astrid felt drawn to this girl.

'The fireplace girl here is always called Peggy, miss. Always
has been, always will be. Mrs McCoy – that's the housekeeper
– says so.'

'And where d'you come from, Honesty Leeming?'

'Everywhere and nowhere, miss. I'm *romani*.'

'Ah yes. I was beginning to think that.' Astrid smiled slightly.
The sing-song tones had told their own tale. 'To be honest,
though, it's very unusual to find a *romani* girl . . .' She left
unsaid that people didn't usually allow gypsies across the
kitchen threshold, much less in their back parlours, their
corridors and their bedrooms. The epithet *thieving gypsies* was
easy in the mouths of people of all classes.

Honesty sat back on her heels and turned round to see
Astrid properly. She stared at her for a few moments, then
relaxed. There was something about this lady, sitting there
with the window behind her, her hands folded quietly in her
lap. 'You're thinking why'd they let a gypsy work indoors,
miss? Well, I came here well recommended. My mother knows
the lady that obtained this place here for me. I wanted to work

in a house. My mother hates houses but she knows that I like them. She says to me that working here would mean I would always know what went on behind such doors as these. Nothing lost. She's a bit of a queer'n, my mother.'

'Your mother found you this place?'

'In a roundabout way. My mother's a very . . . well, she always gets what she wants.'

Astrid leaned forward to look more closely at Honesty. A child, really. No more than fourteen. And those fine dark looks. She should have realised at the outset that she was *romani*. 'So where does your mother live? Is she travelling?'

'She lives by Benbow Hall, miss. At the forge. She's married to the blacksmith there. This man's not my father, you understand. My father's long gone.'

Asrid laughed. 'I know Benbow Hall very well.'

The girl nodded eagerly. 'It's a lovely place, miss. And they like the *romani* there. They say the man of that house was a *rai*, a scholar who knew much about the gypsies. He's dead now but it's still a good place to call. Known for it. The signs are always left. They say when he died they burnt his van. He'd had a van and he'd done some travelling himself.'

'I know all about that, Honesty,' said Astrid. 'I knew this *rai*. I knew him because he was my father.'

The girl shook her head, smiling broadly. 'Can you believe it? I see it now, miss. You're Ambrose's sister. Daughter to the old *rai*. You live in the city. In London.'

'You know Ambrose?'

Honesty's smile faltered a little. 'I used to, when I was there. I went fishing with him when we first settled at Benbow. He knew nothing about fishing. We used to play in my mother's *vardo*, her van. And he would pretend to be king of the gypsies. I would dress up in my mother's skirts and he would draw pictures of me. He was always round Freddy Leeming's forge. That's the man my mother married.'

Astrid relaxed completely. Freddy Leeming was the quiet blacksmith who always shod the Benbow horses: a dour fellow who lived in the house by the forge with his equally dour sister. But Ambrose had always been fond of Freddy. More so than Michael John, her other brother. That one was contemptuous of Freddy but was fascinated by the massive strength of the blacksmith and the power of fire over iron. On his long holidays from school he liked to hang around the forge.

Freddy Leeming married! Astrid's mother had always said Freddy, with his sister to take care of him, was the primal bachelor, a man destined to be alone.

'So you took Freddy's name? You call yourself Leeming?' she said to the girl.

'Well, my mother married the blacksmith proper. In the little church at the hall. Our real name is Lomas. Our Jack's father was a Lomas, so he is pure gypsy, but me, my mother had me with this *gorgio* horse-doctor she took a fancy to. Never married him, but. She says that's why I like houses.'

'So why call yourself Leeming?'

Honesty shrugged. 'She says to me to use Leeming, as it would get us more places in the *gorgio* world than the old name. She said the old name was always there when we needed it. But our Jack refused. So he's Jack Lomas.'

'And is Edith gone from the forge house? Freddy's sister?'

Honesty shook her head. 'My ma says *no fear*. Edith takes care of Freddy. My mother keeps her *vardo*. That's her home. And then she has her business.'

'Business?'

'She's a horsewoman. Known for it. She breeds and breaks horses. Trades with the *gorgio*. She's trained horses for Mrs Benbow.'

'How did she end up at Benbow?'

'Well, she was travelling through Durham to Appleby Fair and her horses needed shoeing. Freddy Leeming did a good job on them. He wouldn't take money off her. Not a penny.

15

Then she moved on. He followed her. Followed her to Appleby and brought her back after she'd sold her horses there, at the big fair. She must've wanted to do it – get married – 'cause my mother never does nothing she doesn't want to.'

Astrid frowned. 'So she's a horsewoman. She rides horses?'

'Nah. Not really. She breeds'm, breaks'm, heals'm, sells'm.'

'That's very strange, a woman doing that.'

'Aye. And it's even stranger than that. She's *romani* and among us only men do the dealing. At the fair she deals through a man, an old friend of hers. The kings, the *romani* kings, they say she can't deal herself.'

Astrid knew about this. Her father had written learned papers on the kings, the tribal chiefs held in such great respect. 'So,' she ventured. 'Your mother fell in love with Freddy Leeming?'

'Love? Dunno about that. More like he fell for her. And he's mebbe fourteen years younger than her. Not much older than my brother Jack who's seventeen. Freddy had to persuade my ma, I'm telling yer. He kind of heated her up and wore her down, like she was a bit of old iron on his anvil.'

Astrid laughed, shaking her head.

'She's still only half-house, like. She stays at the forge a lot. But she keeps her *vardo* in the field so she can breed her horses and keep her chickens.' Comfortable now, Honesty squinted up at Astrid. 'That Mrs Benbow, I suppose she's your mother, Mrs Benbow, isn't she? She's a bit of a queer'n herself, if you don't mind my saying so. Not bothered about the *vardo* nor the horses. Doesn't worry or nag. That's not common. Other people're sniffy about it, like. That Mr Tyler, odd man at Benbow Hall, he don't like us, no more than his wife. They'd like my mother out of there tomorrow. But not your ma. Half fairy herself.' The girl put her hand to her mouth. 'Sorry, miss, I shouldn't . . .'

Astrid shook her head, unwilling to end the conversation. So much better than that going on round the breakfast table downstairs.

'Her ladyship'll skelp us for talking to you. But it was nice, talking. Bit of a fairy yourself. Helped us forget me own troubles, to be honest.' The girl reached for the metal mantelpiece and pulled herself to her feet, wincing a little. 'Never talked to no one in this house like that. Not ever.'

'What is it?' said Astrid sharply. 'Is there something wrong?'

The girl stared at her. 'I've got these bruises, miss,' she said slowly.

'Bruises? You have bruises?'

The girl stared at her and sighed a deep sigh, the shadows under her eyes darkening. Then to Astrid's horror the large eyes filled, then spilled over with tears. Honesty stood there, arms loose by her sides, and started to sob.

'Goodness, child!' Astrid went and put her arm round her shoulder. 'Come. Sit down.' She drew her towards the window seat. The girl pulled away, sniffing. 'No, miss. I canna sit there. Her ladyship'll have us. Her or Mrs McCoy.'

Astrid forced her down in the seat. 'Sit down and do as you're told. Now tell me. What on earth is wrong with you?'

Honesty reached down and pulled her apron up over her head, sprinkling the room with fire dust that glittered briefly in the morning light. For a few moments the sacking apron muffled her sobs. Astrid sat on the seat and carefully lifted the apron down to reveal the girl, her cap now quite awry and her honey skin sprinkled with coal dust. 'What is it?' Astrid said again, her voice very severe. 'Whatever has happened?'

The girl sighed very deeply, hiccoughed and stopped crying. 'It's the King,' she said sadly.

Astrid blinked. 'The King?' She thought of the gypsy kings. The men who said what could or could not be sold at Appleby.

'Last night. It was the King. The big man, he was . . .'

'What happened?' Astrid took the girl's hand and held it tight.

Honesty sat in silence.

17

Astrid put out her other hand and clasped the girl's fingers between her own. 'Start from the beginning and tell me what happened.'

Honesty looked at her and then down at their joined hands. Then she gave a small nod and took a deep breath. 'It was me own fault, miss. I do these cartwheels and things, walk on my hands. I can put my feet right by my head. I used to do it on the road to earn a few pennies. Well, the staff here, they like me to do it for them. Give them a laugh when they have a minute off. Mebbe after supper in the servants' hall. They'll give me a penny. Miss Mason, that's her ladyship's maid, was quite taken with it. Told her ladyship, who watched me do all this, just outside the laundry. She watched from a window. Then yesterday afternoon I was doing my last round with the coal scuttles. Her ladyship caught me on the back corridor. I'd turned my back like they say we should. But she called my name.'

'And . . .'

'She told me then. "Peggy," she said. Like I said, they all call me Peggy here, not Honesty.'

'So she said *Peggy*? What else?'

'She said "Peggy, you are to go to the King's room tonight at eleven o'clock." ' Lady Seland's clipped voice filtered through in curious echo within Honesty's sing-song tones.

'I told her I'd seen to the King's bedroom. The scuttles were full in the dressing room and the little study as well as the bedroom.' She stopped. 'Turned out it wasn't *his* bedroom she was talking about.'

'And she said . . .?'

'She said that was *immaterial*. I was to go to the King after they'd all had their dinner. That the King would be entertained by my acrobatics. That the King had seen me and liked what her ladyship called *my dark looks*.' Honesty paused. 'I tried to ask more but she put her hand up like this.' She wrested her hand from Astrid and spread out her fingers and put them over her face. 'And before I could say anything else she'd swep' off.

18

Why, miss, I sat there at the top of the stairs and cried my eyes out. I an't ever cried since I was six and fell off this big mare my mother had bred. The man that bought it called it Catherseed. It won races after. Anyway I fell off and cried and my mother threw me right back on again.' She paused.

Astrid frowned. 'About last night, Honesty. That was it? They left you crying on the stairs?'

Honesty shook her head. 'The second footman nearly fell over me there on the stairs. He took me to Mrs McCoy. This feller told me she was the hardest housekeeper he'd ever had the privilege of working with. Even so, she didn't like her girls crying. Couldn't stand it. Her that could make grown gardeners cry! Anyways she sent him away and set me down on her own chair. She gave me a drink with a nip of something strong in it. A cup of tea from her own hand! Can you believe me? Then she put her hand on my shoulder. Seems she knew all about it, what her ladyship said. And she wasn't pleased, I could tell that. So she put her hand on my shoulder. Her hand! Do you know, miss, no one has so much as touched me, not once, since I came to this house six months ago? Not one person. But d'you know Mrs McCoy was as kind to me as your mother ever was? She listened to what I told her and then gave a sigh, like she was this very old and tired horse. Then she says this. "It's the King's command, Peggy. It's the King's command." '

Astrid shivered. 'What did you say then?'

'I telt her my name was Honesty, not Peggy, and she must call me that. I was still crying, then, like.'

'Is that all she said?'

'Nah. She said that I should not worry. And she called me by my real name. She said that the King always took care of people. He always did. That he was a great man.'

'So what did you do?'

'Well, miss, Mrs McCoy was very good to us. She let us have half an hour off that evening. She got that footman to fill the hip bath in her sitting room with hot water. All in secret, 'cause she said we must tell no one about this. She gave us her own scented soap. She blazed up her fire so I could dry my hair. She brushed it and spread it like a curtain over her fireguard. Then she tied it with a new green ribbon. She even gave us a cotton nightdress of her own to wear. And this really nice shawl with a fringe and a checked pattern. She told me her ladyship had got it in Scotland and when it was worn a bit, she gave it to her.'

'And then?' Astrid sighed in savage anticipation.

'And then she took me to this little room along by the King's room. Then he came in, in this long embroidered coat and a nightshirt under.' She paused. 'He had bare feet in his slippers. Fancy! The King in bare feet.'

Astrid looked past the girl's white face out of the window. How long had she been in London? Five years? Six? She was little interested in society. She did attend an occasional restrained soirée in her aunt's house in Devonshire Place. She'd endured the odd card party or dance. Most of her time was spent improving her drawing at the studio in Chelsea, quietly relishing the ebb and flow of the people who drew and painted or bought drawings and paintings. And those who wrote bad poetry and half-plays. And those who pretended they did these things and did virtually nothing. Such people were free, unconstrained by petty morals; ultimately they made love with whom they wished. Astrid, constrained by her own reserve, had managed to keep herself slightly apart from all this. Merely to survive among those lively people, she'd created a little repertoire of mild flirting and teasing. She felt no obligation to take it any further. Not one person, man or woman, had such an impact on her as to make her abandon her self-imposed code. But their behaviour no longer worried her. It was their way of showing their freedom and for that she quite admired it.

But the account she was listening to now was not a tale of freedom and experiment. Instead, it was as though the last thousand years had not been: feudal rights were still being exacted. They were as old as castles and moats, as outdated as knights riding with squires.

And wasn't this the twentieth century? There were railways and canals, bridges and great steam engines. There were trains you could travel on at as much as sixty miles an hour. All life was turning wheels. Motorcars buzzed along on roads. Bicycles meandered along pathways. Women wore trousers under their skirts to make the cycling easier. They would even be voting for Parliament if the recent ferments were anything to go by. Things were changing. Think of Constance riding astride on her black mare.

Honesty was watching her anxiously.

'What then?' she asked quietly.

Honesty took a deep breath. 'The King told me I might show him my acrobatics. But I should take off my nightie or my legs would get tangled in so much linen. So there I was in my shift and drawers . . .' Her voice faded away for a second. 'Anyway, I did some tumbles and, well, he clapped his hands and said "Bravo!" and to be honest I felt quite nice.'

Astrid became aware of the girl's eyes boring into the side of her face. 'What happened wasn't my fault, miss. It was not my will,' said Honesty. 'What could I do?'

Astrid almost laughed. 'Of course not. Of course it wasn't your fault.'

'He says then I am a naughty girl and'd caught his eye with my dark looks. He said I was an exotic flower. And then he says I should come and sit on his lap, right across, a leg each side.' She paused. 'He says I was to show him what acrobatics I could do just there. He asked me to fasten my hands behind his neck and I did this. He told me to loosen them and I couldn't. "Oh dear," he says again, "what a very naughty girl you are." '

'No, Honesty.' Astrid was shaking. 'You were not naughty. It was not your fault.'

'I did – I do – know about that thing that happens, miss. Haven't I seen stallions serving the mares since I was a little'n? I've seen that. But I couldn't quite reckon what it was really like with humans. I reckoned that they couldn't really mount you, can they?'

Astrid shook her head.

'I thought you'd have to kind of lie side by side, kind of facing for it to happen.'

Astrid blushed. She'd thought something similar. Once, when she was eighteen, she'd lain on her side in her own bed, mimicking the actions she thought might be involved. It seemed impossible. Really. Then one of her poet friends gave her a Persian book that seemed to solve some of the problems in picturesque ways. The figures on the pages looked beautiful but what they were doing looked tortuous and laughable.

And she knew about men's bodies. She'd seen the great statues in Florence that showed you the whole of a man – beautiful satiny flesh compelling your attention on the pulsing muscle and sinew beneath. The *thing* that proclaimed the manhood of these glorious sculpted men seemed small and budlike, unlike those in the Persian pictures. The thing that men and women did together still, to her, seemed impossible, even laughable. But this was no laughing matter, she thought soberly. Not for Honesty Leeming.

The girl was ploughing on, her voice slightly hoarse now. 'I'd not realised, miss, that they could do it to you, just sitting there. Suddenly he grasped me and pressed into me. He held me so tight that he pushed all the breath out of me. I gasped out then that there was no place at all to put that thing, I told him that. There was no place to put it but he just laughed heartily and reared away. It hurt so very much. I tried to unclasp my hands but it was like they were stuck with glue.'

'Oh, my dear girl!' Astrid's flesh was creeping with shame; her heart was leaping with pity for what had been done.

'He kept on gasping and sayin, "Don't worry, child, don't worry, child" over and over again. In this kind, gruff voice . . . I can tell you miss, it really hurt. Hard to say how much. Then he put his head back and was snoring in a second. I dare not move a muscle. It seemed like there was sticky fire between my legs, in my belly. I just lay there sprawled on him. Then he woke up again and stretched and yawned. He lifted me off quite gently and put me on the bed. Then he stood there beside me and pulled my nightie right over me, tucking it in like I was just a babe! He took my hand quite kindly. He pressed a gold sovereign in my hand. Gold! Then he chucked me under the chin like I was a little'n. "You're a good girl, my dear," he said. "A very good girl." And he'd gone. My own blood was on the bed and on the sheets. You know what I was thinking? I thought about them maids that do the beds. What would they think of me this morning, when they stripped that bed? I was crying my eyes out. What'd they think of me?'

'It was not your fault.' Images were cycling through Astrid's brain.

'Mrs McCoy kept saying that. She was there when I got back to my room. When I saw her I bawled like a young'n. She had my little fire on, the hip bath squashed in there beside it. The water was steaming. She helped me with the bloody nightie. But she gave me warm milk with honey in and told me not to worry about the bed in that room by the King's room. She'd change it herself. No one would know. I must not say anything and no one should know. She musta put sommat in the milk 'cause I slept like an old dog. I was late up this morning but no one shouted at me. She musta told them to lay off me.'

Astrid put her hands over her face.

Honesty placed her hand, small and square, rough-skinned and covered with coal dust, on the silk shoulder of Astrid's dressing gown. 'Nowt for you to be sorry for, miss. Nowt to do with you, after all. D'you know what Mrs McCoy said when she was drying me down like a baby? She had this big dry towel. Like one from her ladyship's closet. I've never been so clean. Two baths in a day!' Honesty paused again. 'Do you know what she said?'

Astrid put her hands in her lap and sat up straight. 'What did she say?'

'She said that she was sorry, but we had to endure things we knew weren't right. This was our destiny. *Destiny*. Endure it. That's what she said. And she told us not to tell anyone. That wasn't allowed.' Honesty, dried tears now streaking her blackened cheeks, stood up. She caught sight of herself in the narrow mirror of the dresser. 'Hah! Just look at us! What a sight. I'd better get on. I'm late as it is, and Mrs McCoy's good mood won't last all day.' She collected her wooden box and her brush.

Astrid opened the door for her. 'Can't I do anything for you, Honesty?'

'Nah. There's no going back in this, miss. I'll not be the same again.' Her eye wandered down to the little name card in the door-slot. *Miss Astrid Benbow* in Mrs McCoy's immaculate school copperplate. 'I never saw you here before, Miss Benbow. Or at Benbow Hall, come to that.'

'I have never been there since my father – your *romani rai* – died. I have lived in London for six years now. Since I was eighteen.'

'Never?'

'Not till now. I am going to Benbow Hall to visit my mother tomorrow.'

'Hey, how I wish I could go there! I wish I could see my mother and my brother Jack. My brother Jack, you know? He is a magician. He makes you laugh. He can conjure things from the air.' She sighed. 'I wouldn't even mind seeing Freddy or Auntie Edith.'

Astrid fought off a feeling of helpless lethargy; she was suddenly exhausted with this unusual conversation. 'You could come with me and my friend Miss Redoute, Honesty. Then you can see this brother of yours. Her ladyship has offered her

carriage and her coachman. There'd be room for you.' One part
of Astrid wondered what on earth she was doing, offering to
share a carriage with this distressed gypsy girl. Even in Chelsea
you'd think twice before making such an offer.

Honesty Leeming shook her head. 'Canna do that, miss.
Days off cancelled this Sunday, because of the shooting party,
like. Even on an ordinary Sunday I only have the afternoon off.
I've tried walking home a few times.' Her grimace was nearly a
laugh. 'I'm no sooner there than I have to start back. Once I set
out in the rain that turned to a storm. I had to take shelter, then
had to turn round before I arrived!'

Astrid was angry. 'Just come back with us, will you!
Tomorrow. After what has happened to you, just come! At least
you can see your mother and your brother. And tell them . . .'

'I'll tell them nothing. It was a mistake tellin' you anything.
It was just you sitting there with that look on your face, and
you being the daughter of the *rai* . . .' Honesty's voice hardened.
'And you must tell them nothing, miss. If he hears about this
our Jack'll go and stick a knife in the King's gizzard and then
where'll we all be? In the Tower of London? Anyway, if I went
home now Mrs McCoy'd give me my notice right off. No
references.'

'She couldn't do that. I'll talk to her. I'll make it right with
her.'

The girl's shoulders raised in a shrug and then she turned
away. 'Like I say. I gotta run,' she said over her shoulder. 'Don't
bother about this, miss. You shouldn't really know.' Her eyes
were no longer red. Her face was closed and stubborn.

Astrid flushed at the innocent patronage in the girl's tone
and watched as the maid walked, straight and tall, along the
corridor, her box of tools clanking. She pulled back into the
room shaking her head hard, trying to rid herself of the image
of the King plunging like a whale into the young girl.

The talk she'd just had with Honesty Leeming had been the
longest conversation she'd had with someone who was not her

equal since she'd been a child in the nursery at Benbow. Her nanny, dead now, had loved to talk and talk. After tea she'd hit the table with the flat of her hands and say, 'Now, my dears, what shall we talk about today?'

They would talk a lot about the old Queen. About Nanny's own heroine, Florence Nightingale. And about a very bad man called Charles Darwin who had some preposterous ideas about men being monkeys. They talked about Mr Disraeli who had charm, and Mr Gladstone who had dignity. They got quite deeply into the dastardly murders that happened in the streets of London and considered how lucky they all were, to live in the north where such things didn't happen. (When she was eighteen her fond memory of these tales made London seem a very alluring place to Astrid.)

They also talked of Nanny's own childhood in County Kerry, where there were small magical people and very surprising events; where there were all these streams and pools that glittered darkly in the early evening light.

In all of her life since (at her aunt's house in London; in the studios in Chelsea; more recently travelling in France and Italy), the people employed to make her life smooth had all merged into two collective individuals – a woman, probably called Peggy or Maisie and a man usually called Fred or Tom. She looked on them kindly, talked to them about the business of whatever house they happened to serve; but if she were honest, to her they were no more than cut-outs in a toy theatre.

But Honesty was much more than any cardboard cut-out. She was flesh and blood, a person who had been savagely wronged. Astrid blushed again at the thought of what had gone on in that small room with the red couch. Her cheeks were still hot as she wandered back into the room and opened her wardrobe. What to wear for lunch? Most of the ladies would be at the round table in the summer salon with its seven windows.

Astrid forced herself to think of these things, screwing her eyes tight to stop herself imagining again the threshing figures of Honesty and the King.

Still battling to keep thoughts of the King from the front of her mind, Astrid selected a neat violet gown, finely cut and stitched by a dressmaker who copied the Paris models. (Constance, of course, wore the genuine thing). Yes, the violet gown would do the trick. She had to keep some kind of standard even in the chirruping company of rather mature female pigeons who fluttered around the King: Mrs L., the Jersey Lily, still beautiful though a little stout, was Astrid's favourite. It was said that when she first came to London and caught the future King's fancy, she wore the same simple black dress on every occasion, her beauty rendering competition irrelevant.

The future King. The King. How could she sit with other, more eager guests this evening and respond to his heavy humour, his beaming gaze? It was not difficult to respond. There was something undeniably likeable about him; he was often less stuffy and self-absorbed than the people around him. He was sharp and watchful yet he laughed very naturally when he was pleased.

She retied her corset at the front, then spilled the dress over her head and allowed it to slither and settle over her petticoats. She stood before the mirror using her long hook to fasten the last little buttons at the back. Most of the other women here would have a maid to do this. She'd always preferred to see to her own toilette, treasuring time on her own in what sometimes seemed to be a crowded life. She so loved these moments of freedom that she had her dresses made, her hair simply dressed, so that she could deal with them herself. Alone.

Some ladies of her acquaintance were never without their maids. The poor creatures had to wait up, yawning, ready to unlace, undo, brush and braid their mistresses. Some even slept on low couches outside their mistresses' bedrooms. It seemed to Astrid that these maids were more intimate, more part of their mistresses' lives than their husbands. As these brushing and braiding intimacies proceeded, the men would probably be snoring in another bedroom, or playing a late hand of cards at their club, fifty, a hundred, two hundred miles away.

Astrid pinned up the last fair curl, pinched her cheeks to make them redder, and made for the door. She thought she should hunt down the usually fearsome, occasionally benevolent Mrs McCoy before the gong called the remaining ladies to luncheon in the company of the obliging Mr Marquand, a non-sporting gentleman specially invited to play cards with the ladies and entertain them at the piano.

The King! He would still be at the butts: allowing his guns to cool and probably downing some warming drink before settling down to enjoy a picnic feast and teasing and chaffing the attentive company.

Astrid closed her bedroom door behind her. Luncheon with the ladies and Mr Marquand would be tolerable. But this evening's dinner would be a trial. That was certain. She didn't know whether she could bear it, whether she could sit around that crowded table, listen to the rough putt and glide of conversation where two things were always going on side by side. One of these things was the humour and wit of one's dining companions. The other was the necessity to keep a sharp ear for the growling voice of the King: the reason why they were all there.

Walking along the echoing corridor she came to a decision. It would be better if she and Constance went straight on to Benbow Hall. She could not spend another evening here in this palace of sycophants. She would go home to Benbow. This afternoon.

Two

Journey to Benbow Hall

Constance was more than a little miffed when she realised that Astrid had arranged for them to move on. She watched with a scowl as the Selands' third groom loaded their boxes onto Seland's third best carriage. 'Why must we do this, Astrid?' she said crossly. 'I thought we were to be here for the weekend before going on to Benbow.'

'I don't want to stay here.' Astrid looked round. Lady Seland's anger at their departure meant there wouldn't be a mannerly farewell.

'But why?' pouted Constance. 'Weren't we having such a good time? The King . . .'

'I don't want to stay where he is.'

'But Astrid . . .'

'Don't talk about it. Any of it.'

They clambered up the steps in silence and sat in opposite corners of the carriage. Constance sulked a little as the carriage made its slow way though the park and out onto the road. In the end she could bear it no longer and bounced across the carriage to sit beside Astrid. As she did so the carriage swerved round a corner and she almost landed in Astrid's lap and they both ended up laughing.

'Oh, bother it all!' gasped Constance, settling beside her friend and linking her arm. 'Bother the King and all those stiff-necks and their port-drinking wives. If you don't want to be there neither do I.'

Astrid relaxed. 'Good,' she said. 'Let's talk about something else.' She wanted to talk. She didn't want to think of Honesty, and her own lack of courage in dealing with that matter.

The carriage rocked on in silence for a while.

Constance asked, 'So, when will we be at Benbow?'

'About half an hour. Probably more. This driver does not seem to be in a hurry.' They surveyed the driver's stiff uniform and the thick neck that somewhat spoiled his rather good proportions.

'Then you can tell me about it. About your house. When I get there I will be an expert on Benbow Hall. I will be able to write to tell my dear momma all about it. I think it must be like Seland only prettier.'

Astrid laughed. 'It's not even a tenth of the size of that place. Though once there was a place as grand as Seland on that very site. The Benbows were grander than the Selands then. But that was burned down. The house we live in is merely forty or so years old.'

'Merely! Back home that's real, real old.'

Astrid sat back against the padded backrest. 'The site goes back even before the house that was burned down. You'll be pleased to know, Connie, that my family is *real, real, real* old. My father wrote a little book about it all. So I know it by heart. When I was little I could chant it like a fairy story.'

'Just how old is that old?'

'Well, there's been a house on the spot since Saxon times. An old book mentions a "small manor with fifteen villeins, ten farmholdings, three small lakes with plentiful fish, including roach, a number of free-roaming deer".' Her voice took on a child's sing-song tone. 'In those days the lands were important enough for the Normans to chase away a rather peaceable Saxon from the Hall and install their own more amenable placeman. Now he was son of a brave archer who had married a Saxon princess down in Wessex. Ben-b-o-u-g-h, the name of that hardy archer, transmuted itself through the ages to Benbow.'

'Saxons! Go on.' Constance, the daughter of a committed anglophile, knew her English history.

'It seems this Benbough tore down the Saxon Hall and built himself a house with "high sloping walls snugly fortified and with a narrow wary eye to the north".

'Then at the Reformation, a Robert Benbough joined the King in distancing himself from Rome. He grabbed some rather useful church lands, including some lucrative coal pits and a lead mine further up the valley.

'In the Civil War the Parliamentarian Edward Benbow managed further to extend his land at the expense of a Royalist neighbour. At the Restoration his son eagerly paid his fines to the King and forfeited the incorporated land.'

'A roundhead then a cavalier.' Constance clapped her hands.

'In a later generation a younger Benbow son, called Matthew, fought under Wellington in Spain and died. They said this was a hero's death but there's no real evidence for it. That was the Benbow who brought home a black ship's cat called Scat the Spanish Cat that was the ancestor of a line of black cats at the Hall. The cat these days is called Susannah. She has a high temperament and is a good fighter.'

Constance shuddered. 'I can't stand cats. They bring me out in hives.'

Astrid laughed. 'I'll tell Susannah to keep out of your way.'

'Go on! Go on!'

'Well, Matthew's brother, Michael John, fought with Nelson at the Battle of the Nile and returned to Benbow Hall with crates of booty including sacks of fine finished mahogany that had once been the deck of a French merchant-man. This has been our drawing room floor in two successive houses. They ripped up the oak in that first house and put down the mahogany. The inherited instruction to generations of housekeepers is that the floor should "shine like conkers". And so it does. When we were small my brothers and I used to slide on it with dusters tied to our feet and pretend to be pirates. Just think! This floor was salvaged twice: once from the wrecked merchantman; once from the big house which was burnt down. As I said the Benbows were grander than the Selands in the old days.'

'A poke in the eye for her ladyship!' said Constance.

'You could say that,' agreed Astrid.

'Where'd they get all their money, your people?' said Constance with her American directness.

'They had the wealth in the thousands of acres here. They invested in shipping. They made a great flush of money from slaves and sugar, and later from coal. They made it and spent it just as easily on stone and marble, on the laying down of floors of fine oak, the purchasing of furniture and interior features in the new clean styles from the pattern books of Mr Chippendale and Mr Adam. This easy money paid garden designers, Italian carvers of marble pediments, German silversmiths for sconces, lamps and elaborate crystal.'

Constance whistled. 'Kings of all they surveyed. Just like my own poppa out West, sending to Europe for the baubles to show him better than his friends.'

'It seems one Benbow, made Sir John Benbow by King George for his services in the Battle of Culloden, even took the trouble to move every stick, stone and boiling barrel of Benbow village, with its mean houses and narrow streets, half a mile down the road to a point where the village didn't spoil his view of his three small lakes and the landscaping of Mr Brown, which was now a growing treasure to the eye.'

'But the big house is gone?'

'Most of it. The library's still there. That has fine shelves and fittings, and a central raised roof of glass. Other bits – such as the ship's deck floor in the drawing Georgian portico – were salvaged.'

'But your house is different?'

'Our house is a mish-mash of a place, like the low-browed offspring of a fine father. The Georgian portico sits uneasily on this much cosier, lower building, and the square block of the old library sits oddly by it. It faces towards the park, away from the new house, as though trying to ignore its plebeian presence.'

'What about the people?' demanded Constance. 'Tell me more about the people.'

'My father Rufus . . .'

'Is he a sir?'

Astrid shook her head. 'The sir business got lost somehow in the generations.'

'So, your father Rufus?' prompted Constance.

'Well, he discovered in his researches that there had once been two black servants at Benbow Hall, retained as fancy trophies from the second leg of the sugar trade between West Africa and the West Indies. They are shown in a family portrait like the trophies they were. My father was ashamed of this, and the source of the Benbow wealth, so he started to give it away, to worthy and unworthy causes in Africa and the West Indies.'

'Was he crazy?' Constance was really puzzled.

'No, I don't think so. He thought that wealth was immoral and this was the only way to deal with it.'

'Can't see it,' said Constance.

'He sold much of the fine silver from the house, even some of the furniture. He spent this money on early ventures to finance archaeological digs in Mesopotamia and later to travel in a gypsy van through Europe. He became an expert on gypsies, writing down the histories from the *romani*'s own mouths. He comforted himself and his conscience by distributing largesse as he went.'

'He *was* crazy,' said Constance.

Astrid found herself going on and on. Anything to keep thoughts of Honesty out of her head. 'Money still dribbled in from the coal and, to a lesser extent, the farms, and the shrewd railway investments made by Rufus's father. Benbow coal, moved by these same railways to Sunderland, and thence to

London, is of a high quality. They say Benbow coal, especially that from the Red Daisy Pit, burns in the grate of the Prime Minister.'

Constance peered out of the window. 'The coal might bring in the money but it ain't very pretty. See that coal heap like a great scar against those woods?'

'Ah. But we don't see any of that from the house. They're all masked from the Hall by successive landscapers and gardeners, by the judicious banking up of the land and the planting of swaths of trees.'

'Tell me more about the people,' pleaded Constance.

'Well, generations of Benbows married quite appropriately and settled down to a steady production of daughters who married within their class and sons who went to sea, fought for whatever king – or queen – was on the throne. A few were drawn to the church, more as scholars than shepherds. The more decorative and decadent Benbows provided the occasional ornament for London society. They stayed at Benbow House in Sloane Square as the Season demanded, then fled north with a covey of friends and cronies to test their shooting and hunting prowess and blow off the fetid closeness of London life. My father sold Benbow House in the end.'

'Tell me more about him.'

'My father, as I've said, was a Benbow of the scholarly persuasion; in fact he was a scholar of some repute. He married my mother when he was in his forties and still, basically, lived like a bachelor. Before their marriage he spent a quarter of the year in Mesopotamia, digging to satisfy his curiosity about dead civilisations. Half the year he spent in Benbow House in Sloane Street. He walked each day to work in the British Museum and dined at his club in the evenings. The scattering of days that made up the fourth quarter of the year he spent at Benbow Hall, checking his resources and deciding what to sell to fund his next piece of scholarship.'

'Where did he meet your mother?'

'In the British Museum. She was studying prints of old roses from China. Carmel. She was a self-determined old maid of twenty-six, who lived on a tiny annuity from her grandmother and the proceeds of delicate flower paintings. She loathed London and loved the country and was quite happy to exchange a light-minded London life for a house, and even better a garden, in the far north. She is obsessed with her garden.'

'Was she happy? After all, he was a crazy man.'

Astrid shrugged. 'After the early years when she travelled with him it didn't seem to bother her that my father only had a few days through the year when he came home. He would sit in the library and write his articles and rest and walk and talk with Colonel Carmedy, the agent, about the running of the estate; he would admire her fine garden and plants. We saw very little of him but I remember being delighted when he was at home, how he seemed to light the whole house up.'

'My poppa is like that,' said Constance. 'You always know he's around. Everyone loves him. Right from his old soldier buddies to the youngest houseboy.'

Astrid went on, caught up now in her own story. 'Then he contracted some kind of lung disease on a winter trip to Romania. Losing him seemed to make little difference to my mother's life. Through the years when he was alive I think she developed the ability to imagine his presence when he was away from her.'

'Was there a very grand funeral?'

Astrid laughed. 'Well, she followed the *romani* tradition and burned his van and some of his books in this special ceremony with crowds of gypsies from all over the world who had turned up at the funeral. The burning was supposed to set his spirit free but he is still there somehow. Mostly in the regular presence of gypsies who turn up at the back door offering work, baskets, flowers, and small birds in cages, in return for food and a little bit of money. They are never turned away.'

'Now that's unusual.'

'When my mother is up at the Hall, as opposed to in her walled garden, she talks with the visitors herself, about my father's travels in Europe. She shows them his old maps. If she's not there they're given some scraps and then shooed away by the servants. They are under strict instructions to give the travellers something, but often they give with bad grace and are relieved when they go away.'

'Fascinating,' said Constance. 'So romantic.'

Astrid yawned. 'Doesn't feel that way when you grow up playing second fiddle to a rose bush and a tribe of gypsies.'

'Don't you be such a sourpuss, Miss Astrid. You are proud of your parents. I can hear the pride in your voice. You English are so irritating. Too screwed tight to show your feelings, admit your pride. I come to the conclusion, my dear, that it is a very clever way to be one up on us simpler mortals.'

Astrid leaned over and looked through the window. 'Oh good,' she said. 'Not long now.'

Three

Constance Redoute

2pm

Constance Redoute leaned forward and tapped the Seland groom on the shoulder with her parasol. 'Sir, would you stop?' she said.

Unaccustomed to such civility the thickset groom lifted his shoulder and pulled too hard on the reins. The sturdy cob on the left turned his head and jumped, making the carriage tilt slightly. Astrid, whose mind had returned to Honesty Leeming, lurched into Constance and they both laughed, easy now in their intimacy.

'How very quaint,' gasped the American girl, her white teeth gleaming. 'Just look at *that*, Astrid dear.'

'What is it now, Connie?' Astrid was used to Constance drawing her attention to the most ordinary of things.

'Look at *that*. Those people! So engaging.'

That was a small procession of two heavy-wheeled bow-topped vans, each pulled by a bony horse plodding in a resigned fashion down the metalled road. Crooked metal chimneys thrust their way through the dingy canvas. Behind each van, tethered on an easy rein, trotted a less burdened and rather finer horse than the poor creature that dragged the family and their life's jingling possessions.

Alongside the first van walked two men. The first was grizzled, perhaps in his forties, though it was hard to tell. He wore a scarf round his head held down by a wavy-brimmed felt hat. The other was younger, bareheaded and barefooted. A third man sat up front in the first van, the reins loose in his hands. Beside him a very old woman leaned sideways, her eyes closed in sleep. On the second van three children sat up front. The oldest, a girl, had a sleeping baby lying flat across her knee like a cat. The reins lay across its back and were looped once round the girl's wrist. All of the family, for family it must be, had gleaming copper skins and hair black as liquorice.

The men on foot gazed openly at the two young women who were staring at them through the window of their carriage. The younger man called loudly in a strange tongue up to the driver of the first van. The driver chuckled. Then he clicked his teeth at his horse in a theatrical attempt to urge it on.

Astrid sat back in her padded seat. 'Drive on, will you?' she said wearily. 'We shouldn't stare at these people.'

'Are those folks Indians?' said Constance, settling back beside Astrid. 'They bring to mind the Indians back home. The Ute nation. They were stubborn creatures, according to my dear poppa. Took some moving.'

'Not Indians,' said Astrid, closing her eyes, 'gypsies. Some say they're Egyptians who came here hundreds of years ago. But my father, who as you know studied them, thought that quite possibly they may have come all the way from India. There are similarities of language. Today, you may be pleased to hear, those people will have come from my house, where without doubt my mother will have welcomed them warmly.'

'Goodness,' said Constance. 'How very amazing.'

Astrid was amused as always at the open-eyed amiability of her new friend. 'My father used to love the gypsies. He had a feeling for all such people; for outsiders. He learned their ways. He took their photographs. He called them "people out of time".'

'How quaint,' said Constance.

'Oh, Constance!' said Astrid, irritated at last.

'Dear Astrid, what have I said?' sighed Constance, settling back comfortably against the cushions. 'You English. How am I ever to understand you?'

'I'll tell you about quaint.' Astrid eyed her coolly. 'My mother used to leave me and my brother and travel with him. She wore gypsy clothes. She cooked gypsy food.'

'How very . . .' Constance encountered the stern look of her friend. 'Well, dearest Astrid, what did *you* think of that? What should *I* think? So often I don't know *what* to think in this country.' Constance could feel rather than see Astrid's shrug. She persisted. 'It does seem a little strange, a mother going away like that and leaving her children.'

'It was what we knew,' said Astrid. 'Our nanny took care of us.'

Constance knew about this. Her own mother had left her regularly to come each year to England to hunt. She and her sister Delphine had been left at home with her father and her black nurse Aunt Beatrice, and the crowd of adoring servants. With her beloved father there and the ponies, then the full-blood horses, it had been fine. Her mother, when she was not in the hunting field, was somewhat obsessed with her health, which made a person weary. 'Was that too awful?' Constance said now to Astrid. 'Being left like that?'

'It was quite all right, as a matter of fact. We knew no other.' Astrid paused. 'Then, as I said, my mother stopped going with him. She left him to travel on his own.'

'And that would be much better for you, dearest Astrid. To have her at home with you?'

'Not really. She was only barely with us. She found another obsession. As you will see.'

Connie Redoute wriggled against the well-buttoned cushions of Lady Seland's carriage as it swayed gently along on its fine springs. She thought to herself that she must learn to curtail her curiosity and cultivate a modicum of discretion. She was grateful to Astrid. Had not she and the dear girl just spent half of a charming weekend ... well, almost ... in the company of – amongst many others, it was true – the King of England?

Three months before this day, when Constance had first met the gawky young English woman in her drawing class in Chelsea, she'd never imagined the girl to be so well connected. In fact she'd written of her, in her daily letter to her momma in Torquay, England, where she'd lived, for her health, for the past two years: *You'd find her, dear Momma, quite dull. She dresses in a strange way, somewhat dusty. And my, she is so intense! She has very little light talk. I have to say that she is not much of a drawer and less of a painter. And yet, and yet ... I like her. She does not pull on the haughty and simpering armour of many English girls whom I have met. And Lady Parlellum seems quite to approve of her. Talks of her family as 'very old'. How they love old things in this old country!*

Lady Parlellum was Constance's hostess and chaperone for the season, paid handsomely by Mrs Redoute to launch the daughter of the legendary General Redoute into English society. Constance was rather old for the Season at twenty-two, but she was, after all, American.

Although the Redoutes were less of a pull than the great bankers and politicians from the eastern states of America, Lady Parlellum did her best. She organised the whole matter with a rigid and reassuring correctness: a trip to Paris for the right clothes, to Bond Street for the right jewels; some drawing lessons, some bridge instruction; a little gentle language coaching. Above all, in the Byzantine jungle of exclusiveness that was London society Lady Parlellum tried her very best to secure for Miss Redoute a reasonable number of introductions to the right people. But of all the unctuous and impressive people that Constance had met, it was the dusty girl in the drawing class to whom she was most attracted.

Lady Parlellum was sceptical when she heard Constance's description of the girl, but delighted when she heard the name. She raised her sparse eyebrows and clapped her mittened hands when she heard of the invitation to stay with the Benbows. It was a great coup. Eccentric they were but this was really an old family. And apart from anything else it meant that Lady Parlellum could retire for a while to her own little dower house in Wiltshire and submit to the indulgent care of her sister Violet and their old housekeeper. As she regularly explained to Violet, taking care of these American girls, though lucrative, was *so* wearing.

After meeting Astrid, Connie had begun to find herself attending more interesting parties than those provided by Lady Parlellum. At these gatherings titled people rubbed shoulders with artists and poets and the conversation veered sometimes from sheer gossip to ideas, like the photographing of things in motion and the possibilities of flight. As well as Mr James, whom one would barely recognise as American, one caught sight of the *ebullient* Mr Morris, the *affecting* Mr Millais, the *witty* Mr Holman Hunt, the *shy* Mr Singer Sargent (yet another American but *so* fashionable these days) and that fine actress Mrs Patrick Campbell. Once, she'd even come across the *growly, twinkling* creature who was George Bernard Shaw, in the company of his deaf wife, both Irish. So it was that Astrid Benbow's connections established for Connie Redoute experiences that would be the staple ingredients of her 'English stories' for the rest of her life.

This present adventure had started one day when Astrid ceased labouring over a rather wooden rendering of the goddess Diana breasting her longbow, and asked Constance what she was doing at the end of August.

Lady Parlellum had explained to Constance that London was as empty as a soldier's drum in August. One always, she said, either went abroad, or to the country. Ireland was a possibility. Good shooting there. Constance's mother had from time to time some very good hunting there though not, of course, in August. Lady Parlellum thought she herself would go to the country. Constance toyed with the idea of going down to Torquay to spend a week or so with Momma and her sister Delphine as (to her great surprise) she had rather missed them. Such a pity about their shared affliction of delicate chests that prevented them from enjoying the delights of London. Hunting, of course, was very good for one's health. Mrs Redoute, who had despised from the first day of her marriage the dry expanses of Colorado, thought England was the Mecca for any civilised person. She refused to admit that the damp, befogged English climate was the worst thing possible for the delicate pulmonary systems that the good Lord had visited on herself and her younger daughter.

So Constance was very pleased when Astrid asked her to come north with her. 'It's not terribly exciting, Connie. Can be grim, actually. There's good riding. I should go home for summer. It's two years since I made a flying visit for my father's funeral.' (That remarkable funeral.) 'My mother has written especially to say she'd like to see me.' Astrid smiled and her face lit up and Constance Redoute thought, not for the first time, that perhaps Astrid might be quite beautiful after all. Though she was restrained and sometimes too quiet there was a spark about her that made her very attractive.

Astrid went on. 'A mere request from my winsome mother is more like a royal command than anything else.'

'And would I be able to take Diamond?' Even in London Constance rode her black mare every day.

Astrid, who was not troubled with a love for horses, had shrugged. 'I'm sure the railways will move her and take care of her.'

'Someone would have to travel with her all the way.'

'I am quite sure they'll have men to do that for you.'

It was on the train that Astrid had dropped her rather pleasant bombshell. 'I forgot to tell you. When we arrive we're to stay one or two nights with Lady Seland, my mother's oldest friend. Then we'll go on to Benbow.'

Constance could not protest. She was in her friend's hands after all. Staying with some old lady *en route* was a small price to pay for a month in the country. It was not only poor old Diamond who needed to shake the sooty London cobwebs out of her brain. When Constance had first arrived in London the sheer tapestry of people and events had been endlessly engaging. But just now and then she felt hemmed in, bowed down by the high dirty buildings and the lowering, sulphurous sky. Even on her daily rides in the parks and on the Heath she had to endure the close proximity of dozens – it sometimes seemed like hundreds – of others clip-clopping along the paths, many of them displaying like peacocks at mating time.

But when the old lady's carriage with its coat of arms and the groom in livery collected them at Darlington railway station, and when that same carriage drew up outside the Palladian mansion set in a thousand acres of park, she realised that her enigmatic friend had something up her sleeve.

Later, meeting the dowdy Lady Seland in a crowded boudoir which smelt of cats and lavender, Constance was drawn to reflect yet again on the sheer understated confidence of these upper-class English. Lady Seland had offered a powdered cheek to Astrid, and a limp hand to Constance. 'America? The West? How charming.' Constance knew enough now to know this meant the opposite. It really meant, *How terribly boring and provincial. How frightfully alien.* The English could just about tolerate the anglophile Easterners who aspired to be English anyway. But Westerners! *My dear, completely bizarre!* Constance had lost count of the number of times someone told her at a party of the time 'Buffalo Bill' Cody put on a show for the old Queen and how enchanted Her Majesty had been with the galloping Indians. No matter how many times Constance protested that all Americans weren't whooping cowboys, people would still ask if she had brought along her lariat or her six-gun. No wonder her mother preferred to hold her own kind of court in Torquay.

Bored with contemplating such wildness, Lady Seland had turned to Astrid with a faint but distinctive warmth. 'How delightful that you came, darling Astrid.'

'I told my mother of your kind invitation and she wrote to me, Lady Margaret, and instructed me to come. Your very word is her command. I am to bring her news of you. She reminded me that it was only ten miles from here to Benbow Hall. So I am to go on to Benbow from here.'

Lady Seland emitted a sound that was something between a child's laugh and a horse's snuffle. 'Ten miles is merely a notional distance, darling Astrid. A distance of the imagination. Your dear mother could as well be on the moon. She does not move in society. One calls and she is off somewhere in those dreadful gumboots of hers.'

Astrid raised her fine brows. 'But my dear Lady Margaret. How *could* she receive in gumboots?'

Lady Seland stared hard at Astrid then relaxed. 'You are such a tease, child. How much you favour your mother at the same age. Now!' she went on briskly. 'I am afraid we have had to tuck you away on the blue corridor. The Hall is overflowing with guests.'

'We are very comfortable, Lady Margaret, I assure you.'

'Good, good.' Her ladyship's gaze went past them and wandered round the room. It dawned on Constance that she and Astrid had been deliberately kept standing so that, presumably, they would not be tempted to dally. She'd read somewhere that the old Queen had done that with the Privy Council to keep the meetings short.

Lady Seland's gaze returned to them. 'Perhaps you would like to rest? The dinner gong will sound at three minutes to seven. His Majesty does not like to be kept waiting.' She transferred her mild gaze to the door, appearing to will them to move.

As she trailed out after Astrid, Constance glanced back at Lady Seland who was adjusting a frill on her sleeve. Then, as they made their way along the marble floor of the upper corridor, she said, 'What secrets have you been keeping, you bad girl?' She gave her friend's arm a shake and a squeeze. 'I thought I was coming to see this old dame living out her dotage amongst cats and you bring me to a palace and we're to dine with a royal guest. Who is she, this old lady?'

'Lady Margaret is my mother's oldest friend. Some kind of cousin, I think. She was brought up across in Cumberland with my mother when her own family drowned in a yacht just off Naples. They say she used to be a great beauty. Lord Seland was a friend of my father's – he was just a "Sir" in those days – he fell in love with Lady Margaret, married her and brought her to this "palace" as you call it. She's my godmother, and my mother is godmother to her daughter who's also my friend. It seems *she* just ran off with a diamond prospector and apparently brought shame on us all.'

Constance didn't bother to ask herself whether or not Astrid was being ironic. 'And the royal guest is in this house? This very minute?'

'I would think so. The King is never late. People are never late for him. Lord Seland has a first class shoot across on the great moor.'

Now, as the Seland carriage bumped along on worse and worse roads on the way to Benbow Hall, Constance wondered idly what Lady Parlellum would think of their early, rather scrambled departure from the shooting party at Seland Hall. Constance herself had been puzzled by the haste, concerned that they may have offended the King. It appeared that dear Astrid was experiencing some kind of black foreboding, which she did not wish to communicate. It even seemed that the King himself may have offended her. Constance, as her friend and fellow-guest, was honour bound to leave with her.

45

Now the Seland carriage creaked in protest as it squeezed its way down even narrower roads. Here and there the high, untended hedges lashed out at the coach. In the spaces made by field gates Constance could make out the breasted humps of the hills of Durham as they stretched to the horizon. They were pockmarked by much duller symmetrical heaps of mining spoil and slag. Tucked in beside these were the cables and wheels of pitheads surrounded by low huddles of blackened houses. Constance had seen prettier vistas in her travels in England, Palladian palaces notwithstanding.

'Stop!' This time it was Astrid instructing the driver. 'Stop, will you?' She leaned out of the window and peered back at the figure making its careful way along the edge of the narrow road. 'Look who's here.'

Four

Jack Lomas

Constance peered past Astrid to the slight trudging figure hurrying towards them along the road. She was tall and golden-skinned and wore a shawl over her head and crossed over her chest and tied at the back. In her hand she carried a bundle, the top so tied as to make a handle.

'Honesty Leeming!' Astrid called. 'What are you doing? Where are you going?'

The girl caught up with them and stood beside the Seland carriage breathing hard. 'I'm gunna see me mother, miss. Talking to you made us think I should go home.'

'So you decided not to stay?' Astrid was smiling, relieved. She felt a burden had gone from her shoulders.

The girl stared blankly at her for a few moments. 'Would you, miss? Her ladyship says mebbe I *should* go. That is, when I tried to say something to her, like, about what happened. She give us a month's wages and promised us a reference. So no problem there.'

Astrid felt guilty that she'd not seen Lady Seland herself about this matter. She had not even seen Mrs McCoy. And here Honesty had dealt with it herself.

The silence stretched out. Astrid was rigid beside Constance, who wondered why her friend was so focused on this servant girl. She felt again the anger that her friend had shown as they departed Seland. But it didn't seem to be anger

47

against the girl. So many things in this country were beyond her interpretation. What had happened with this girl that had so affected Astrid, who was so hard to offend? The air between these two crackled with meaning, which the American girl could not begin to decode.

'Well, Honesty,' said Astrid finally, sitting back in her seat and bunching her skirts tightly under her knees, 'perhaps you'd travel back to Benbow with us? We're going the same way, after all.' She pushed open the door and Honesty took a step towards her. 'Climb up,' said Astrid.

'Miss . . .' the thickset Seland groom protested, wrinkling his nose at the girl with her wet boots, her muddy skirt and her uncertain smell.

Honesty hesitated on the high step and flashed a hard look at him. 'Don't you worry!' she said. 'I'll not soil your precious rig. I'd rather bliddy walk.'

Astrid was just reflecting that Honesty was no longer the trembling creature of this morning when there was a clatter on the metalled road behind them. They turned their heads to see a large grey horse being hauled to a stop by a heavily built young man who was riding the horse bareback, hanging on to its streaming silver mane. 'Whoa, lass, whoa lass!' The voice was deep. The hands that grasped the mane were strong; the feet that turned inwards over the horse's belly were bare. He pulled the horse up and it shied into the lead horse of the Seland carriage which swerved so that the reins were almost wrenched out of the groom's hands.

'Steady now! Steady now!' said the groom, glaring at the young man on the horse.

The horseman ignored the two watching women and spoke to Honesty. 'Hey now, Honesty, girl. How d'ya come to be down this road on this day?' He walked the horse round until he was beside her on the grass verge. 'Goin' back to Benbow, are you?'

Honesty was beaming, almost laughing up into his face. In that second the sun emerged from the shuttering clouds and touched her face. 'Jack, well, if it an't our old Jack,' she giggled. 'An' it's true I'm goin' home to see Keziah.' She shot a flaunting glance back at the women in the carriage. 'These ladies here offered us a lift back but their driver's dead scairt I'll mucky his rig. Seems this lady here's daughter to Mrs Benbow.'

'Is that so?' He turned his head and looked hard at Astrid. She felt the cool appraisal like a physical blow. His eyes were very pale gold, and in that, very strange. He nodded to her, then lifted his battered hat and bowed precariously from the waist. 'No finer woman than Mrs Benbow, miss. Me own mother thinks a lot of Mrs Benbow.' Somehow he made the mild words seem like an insult. He held on to Astrid's gaze for a full ten seconds. She blushed.

The boy looked back at Honesty. 'Give us yer hand, *charver*. Regent here don't mind a bit of muck.' He held out his hand and she swung up confidently behind him, her bundle swinging precariously over her arm. Then he clicked his teeth and the big horse started to move smoothly forward, its flanks gleaming in the sunshine.

'Them gypsies is beggars,' said the groom sourly. 'I'd string up the lot, me.'

'Walk on,' said Astrid sharply. 'Walk on, will you?' She sat back against the cushions, closed her eyes and reflected on her second meeting with Honesty that day.

Astrid was displeased with herself. It was true that she'd made her gesture in not staying, but really it was a feeble gesture. In the end she'd been too shy to tackle Lady Seland or even the housekeeper properly about Honesty Leeming. She'd even avoided seeing Honesty again. What a weakling she was. All she'd done was creep away like a dog with his tail between his legs. In her heart of hearts she felt she deserved the laughing contempt in the gypsy boy's eyes.

* * *

49

Freddy Leeming's forge at the crossroads at the edge of Benbow village was the oldest house in the whole district. It existed as a forge when the eighteenth-century Benbow relocated his village away from the Hall. The low building stood at the point where the old coal-carrying road crossed the main Durham road. In the days when the coals were hauled across country on the backs of mules or behind patient heavy horses, it was convenient to have a blacksmith on the spot to refit a thrown shoe or even doctor lame animals. By the time the railways took away that trade Freddy's forebears had established a good reputation making farming and mining tools, iron gates and fenceworks. That, and the more regular shoeing jobs for farmers and tradesmen, had kept the Leemings in a decent way of life for generations.

One forebear, Lemmel Leeming, had gone to sea in the sixteenth century with the first Michael John Benbow. They'd fetched up once in a Spanish port and Lemmel had worked with a Spanish ironworker for three months while the ship was repaired. He'd returned with some very fancy ideas about ironwork and it was he who designed the great iron gates that always stood open at the entrance to the park. An etching of his design of anchors and seahorses found immortality in a famous ironwork pattern-book. The motif had been frequently copied, on a more modest scale, by farmers who became rich in the 1860s and for a while fancied themselves gentlemen.

When Honesty and Jack finally arrived at the forge, Freddy was hammering and stretching a slug of molten iron, destined to be part of a new garden gate for Mrs Benbow. A scribbled design on a piece of blackened paper hung from a nail on the wall. It showed Freddy's signature seahorses sitting somewhat incongruously with Mrs Benbow's stylised drawing of a rose.

Freddy looked up as his massive stepson blocked the light from the open doorway. 'Now, Jackie,' he frowned, still concentrating on getting an even pull on the iron, nudging it into an ellipse to make the top half of the rose.

50

'Now, Freddy!' Jack moved forward to make room for Honesty behind him. 'Look what I found in the road.'

'Now, Honesty,' grunted Freddy. 'You back?'

' 'Lo, Dad,' she said.

'We lookin' for Keziah,' said Jack. Like everyone else Jack called his mother by her given name. She was no *Ma* or *Mam*, though she'd given birth to both himself and Honesty. She did not cook or clean or wash clothes like other women. Freddy's sister, Edith, did the cooking and cleaning. She'd kept house for her brother for most of her forty years and this didn't stop when the gypsy horse trader, trailing two barefoot children, called at the forge with a request for a special kind of shoe for two Welsh cobs that'd never had a shoe fitted nor walked on a man-made road.

Despite the fact that Keziah was fourteen years older than Freddy, and that she was pure gypsy, the two had been married in the little Benbow estate church a month after their first meeting. Freddy's sister Edith had held her breath and waited to be put to one side (as is often the fate of loyal sisters). This did not happen. Freddy negotiated with Colonel Carmedy, the Benbow agent, for two three-acre fields behind the forge. This land was to accommodate Keziah's two mares in foal, her donkey and her small cage of chickens. She also used the field to fatten up the two Welsh cobs she'd bought at that year's fair and would train and break and sell at the next year's fair.

Into the corner of this rented field she drew up her *vardo*, the van in which she and her children had led all their lives. She told Freddy that her first husband had been killed in a bare-knuckle fight near Reading. She told Edith that he had been killed fighting for the British against the Boers. After that she never mentioned him at all.

Most times Keziah slept in the van. She washed her own clothes. She cooked her own food over a fire set on the lee-side of the stone wall that surrounded her fields. She called Edith's way of cooking 'unclean' but Jack and Honesty were not so fussy. They took rather a liking to Edith's flat bread and teacakes and they loved her lamb stew laced with pot-stuff.

Sometimes Keziah took off in her *vardo*, pulled by her oldest cob, Goggy. Sometimes she harnessed one of her other horses to the van, to train it for a lifetime of haulage. Sometimes she tethered one of her brood-mares behind the *vardo* and took it off, either with a view to hiring it out or to put it to some desired stallion.

'Looked all round the place,' said Jack now to Freddy. 'Keziah an't anywhere here. What about our Honesty? Didn't they go and give her notice at that house?'

Freddy nodded. 'No good working in their houses. That's what I say. No Leeming's ever working in another man's house.' He picked up the half-formed rose and dipped it in a vat of water, making the water sizzle as it cooled down the iron. 'Keziah took a load of hoss-shit up to the house for the woman in her garden.' He held the cooling rose to the light and squinted at it. 'Any luck with the mare? Did the livery man bite?'

Jack nodded. 'Got me a good price. Feller wanted the grey as well but I told him no chance. I've other plans for him.'

Freddy grunted. 'Th'art thy mother's son.'

Jack took this as the compliment it was. Freddy was a queer old *gorgio*. Strong as an ox, silent as a tracking fox and nobody's place-man. But still he bowed to the wisdom and ways of his *romani* wife who could quieten panicking horses with a whisper. He was content.

'Owt for me?' Jack looked around.

'The mole catcher needs seein' to.' Freddy nodded towards an elaborate torture-device flung carelessly on top of a heap of new garden tools. 'Slip catch not quite right. That done, I got orders for seven. One farming lad said he's never seen anything like it.'

Freddy's garden tools and farm implements were prized even beyond the county boundaries. Colonel Carmedy took a small royalty on each one Freddy sold and did not make a fuss at the Benbow blacksmith's failure to confine himself to estate work. With the extra pairs of hands provided since Keziah had turned up with Honesty and Jack two years ago, Freddy had been able to take on even more work and was now building a tidy little nest-egg. The boy Jack was hard-working and inventive. Every tool nowadays had some little modification that he'd dreamed up, making Freddy's tools even more desirable and the business more profitable.

That being said, Freddy always watched Jack very carefully. No matter how helpful and inventive he was, Freddy always felt that you had to watch him. He sometimes seemed too clever, too eager. It was hard to see what was going on behind those golden eyes of his. He seemed so much older than his seventeen years. Like his mother, he sometimes went off for days on end, leaving promised jobs undone, and he took umbrage at criticism at his absence or his shortcomings.

'We'll get off, then,' said Jack. 'Your Edith'll mebbe have sommat on the hob. I'm that hungry I could eat a dead monkey.'

'Ugh!' said Honesty. 'What I really fancy is Edith's lamb stew. Come on, will you, Jackie? What I want most in the world is to peel these boots off my poor old feet.'

Five

What a Heavenly Place

3pm

'See?' said Astrid. 'Benbow's nothing at all like the Selands' place.'

She and Constance were standing on the sparse gravel, watching the Seland groom hand their bags and boxes down to John Tyler who had just been introduced to Constance as the Benbow 'odd man'.

Connie glanced up at the sturdy stone house with its cosily curtained mullioned windows, its unlikely stone portico. Certainly this wasn't an ancient house, in English terms. 'I would say not,' she said tentatively. What was the right thing to say? 'But . . .' She turned round in a circle. 'It's set so wonderfully in this park, with those rising hills. And the wonderful meadow. A beautiful setting.'

To her relief Astrid nodded, and pointed to a square block-like building alongside the house. Its bulky shape was softened by rampant Virginia creeper that was now dying off. It was crowned with an odd glass construction on its flat roof. 'That's my father's library, the only part of the old building which survived the fire.'

'Didn't they want to rebuild the whole thing? Just as it was?'

Astrid shrugged. 'Apparently my grandfather said he wanted no draughty old mausoleum. He put in the skylight on the library roof to improve the light. But as for the new house, his fancy was something modern and comfortable. Such a place would take half the staff to run and would leave more money for his journeys and his life in London. Like my father he was a bit of a traveller and a scholar. There was trouble over the corn then, and the rents were falling. So he wouldn't waste money on a grand building.'

Just then, round from the side of the house came a tall, heavily built, rather attractive young woman dressed in black. Her face was as watchful as a ticking clock. She stood there surveying the unloading, her hands folded beneath a jutting bosom.

Astrid looked at her friend. 'Is the house where you live like this? Or is it like Seland Hall? Or . . .' She blushed at her own curiosity. Constance's openness was infectious.

Constance laughed. 'Well, dearest Astrid, my place is not a log cabin, nor is it a teepee. It's not like this cosy place, nor is it like Lady Seland's pile.' She paused a second. 'It's a castle. You know? Like a Scottish castle? With turrets and a moat and a central keep? Set among high redstone mountains?'

'My goodness,' said Astrid.

'As you say, *my goodness*. The house was my dear father's fancy, of course. He saw a print of your old Queen's castle in Scotland. He had our castle built so my mother could live in great style. She could be queen of all she surveyed. That way, he thought, she'd not miss the sophistication of life back East. It didn't work, of course. Not only did she hate the castle, she returned East. Then she got on a boat and kept coming and landed up here in England. Poor Poppa.' She sighed.

Astrid didn't know whether or not she should laugh, but she decided against it. She swallowed the chuckle and nodded gravely.

The Seland groom clambered back up onto his empty carriage. He turned the horses with some expertise and set them off at a trot down the winding drive. Astrid could have sworn she heard him whistling.

The woman was bearing down on them. 'Miss Benbow.' The bottom of the clock-face dissolved into a brief smile. 'Welcome home. We'd thought you'd be here tomorrow?'

'Change of plans, Mrs Tyler. This is my friend Miss Constance Redoute who will be staying with us. Constance, this is Mrs Tyler, my mother's right-hand woman. And married to John, over there.'

Constance put out a hand, which was not taken. The woman ducked her head forward like a pecking bird. The sturdy body creaked in a grudging curtsey. 'Good afternoon, Miss Redoute. I hope you enjoy your stay.' Her mouth barely opened when she spoke and her voice was like a whisper on the wind. She turned back to Astrid. 'Mr Tyler and I will attend to the luggage, Miss Benbow.'

'My mother, Mrs Tyler? Is she at home? My brothers?'

'Mrs Benbow, of course, is up in the walled garden, miss.' The dry tone in her voice suggested that the question had been unnecessary.

'And my brothers?'

'Master Michael John and his brother have gone up to the High Wood by the ice house, to shoot rabbits with Jacob Ellenberg. Let's hope that's all they do shoot,' she added darkly.

The boys, more especially Michael John, had shot many things in their time, including crows strung from trees, squealing piglets escaped from their sty, a prize cow from the home farm and, once, Jacob Ellenberg himself. The old man had been seeing to some pheasant pens and had wandered into Michael John's line of fire. It was called an accident, but Michael John, young as he was, was a very accurate shot. And he liked his fun.

Mrs Tyler, who would have whipped the boy for it, was very disappointed when Mrs Benbow merely sent for the doctor to bind old Jacob's flesh wound and told the boys to put the guns away and go off and play something else. Really, Mrs Benbow was far too preoccupied with her garden. She knew more about her garden boys than she did about her own two sons. Those Benbow boys, Mrs Tyler frequently told her husband, would come to a sticky end.

'Well then, shall we brave the meadow and go and see my mother?' Astrid asked. She took off her hat and cloak and handed them to Mrs Tyler. Constance did the same.

Mrs Tyler sniffed. 'She'll be talking to that gypsy woman, no doubt about that. I saw the woman wheeling that dreadful cart up through the meadow. It was loaded with horrible-smelling stuff.' She sniffed again. 'Do you know Mrs Benbow has taught that woman and her lumpish son to read? To read? Gypsies, reading, what next? Dogs singing duets I shouldn't wonder.'

'Mrs Tyler!' warned Mr Tyler, from behind Constance's largest box. 'That's quite enough! Now pick up those bags and let's get them inside.'

'So where is this garden?' said Constance.

Astrid nodded towards the horizon. 'Across the meadow and behind that belt of trees.'

'Hidden away like that?'

'The old boy who built the first great mansion didn't want to look at anything as vulgar as a garden that produced cabbages and apples. So he hid it away. I think that's why my mother loves it. It's a place to hide.'

They set out through the tall grass.

'Your Mrs Tyler's a bit of an old sourpuss,' said Constance, linking Astrid by the arm as they crossed the low bridge that spanned the river. Their skirts swished as they made their way through the long grass of the meadow towards the belt of trees that masked the long brick walls of the garden.

Astrid laughed. 'Poor Melanie Tyler feels she's married quite beneath her, I'm afraid. John Tyler was my father's under footman in better times, hoping perhaps to be made butler. Then my father halved the staff and poor Tyler ended up as jack of all the house trades. Melanie was one of the under parlourmaids at Seland Hall. She had high aspirations, had Melanie. John was very handsome. When I was very small I used to think he was like the prince in Sleeping Beauty. But when Melanie kissed him I think he turned into a very craven frog. A shock for her. I'm certain that she thinks all of us at Benbow very *déclassés* compared with the Seland clan, even the fugitive Gertrude. I once overheard her say to John that they were all proper quality there, but at Benbow you never knew who you were going to meet. She thinks she has come down in the world and she is most definitely right.'

This was familiar ground for Constance. She'd learned a complicated matrix of snobbery at her mother's knee which involved rich relations and poor white folk, poor relations and dear sweet coloured folk. Now she reflected on the refinements of snobbery she'd met since she had arrived in England. This was a new one – the maid looking down on her mistress. *Déclassés*, indeed. Back home things were somewhat simpler. There, it was all about money. In Colorado even Mrs Tyler might be able to transform herself into a lady if she were to be lucky up in those hills. There was a saying *one day a laundress, another a millionairess*. Of course, according to Momma, back East it was different. That blatant worship of the golden dollar would be seen as entirely vulgar. Back East they were very keen to ape the refinements and the gentilities of the English. That was one of many things, according to Mrs Redoute, which made the East so very superior to the West. Colorado was most definitely too *déclassé* for Momma. For those exotic Easteners (and, she supposed, for these English), a millionairess laundress would be anathema. As bad as a millionaire gypsy.

Even so Constance had never quite grasped why her mother, despite her Eastern sensitivities, so loved the English that she'd left her doting husband and his castle to come to live here, in this crowded and parochial country. In the two years she'd been here Constance had not learned to love England half so much as her mother. There were so many peculiarly needy people here. So many snobbish traps into which one could unwittingly walk. Constance's first year in Torquay had been a trial.

As Astrid and Constance approached the high-walled garden they passed a young lad shovelling horse manure from a large hand barrow into an open bay, set beside a row of stone garden sheds which abutted the south wall. They entered through a narrow gateway in the high brick wall, first dodging the looping exuberance of a large-flowered honeysuckle in its last autumn excess whose tangle of leaf and battered blossom still hummed with fifty or so feasting bees. Standing on the gravelled path Constance looked round. The high brick wall enclosed an acre of land. The whole space was bisected by two paths that crossed at the centre giving four equal squares, each pencilled in by low box hedges. Another gravelled path outlined these, and between this path and the high walls borders twelve feet deep were edged by lavender cut like a line of pale velvet rope.

The south wall was covered with a row of glasshouses; the central house, a round structure with a high double-height dome, was reached by a flight of shallow steps. Close in front of these glasshouses each quadrant in season was planted up in its own style – rows of potatoes, beans, peas, saladings, blackcurrants, white currants, blackberries, and climbing peas. In high summer one border spilled out with fading perilla, salvia, perovskia, penstemon and scabious: a great drift of mauves, blues and pinks. Another border glistened with flax and nigella backed by delphiniums, foxgloves and lupins. The third border was strewn more loosely with valerian, stachys and very nearly wild geranium. The other border had been stripped bare and was being deep-dug by a boy with very heavy shoulders. In the far quadrant another garden boy was lifting the lights from a row of growing frames.

Behind and above the plants towered warm pockmarked brick walls against which were pinned wide-spreading espalier fruit trees, whose slender upper stems belied the great age of their horny trunks. A boy was up a ladder by the west wall, gently pulling peaches and placing them in a shallow basket that hung from his arm.

Where the main paths crossed at the centre there was a raised pool, planted round with the last of marigold and larkspur. It was crowned with an ornamental iron cupola supported by Freddy Leeming's signature seahorses. Leading from here to the wrought iron gate in the back wall were a series of arches looped now with late blossoming honeysuckle and tiny, nodding white roses. The air was filled by the twittering of birds and the hum of bees and insects.

'My goodness.' Constance breathed in deeply. 'What a heavenly place this is.'

Astrid nodded. 'I suppose you must meet the presiding angel.' She led the way towards the round glasshouse. As they drew near they could hear the steady lilt and rasp of voices pinging against the glass. Inside, beside a round pool that freshened the stifling air, two women sat on high-backed white wire chairs.

The nearer woman sat tall and very straight-backed; she wore a man's jacket and a chip hat set at an angle on black hair that gleamed in the light that was refracted through the glass roof. Her face, too, was masculine, with long flat-planed cheeks scored by deep vertical furrows. Her large eyes, set over her hawk-like nose, showed barely any white of the eyeball. Heavy boots peeped out from the woman's coarse skirt of embroidered cloth. The hands that lay peacefully in her lap were large-boned and heavy-knuckled.

The other woman wore a long cotton jacket over a wide hessian skirt whose gaping pockets were weighed down with trowels and heavy garden clippers. On her head was a purple silk scarf, tied backwards and topped by a shady straw hat. The face underneath the hat was rather too brown and weather-beaten to be admired. However, in its fine bones and heart shape, Constance noted the resemblance to Lady Seland. Like her companion, this woman too had heavy boots beneath her hitched-up skirts.

She stood up and shook out her skirts, freeing leaves and petals into the bright interior air. 'Astrid, my dear girl. What a surprise. I thought perhaps tomorrow?' Her voice was soft and unemphatic.

'We came early from Seland Hall, Mother.' Astrid kissed her mother on her left cheek. Constance wondered what she should do, so she did nothing.

Carmel waited for further explanation from her daughter.

Astrid opened her arms wide. 'I could not tolerate all the fawning and flattering that was going on . . .' She was trying not to stare at her mother's strange companion whose wide golden eyes were set hard on her. The reality of Keziah Leeming was both more and less than what she had expected. More, because of the sheer presence that filled the space to the creaking windows. Less, because she appeared to be peaceful and very still, like the deepest pool.

'By all accounts the King is a very amusing companion.' Mockery and reproof mingled in her mother's voice. 'Isn't this the second time you have met him there? I have not myself had the privilege of his company.'

Astrid thought briefly of Honesty Leeming, who had 'enjoyed' that very company. 'I don't quite know that I agree, Mother. Those around him, of course, seem to think he's amusing. But they would laugh with him and cheer for him even if he were not.'

Carmel turned to Constance. 'And this is your friend?' She put out her small, rough hand and allowed it to be enveloped in Constance's rather longer and more tender one. 'This must be Miss Constance Redoute. A charming name. Perhaps your family were French?'

Constance found herself liking this woman. 'Some generations ago, ma'am. My great-great-grandfather was born in Louisiana, then went to Virginia.'

'But not now?'

'No. My father fought in the war and then created a company that brought the railroad to the midwest.'

'Ah. The outstanding General Redoute! His exploits are a legend.' She released Constance's hand and turned to her daughter. 'Now, Astrid.' She gestured towards Keziah, still sitting in her chair. 'You should meet my friend Keziah Lomas Leeming.'

The dark woman stood up. She towered over Carmel; even Astrid had to look up to her. Keziah neither offered her hand nor bent in the expected curtsy.

'Hello,' said Astrid, her hand dropping to her side. 'Hello, Mrs Leeming.'

'You should call me Keziah.' The woman's voice was deep and resonant. Astrid thought of the gypsy boy on the grey horse. 'Everyone calls me Keziah.'

'Hello, Keziah,' said Astrid uncertainly. She broke the ensuing pause. 'Keziah, this is my friend Constance Redoute.'

Constance clumsily grasped Keziah's hand before she could avoid it. Then she turned back to Carmel. 'I sure am grateful, ma'am, for your kind invitation. I have not experienced it as yet but they do say that London is quite deadly this late in August. July was a different matter entirely.'

Carmel opened her blue eyes wide. 'Of course, your first season here. I'd forgotten.' She sat back down on her seat. As Keziah resumed her own seat, her chair creaked and settled.

'I was in Torquay last year,' said Constance. 'No season there!'

Carmel looked from Constance to Astrid then back again. 'Perhaps you would sit with us and enjoy the flowers? Or are you too tired from your journey? Perhaps you wish to rest?'

They sat down side by side on the opposite side of the pool to the older women. On the benches were rows of species pelargoniums. A sprawling old fig tree scrambled up the walls behind them. The air was almost unbearably drenched with the mixed perfumes of rose and stephanotis. Constance's head started to swim.

Carmel waited for them to settle in their seats, then said, 'Perhaps some coffee would be reviving?' She picked up a hunting horn from the bench beside her, took an enormous breath and blew it with all her strength. The sound echoed and re-echoed through the glasshouses and made Constance jump.

They all waited in awkward silence until John Tyler came stumping through the gate with a tray designed like a handled basket holding a large flask and four cups and saucers. He placed the tray on a bench while he cleared the low table beside Carmel's chair of plant catalogues and notebooks. 'We assumed the young ladies would partake,' he said as he arranged the cups and poured out the steaming coffee. He avoided looking at Keziah Leeming.

'You assumed quite correctly,' said Carmel gravely. 'I thought perhaps Mrs Tyler might bring it up?' she added innocently. She knew quite well that her odd man's wife would not deign to bring the basket over the meadow and serve tea to Keziah Lomas Leeming.

'Ah no, Mrs Benbow. Mrs Tyler is busy instructing Cook for this evening's dinner.' He struck one hand against the other and backed out, uneasy in the lie. 'There being visitors, like,' he called from the door as he departed, 'she thought they'd need to fix something special.'

Astrid thought ruefully that her mother did not change. She always teased and tested one without seeming to care about the result. Astrid looked over the rim of her cup at Keziah, this newcomer to Benbow who seemed to have had a meteoric effect on them all, including Mrs Tyler. 'I met your daughter Honesty, Mrs Leeming. At Seland Hall.'

'My name is Keziah,' she said, her strong brow rising into her hairline. 'I telt yer, yer mun call me Keziah.' She drank a gulp of the hot coffee. 'She works in that place, our Honesty.'

'No longer. We passed her on the way. She's coming home.'

Keziah frowned. 'She has a holiday?'

'No. I'm sure she's come home.' Astrid hesitated. 'Perhaps she'll tell you why.'

Keziah glanced across at Carmel. 'I telt you she'd be no good. Inside a house like that. She likes to be inside but it's no good for the likes of her!'

Astrid, stung by the familiarity of Keziah's tone, fought back the instinct to blurt out the truth that had been burdening her since early morning.

Carmel shook her head at Keziah. 'The child was eager. She was neat. Such training will do her no harm.'

'No place for a *romani* girl, skivvying for others in a house. Eating dirty food.' Keziah would not let it go.

'The child was eager,' repeated Carmel.

Astrid tried to change the subject. 'Honesty told me you were a horse dealer, Keziah, and that you can cure horses. Have you always done this?'

'She says that, does she? Well, it be better if the girl kept her mouth shut.' Keziah cast a hard glance at Astrid. 'Better if all keep their mouth shut, I say.'

Astrid looked back into her golden eyes and thought that perhaps this woman knew everything. About the King. And Honesty. Everything.

Unbidden, her thoughts went to Keziah's son, who had those same golden eyes and that same inner strength. She could see his face before her even now. There was something about him that stuck in the memory, however one wished to dismiss it.

Six

Carmel's Lair

4pm

I have to admit I rather relish seeing my daughter Astrid treading the difficult conversational path with my friend Keziah Leeming, sometimes called Lomas. To be perfectly honest, Keziah can be as taciturn as any of her kind in the wrong company. Sometimes she'll talk at length and in elaborate detail about her travels and her horses and the long lineage of her own family. There are some strange tales. I often think she borrows stories from other memories and makes a whole new truth in her own mind. She once told me a story of how she magicked the death of a man who had poisoned her best horse. Another time she told me of how she saw the birth of a child with two heads and supervised the ritual burning of the poor creature in the very dark of the night. How later, when the next was due, the young mother stayed with her in her *vardo* for the whole of the birth time, to ensure there were no more monsters. She told me of a potion in her possession that she used from time to time (very sparingly) to ensure the birth of a stallion.

So often I think that Rufus would have loved her! She'd have been such a prize in his laboratory. His notebooks would have been filled with her words laid out in his neat, tight writing.

Today she's being quite polite with Astrid and her friend Constance – very direct, not saying too much. She cocks her head to one side as she listens to them, like a fisherman playing a fish to test its cunning and its strength. Suddenly there is tension in the air. I can feel that she wants Astrid to tell her something and Astrid is resisting.

Astrid has a strength of her own that I quite admire, even though, to my regret, we're not close. She was always such a watcher, Astrid, even when she was a child. It was quite a relief to get away from her quiet gaze. One always thought she saw far more than she told.

Even so, in my experience Keziah holds the whip in most conversations. It was so when we first met and has been so ever since. She comes to see me and goes away in her own time. Whatever is to hand has to be put to one side, even if it is a very needy rose.

The day she first came – a warm June morning – I am down at Freddy Leeming's checking the details for the gate for the rose-garden in a vain effort to persuade him to incorporate one less seahorse. Keziah turns up at his door in her *vardo* with the girl child Honesty on board and that very fine-looking boy leading the draught horse. At the back of this equipage hangs a home-braided rope trailing two highly bred but rather dusty Welsh cobs.

Freddy abandons my querulous enquiries about the gate and takes a closer look at the cobs and their owner. This big dark woman takes Freddy from one horse to the other, showing him how their feet are unshod and sore. Her blunt finger jabs at Freddy to make the particular point about her demands on his professional skill. He unties the horses and tethers them to his blacksmith's rail, his every move showing his anxiety to please.

The young girl wiggles her bare feet and watches from the *vardo*. I see her lick her dusty lips. I am drawn to the fine clear lines of this child's face, the trim jawline, the rosy tinge on the high cheekbones, the hair springing from her brow like fine black moss. She has the simple beauty of the wild hedge-rose.

I offer the children food and drink and a ride in my dogcart. The girl smiles an enchanting large-toothed smile and the boy glances at his mother, who says something in their tongue.

'What does she say?' I say, more sharply than I should. The woman has me on edge.

'She says we may take food and milk but must not go in the house.' His bold gaze meets mine. 'She says the houses of the *gorgios* are dirty. That they wash and cook in the same dish.'

I've heard this before so it does not disturb me. 'That is fine. You do not need to come into the house. You can eat in the yard.'

This they do, under the baleful eye of Mrs Mac and Melanie Tyler as well as the more disinterested eyes of Susannah the Spanish Cat and the yard cockerel of no name. The disapproval of the two women spills over onto me though they dare not voice it. I can see that they ask themselves what am I doing to encourage this scourge of travelling people who call at the Hall as regular as clockwork? I know they both hoped when Rufus died it would be an end of all this. Then, surely, the place would be free of these people who move through the country following the seasons with the regularity and the disturbing flurry of migrating birds; people who are unpredictable in their moods and preferences and have only a dim view of the integrity of property and territory.

The baleful looks bestowed on me by these two women make me defiant. I order the unwilling cook to pack a basket with bread and cheese and vegetables and bacon, as well as a tin jug of milk from the cow. My son Ambrose, just in from playing catchball on the pasture, pours the milk for me and carries it to the dogcart, much to the disgust of his brother Michael John who stands scowling in the kitchen doorway, as cross as Mrs Tyler and Cook at these shenanigans. Michael John often stares in disgust – at me, at poor Jacob Ellenberg, at Ambrose. He is such a very discontented boy. It can be so distracting.

By the time we get back, Keziah has drawn her *vardo* into the field behind Freddy Leeming's forge. She sits on a hay-bale and calls instructions as she drinks water from a great pot mug. She watches Freddy closely; there is not a single thing he does to her horses that she does not see with her sharp, golden eyes.

The child, who tells me her name is Honesty, runs across to show her mother the basket. Keziah nods in my direction but does not trouble to say thank you for the food. So, somewhat chastened by my craven expectation of servility, I make off in my little cart.

The day after her arrival Keziah set the old draught horse free to graze alongside the newly shod cobs. Freddy and Keziah were married in a few weeks. For her wedding gift Freddy rented from us the three-acre field behind the forge and one beyond that. On this she let out the horses to graze, allowed chickens to scratch and finally found a home for a donkey that another gypsy had been housing for her. Her turkey she tethered by a string to a wheel of the *vardo*.

Since then the boy Jack has made a living mending wagons and rigs not just for gypsies but for other horsemen in the county. He is his own man but is very clever and inventive, solving problems of haulage and balance in ways never seen before. His intricate skills ensure that his relationship with his quiet stepfather flourishes in the soil of mutual appreciation.

The little girl (more hedge-rose than honesty) was my shadow for more than a year. I hauled out Rufus's photographic equipment and took pictures of her while she played and helped her mother and brother about the place. She came up to the garden a good deal and helped me pot up plants and fertilise my new roses. She was very neat and organised and I came to watch for her coming to the garden. I would plan little tasks suitable for her small hands. Here I have to admit that where I would shoo Astrid and her brothers out of the garden, I looked forward to Honesty tripping her way down my path, and dealing with Jack over garden tools.

The boy, though, always refused to have his picture taken and I was reminded of Rufus who told me of one tribe he met who accused him of taking their spirit when he showed them their photographs. Towards the end of that first year Keziah, just back from a selling trip to Scotland, came across to the garden to find her daughter. She'd never been here before and Honesty watched through the window of the glasshouse as her mother walked slowly round the garden to look and to sniff, to touch and to pinch between her fingers. She nodded and talked to herself as she went. Then she walked through the grape and the peach houses and came through the plant house to the round glasshouse, which is my lair. She sat on the seat beside me and asked me if I knew that my garden was full of medicine and good things.

'Thank you,' I said. I bathed in the warmth of her compliment and at that moment felt I would do anything for her. I wondered whether this was how Freddy Leeming had become Keziah's slave and married her so quickly, despite being a confirmed bachelor half in love with his sister Edith. How wise Keziah was about Edith, leaving her her territory and three-quarters of her brother's attention.

'My daughter works very hard for you,' she stated then.

'Yes, yes,' I said, too eagerly. 'She is a wonderful help.'

'You have no daughter?' she said.

'Yes, I do. She's in London.'

'Did she help you?'

I shook my head. 'I was often away in the early days, travelling with my husband. When I came back she had her own preoccupations. And I wanted to get on with the garden.'

'Freddy Leeming tells me your man was the scholar? The *rai* who wrote down the history of the gypsies.'

'Yes. His notebooks are in the house if you want to read them.'

'I cannot read, but I imagine it is an easy enough matter. Will you teach me to read and then let me read them?'

I was flustered by this, though I shouldn't have been. 'Well . . .' I said.

'I will learn,' she said. 'It is my history. I wish to read it.'

'Of course, of course.'

That was how the lessons and the talking and the quiet times in the round glasshouse began. Sometimes I was pleased when Keziah went off on one of her selling trips so I could get on with my roses. But I always looked forward to her return. It was in the glasshouse that we cooked up the turn in Honesty's fortunes. It started by Keziah telling me that Honesty's father was a *gorgio* and that the child wasn't a proper *romani*. It seemed there was always a worry, with such people, that travelling would not suit. So it was with the girl. Honesty had settled very cosily there at the forge cottage with Edith, as though she'd never been in a van in her life.

In the end it was I who suggested we should try Honesty with a domestic place. This was how she ended up in Margaret Seland's household. I missed her when she went away but I knew it was for her own good and I got used again to my empty lair.

But Astrid says Honesty is back. There must be something amiss.

When I finally get down to the forge and see her I can see there is really something amiss. She's back from Seland Hall as Astrid said. But there is more to it than that. The child's own demeanour is carefree enough but there is something the matter. I saw this in the glasshouse in the face of my own Astrid. She knew something and was keeping me out. But I will not pursue it. There is work to do here in the garden.

Seven

The Shooting

5pm

Apart from the burden of keeping a very watchful eye on the troublesome Michael John Benbow, Jacob Ellenberg was grateful for many things in his life. He was guiltily grateful even to be still alive. He was most grateful of all to Rufus Benbow for rescuing him on the Liverpool docks when he arrived in 1895, having made his escape from the savage persecution against Jews in Russia.

With characteristic generosity and originality Rufus had decided that Jacob should share a house with Seb Golightly and learn from him the role of gamekeeper. The fresh air would put colour in his cheeks and take the strain from his eyes. The urban Jacob found this all very strange but oddly congenial. The Benbow gamekeeper's job was not onerous. Unusually in that district, there was no hunting on Benbow land; more surprising, there was very little shooting. Seb Golightly did make a half-hearted attempt to curb the poaching on his domain. However, Jacob soon learned that there seemed to be some kind of tacit agreement about this, which involved not arresting the poachers they apprehended. They merely gave them a good talking to, which did no good at all.

Seb Golightly's main responsibility, now to be shared with Jacob, was the scholarly recording of the seasonal movement of the birds, the multiplying of the fish, and the growth of trees and plants, on this rambling, altogether decrepit estate. A large part of Jacob's job was to take the notes and drawings that were scribbled in their notebooks out in the field and copy them into great ledgers in Rufus Benbow's library. Rufus had rightly thought that this was where the clerkly Jacob would come into his own. And so he did, spending many absorbing hours in Rufus's library, copying images from the notebooks into the ledgers, the sunshine streaming down from the skylight onto his balding head.

In the weeks before his death Rufus Benbow had sat in that library, huddled in blankets by the blazing fire. He turned the leaves of his ledgers and peered at them through a large spyglass. He commented in a wavering voice to Jacob on how the patterns made by the migrating birds reminded him of the movements of gypsies in Europe. 'There is a pattern to the movements of those people, Jacob. A cosmic, natural pattern. It is not always to do with flight.'

'Not like the Jews,' Jacob had said.

Rufus had shaken his head. 'Perhaps not. But I know very little about the Jews.'

At Rufus's funeral the distraught Jacob had wept for his friend and for his own murdered wife and lost daughter, for whom he'd never been given real time to mourn. He tore his hair and rent his clothes and caused some disturbance in the congregation. Carmel Benbow had led him to the vestry and patted his shoulder. 'We will all miss him, Jacob. Even those of us who barely saw him.'

Only after the ritual burning of Rufus's *vardo*, when the great crowds had departed from Benbow Hall, had Jacob begun to wonder about his own fate without his patron. He sat for days in Golightly's cottage without sleeping, his clothes torn and his hair dishevelled, concern for his own fate gradually subverting his grief at the loss of his friend.

In the end, though, Mrs Benbow was kind. It seemed that Rufus's wishes had been made clear. Jacob was to have the tiny cottage next door to the one he shared with Seb Golightly. In addition, he was to have the deeds to an acre of land three miles down the River Gaunt, and the perpetual lease of Carafay, the small run-down coal pit that stood on that land. Jacob was also to continue to work on the estate with Seb Golightly, ensuring that the ledgers were kept up. His main task was to be to create a kind of index for them. As long as Jacob did this he would receive two hundred pounds a year from a special reserved fund. This was well in excess of Seb Golightly's remuneration and was clearly a sign of genuine affection.

So Jacob Ellenberg was happy at Benbow. The only thing that troubled him was the enforced occasional contact with Michael John Benbow, Rufus's older son. Even to Jacob it was clear to see that Michael John had never been a happy child. His father had no patience with his demanding ways and took little notice of him. His mother was bewildered by his destructive outbursts, even slightly bored. It seemed a relief to them all, including Michael John, when he went off to school. When he came back he was a changed boy. At school he had absorbed a sense of the world and the way it should work. No longer complaining or demanding, he was imperious, self-confident, and had distinct ideas of what he wanted to do in the neglectful freedom of Benbow.

In the ten years Jacob had been here he'd had many occasions to follow Master Benbow's trail in the woods and the fields: he had dealt with the skinned and dead and the half-dead creatures, the charred bones and the desecrated nests of rare birds. He'd silently cleared up the mess and, as far as he could, restored the damage. Seb Golightly had told him this was the way you had to do it up here at the Hall. In the past Mr Benbow had mostly been away and Mrs Benbow, busy with her garden, did not wish to know of any trouble regarding their children, particularly not the exasperating Michael John. Seb told Jacob of the time he'd given the lad a thrashing and had been offered his notice by Mrs Benbow. He'd not risked that again.

There were respites, of course, during the school terms. Still, in the holidays Michael John, seventeen years old now (six feet tall and immaculately handsome), showed that he did not improve with age. His particular game this summer was to insist his young brother Ambrose should serve him, jump to it, like his fag at school. He also dropped the *Mr* from Jacob Ellenberg's name and took to ordering him around on matters regarding the condition of the guns and the state of the ground cover. More than once he'd ordered Jacob out of the library for no reason at all.

Jacob, obsessed now with protecting Rufus's domain, took to following the boy on his shooting forays, so that he could properly identify the damage done, and note it. He had an idea that one day he would be able to go to Mrs Benbow and show her the pattern of Michael John's destruction just as clearly as he could demonstrate the presence of golden plover and bullfinch in the Bottom Wood. He persisted with his surveillance even after that time Michael John had winged him with a glancing shot, then had protested to his mother that Ellenberg had been hiding in the undergrowth, skulking like a gun shy dog.

The day Astrid Benbow returned to the Hall from London, Jacob was tracking Michael John. A few hundred yards into Bottom Wood Jacob heard a shot, followed by screams and groans. Then there was silence. Very quietly he moved forward through the trees to the edge of a small clearing. The boy Ambrose was tied to a tree with rope, tears flowing down his cheeks, lips pressed tight together. The bark on each side of his head was mangled and smashed.

Michael John stands twelve feet away, cocking his reloaded shotgun. His voice is quiet, threaded through with deadly calm. 'There now, Amby, I told you there was no danger. But the rule is that you mustn't shout out or what might happen? What?'

The child's lips form the whisper. 'You might lose your aim.'

'And then what might happen?'

'You might shoot me.'

'Where?'

'Through the heart.'

'Or?'

'Through the head.' Sweat is running down the child's face.

'Well then . . .' Michael John raises the gun to his shoulder. Before his finger can squeeze the trigger Jacob moves out of the shadows, walking forward very steadily. He stands still with his body between Ambrose and his brother.

'Ellenberg! Clear out!' says Michael John sharply. 'Mind your own business.'

Keeping his back to Michael John, Jacob takes out his pruning knife and sets about cutting through the ropes that tie Ambrose. The boy looks up at him from a face lumpy with terror. 'I've wet myself,' he wails. 'Mr Ellenberg, I've wet myself.'

'Do not worry about that, Ambrose.' Jacob pulls the boy away from the tree and, still shielding him with his own body, guides him to the edge of the clearing. 'Now then, boy, you run home. Mrs Tyler will take care of you.'

He turns back to Michael John who is standing, feet apart, his shotgun at the ready in his hands. The boy raises it and nestles his smooth cheek to the stock and aims. 'Go on, dirty Jew, you run!' He says the words through clenched teeth.

Jacob looks at him calmly. 'You are a very wicked boy, Michael John. Your father would very much regret it. But I must tell you I have been pursued by people far better schooled in evil than yourself.'

Michael John tightens his finger on the trigger. 'You're a scheming slimy Jew who's wormed your way here, who's stolen our money . . .'

Before Michael John can pull the trigger a blow from a heavy stick puts him on his knees and sends the gun spinning from his hands. A rattling crack resounds through the clearing as the stray bullet brings down a shower of leaves and branches.

Jacob walks forward, picks up the gun and smiles faintly at his saviour, a dark-haired young man with bare feet and a soft hat on his head. 'A close thing, young sir.' Jacob keeps his eye on Jack Lomas's face. He ignores the two dead rabbits at the gypsy boy's feet and the frisky Jack Russell – a fine hunting breed – at his heels. 'I thank you from my heart.'

Jack winks, then nods towards the kneeling Michael John. 'Me, I like a good scrap but that was too uneven for my blood. Tying up the *charver* like that. It ain't right. Then you, standin' there like a sitting duck.'

They watch as Michael John hauls himself to his feet and attempts to brush down his immaculate jacket with flapping hands. He takes a kick at Jack's dog, who has come to sniff at him. He scowls at Jacob. 'Hand over my gun, Ellenberg.'

Jacob shakes his head. 'I think not, sir. I think perhaps I should return the gun safely into your mother's hands.'

Michael John takes a step towards him. 'I warn you, you dirty Jew . . .'

He is hauled back by huge hands. 'Settle down, will yer? Leave the old man alone,' says Jack Lomas. Then he puts a bare foot into the lower part of Michael John's back and kicks him on his way. 'Get yourself out of here. And next time pick a real man to fight, not an old man or a *charver*.'

Michael John runs to the edge of the trees and turns to face them. 'Jews and gypsies, poachers and thieves, that's all you are.' He is trying to deal with very inconvenient tears. 'That's all you are.' Then he walks off in the same direction as Ambrose. When he thinks he's out of sight of the watching man and boy he starts to run. He doesn't know where he is running, or to whom. Not to his mother, that's for sure. He knows she will not listen to him. She will have that blank look on her face and her gaze will move somewhere to the left of his head. Even the worst – or the best – thing he could do would be of little interest to her.

Jacob breaks the stock of the gun and puts it under his arm. He shakes his head. 'His father would be very disappointed. It seems that the boy learns very strange ideas at his grand school.'

'About Jews and gypsies, mebbe?' Jack picks up his rabbits and his heavy stick and turns to go.

'Thank you, boy!' calls Jacob to the lad's receding back. His only acknowledgement is a brawny arm raised into the air as Jack Lomas melts again into the promiscuous tangle of foliage that still rages through the Bottom Wood in late August.

Eight

Walking the Bounds

5.30pm

The Benbow odd man, John Tyler, came back from the walled garden laden with an armful of pink hydrangea, several long purple spikes of Russian sage and fifteen long-stemmed dahlias. On the other arm he had a basket filled with cucumber and capsicums, parsnips and beetroot, carrots and salsify, all nestling in a bed of cabbage leaves.

He left the flowers in the back scullery and took the vegetables in to Mrs McInerny, the cook. 'I see we've got a big dinner tonight, Mrs Mac, according to Mrs Benbow. We're to have all our buttons on. We're to fly the flag for England, so to speak, as we have this American friend of Miss Astrid to entertain.' He took a note from his pocket and read from it. 'She says to do the pork loin as planned but that she'll get Seb to wring the necks of a couple of pullets as well. And she'll send the boy down with fresh grapes and late strawberries. She requests your special lemon jelly with the nasturtiums. There are a few in here, beside the capsicums.'

The cook made a great play of peering under the table and out of the window. 'And where, John Tyler, does the missis think is the army that'll help a poor woman to put such a feast on the table?'

John Tyler smiled. He knew Mrs Mac wasn't averse to a bit of a show. She sometimes complained that food, though always good and fresh, wasn't given its due place in this house. For heaven's sake, these days people never ate at the Benbow table without they had their nose in a book or a plant catalogue! He went on, 'I'll go down to the village to get hold of your niece Kate and young Leonie Liss. They won't say no to earning an extra shillin' or two. And I'll do the table, of course, and get Mrs Tyler to do the flowers. And she can help you in here as well.'

Mrs Mac shook her head. 'No offence, Mr Tyler, but I'll manage with the girls. Wouldn't wish to disturb Mrs Tyler, not in a month of Sundays. I've heard all about true love, Mr Tyler, but your missis must have charms hidden from us common folk. To be honest with you I don't like her to set foot in here.'

'Aye, I know that,' he said patiently.

'Don't get me wrong, Mr Tyler. Your wife is wonderful, I'm sure, with the polish and duster and the smoothing iron, but she's curdled my custard more than once.'

John Tyler smiled helplessly. The domestic territory of Benbow Hall was carefully carved out between Mrs Mac and his wife. John, who had to breach the frontiers regularly, had developed a survival technique that involved smiling in impotent agreement with whichever woman was on the genteel attack.

He went upstairs to the linen cupboard to break the news to his wife. 'I thought you could do the flowers, Mellie. Mrs Benbow sent up some lovely dahlias for the table and a big mound of pink and purple stuff for the fireplace. Asked specially for you to do them. Said you had the touch. You always do the house great justice. That's what she said.' John indulged in many white lies to keep his life smooth.

Melanie sat back on her heels. 'I bet that Mrs Mac's in a flap. Can't cope with anything the least bit out of the ordinary. Never could.'

John smiled his smile of helpless agreement. 'I'm going down to Benbow on me bicycle to get Kate McInerny and Leonie Liss to give her a hand.'

Melanie sniffed. 'Good thing too. You won't get me to skivvy for that Mrs Mac. Not in a month of Sundays.'

John smiled on. 'I'd never agree that you should, Mellie. Surely you know that?'

'The table must be right, John. You should take trouble with the table.'

'Oh, the table will be right. You can be sure of that. We've got to show these Americans what for. We must be on our mettle.' He put out a hand to help his wife to her feet. Her smaller fingers fitted there very comfortably. For all her prickliness John Tyler still thought he'd got a treasure when he married Melanie. He squeezed her hand. 'I tell you what, Mellie, I read in the newspaper that this Miss Redoute is the daughter of a general. A piece about the King visiting Seland Hall. Said the General was a hero of the Civil War and what's more he's a millionaire.'

'The girl probably eats off gold plates where *she* lives.' Melanie Tyler pulled her hand away and smoothed down her immaculate apron, and sniffed again. 'Can't make a silk purse out of a sow's ear, John. Even at Seland Hall it will only be the best Sèvres porcelain. Here we just have Spode. Any dinner here wouldn't be a patch on those affairs I used to wait on at Seland Hall. They are very superior there. How Lady Seland and Mrs Benbow come to be cousins I'll never know.'

'Mellie!' For once John Tyler's tone was firm. 'That's very disloyal.'

Melanie Tyler, as Mrs Mac had done minutes before, made a play at looking around for invisible people. 'Disloyal? Are there spies here? Oh no! Will you report me to Mrs Benbow? Or will you remember that I'm your wife?'

John Tyler stared at his wife and smiled helplessly.

Astrid left Constance to unpack her own trunk and set off from the house to walk the bounds. She'd always enjoyed walking the bounds with her father each time he returned from his travels. When she was a small child her greatest delight had been to be his silent companion, trudging three steps behind him all the way. Her father was an occasional enchantment in her young life, a beloved mystery. He said very little but she picked up the slightest statement and put it away in her memory, like a treasured ribbon in a locked box. He was never there to hear her woes about school, or to witness her despair about her vanishing nanny, her mother's neglect, her isolation when the boys finally went back to school. Her inevitable escape first to Paris, then to London was barely noticed by either of her parents. She exchanged the usual polite, quite informative letters with him, but the only time she returned to Benbow was for his funeral.

At the funeral she saw him through the eyes of other people. The stories they told painted a picture of a spirited, convivial man, a battler for the underdog, a great humanitarian. Not for the first time she contemplated the fact that the man they described must have come home to rest from all that. He simply left that convivial man behind. At home he was quiet, reflective. She and her brothers enjoyed less attention from their father than any passing stranger. Think of the way Jacob Ellenberg – nice as he was – had become a fixture in the household. She reflected now that she'd had more real conversations with the quiet Mr Ellenberg than she'd had with her father.

Today she set out on the route her father had always taken: up behind Benbow Hall, down the lane to the village that sat with its mud streets and low rows of houses among the spoil-heaps and tangled headgear of Benbow Colliery, thankfully invisible from the Hall.

If she remembered rightly, they would go along the ancient overgrown path by Bottom Wood to Carafay, the little pit which had its own small slag heaps and sent its chaldrons of coal down to Benbow pit by the small railway spur that joined them, and then on to Hartlepool, on the coast. Carafay was run by Colonel Carmedy as part of the estate, though it was now the property of old Jacob. In one of her mother's rare letters she wrote that Carafay just ticked over with twenty or so men.

Then they would go on down past the lakes and the hump of land under which lay the icehouse. Her father had once allowed her to peep into its dark mossy interior. She had asked him whether it was *the very jaws of hell*, as she'd heard Mr Golightly call it once. Her father replied with a laugh that he thought hell was a rather warmer place.

After that, on down to where the River Gaunt flowed into the broad reaches of the Wear. And back up through the bluebell wood that edged the slag heaps and the tangle of buildings and the great wheel which was the big Red Daisy Pit whose coal was said to keep the Prime Minister warm. Then came the long walk along the high ridge that finally led down by the walled garden and back across the meadow to the Hall.

There were illusions. Parcels of land had been sold off, like bites taken out of a cake. Her father had once told her, 'One must be honest, Astrid. We're not actually walking the true bounds of Benbow. But from this pathway wherever you look, as far as the horizon, has been Benbow land.'

Astrid was thinking ahead of herself: she was barely at the beginning of her walk. She paused at the gate of the forge cottage. Freddy's sister Edith Leeming came out, leaning against the weight of a washing basket on her hip.

'Good evening, Miss Leeming,' said Astrid. She and her father had always stopped there for a drink. In those days, though, there was just Edith and Freddy Leeming: a quiet self-sufficient brother-and-sister couple at the forge. In those days there was no woman horse-dealer with a wild son and a striking daughter.

Edith nodded at Astrid and put down her heavy clothes basket on the grassy path. 'Evening, Miss Benbow. Long time since we had a sight of you. You out for a walk, I see.' She had a soft Durham voice and a settled, uninvaded manner. 'I just have scones out of the oven, should you wish . . .'

Astrid smiled. 'You might lose the weather for drying the clothes, Miss Leeming.' She sat down on a low wall by the gate.

'Aye. But our Honesty'll hang the stuff out while I get the kettle on. You just sit there now. I'll bring your tea out. Honesty!' she called.

'Right, Auntie.' The girl came out, glanced blandly across at Astrid and set about pegging out the clothes. Her curly hair was hanging free and her petticoats were pinned up. Her brown legs were strong and her feet were bare. She was hardly recognisable as the demure fireplace maid from Seland Hall. Astrid watched silently as she pinned up two white shifts and three pairs of drawers.

'How are you, Honesty?' she called at last.

The girl took the peg out of her mouth to answer. 'There's nothing the matter with me, miss,' she said firmly. ''Part from being happy to be home, like, just for now.'

'I'm pleased to hear that.' Astrid lowered her voice. 'Have you told your mother . . . your auntie . . .?'

The girl shook her head. 'Nah. Couldn't do nowt about it anyway.'

'But that was an awful thing. You should do something about it.'

'What should I do? Send down our Jack to put his fists up to him? Have me mother put a spell on him?' She picked up a bundle of socks, shook them out and laid them in a line one by one along the edge of the basket. 'I've been thinking about it, see? That – thing – was no worse than it might be with any man. I admit that before that I didn't really know what it was that happened with a man and a woman. And now I do. And I know whichever man it was first time it would have to be like that – like, *forcing*. You'd have to be forced. There's no way you could do it otherwise.'

Astrid could feel colour rising in her cheeks. 'I don't know, Honesty, that that's the way to look at it.' Her own ignorance of the process had never been more troubling. She'd no notion, truly, about the nature of the thing that had happened to Honesty.

'And he wasn't a bad old man. He gave me the guinea.'

'And you haven't told your mother or your auntie?'

Honesty started to peg up the socks. 'They'd make more of it than it was. It'd be a seven day wonder round here.' She finished off the socks. 'Keziah knows sommat's happened, though. She always knows.'

Astrid thought how odd it was that Honesty called her mother by her given name. 'Does she?'

'I can tell it in her eye.'

'So will she not say something?'

'Not if I don't.' Honesty picked up the basket and put it on her hip. 'She wouldn't.'

'So you will stay at home now?'

Honesty shook her head. 'Nah. No fear of that. There's plenty here to do the work with Auntie Edith and Keziah. I'll be off again soon.'

'Will you go again into "place"?'

Honesty shook her head. Her dark curls trembled in the low brassy light of early evening. 'No fear of me skivvying like that again, miss. I thought I might go to some town. Our Jack says York's a big town. There might be something for me there. I thought of a shop, but I'm not sure about standing there all prim. Lifting and carrying I could do. I'm very strong. But not in a house. I'm never going near anyone's bedroom ever again.' The faintest of smiles passed over her face. 'Not ever again.'

She vanished into the house and Edith came out with a china cup and saucer in one hand and a plate bearing a scone on a small doily in the other. She stood and held the plate while Astrid sipped the tea. This was in the tradition. Edith, and her mother before her, would stand and watch as Rufus Benbow, and his father before him, drank their tea and ate their scone. It was inconceivable that Edith or her mother should actually eat and drink with any Mr or Miss Benbow.

'You have a new family now, I see,' said Astrid.

HONESTY'S DAUGHTER

'Seems like. The woman is a strange'n but at least she never tipped us out of me own kitchen. The boy's strange too but a good hand for Freddy. Right clever at making things.'

'And the girl?'

'Honesty? Why, I love her like she was me own. Was put out when they sent her away. But that seems to have come unstuck, though I can't think why. She's a good girl.' She frowned. 'Mebbe she blotted her copy-book.'

'Honesty did nothing wrong, Miss Leeming. I was at Seland Hall. I'm really certain she did nothing wrong.' Astrid ate the last crumb of scone and handed the cup and saucer back to Edith. 'Lovely scone, Miss Leeming. I'll get on. I'm walking the bounds.'

Edith stood very still, looking at her. 'Aye. Old Mr Benbow always did that. He's a big miss round here. We were very sorry when he was taken. He was only here now and then but he left his presence behind him. More ways than one.'

Astrid laughed. 'Mrs Tyler's not too happy about the travellers who keep calling.'

Edith shrugged. 'Melanie Tyler can't see further than the keys to her linen cupboard. Mr Benbow explained it to me one day. Those travellers are part of the pattern; they were here before she came and'll still be there after she's gone.'

Astrid stood up, away from the wall. 'Take good care of Honesty, Miss Leeming,' she said. 'She really is a good girl.'

As she strolled further along the lane she reflected on how, within a day, Honesty had become important to her. Then a story leapt into her mind, one her father had told her, about a Chinese legend which said that if you help someone at a critical time they become part of your life for ever.

She paused at a gap in the hedge. In the field beside the road Keziah Leeming was schooling a young grey horse on a lunge rein. As Astrid watched, the horse pulled and jumped away, making Keziah drop the rein. The sweating animal cantered to the corner of the field, the rein trailing behind him like a snake.

85

He stood there and raised his head to look at Keziah. Very slowly she picked up the rein from the ground and, gathering it in loops in her hand, approached the horse until they were nose to nose. Astrid could hear the rough rasp of her voice as she spoke to the animal. The horse's head went down to her face, then pulled back, snuffling. She said something into his nostrils. Then, without lengthening the rein, she trudged back to the centre of the field, making the horse follow closely just at her shoulder. Pulling in the rein even tighter she got him to walk round and round her in a narrow circle, talking to him all the time. Then bit by bit she lengthened the rein again and the horse stepped calmly round her with light steps in wider and wider circles.

'She's good at that, is Keziah.' A deep voice from behind her made Astrid jump. She turned and had to shade her eyes to look up to see the man on the big grey horse. A sack was thrown across the horse's bare back in front of him, with a soft-brimmed hat perched on top of it. Then she realised that it was not a man. It was the boy, Honesty's brother. He had a long stick slung across his back, held by a red lanyard. 'It's Jack Lomas,' the boy said. 'I picked up our Honesty out there on the road.' His bright eyes met hers.

She found herself blushing. 'I know who you are,' she said. Then to escape those eyes she turned again to the scene through the hedge.

'The old fellers would have given that old hoss a thrashing, face on, to settle him down.' Jack Lomas's voice, softer now, came from behind her. 'It's true that you have to master those old hosses, to get them to heel. But she has her different ways, has Keziah.'

His voice made her conscious of herself, of her hair, of her neck, of the way her dress sat on her shoulders. She breathed out very slowly to cool down then turned to look back at him. 'She's remarkable. Does she really talk to it? Does it understand?'

He smiled and she blushed again.

'Every word,' he said. 'No need for thrashing. Never a mark

on them. We'll be able to add thirty guineas to the price. Never any bother selling Keziah's horses.' The golden eyes blinked at her. The boy seemed easy, not as angry as he'd been in the road. 'A bit of a magician, is our Keziah.'

Astrid made to walk on. Jack moved his horse very slightly, blocking her way.

'I . . . I hope she didn't think I was spying on her.' Astrid didn't understand why he was challenging her. The normal thing would have been for such a boy to pull back, even touch his cap. His head was bare but he made no attempt to touch his curly forelock.

Jack shook his head. 'Keziah wouldn't care tuppence about any of that. She's about her work and don't care who sees. No more than I would.'

'Well.' She moved to one side and he turned the horse the same way. 'What is it?' she said. 'For goodness' sake, what is it?'

He looked her in the eyes. 'I wanted to say to you thank you for looking out for our Honesty up at Seland. She said you'd been all right with her. Really good.' He didn't sound too grateful.

Astrid gave up trying to get past him. She glared at him. 'She is a very nice young woman. I like her. I liked her when I first saw her.' She groaned inwardly. Why on earth had she said that?

'I'm sure our Honesty feels the honour. Me, I told her she should never've gone to that place. Slavery for pennies. I told her it was slavery before she went. But your ma persuaded her.'

'It's not slavery. You're wrong. It's a very respectable . . .'

'Respectable! A respectable slave then. But still, we have to thank you.' He paused. 'For your kindness.' He clicked his teeth and his horse moved on past her. All she could see was his straight, sturdy back swaying above the haunches of his horse which shone like silk in the late afternoon sun.

She stared after him, the muscles in her face aching as she controlled the desire to call after him to come back and dismount and talk some more. About Keziah. About Honesty. About anything.

Nine

The Propagator

6pm

As Carmel Benbow tied the last of the paper bags round the necks of her stripped rose cuttings she reflected that, if she were honest with herself (she very occasionally was), she'd never really cared for her children. She made a note in her battered book: *Rosier de L'Iles + Hume's Blush China – NB inside only*.

She had not really thought she would have children. At twenty-six she'd been plucked from the dry, inevitable disadvantages of third-daughter-non-hunting-spinsterhood by the scholar Benbow. At least it was not spinsterhood-under-the-parental-roof, thanks to a small allowance from her grandmother that prevented her from starving in London while she studied the history of roses. After their meeting at the British Museum Rufus Benbow followed her on a visit to Cumberland. His excuse was that he wished to sell her father some antiquities he'd picked up in Mesopotamia. He'd also tried, unsuccessfully, to interest the old man in the funding of a new expedition into Europe, this time to investigate the genealogy of travelling people.

On the second day Rufus had returned and come upon Carmel in her father's garden. Banned by the gardener from the glasshouses, she was ensconced in the old summerhouse, busy doing her plant experiments. Propagation was her passion.

Bowled over by Rufus Benbow's evident and pursuing interest she'd not had the time to cover herself with her usual mortifying shyness. He questioned her closely about the cross-fertilisation process and she even explained it to him without blushing. He looked at her meticulous notebooks and commented on the unusual quality of her mind, unschooled though it was.

While Rufus was a guest in her father's house, Carmel lived through the days in a state of heightened consciousness and lay awake each night savouring in her head every contact she'd had with Rufus Benbow that day. Downstairs she would blush when she heard the rumble of his voice before he came into a room. She felt the heat, smelled the tobacco-spicy smell of him when he was within six feet of her.

In the end Rufus extended his stay to five days and on the fifth day he asked Carmel's father for her hand in marriage. Within a month they were married in the family chapel up in Cumberland and set out immediately on a journey to Romania in a van – which she learned to call a *vardo* – purchased for them by her delighted father. To get a twenty-six-year-old daughter off his hands was no mean feat. Her parents were relieved to dispose of the daughter they had thought unmarriageable; who stubbornly refused to be presented, to 'come out' in Society and marry someone suitable. The girl was interested in nothing but her blessed plants, her bags of seeds, her catalogues and her garden trowel.

In the first years of their marriage Carmel travelled with Rufus on his European journeys, acting as his amanuensis and helping him to develop his photographs. Rather to his and her own surprise, she took to the physical processes involved in human cross-fertilisation with some sensual delight, although much of this intimacy stopped when Astrid arrived on the scene. She came as quite a shock. Rufus and Carmel were attending a big gypsy gathering just outside Paris. A Frenchwoman, the wife of another scholar, had guessed Carmel's condition by observing her very closely, and had asked her some further questions. At that point it dawned on Carmel that she might be in an 'interesting condition'. Then the Frenchwoman had helped her to work out that she was probably eight months pregnant, although it barely showed under her flowing skirt. The ever-practical but distracted Rufus had packed her on the train with picnic baskets and instructions about how to get home to Benbow Hall. He waved her off at the Gare du Nord and went back to his discussions.

She'd arrived at Benbow Hall on a bitter September day. Crowner, the old butler, had welcomed her like a princess. In the middle of that night she gave birth to Astrid with the help of the cook. Mr Crowner put on his black apron and instructed the boy John Tyler to boil water and do exactly what Cook said. He sent to Bishop Auckland for the doctor but, the road being bad, the latter arrived only in time to congratulate the mother on the delivery of a fine, fit daughter.

The birth was painful but quick and after the doctor had gone Carmel barely stirred for a day and a half, sleeping off the long journey, the childbirth, and the pain of leaving Rufus.

When she woke properly she was not in the least interested in the baby, unwilling to put her to her breast or even to look at her. To tide them over, she got the cook to hire a wet-nurse through an agency in Bishop Auckland. Cook put the crib in a warm corner of the kitchen and crooned and rocked the baby when her chores permitted. She fed the wet-nurse wholesome food and set her light chores around the house.

Every day Cook brought the baby to Carmel. Every day Carmel turned her face to the wall. In the end Cook dosed Carmel with something bitter to get rid of the troublesome milk, and the pain and the leakage stopped. For three days she insisted Carmel get out of bed and walk the corridors of the house. On the ninth day she insisted that she put on her clothes and eat in the dining room. On the tenth day, serving a delicious raspberry syllabub for pudding, she said, 'And the christening, madam? The babe must be christened, after all. And you should be churched.'

Rufus got back to Benbow just in time for the christening and insisted that the child be called Astrid, as he'd once met a very interesting woman in Hungary who was called Astrid. If the child had been a boy she would have been called Michael John, that old family name, a favourite of Rufus. Happy that Rufus was back with her, Carmel shed her lethargy like a sloughed skin. She was bright and interested in his tales. She started to transcribe his notes into the big ledgers. He talked of acquiring a typewriting machine to do all this. Many of the scholars had these typewriting machines. He spoke now of a scheme he had for a new trip, this time as far as Poland. Her eyes shone. She told him the baby was fine and Cook had full charge of her with the help of the wet-nurse. So Rufus told Carmel that if she got herself back into proper fettle she could come with him.

One morning while he was at home Rufus took her to walk the bounds. They stopped at Leeming's forge and were given tea and scones by Edith, the old blacksmith's daughter, a very steady girl for such a young age. They walked on and as he pointed out his family's signposts to the past Carmel suddenly realised just how much all this meant to him, even though he spent his life wandering the earth away from it. In the last stage of their walk they let themselves into the walled garden. It was a dreadful, grey sight. Only half the beds were in rather higgledy-piggledy use, the rest were overgrown with ground elder and bramble. The gravel paths were tangled with weeds. The walls were matted up with unkempt climbers. The glasshouses were in a muddle; much of the glass was broken, the plants inside parched and overgrown. Carmel sat in the central house by the brackish pool and breathed out. Rufus came to sit beside her. 'When I first saw you in your summerhouse, Carmel, I thought of this place. What great things you could do here, my dear. What propagation!'

That was all he said and that, really, was how it all began.

An hour later they walked back to the Hall and he went to the library to work on his notes. She went to rake around in the box room, among her luggage from home. She filled a satchel with catalogues, paper bags of seeds and her own old garden ledgers. Then she sat in the breakfast room and started to make lists.

The next day she visited Colonel Carmedy and told him to move the gardener to another job on the estate, as he was obviously quite useless in the garden. Also he was to find her two strong men to clear up the mess and three bright boys whom she could train up to do things her own way.

Then she sent for Cook and asked her advice about a proper nanny for the baby. Again the Bishop Auckland registry supplied an admirable woman, just over from Ireland.

That was how the making of the Benbow garden began, and how Detta O'Farrell came to be nanny first to Astrid and then to Michael John and, briefly, to Ambrose, before she was called back home to Kerry to care for her dying mother.

Detta was at Benbow Hall for fourteen years, a mother to Astrid and the boys in every sense. This was exactly how Carmel wanted it. She watched the children from a distance with a kind of detached interest but her passion was for Rufus, her garden and her flowers. She viewed the children as through glass. She saw them moving, knew they were fit and fine, noted how Michael John was even beautiful. But she heard little that they said and came to avoid their direct, enquiring gazes.

In the end the garden won out even over Rufus: in the end, after some years, she stopped travelling with him at all. Didn't her new plantlings need more sustaining care than did he? When she was away, Colonel Carmedy did not have the time to monitor the garden boys as she would have wished. She could go on the road no more. Rufus loved her no less and accepted her decision with grace.

It was for the garden that Carmel finally came home to stay. She supervised the garden boys ruthlessly until they did all their tasks to perfection. Then when they got to twenty she gave them excellent references and sent them off to good jobs in other gardens. She wanted no old gardeners here, taking charge. The tyrant of a head gardener employed by her father had been the bugbear of her youth and she would not have that here. So, in the years that the garden had been her life, she'd had three cohorts of boys who did exactly as they were told and contributed to the perfection of her work. She became quite fond of them in her own way and she always made sure they went home each week with full baskets.

Her own children were also to be supervised, of course. But the boys went off to school – albeit unwillingly – when each of them reached the age of seven. Michael John ran away twice and had to be dealt with severely by Colonel Carmedy, who dragged him back bawling. After that he settled very well. Young Ambrose took to sending her pathetic little poems and notes of despair. She wrote to him in her fine hand of her garden and the growing plants.

She did mention the boys' distress in her weekly letter to Rufus, but he wrote back that she was not to worry, as this was quite normal. Hadn't the boys run wild since they were born? Had they not been spoiled by their nanny and indulged by their tutor? So this revolt was only to be expected. And did she not put her plants into the air to harden off? Didn't they indeed harden off and thrive in the end?

It was very convenient to think Rufus was right. Michael John had developed into the perfect little schoolboy, robust and challenging and full of little games and school argot. He was a little too robust at times if one were to be honest. But Carmel was lenient with him. He was home so little. Young Ambrose had never become hardened in that fashion. In fact

93

he seemed perpetually on the brink of tears. But at least now they were in the same school he had Michael John to show him the way. These holidays Michael John certainly seemed to have taken him under his wing. Even Carmel had noted that he wouldn't let his brother out of his sight.

And now dear Astrid was home for a while from her travels! Quite like her father in her delight in travelling and in her rather plain looks. But she did not bring back with her, as he did, the whole of her life. She did not flood the house with interest and passion. She was mysterious. She liked to paint a little. She read. A delightful talent. But silent. She'd been little trouble as a child. A shadowy figure in the kitchens and pastures. It was true that she'd taken a little fit when Detta O'Farrell had gone back to Ireland. But then Mrs Mac came and old Crowner had moved on. So they'd promoted young John Tyler and the house ran smooth as silk. He was not so grand as Crowner, but was easier to have around.

Astrid had shared governesses and tutors with young Gertrude Seland up at Seland Hall. Carmel's cousin Lady Margaret Seland had been quite keen on that, having espoused a theory that children behaved and learned better in the company of others.

Carmel mused on the fact that she'd never really known Astrid, any more than she'd known the boys. They were people on her periphery whom she'd never known well enough to like: not even as much as, in a passing way, she liked her garden boys. Or Honesty Leeming, who had been such a help in the garden and was so easy and unquestioning to have around.

And now there was this dinner to be faced. And the American girl, Constance Redoute. Ah well, Carmel would do her duty. They would be gone soon and she would have her house back.

She heard the iron gate to the garden creak and stood up. It couldn't be the garden boys. They were digging peat at a special spot down behind Bottom Wood. It would be an hour before they were back.

She watched a shadow pass the glass and was surprised to see Mr Ellenberg at the glasshouse door. Mr Ellenberg never came into the garden. He looked hot and flustered in his cut-down tweed suit (another part of his legacy from Rufus). His slightly protuberant eyes were red rimmed, as though he had recently been crying. He was carrying a ledger in one hand and a disabled gun under the other arm.

She held out her hand. 'Mr Ellenberg. An unusual pleasure. I don't think I have ever seen you in my garden.'

'*Madame*.' Jacob put down the gun and carefully placed the book on the cast-iron table. Then he found himself bowing very low over the hand, his lips six inches from its dirt-ingrained surface. A flutter of memory in his heart from other times. A rare gesture of equality. 'Your garden is a paradise, *madame*, a paradise of colour and warmth in your cold country.'

Carmel seated herself. 'Won't you sit down, Mr Ellenberg?'

Jacob shook his head. 'I should not sit down, Madame Benbow, in this, your sanctuary.'

'Well then, Mr Ellenberg?' She put her head on one side like a rather weatherworn thrush.

'You will excuse what I have to say, *madame*. And if, when I have said it, you wish to send me away, then I will bow to my fate.'

'Mr Ellenberg! You are so dramatic. You must say what you want to say or we will both expire with the heat and impatience.'

He put a hand on the gun where it lay on the wrought-iron table in front of her. 'I take this gun from young Mr Benbow not an hour ago. He asks for me to return it and I refuse.'

'Why? It's his gun. It's a Purdey. A very fine gun. It was a present from his father. Those are his initials.'

'I take it from him because I see him shoot directly at his brother whom he had tied to a tree . . .'

Carmel listened carefully to the whole story. 'And Keziah Leeming's son struck him?' she said sharply.

95

Jacob shrugged. 'If he had not done so, I fear I would not be standing here. The gun is pointed directly at me. It is cocked.'

'Surely they were playing games, Mr Ellenberg? They are merely boys.'

He sighed heavily and shook his head. 'I think not, *madame*.' He leaned over and opened the book at a back page. 'I noted here for more than a year now. Young Mr Benbow has no qualms about hurting things, *madame*. I was concerned that today it would be a human being, not another poor creature. Perhaps you'd be so kind as to look in this book? You will see there I have made a note of each incident for the past three years now. The time and the place. Too many poor creatures.'

He stood very quietly as she looked carefully down the list. Then he said, 'You will remember the time, *madame*, when he shot me "by accident"? Now it is not just a concern for the creatures in your domain, *madame*, but for your own little son. For both your sons, perhaps.'

She stared at him, one part of her annoyed with him for breaking into her peace, remembering the time she nearly sacked Seb Golightly. Another part of her realised that this time, this time she would have to do something about Michael John.

She stood up, closed the ledger and handed it to him. 'Thank you, Mr Ellenberg. Perhaps you'd take the gun and hand it to Colonel Carmedy? Tell him he is to keep it until I tell him otherwise. And would you be so kind as to ask him if he will join us for dinner this evening? Seven sharp. You may tempt him by telling him he may discuss American farming with our guest. Before that, though, would you ask John Tyler to bring the pony and trap for me to the bottom road by the meadow?' She put a hand lightly on his arm. 'And you must not trouble yourself about Michael John, Mr Ellenberg. He will be dealt with. You may be sure of that.'

Ten

The Need for Reparation

Carmel put her satchel on her shoulder and made her way down across the blowzy late August meadow to the lane where John Tyler, as requested, was standing with the pony and trap. She climbed into the driving seat.

'Off somewhere, now, Mrs Benbow?' He looked up at her.

'Just some small errands, John. The dinner arrangements are in hand?'

'Mrs Tyler's done the flowers beautiful, Mrs Benbow. The table's fine and Mrs Mac has a glint in her eye over the dinner.'

'Ah.' Carmel fiddled with the reins so they sat comfortably in her gloved hands. 'Well, as we know, John, a glint in Mrs Mac's eye can mean a triumph or a disaster. We've known both, have we not?' She looked at the ears of her pony and made kissing noises into the air. 'Walk on, Laurel, walk on.'

John Tyler smiled as he stood and watched the pony and trap until it disappeared round a turn in the lane. He was very fond of Mrs Benbow. She might be a bit of a cut in her gardening hat and her boots but she'd always been good to him, right since he arrived as hall-boy when he was thirteen. She'd intervened once when old Mrs Crowner wanted to sack him for being late back on his day off. Then when the staff was radically reduced and finally the Crowners moved on, John Tyler found himself filling all the roles between butler and hall-boy, much to the disappointment of Melanie who'd expected better things when she took him on. Still, it was a trim ship, crewed by himself and Melanie and Mrs Mac, and the occasional extra hands when required.

He'd always had the feeling that Mrs Benbow had been glad to be rid of Crowner and his prim, fussy ways. She didn't like any man bossing her about. She'd never allow a proper gardener in that garden of hers: only garden boys not much older than John himself when he first came to the Hall. John Tyler had a real soft spot for Mrs B. No matter how much Melanie went on about their getting a 'proper' place together, he would never, never desert Mrs Benbow.

At the forge Carmel wound Laurel's reins round the top bar of the gate and waved a hand at Edith, who was swilling the back step of the house with the last of the washing water.

'Your Astrid was here, Mrs Benbow,' called Edith. 'She had a cup of tea.'

Carmel smiled. 'Walking the bounds,' she said. 'So like her father, that girl.'

Edith nodded. 'She has that nice quiet way about her. Same as him.'

'I'm looking for Keziah, Edith.'

'She's along the field by her van,' said Edith. 'Round the corner. Just follow the smell of rabbit stew.'

Round the corner, between the dry stone wall and the van, there was a long shallow fire hole. Set above the fire was a cunningly designed iron rail from which hung a round black pot and a heavy black teapot. The smell of smoke, herbs and rabbit impregnated the cooling evening air. Three chickens were roosting under the axle of the van. Two goats lurked malevolently behind it.

Keziah was sitting only two feet from the fire on a low stool, legs akimbo, and Freddy Leeming lounged back on the second step of the van. They were both smoking pipes. Honesty was sitting on the top step of the van, her legs and feet bare and her skirt up over her knees. Beside her on the step, ears sharp, eyes watchful, lay Slow, one of Keziah's Jack Russell terriers. Swinging above her head in a home-made willow cage Keziah's canary-finch whistled sweetly into the evening air. For a second Carmel wished she had Rufus's camera to record this familiar sight. There were many such photographs in his collection: people contemplating a fire under open skies.

Freddy got to his feet when he saw Carmel but she shook her head. 'No, Freddy. Stay where you are.'

He clambered over Honesty, vanished into the van and brought out an intricately carved chair with a low back. He put this near Keziah and waited for Carmel to sit down before he followed suit.

Keziah looked hard at Carmel then took her pipe from her mouth and called up to Honesty. 'Go see your Auntie Edith, *charver*. Mebbe she has some of them dough-pieces of hers to gan with this stew.'

Honesty jumped down and smoothed her skirt.

'An' tek yer time!' said Keziah.

Carmel peeled off her gloves and waited. They watched Honesty skip down the path, the black soles of her feet padding along the shady path.

'Seems our Honesty's had some kinds of bad time at the house of that friend of yours, Carmel,' said Keziah. '*Charver* won't say what.'

'Do you want me to talk to Lady Margaret?'

Keziah shook her head. 'Raking up's no good.' She drew on her pipe. 'I had a notion, mebbe, your Astrid'd like to take our Honesty on. My lass likes her. Like we said afore, she's not right for the vans. Heart's in the right place but she does like houses . . .'

Freddy drew on his pipe, then said, 'Not like our Keziah here. Cannot even get her in a house when it's ten feet away.' He sounded quite content.

'I'll certainly talk with Astrid. I don't quite know how her life is . . . what her plans are,' Carmel apologised.

'There'll be changes in her life and there'll be room for our Honesty in those changes. I tell you this.'

Carmel was used now to Keziah's confident, prophetic tone and was not too disturbed by it. Keziah's statements had the resonance of prophecies and often, not always, turned out to be true. But in Carmel's view this was more to do with her wisdom and insight than any magical powers.

Carmel said now, 'I'll do everything I can about Honesty, Keziah. But today I've come about Jack.'

'I was going to talk to you about our Jack. I want you to find us some *gorgio* who'll teach him figuring on paper. He's clever, mind. No better reckoner in his head than our Jack.'

'No better,' echoed Freddy. 'The lad's a wizard with measurement. A natural. Knows to the quarter-inch.'

'Do him no good less he figures on paper,' insisted Keziah. 'World's changin', Freddy.'

'Aye, it is. No doubt about that.' Freddy sucked thoughtfully on his pipe.

'I know someone who might help him.' Carmel thought of Jacob Ellenberg. 'But I want to talk to you about something else, Keziah. A very bad thing happened today. Your Jack attacked Michael John in the Bottom Wood. He knocked him to the floor with that stick of his.'

Keziah took a long drag on her pipe and stared hard into the fire. 'He'll be here very soon,' she said. 'We'd better wait, Carmel. See what he says.'

Keziah was right. Within a minute, as if called silently by Keziah's will, Jack was there, hauling a sledge of sticks and branches tied round with twine, his dog Fassy leaping at his heels. He dragged the sledge to one side of the van, took the branches up in a bundle and threw them onto a straggling pile of branches that was already shoulder high. 'Aye.' He nodded to his mother. 'You wanted us?'

Carmel reflected on the intimacy between these two. She thought of herself, and her own sons. She had to admit there was none of this peculiar closeness with them.

'Get across here, Jack,' instructed Keziah. 'An' tell us what happened over Michael John Benbow.'

He stood beside his mother and talked rapidly in *romani*. His face was less than a foot from hers and he talked with his eyes as well as with words.

Carmel put up her hand to stop the flow. 'I understand that Michael John had Ambrose tied, Jack; that there were shots at the tree; that Mr Ellenberg intervened.'

'Has some guts, has that old *gadgie*,' said Jack.

'He tells me you saved him. That Michael John was aiming the gun at him.'

Jack shrugged his shoulders. '*Gadgie* saved hisself. He got hold of the gun.'

'He told me you made sure the gun flew out of Michael John's hands. By hitting him with your stick.' Carmel nodded at the stick still slung over his shoulder.

'That's so, missis.'

Carmel stared at him then nodded slowly. 'Well, I have to tell you the gun will be right out of Michael John's hands now. For good.'

'That lad doesn't need a gun to do damage in them woods.'

'So I understand now, from Mr Ellenberg.' She stood up. 'Michael John will be made to stay away from the woods for the rest of his time here. Thank you for protecting Mr Ellenberg, Jack. And Ambrose too. It was a risky thing to do. Guns can go off.'

He grinned suddenly. 'That's true. Ask anybody that tries to snare their dinner.'

''S enough, Jack,' growled Freddy Leeming.

Carmel kept her eyes on the boy. 'Keziah tells me you want to learn mathematics? Proper numbering? On paper?'

The boy nodded slowly. 'Aye. She's right there. But I can't pay no teacher.'

'Mr Ellenberg could teach you. Perhaps you saved his life today, so he owes you something.'

'That sounds fair exchange,' said Freddy. 'Teck Mrs Benbow up on it, lad.'

'All right then,' said Jack. 'I'll do that.'

'Come down to the house tomorrow at six. Tell John Tyler to take you to the library. Mr Ellenberg is always there after four in the afternoon. He will teach you your mathematics.' She pulled on her gloves and turned to go.

'Stay, Carmel, and eat,' said Keziah suddenly.

Carmel smiled and shook her head. 'How I wish I could join you. But I have to go and play hostess and fly the flag, as well as deal with the problem of a very bad young man.'

'Fly the flag?' Keziah raised her considerable brows. 'What're you up to now, Carmel?'

On her way back to the trap Carmel passed Edith and Honesty, who were walking along the narrow path. Honesty was balancing a plate covered with a cloth in her hand. As Carmel approached, Edith pulled Honesty to the side of the path and dragged her down in a bobbing curtsy. Carmel took her seat in the trap and called after them, 'Enjoy your supper, won't you?' Then she kissed the air and told Laurel to 'walk on'.

By the *vardo* Edith sat on the chair that Mrs Benbow had just vacated. Honesty held the plates while Keziah doled out the stew. They all ate in appreciative silence and when they finished they waited while Honesty piled up the plates. Then Freddy took up his pipe again. 'Bad business with the boy,' he said. 'Would he have shot old Jacob, Jack? Was he that set?'

Jack leaned back against the wall, fondling Fassy's ears. 'No tellin',' he said. 'He'd been shooting at his brother. The tree was all smashed up. I'll tek yer to show yer if yer want.'

'He's a dangerous lad.' Freddy nodded. 'A sly, interfering lad. Never keeps his hands to himself in the forge.'

'Lacks a man's control,' said Edith. 'And Mrs Benbow has no hold of him. Can see no wrong in him.'

'Not till now,' said Keziah. 'Not quite till now.'

'Aye,' said Freddy, taking a suck on his pipe. 'Yer right there, Keziah. Not till now.'

Carmel's next port of call, the Old Lodge, had been built for his own use (at Benbow expense) by the then agent who had commissioned and supervised the building of the old Georgian mansion for Rufus's grandfather. In consequence, with its touches of elegance, the Lodge was a grander house altogether than the present, rather squat and comfortable main Hall.

The occupant of the Lodge, Colonel Jerry Carmedy, was the Benbow agent in this generation. An old comrade of Rufus from the Mesopotamian digs, Jerry lived in higher style than the occupants of the Hall. He was not above using the money that came his way for his own comfort. He had more servants than Carmel (including one who wore a turban) and a better carriage; he kept a grander table.

His butler bowed and asked Carmel to take a seat in the drawing room while he informed the Colonel of her presence. Carmel stood by the wide bow-shaped window looking out across the immaculate lawns and through the trees to where the church spires and pitheads of Bishop Auckland spiked the evening sky. Back at the Hall this view was masked by great belts of trees specially planted for the purpose. Carmel sighed. She had no desire whatsoever to have the pits and the blackened villages of Durham brought to the front of her mind. She much preferred her garden, its flowers, its fruitful rows and its tumbling climbers.

'My dear Mrs Benbow, a rare honour. A surprise too, as I understand from Tyler I am to join you for dinner.' Colonel Carmedy came bustling in, buttoning his jacket. His long face was yellow from old malaria and lack of recent sun, and a fringe of silver hair wound round his high-domed head. There was a small dent above his left eye where he'd been winged years before in India by a sepoy with a poor sense of direction. He'd told Carmel the tale many times. 'I should order tea, perhaps?' He leaned towards the frayed bellpull by the fireplace.

Carmel sat down and removed her gloves. 'No, Colonel. I don't wish for tea. I wish to consult you.'

He sat down opposite her, his back very straight, his chin up. 'Anything, dear lady. Anything.'

She told him the tale about Michael John.

He sniffed. 'It's not this scallywag of a gypsy getting your son into trouble?'

She raised her brows. 'I'm surprised that you should say such a thing, Colonel. Rufus would have been rather miffed at your lack of charity.'

'Of course, Mrs Benbow. How remiss of me. So you are wondering . . .?'

'What I should do with this very naughty son of mine.'

His shoulders moved under his closely fitting jacket. 'Boys will be boys, Mrs Benbow. Michael John is perhaps too playful. It is not of much import. I fear I was up to such mischief myself, at his age.'

Carmel was not pleased at this. 'Colonel, my oldest son has been shooting at his brother. He has tied him up and shot at him.'

The Colonel sat up even straighter. 'Young Michael John is too good a shot to hit his brother. I know because I taught him myself. It was a game. A jape, Mrs Benbow. As I said, I myself got up to such mischief as a youngster.'

'He could have shot him by accident, Colonel. Had it not been for Jack Lomas and Mr Ellenberg, Ambrose could be injured. Perhaps dead.'

Colonel Carmedy stared at the mild face of the woman before him. Like Rufus Benbow, Carmel interfered very little in the normal running of the estate. Rufus had merely wanted the estate run in an efficient manner so it would produce the income to allow him to travel and write, and to indulge in his various philanthropies. Mrs Benbow gave him the same freedom although, being no traveller, she was much less of a drain on capital. Her preoccupation with Benbow strayed no further than her garden. This was a very good thing.

She knew little of the fact that the need to sell off four of the farms in the nineties reflected their reducing income. And that the collieries, though they produced very good coal now and then, threw up a beggaring need for investment. There had been roof-falls since January and seven deaths. The coal, though fine, lay in narrow seams and the miners were always at risk. Worse than this, the seams were finite and new shafts had to be sunk, which was expensive.

But Jerry Carmedy flattered himself that the estate was in quite good heart, all things considered. Mrs Benbow was content; Carmedy himself had a good life and had built up a tidy – a very tidy – bank balance to show for his efforts. Not that the dear lady knew the details of that. Absolutely no need. He appreciated the fact that she made so few demands. Now that she obviously wanted something done about the boy, he would do his damnedest to get it right. 'Was he not to go to Cambridge?' he said. 'Magdalene, like Rufus?'

She shook her head. 'They would hold a place for him, but lately Michael John has been lackadaisical with his studies. The school has no regard for his scholarship. His sister is the one with the brains. He needs something . . .'

'Ah!' So this was why she was here. He could come up with exactly the right answer. 'Those old, wild excesses to which I just referred, Mrs Benbow, were curbed in myself by army discipline. More, I think that military life harnessed this wildness and fused it into a weapon of use, in those days to the Queen and Empire. Now of course it would be to the dear King. So popular now, don't you know? Brought the monarchy into the light of modern day.' He coughed slightly. 'No disrespect to the old Queen of course. Now, then, Mrs Benbow. You speak of the army, I think?'

She nodded her head. 'If he is to fire shots in anger I would prefer it to be in the right direction.' She stood up. 'Could you help me with this? Today?'

'Today?' He stroked his chin. 'We would need to find funds for him. Perhaps I should ride into Bishop Auckland. I believe they have telephonic apparatus in the club. Perhaps I could speak directly to one or two fellows I know.'

'Speak to them?' She pulled on her gloves. 'How very amazing.' She put a hand on his arm. 'Now, Colonel, I want this done now, today.' She smiled very sweetly. 'And don't forget to join us for dinner tonight? Then you can break the news to Michael John. I know dining is a bore but perhaps it should be quite entertaining tonight. My daughter has her American friend to stay. The girl's father was a hero of their Civil War.'

She stood up. He stood and bowed stiffly from the waist, hiding his disappointment at having to miss a night of snooker and whisky at the club with his chums. He had been winning good money at snooker lately. Still, yarning about Yankee heroics might provide some amusement.

'No need to dress, Colonel,' said Carmel, turning at the door. 'As you know, we are very informal at Benbow. These days I fear we lag far behind all those royal goings-on at Seland.'

Eleven

The Long Game

6.30pm

Although Carmel did not resort to the chilly bathroom, on this special night she took more trouble than usual with her toilette: a footbath as well as a strip wash. Melanie Tyler came up to help her with her hair: she pinned it up properly at the back and padded the sides so that she could sweep back wings on either side of Carmel's face.

Rufus had always liked her hair like that. He would touch her cheek and call her *the innocent*. But when they were away travelling on the road he liked her to wear it falling down her back in a thick pigtail, worn with a shady hat to protect her fine skin.

Now she creamed her face in an attempt to reduce the rather ugly weathering which was its salient characteristic these days and worked more cream into her hands to bring out the ingrained dirt. She hunted out her corset to replace the easier boned bodice she usually wore, and told Melanie to get out her Polish turquoise choker with the matching earrings: Rufus's wedding present to her. 'I thought you eschewed things of vanity, my dear,' her mother had rather stiffly said on the eve of the wedding. 'This is vanity to excess.'

Melanie also disinterred the green moiré taffeta dress, still stored in its Paris-labelled box. Though twenty-four years old and smelling just slightly of mothballs, the dress had kept well in its swathe of tissue and was barely creased.

Melanie stood back and admired the effect. 'Now that's something like, Mrs Benbow. You'd stand against anybody, looking like that.'

Carmel smiled at her. 'Poor Melanie. So little life for you here at Benbow.'

Melanie's cheeks went red. 'I chose John Tyler and there's an end of it, Mrs Benbow.'

'Perhaps you often wish you were back at Seland Hall?'

Melanie looked at her through the mirror. 'Well, there's less work here, overall,' she said slowly. 'Down there at Seland it was like a great big machine that spewed out a rich life for Lord and Lady Seland and their friends. And you were just a little cog in their wheel. They barely noticed you.' She paused. 'But there was colour there, and excitement. Music sometimes. Here there's just Mrs Mac and her stories. And John, who almost never gets dressed. He's always in that dratted black apron.'

'But not tonight?'

'No. I've pressed the old livery and the white linen. And cleaned his patent shoes. Looks more like he should do. He looks very handsome.'

'I'm sure he does. He was always such a handsome boy.' Carmel leaned forward and looked at herself closely in the mirror. She glanced up at her maid's reflection. 'I think perhaps you and he should go out from here more, Melanie. Get dressed up for your own benefit. You can go into Bishop Auckland. Have lunch in the Co-operative Society's new restaurant. Go to the theatre.'

'It's getting there, Mrs Benbow, that's the problem.'

'Take the pony and trap. Or the wagonette. Now then, go downstairs and see if your John has everything in hand. Go.'

Melanie bobbed a grateful curtsy. 'Very well, Mrs Benbow.' She stopped at the door. 'And thank you, Mrs Benbow.'

Carmel waited until Melanie had gone before reading the note brought down by Colonel Carmedy's man. Then she followed Melanie downstairs at a more leisurely pace. She paused at the chess table by the fire in the hall.

'White plays King's pawn,' she murmured, and made the move. Then she pulled the little mechanism on the side of the board to show that the next move must be black. The chess game was always set up and in progress. The board had been designed by Rufus. Everyone was designated a colour when they came to the house. Rufus was already black when Carmel came, so Carmel was white. Astrid was black. Michael John was white, Ambrose was black. Everyone was allowed to make one move as they passed through. A game could last weeks. It stopped altogether when the boys were at school. Melanie kept the chessmen dusted and put them back on their spots. Carmel thought perhaps she should assign Jacob Ellenberg a colour, then the game would move along rather faster. He was in the house every day, after all.

She went across to look over the dining room. The linen and the old crystal were perfectly laid. The slightly battered silver gleamed with reflected firelight. Tweaking the anemones and dahlias which made up the centrepiece, Carmel felt the ghost of her mother pass through her. Her mother had adored a well-dressed table.

She went across the hall and down the corridor to the library. The familiar smell of dust, old leather and sweet, dead tobacco assailed her as she opened the door. Even at this late hour the room was suffused with soft evening light streaming down from the glass turret in the ceiling.

Tucked under the corner of the gallery, almost hidden by the piles of books before him, sat Jacob Ellenberg. He stood up hastily as she moved towards him, brought his heels together and bowed very deeply. 'Good evening, *madame*. I am impertinent but I must say that you have a very fine appearance this

109

evening. Very fine.' He blinked up at her through his round glasses.

'You're very kind, Mr Ellenberg.' She smiled and took a seat at the table. He sat down opposite her. 'I should tell you that all this is a vanity, in honour of the American visitor. It occurred to me that Rufus would say we must fly the flag. And also I find myself very pleased that my daughter is here in my house after these years away.'

'Ah. A daughter is a very fine thing, Mrs Benbow. And sons of course.'

She blinked away an image of Jack Lomas talking intimately with Keziah. Ah yes, Jack Lomas. She explained to Jacob Ellenberg about the tuition in mathematics.

Jacob nodded. 'A very fine idea. The boy has a good brain. Very quick and inventive. Those pieces of farm equipment he and Mr Freddy Leeming sell at the markets are ingenious.' He paused. 'I must say, Mrs Benbow, that this is a synchronistic moment. I was about to ask permission to allow the boy to borrow Mr Benbow's volume on the inventions of Leonardo da Vinci. I thought they might serve as inspirations for his little innovations.'

Carmel nodded. 'Rufus would be pleased. You will enjoy teaching him, Mr Ellenberg. The boy learned to read very quickly indeed.' She'd thought a children's primer might be too childish for Jack, so she'd used one of Rufus's catalogues of the Great Exhibition of 1851. Jack had been so fascinated by the contents that once he had the alphabet off by heart, he'd virtually taught himself to read.

Jacob's face shone with admiration. 'You are like a mother to these people, Mrs Benbow.'

She frowned and shook her head. 'The thought has been pursuing me all day, Mr Ellenberg, that perhaps I may be a very poor parent. I have so little intimacy with my children. In all my life here at the Hall I've been absorbed only in matters to do with my husband and my garden. I've barely noticed there were children here. And now my daughter makes her life away from me, so that I hardly know who she is. My son persecutes his brother and goodness knows who else and will take no reproof. I am a very poor parent.'

Jacob thought briefly that it was hard to make out regret in her tone. It was as though she were rehearsing some observed fact about the habits of a plant or an animal. He shook off his critical thought. 'I am certain this is not true, Mrs Benbow. Your children have been nurtured, taken care of here at Benbow . . .'

She shook her head. 'Like my beloved husband, I give more real attention to the strangers at the gate than to my own children. Perhaps that is always easier.'

Jacob sat very still. 'I myself am one of those strangers, Mrs Benbow, and the care of Mr Benbow and yourself has given me the means of having a life. I cannot regret that.'

'No more do I, Mr Ellenberg. But the children . . .'

'But today it is only Michael John, Mrs Benbow. Only one incident. Now I must feel great guilt about coming to you with my tale of his misdoings.'

'Is what you said the truth?'

'The absolute truth.'

'Do you know that Seb Golightly came to me once, many years ago, with a similar truth? I hid my eyes from it then, pretending nothing had happened.'

'I have heard of this,' he said gently. 'So perhaps sometimes the truth needs to be brought out to the surface. There it can be dealt with.'

There was silence between them until Jacob went on quietly, 'Your children are a true blessing, Mrs Benbow. You are indeed fortunate.'

She stood up. At the door she turned back. 'Have you had your supper, Jacob?' His name slipped out without her thinking. A new element in their acquaintance sat now in the air between them.

He shook his head. 'I always eat when I return from the library. I find preparing something to eat very restful after a long day.'

'Then perhaps you will join us here for dinner?'

He spread his hands helplessly, looking down at his tweed suit; then he touched his soft cravat. '*Madame*, I could not . . .'

'You must. The dress does not matter,' she instructed. 'I am concerned to make it an interesting evening for Miss Redoute. You will help me. We will talk of my husband. You will be able to explain his theories of the migration of people across Europe. And here at Benbow, how he pursued his notion of the seasons and the movement of the animals and birds. How you note it down every day in those great books of his.'

Jacob stared at the door as it clicked behind her. *A daughter is a very fine thing, Mrs Benbow*. The last time he saw his own daughter she was being jumped on, in turn, by four thickset boys – younger than her – in uniform. Beside her lay his wife, bayoneted through the heart for being too old and ugly to bother with. Jacob had clambered onto the back of the one who was about his business and the others had dragged him off, jeering. Then Jacob had run through the empty door and down the ever-narrower back alleys, holding his hands over his ears to cut out the tearing sound of screaming. *Daughters are a good thing*. But Jacob Ellenberg had no idea whether or not he had a daughter in this world. Still, sometimes he did not think of the screams for days at a time now.

He stood up and looked at his shadowy reflection in the glass front of a tall bookcase. Large head, thick hair receding, white face, round spectacles, messy necktie. He pulled off the tie and straightened the soft collar of his shirt. Then, very carefully, he retied the necktie and adjusted the bow to show the jacquard weave to its best effect.

A peremptory knock on Astrid's bedroom door, the whisper of silk, the rush of heavy rose scent announced the presence of

Constance Redoute. 'Oh, Astrid dear, are you not ready for dinner?' she drawled. 'Dreaming by the window again. Framed there in the lamplight I swear to heaven you look like a painting by that strange little Mr Rossetti.'

Astrid turned back to the room to see Constance, who had slipped off her long silk dressing gown and now stood before her, naked but for her underpinnings. Constance had a fine figure. Her shoulders were very fine, smooth and fleshy, her ankles were narrow and her feet were slender.

'Would you be so good as to lace me?' Constance turned round so that her back was towards Astrid. 'How I miss Lady Parlellum's little Maisie. Do you know, at Seland Hall I had to go onto the corridor and grab a housemaid to help? My dear momma always says it's a bigger mistake to travel without your maid than it is to travel without your husband.'

'I don't know. In my view having a maid is like employing a jailer or a nanny.' Astrid started to fiddle with Constance's laces, pulling each crossover as tightly as she could. Above the stays Constance's flesh, covered by fine lawn chemise, began to bulge. 'One is responsible *to* one's maid and *for* her, every minute of the day. She is the first person one sees when one wakes up, the last before one goes to sleep. My empty rooms in Chelsea are so much more agreeable than any of that palaver.'

'That's better,' said Constance approvingly, feeling the cage of her corset digging tightly into her body. She walked stiffly across to the bedpost and grasped it firmly. 'Now pull! Hard as you can!' She gritted her teeth a little. 'Yes, of course, honey, maids're around all the time. But ain't it like there's no one there at all? They're there to take care of you. Of course you have to have them around. Perhaps it's easier for us back home. Over there, our maids are dear things, we're truly very fond of them. We grow up with them. But they're just black shadows in one's life. Pull harder, tighter, there's a dear.'

'That's enough,' said Astrid, tying the last secure double

bow. 'You'll break in two, Constance. You are in great danger of fainting over dinner and Mrs Mac would be so very upset at the waste.' She sat down on the bed and smiled up at her friend. 'I can't think why you are going to all this trouble, old thing. There are no kings and lords around the Benbow table. Just my old mother, perhaps Colonel Carmedy and the two brats of brothers. Perhaps some other oddities. There are frequently some oddities. My mother is no better than my father on that count. Do you know, we once had two gypsy kings to dinner? And their acolytes, complete with tambourines? We've had some very colourful tables, through the years.'

'My!' Constance sat stiffly upright beside Astrid and took her hand and kissed it. 'Dearest Astrid. I dress to my very best because it's such fun. And because I have respect for myself. I look into the mirror and if I see less than perfection I'm disappointed. My momma says that the best thing about daughters is that one can rise to new realms of perfection in each generation. But I look in the mirror and wonder just how this may be surpassed.'

Astrid squeezed her hand and chuckled. 'You're so vain, Connie.'

'Oh my! A deadly sin. How can I cope?' Constance jumped from the bed. 'Now, can I be your maid and pull your laces?' She looked round the bedroom. 'Where are they?'

Astrid stood up beside her and gave her a little push. 'Go and make yourself even more beautiful. Go on! I can do my own lacing.'

'That ain't possible, honey.'

'Oh yes it is. My corsets are already back-laced. I just need to hook them at the front. It might not squeeze my waist to eighteen inches, like yours, but it suffices.'

Constance planted a kiss on her brow. 'Dearest, dearest Astrid. You are the least vain person I know, and I love you for it.'

Astrid smiled as she watched Constance skip stiffly from the room. She rubbed the grease from her forehead where her friend had planted her kiss. Constance might be a vain soul but she did sprinkle a little joy wherever she went. Astrid thought of her at Seland Hall, flirting with the King before he went off to shoot his thousand birds. Constance could step outside all the leaden court protocol that existed even in the most informal situation and still charm the pernickety King.

Please the King. In the darkness at the back of her head Astrid began to fret again about what had happened to the child Honesty. She should really have done something about that. She should. Even now she should be doing something – she should tell Keziah Leeming, or even her own mother – so they could all share the despair, the impotence. Only that. One thing was certain. Nothing could be done about it. Nothing at all. Unless, as Honesty had so graphically put it, they let Jack Lomas go and slit the royal gizzard. For a second that was an entertaining thought. She saw those cool golden eyes again. He would do it very efficiently, she was sure.

Ambrose Benbow loved the long chess game in the hall. He'd been taught to play by his father on one of his rare visits home. One week's training in the schoolroom and he was designated a black and allowed, after a little discussion, to make his move. Later on, when he was incarcerated fifty miles away at school he dreamed of his parents: images of his father would dissolve into the Black King and those of his mother into the White Queen.

Now, every day when he was at home, each time he passed through the hallway, he looked eagerly to see if the lever indicated a black turn. If it did, he'd study the board for many long minutes before he made his move. He liked the fact that you did this on your own: nobody watching, no drama, no pressure. Each time he made his move he felt, even if he did not think of, his father.

Today he was in luck. Black move. His mother or Michael John must have taken their turn. He grimaced at the thought of his brother and settled down to make his choice. The best ploy would be to attack with his knight. Or should he move to take the centre?

'Difficult to choose, old boy?' His brother, immaculate in his OTC uniform, slipped into the chair opposite. Ambrose stiffened. Michael John's fair hair was brushed straight back from his broad forehead and he was smiling a broad open smile. *Beware the crocodile* . . . Ambrose wondered if that were a nursery rhyme. He'd heard it somewhere. He put his hand carefully back into his lap, the piece untouched.

'Go on, old boy. Make your move and then I can make mine. Because I always will. I'll always make my move. You know that, don't you?' The smile froze on his face. 'Don't you?'

'Yes, Mick.'

Michael John caught him by the front of his shirt. 'You call me by my name, worm. Only my friends call me that. Do you understand?'

Half choking, Ambrose shook his head.

Michael John let him go and thoughtfully smoothed his collar. 'You know what you are to say, Amby?' he said softly. 'You are to say the gypsy thug tied you up and I rescued you, is that clear? And that old Jew mistook the situation and took the gun from me. Is that clear?'

'But that's not what happened, Mick . . . Michael John.'

Slowly Michael John lifted a highly polished riding boot and pressed it on the chess table, sending the pieces flying. 'Oh dear,' he said. 'No more moves.'

As the pieces clattered on the oak floor Astrid and Constance came down the stairs. Michael John smiled brilliantly and bent over Constance's hand as Astrid introduced her friend. They all turned to Ambrose who had set the table upright and was scrambling for the pieces. 'Poor old Amby has knocked the table over,' said Michael John. 'That game's finished. You'll have to set up a new game, old boy.'

Ambrose put the Black King in place. 'Oh no, Mick,' he said, daring to call him that because his sister and her friend were looking on. 'Every piece will go back the same. I remember where all the pieces go. I always know where the pieces are.' He set about his task with great care. Then he made his move. 'Black challenges with his knight,' he murmured.

They all stood and watched him until he turned the lever, then went together into the drawing room where Carmel was sitting on the couch talking to Colonel Carmedy and Mr Ellenberg, who were sitting in the chairs on either side of the great fireplace. Michael John smiled at his mother: a smile designed to melt hearts and to give the smiler the advantage.

Carmel treated him to a mirror image of his own brilliant smile. For once she had decided to talk to him directly. 'Darling!' she said. 'Wonderful news. Colonel Carmedy has been talking to General Charles Coote – an old friend of his – on the telephone. What an amazing thing the telephone is. From here to York? The General, who knew your father in India, will ensure you a commission with the regiment. So we've decided you must go into the army, straight away. Sandhurst, of course, then . . .'

Michael John flushed. 'But Mother, I can't. I'll go to Magdalene like Father, then . . .'

Carmel stood up and glanced round the company. 'We cannot discuss just now why your actions today out in the woods make all that impossible, Michael John. But as Colonel Carmedy says, the army can take such energies as yours and put them to fine service for our country.'

Michael John's fists clenched and he took a step towards her. The Colonel put a hand on his arm and coughed. 'The army will suit you, young man. The regiment is of the first water. First class.'

Carmel smiled quietly at her son, then turned to Jerry Carmedy. 'Now, Colonel, perhaps you would take me into dinner? And Michael John, you can escort Constance? Astrid, perhaps Ambrose and Mr Ellenberg will be your knights in shining armour?'

As she walked through the double doors of the dining room between her young brother and Mr Ellenberg, Astrid wondered just what was going on. The air was crackling with meaning she could not quite grasp. Then she thought of the unspoken turmoil in her own mind regarding the dilemma of Honesty Leeming and reflected on how, in this family, so little that really meant anything was ever properly spoken out loud. A bit like the chess game, when you thought of it. No moves made face to face.

Twelve

An Evening's Entertainment

7.30pm

The meal, managed with assurance and enthusiasm by Mrs Mac, John and Melanie Tyler, went very smoothly. The diners were offered fresh greenhouse melons with ham, then freshly killed duckling dressed with blackcurrants and served with vegetables cooked to perfection, followed by lemon jelly set with nasturtiums and plain cheese from the old dairy. The simplicity of the meal, accompanied by some French wine and old port selected by the Colonel from Rufus's cellar, allowed the diners to concentrate at first on the pleasures of eating rather than the strangeness of the gathering in the Benbow dining room.

Toying with the melon, Carmel disclosed to Colonel Carmedy that Astrid and her American friend had dined in royal company the previous evening. This allowed the delighted Colonel to tell Constance some of his favourite tales of the Royal Durbar in Delhi when, he said, he'd stood just to the left of the King's shoulder. At that time, of course, His Majesty had been Prince. But still, there had been no greater gathering in India . . .

Michael John sat glowering in the direction of Jacob Ellenberg, who munched his duckling with his eyes fixed in devoted admiration on Carmel, who was sitting at the head of her table as though today had been a very ordinary day and she dined like this every evening. Michael John wondered what his mother was up to. The thing in the wood was no more than a game. She should have known that if she'd known anything about him. But she knew nothing, nothing at all. She knew – and cared – more about those oafs Ellenberg and Jack Lomas. She certainly took more notice of them. If it hadn't been for those interfering cretins, his life would be jogging along just as usual. As it was, his future had changed for ever. You wouldn't have thought it, seeing his mother yammering away to the colonel about one of the garden lads, but it was so. He could kill her, he really could.

Ambrose sat quietly in his corner and cast his eye around the table. Up at its head sat his mother, who looked like a stranger with her high necklace and a feather arrangement in her hair. She was very smart, much smarter than Ambrose's housemaster's wife, Mrs Donald, who creaked a lot and smelt rather sour. Ambrose had always thought his mother beautiful and wondered what it would be like to nestle beside her or to have her put her arms right round you.

To his mother's right was the Colonel with his high stiff collar and fine jacket. You never knew where you were with the Colonel. Ambrose once overheard Seb Golightly say to John Tyler that the Colonel was a slippery one, greasing up to Mrs Benbow's face and doing what the hell he liked behind her back.

To his mother's left was the American woman with her astonishing white face and high glossy hair. She smelt very nice, like his mother's garden. Beside her was Michael John, who had abandoned his usual smiling charm and was sitting very still. Ambrose had seen his face when their mother had told him he was going into the army. Ambrose knew that if Mick had had his gun at that moment he'd have shot their mother through the heart. Michael John was not pleased at the news. Ambrose had a flicker of sympathy for him, being moved around in real life like a chess piece. But Ambrose was happy for himself. He hoped the army would send Mick somewhere where the shooting would keep him pinned down and unable to move. That would show him.

Ambrose's gaze moved on to Astrid. She sat there quietly as always, neat in her soft brown dress which looked quite nice with her shining fair hair. Ambrose reflected that he'd almost forgotten what his sister looked like, she'd been away so long. He wondered how long she would stay this time. She never stayed very long. It would have been nice if she had been around when things were so difficult and he had to endure his perpetual fear of what Michael John would do next.

Further along there was Mr Ellenberg who looked rather like Ambrose's history master Mr Peach, although he didn't nod his head quite so vigorously. Nor did he spit. Mr Peach spat and he nodded his head all the time, as though his neck was a spring. Mr Donald had explained to the boys in his house that it was because of some experience in the South African War. At the time Ambrose couldn't quite make a connection between shooting guns and nodding heads.

When at last they reached the stage of the cheese and port Ambrose started to think of what it might be like to be really free. The story of Cain and Abel, studied in his second year of school, came into his mind. As early as that he had dwelled with some satisfaction on the thought of brother killing brother. But then there was the problem of the *Mark of Cain*. Today, of course, it might have been Mick who killed him. That would make *him* Cain, and he would have had to bear the Mark all his life. It would also have made Ambrose himself the Favoured Son. What must it be like, to be the Favoured Son? Ambrose had once spent a weekend in north Yorkshire, at the home of his friend Spinks Minor. Spinks's father had read them adventure stories, recited poetry to them, played tennis with them and ruffled their hair rather a lot. It had been a strange experience, rather disturbing. But it did give him insight into that strange notion of the Favoured Son. Here at Benbow he felt more like the Invisible Son.

'Daydreaming, dear boy?' His sister Astrid's quiet voice came to him through the booming hubbub dominated by Colonel Carmedy. 'What's going on in that furry little mind of yours, Amby?'

'I was thinking of that Bible story, Cain and Abel.'

'Now that's a funny thing to think of.'

'I was wondering,' Ambrose attended to his cheese, 'who was Cain and who was Abel.'

'I see.'

Ambrose thought that she knew exactly what he meant.

They both looked up, then, to catch the eye of Michael John, who had turned his torch-like gaze on his brother. Astrid dissembled. 'I was just thinking how smart you look in your uniform, Mick,' she said. 'Quite the ticket.'

He scowled at her.

Constance turned her rapt face from the Colonel and cast a melting glance at Michael John. 'There is nothing like a man in uniform,' she drawled, smiling. 'Quite makes the heart flutter. My poppa never looks better than when he puts on his epaulettes, even though he's a very old soldier these days.'

'Mrs Mac says your father's a hero, Miss Redoute,' said Ambrose. 'A real American hero.'

The Colonel stopped crumbling the cheese in his fingers.

She smiled her melting smile. 'They do say he was, Ambrose. It's written in the histories. He has medals. Why, he was a general when he was thirty.'

'There you are, Mick, only twelve years to go!' said Astrid.

Constance laughed and nodded at Michael John and this released some tension in him. The air in the room became more breathable.

After dinner Carmel played the piano and the Colonel sang in a surprisingly sweet tenor. Constance and Astrid sang 'Ah Moon of My Delight' and 'I'll Sing Thee Songs of Araby'.

Ambrose recited Horatius at the Bridge and, in honour of Constance, read ten pages of Longfellow's *Hiawatha*. Michael John had excused himself remarkably politely before the entertainment and left the room. He was not missed.

Carmel ended the evening with a hesitant execution of Brahms's Lullaby on the piano. She blamed the garden for her clumsy fingers but Colonel Carmedy declared her playing 'Capital!' and Constance remarked how deceptive the fingering was for that particular Brahms piece. Jacob Ellenberg had tears in his eyes as he clicked his heels, kissed Carmel's hand and thanked her for a wonderful evening.

Astrid paused at the chess game. The white bishop had gone forward. Michael John must have made his move. 'Black takes control of the centre,' she muttered, and pulled the lever. Then she followed the yawning Constance upstairs and helped to release her from her corset. At Constance's door she declared herself too wide-awake to sleep. She told her friend that she'd go for a walk to clear her head from the fog of the port. In contrast to the practice at Seland Hall, the ladies at Benbow did not leave the table when the port was served.

Constance clasped Astrid to her now more or less naked bosom and said, 'It's always so interesting around you, dearest Astrid. You are the still centre around which all life flows. How I do love you!'

Astrid laughed and pushed her away. 'You're really, really quite absurd, Constance. Now let me get to my walk.'

She made her way down to the kitchen where Mrs Mac and the Tylers were sitting with the last of the port. She waved a hand as they all stood up. 'That was a wonderful meal, Mrs Mac. Miss Redoute said she had never had finer in England. Not even at Seland Hall. And she thought the table looked perfect, absolutely perfect.'

Mrs Mac beamed and straightened her apron very carefully. She stole a glance at Melanie Tyler who, to all appearances, was as pleased with the praise as she was.

'I'm in search of a lamp, John,' said Astrid. 'I thought a bit of fresh air would clear my head.'

'It's getting cold out there, Miss Benbow. Autumn setting in,' said Melanie Tyler. 'Too dark for walking out.'

'Mr Rufus always had a fancy for night walks. Like two peas in a pod, you and him.' Mrs Mac nodded at John Tyler. 'There's that spirit lamp he always used, John. In the back scullery.'

John found the lamp and lit it for her with a spill from the kitchen range. Astrid took it, went through to the hall and pulled on a cloak that was lying over a chair. The lights at the front of the house had all been dimmed, leaving the wide bowl of land that contained the Hall in inky darkness. The lamp made a spidery thread of light in the gloom. Astrid walked forward boldly enough then jumped as something touched her skirt. She quickly breathed out as she heard the companionable *meo-ow* of Susannah the Spanish Cat.

She walked on. The recent velvet certainties of the port and now the clear night air made her think yet again about Honesty Leeming. Tomorrow, whether her mother wished it or not, she'd make her listen to what had happened to the girl. Something had to be done. At least she should know about this savage thing.

The broad path in front of the house lay under a fringe of tall cedars. The trees dipped and rustled in the darkness as she walked down over the little river bridge and turned left down the narrow path towards the row of cottages which tagged on to the back of the Hall like the tail of a dog. Her nose wrinkled at the faint privy-smell of dog-rose and chickweed which always seemed to hang about on this lane. She picked her way along the narrow path. The cottages in the row were all in darkness except the one at the far end that blazed with light from every small window. In the doorway stood Jacob Ellenberg, his hands loose by his sides. He was crying.

124

Thirteen

So Much Wreckage

11.45pm

Carmel sat upright in her bed. Someone was battering down her bedroom door. She pushed her hair out of her eyes, pulled on her gown and went to open it.

'Mother, you should come.' Astrid pulled her out onto the corridor. Carmel wrestled her arm away.

'What is it, Astrid? For goodness' sake.'

'It's Mr Ellenberg's cottage. Someone has broken in. They've torn his books, broken his crockery. He's just standing there. He is heartbroken, Mother. Heartbroken.'

Carmel, looking very young with her pigtail down her back, frowned up at her daughter. 'Broken in?' Such things didn't happen at Benbow. 'No one locks their doors here.'

Astrid almost dragged her along the corridor. 'Well, they broke his crockery and tore down his pictures.' She took the cape from her own shoulders and placed it round Carmel. 'Wait!' She ran into her bedroom to get her heavy carriage coat.

As they made their way down the corridor they came upon a yawning Constance. 'What is it?'

'Just some trouble at the cottages, Connie. You go back to bed. Please.' Astrid pushed her back into her room and closed the door behind her.

When Carmel and Astrid, with an anxious John Tyler close behind, reached the cottage Jacob Ellenberg was still at his door, though now he was dry-eyed. He was staring along the lane. The lenses of his spectacles glittered in the light of their lamps. 'Mrs Benbow,' he said. 'You should not trouble.'

John Tyler walked past him into the wrecked room. Books were scattered everywhere. One wall was spattered with black holes that marked the place where a William Blake print, given to Jacob by Rufus, had hung. Fragments of paper and glass still stuck to the wall. Carmel looked round, anger rising in her throat like sticky phlegm. 'Who did this?' she said. 'Who did this, Jacob?'

John Tyler set off up the open staircase.

Jacob stared at Carmel through his round glasses. Then he shrugged. 'I can't . . .'

She nodded. 'It was Michael John,' she stated.

'I passed the boy on my way back,' he said. 'He had a shotgun in his hands.'

'It couldn't have been his Purdey,' she said quickly. 'That went across to the Lodge with the Colonel.'

Jacob sighed. 'I recognised it. It was the one with the carved stock, the old one Rufus used to stop the pigeons roosting on the roof of the house.'

John came bounding back down the stairs. 'It's worse up there,' he said briefly. He wrinkled his nose.

Carmel took Jacob by the shoulder and pushed him towards Astrid. 'Take Mr Ellenberg up to the house and sit him in the drawing room. John and I will close up here and will be back in a few minutes. You may search out your brother and tell him I will see him, now, in the library.'

Carmel and John Tyler watched the other two walk down the path. 'Now then, John,' said Carmel quickly. 'Just blow out the lamp here and shut the door tight. Then get your bicycle and ride down to the Colonel's. Tell him he must come at once. Even if he is in bed. He must come.'

Carmel went back to the house, first to the kitchen to tell Melanie that John Tyler would be a little while. 'And would you make up the bed in the room beyond the schoolroom for Mr Ellenberg?'

'Him?' said Melanie. 'Here?'

'Make it up,' said Carmel.

In the library Astrid was sitting at the long table, glaring at Michael John who was standing in his dressing gown with his back to the dead fire. He looked handsomer than ever and was staring sulkily down at the carpet. Carmel stood before him, took his chin in her hand and raised his eyes to hers. 'Why did you do that? Why on earth did you do that?'

He twisted his face away and stared over her head. His broad shoulders moved under the silk of his gown in a massive shrug. 'The man's a sneak. A cheat and a sneak. They all are.'

'It is a cruel thing, Michael John. Jacob Ellenberg was your father's friend. He has nothing more in the world than there is in that cottage.'

'Fellow shouldn't have come here. He should have stayed where he was, with his own kind.'

'He has no family, Michael John,' said Astrid from the table. 'They are all dead.'

Michael John scowled. 'He should be with them.'

'That's enough!' Carmel raised a hand and slapped him hard across the cheek. Then she put her fingers to her mouth and felt the heat of their burning tips.

Michael John curled his fist and pulled it back as though he was about to strike her. Astrid stood up quickly and moved towards her mother. Just then there was a commotion in the hall and a caped and gaitered Colonel Carmedy marched in, bringing with him the sharp air of the night. 'What is it, Mrs Benbow?' he said crisply. He glanced across at Michael John. 'What now, young fellow?'

Carmel turned to him, breathing heavily. 'Bear with me, Colonel. I wish you to accompany this boy to his bedroom where he will get dressed. Then I wish you to take him back to the Lodge with you. I do not want him beneath this roof one more instant. Then, if you would be so good, you may return tomorrow to collect his luggage, which will be ready at eight o'clock. Then you should take him to the General, wherever he may be, and set this army wheel in motion immediately.'

'Mrs Benbow, he is merely a boy. Perhaps . . .'

Carmel fixed him with a cold gaze. 'That is what I wish, Colonel Carmedy.' Her tone was weary.

Constance had come out of her room again just as, in response to all the noise down below, Ambrose was treading quietly along the landing. They sat down together on the top step, listening to the commotion downstairs. The soft cloth of Constance's nightdress was spilling onto the edge of his dressing gown and her body exuded a scent of light sweat and old roses, which made his head swim. He was shivering. His hands were sweating. In the end he burst out desperately in a loud whisper, 'Is your farm very big, where you live in America?'

To his consternation she put an arm round him and hugged her to him. 'It's not a farm, Ambrose. You might just call it *land*. We have four hundred square miles of land, a mountain or two . . .' she was exaggerating, of course '. . . with some ranches, two or three little towns.'

He sat very, very still. 'Phew! That's here to Edinburgh, two hundred miles!'

'It's a lot of land, honey. It's very empty.'

'How did you get that much land? It's a whole country.'

By now, Michael John and the Colonel were at the bottom of the stairs. Constance clasped Ambrose even more tightly at her side to make room for the grim-faced Michael John and Colonel Carmedy to pass. A minute later, Melanie Tyler marched up the stairs with Jacob Ellenberg trailing behind. Ambrose stared at Jacob, who looked blankly back at him, as though he wasn't there.

Constance's voice was in his ear. 'My daddy and his friends, some of them from here in Britain, bought the land from the government and built a railroad on it, so they could get the miners into the gold country.'

'So there's gold?'

'Oh yes. There's gold.'

'Phew! Out of the ground?'

'Sometimes *on* the ground.'

'Phew!' Ambrose almost wrestled himself free and stood up. His mother and Astrid were mounting the stairs. 'Do you have Indians?' He turned to Constance. ' "Buffalo Bill" Cody brought his Indians here to England. It was in the newspapers. He made a show for the Queen.'

Constance disentangled her feet from her gown and stood up. 'So everyone tells me.'

Carmel came level with them. 'Now then, Ambrose. To bed. You must not keep Miss Redoute from her beauty sleep.' She paused. 'Not that she needs it, of course.'

Constance's smile moved from her to Astrid. 'Well, ma'am. We children must get our amusements somehow,' she drawled. She linked arms with Astrid and strolled with her towards their rooms. Carmel chivvied Ambrose before her and shut his bedroom door behind him. When she had gone, he opened it a crack and waited.

After twenty minutes his patience was rewarded. He heard the stamp of boots going along the corridor and down the landing. Then he made out the low rumble of the Colonel's voice and his mother's lighter tones as they talked in the hall. He moved across to his window and watched Michael John mount the step of the Colonel's light carriage, followed closely by the Colonel himself. Ambrose went back to the landing and watched as his mother moved a chessman. 'White brings out her knight,' he whispered. Back in his bedroom he drew his curtains and went to sit on his bed. So Cain and Abel was not to be the story. The combination of excitement and relief made his bones sing and he started to cry.

Fourteen

The Wheel of Change

7.45am

Breakfast the next day was early, as was the custom at Benbow. Carmel had already done her garden round with her head boy, and set the tasks for the day, when the gong went at three minutes to eight. The breakfasters were sitting at the dining table by eight o'clock. The fancy china of the night before had been put away and today the company ate off a mixed collection of Spode earthenware, some of it crazed, if not cracked. The wide windows with their view across to the lakes were veiled in sheets of fine silver dart-rain, which pulsed against the window panes.

Melanie Tyler, standing by the door in her morning apron, thought what a funny old crew they looked. She was pleased that for once Mrs Benbow had made something of an effort. She had her corset on and had chosen a proper morning gown, rather than those awful fustian garden britches and overall. The American girl, Miss Redoute, looked very satisfactory. Her mauve crêpe morning gown showed what must be Parisian flair in the exquisite embroidery on the collar. The breakfast gong had clearly caught her unawares because her hair was rather hastily pinned up. But she was, on the whole, a very acceptable vision.

Melanie's eye moved along the table to Miss Astrid Benbow. Now she could be quite smart if she tried, but today she had settled for a sage green gown that did not flatter her pale colouring. Young Ambrose, though, had made a great effort on this special morning and put on a clean shirt and his best Norfolk jacket. He'd come to Melanie in the butler's pantry and requested help with his tie, so it was knotted with exemplary neatness.

Michael John was missing, of course, after that carry-on last night. Melanie had been up since six packing his things. Apparently he was to go into the army. She was surprised by the dart of pity she had felt when she heard. Bad as he was, it must be no fun being shoved around like a parcel.

For Melanie the disappointment of the day was Jacob Ellenberg. When she heard from John the tale of the wrecked cottage, and just what Michael John had done in there, especially upstairs, she'd felt sick. She and John had talked into the night about young Michael John: how she'd always said the boy lacked a father's close hand and a mother's true care. How there had never been bounds for him and how, in the end – as they all knew at Benbow – he had created his own half-dark world. How his mother – her eyes too full of roses – had taken no heed of the boy. How could she not feel responsibility for the way he was?

Poor Ambrose. Melanie had lost count of the times through the years that she'd had to dry his tears over some cruelty wreaked by that brother of his. She'd tried to talk to Mrs Benbow about it but was always fobbed off with some airy statement about boys being boys. There was always some plantling to attend to, some seed box to unwrap. In Melanie Tyler's very private opinion Mrs Benbow – nice woman and good employer that she undeniably was – lacked true judgement in certain things.

Take this foreigner, Mr Ellenberg. After that terrible affair yesterday you might agree that it was only Christian to give him a bed for the night. That was fair. But there were rooms – servants' rooms now empty in this barely served place – that would have done very well for the foreigner. What was he, after all? One of Mr Rufus Benbow's strays made into some kind of glorified gamekeeper. Well, not even a gamekeeper really. A grubbing clerk. No need for him to have a family bedroom. Not least because it meant that John (even, God forbid, Melanie herself) would have to take him his hot water and light his fire as though he were a proper guest. And look at him lurking there at the corner: crumpled suit, dirty shirt. He was a disgrace to the family.

Carmel lifted her hand. 'Thank you very much, Melanie. We will help ourselves now.'

As the door clicked behind Melanie, Carmel raised her eyebrows at Astrid. 'Poor Melanie. She looked as though she had been sucking lemons. I'm afraid we are a great disappointment to her.' She turned to Jacob. 'Did you sleep well, Jacob?'

Jacob, caught with a mouth full of kedgeree, spluttered a little. 'Very well, Mrs Benbow. Such a great relief it was to feel safe. And a lovely room. Mr Tyler very kindly lit my fire for me. A great treat.'

'I thought you might like that room. It was Rufus's room when he was a child and later, when he was a young man, his own little separate hideaway. He loved the view: through the trees to the horizon. He told me that when he was a boy he called it his path to freedom.'

'It is indeed a very fine view.'

'And do you like the desk? I think it may be very old. His father brought it from Jerusalem.'

'It is an intriguing desk. Intricate. It evokes the perfumes of Araby.' Jacob hoped this would be sufficient appreciation. He waited. Then, as Mrs Benbow delicately took a forkful of Mrs Mac's scrambled eggs into her mouth, he risked a spoonful of kedgeree.

Carmel masticated carefully, swallowed, then went on. 'I have given some thought to that incident in the woods and the nasty event last night, Mr Ellenberg . . .'

He shook his head and flipped his hand in the air in a very foreign fashion. 'You should not trouble, Mrs Benbow. I have forgotten it. It is a gift of survival that one learns with the top of the mind to forget.' There was a fleck of saffron-dyed fish on his upper lip.

'. . . so my feeling,' Carmel went on as though he had not spoken, 'is that you should stay here at the house, in Rufus's room. You will feel safer there. And you can concentrate on the work on the charts in the library. Seb Golightly will manage in the woods and the fields without you. I will ask Colonel Carmedy to find him a boy to help. So, perhaps you could go to your cottage with John Tyler later today, with a barrow or something, and collect whatever you need.'

Jacob waited for her eye to leave him so he could finish his breakfast. His mind raced ahead as he thought of this morning's tasks. There was his small collection of worldly goods to gather, the mess at the cottage to clear up. He shuddered at the thought of the mess in the upstairs room. Only he could clear that up. What had possessed the boy to evacuate himself all over that narrow space? How much hate there must be in him. Unbidden into Jacob's mind came the image of the young soldier evacuating himself in another fashion onto his helpless daughter.

He relaxed at last as Mrs Benbow turned to Constance Redoute. 'And what would you be doing today, Miss Redoute?' she said. 'When this awful rain clears perhaps you will ride that fine horse of yours? Astrid is a good horsewoman but rather too spoiled by town life, I imagine, to take the pleasure she once did in the Durham countryside. Perhaps she'll show you a little of the Benbow lands. They are of great interest, you know. Have been in this family for many hundreds of years.' She turned to her daughter. 'I have a new mare called Serion, Astrid, acquired for me by my friend Keziah Leeming. A very sweet animal, barely spoiled. You can put her through her paces.'

'Mother,' said Astrid, annoyed at her mother's sweeping condemnation of her attitude to riding, 'if this is some brawny Amazon of a horse, however well bred, I will not ride her. I promise you I will not.'

Constance looked at her friend. She might appear quiet and thoughtful but it was the quiet of self-containment and power, not the quiet of a dim and indistinct character. She would not be crushed by this deceptively imperious mother of hers.

'No, no,' protested Carmel. 'Serion is as smooth as milk. Keziah knows how to bring out the sweetness in horses. Do try Serion, darling. She'll put a spring in your seat.'

'Can I go with them?' said Ambrose eagerly. 'There are lots of things I can show Miss Redoute.'

Carmel stared absently at him for a second. 'Yes, Amby. I think today will be a better day for you. Perhaps you should have a better day.'

Just then the clang of the doorbell resounded through the house. Constance jumped up in her chair, a loose curl springing from its pin to hang just below her ear.

'That's the door. It'll be for Mick's things,' explained Ambrose kindly. 'Don't you have doorbells in America?'

The bell was not from the great front door of the house. The last time that had been opened was at Rufus's funeral. The door much more commonly used at Benbow Hall was the side door just beyond the archway leading from the stables. It led into a narrow back hall that was furnished with a great coat-and-stick rack and a long oak bench, shiny with hundreds of years of sitting. To one side of the door was a large, very effective bell-pull, a mounting block and three tethering rings for horses.

Melanie checked her white cap in the mirror by the rack before she opened the door. Bran Eggleston, the postman, stood there in the rain, the satchel of Benbow post in his hand. Behind him stood his horse, rendered uncharacteristically sleek by the almost invisible sheet of rain which was covering the Hall. Melanie took the satchel. 'Take Nibs down under the arch there, Bran,' she said. 'And go and knock on the kitchen door. Mrs Mac'll have a cup of tea for you and a slice of spice to warm you up.' Melanie liked Bran Eggleston. He never took for granted that you'd offer him anything, even after his long journey up from Bishop Auckland. Made you want to do something for him. She was sure all the farmers' wives felt the same about him because he never went without.

She was laying out the post neatly on its lacquer tray when there was another, more peremptory knock on the door. This time it was not Bran, with his modest ways and downcast eyes. It was the gypsy Keziah Leeming and that scallywag son of hers. They stood there like a pair of drowned hares. The boy's eyes met Melanie's as though they had a right.

'What is it?' No need with these two for her to bother to be polite. In truth they should have come to the kitchen door.

'We will see Carmel Benbow,' said Keziah. She took a step forward and Melanie had to fall back to allow her into the shadowy back hall. Melanie felt her gorge rise as they brought in with them the scent of honeysuckle, hedge-rose and road-grit, of horse-dung and milk, of burning metal and forge-fire. Behind them the veil of rain had blown up into a lashing storm. Jack Lomas shut the great door with a thud.

Melanie took a good step backwards along the passage, putting distance between them. 'I'll see if Mrs Benbow's in,' she said. 'You wait here.'

Keziah set herself down on the long bench and nodded to Jack who came beside her and leaned against the wall. 'We'll wait here,' said Keziah. 'You tell Carmel not to fash herself. We're in no hurry.'

Melanie took the post tray to the dining room and announced the visitors in the back hall. She'd have been pleased if Mrs Benbow had kept the gypsies waiting. But she stood up straight away. 'Tell them to go to the morning room, Melanie. I'll be there in a moment.'

135

'But Mrs Benbow, they've clogs on their feet and they're covered in clarts ... er ... mud. Soaking wet. That's good Turkish carpet in there.'

Carmel frowned. 'Then tell them to take off their clogs, Melanie, then they won't hurt your precious carpet.'

Melanie went back and conveyed the message but Keziah stayed put. 'Dinnet worry about your carpets, hinney. Just you ask Carmel to come down here to see us. These tiles'll take no harm from travellers' feet.'

Carmel asked Astrid to come with her. 'I have a feeling, darling, that this may have something to do with you. Keziah mentioned a certain matter yesterday.'

They were met by Melanie outside the morning room and she conveyed Keziah's wishes that they should meet by the side door. Walking down the corridor at her mother's shoulder Astrid wondered if perhaps this was her last chance to say something about Honesty Leeming. No doubt Keziah had come to ask why some great lady of the calibre of Lady Seland – Carmel Benbow's friend and cousin – had been the architect of young Honesty's tragedy.

But it seemed not.

'I see you've brought the lass down.' Keziah nodded towards Astrid. She did not get up. Carmel went to sit beside her. Astrid stood beside her mother, too conscious of the bright gaze of Jack Lomas.

'Did you tell her?' Keziah asked Carmel.

Carmel shook her head, then looked up at Astrid and explained the idea that Honesty should be her maid. That it would be good training for the girl who, as Keziah said again, had no feeling for the road and would never make a true gypsy.

'But I don't want a maid,' said Astrid. 'I never wanted a maid.'

Keziah fixed Astrid with a deep gaze. 'Seems to me, like, that our Honesty had no fair time down there at Seland. They treated her bad. She needs a good time now. The best place for her is with you. I see it. I know it.'

Astrid blushed. 'Perhaps I should explain about Seland . . .'

'I know about Seland.'

'Did Honesty tell you?'

'Our Honesty said nowt. Like I say, I know. But now I think she should be with you. She's taken a fancy to you. She likes houses. She's a quick learner. So she can come to you. You can take proper care of her.'

Jack Lomas straightened up, shook himself, then leaned up against the wall again. 'Don't try, Ma. This'n wants nowt to do with our Honesty, nor with us. No space for a gypsy lass in her parlour.'

Astrid scowled at him. 'That's not . . . I do have space. I like Honesty very much.' Her mind was in turmoil at the topsy-turvy thing that was going on around her. 'I don't *not* want her.'

'Well, then,' said Keziah, glancing at Carmel. 'Settled then, seeing as you don't *not* want her.'

'Well, Astrid?' Carmel looked up at her daughter.

'Perhaps we could try,' said Astrid. 'If . . .'

'Right then.' Keziah stood up. 'She's doing some jobs for Edith just now. But I'll tell her to come up here at noon.'

Jack straightened up from the wall again. 'Right!' he said, keeping his eyes on Astrid's until she dropped hers. In the months to come, despite herself, she would dream many times of that golden gaze.

Carmel and Astrid stood in the wide doorway watching Keziah and her son trudge away through the veils of rain. Astrid started to wonder whether now was the time to tell the truth about Honesty. Carmel pre-empted her by saying suddenly, 'Do you know why I like Keziah Leeming, Astrid?'

'To be perfectly honest, Mother, I haven't an idea in the world.'

'Because she is like your father.'

'What?' Surprise made Astrid forget her manners.

'She is a pure spirit. She is out of time. She knows no masters. She has no inferiors. Your father was like that. He saw everything afresh. He mesmerised me.' She closed the door and looked searchingly into the eyes of her daughter. 'I think he sent her to me so that I would not be alone.'

Following her mother along the corridor Astrid felt grateful that she'd not told her mother the truth about Honesty. Carmel was out of touch with reality as it was.

When they got back to the dining room Jacob Ellenberg had escaped to the library, accompanied by the newly liberated Ambrose who left a message with Constance that he'd meet her and his sister at the stable at eleven o'clock and come riding with them. At Carmel's place at the table there was a pile of post and packages. Constance had opened a thick packet of her own and was leafing through a closely written seven-page letter. She looked up frowning at Astrid as she sat down to resume her breakfast.

Astrid looked up at her. 'What's wrong, Connie?'

'My momma writes that my father is very ill and she is very concerned. However, her own health is frail, as is that of my sister Delphine. It is impossible for them to travel from Torquay to make haste to his side. So she asks me – being the "vulgarly healthy and hearty one" – to go to Poppa.' She lifted the paper and peered closer. 'And now here she instructs me to do that. She also *instructs* me to . . .' She scrabbled through the rest of the packet, leafing through papers and tickets. 'My goodness, the dear woman has gone quite mad.'

Astrid thought that it might be something to do with mothers. A stage they went through.

'Do you see this, Astrid? It is a ticket for me, first class saloon, sailing out of Liverpool in a week's time.' She held up another piece of paper. 'And do you see this? This is a ticket for *you* on that same voyage. Dear Astrid, I must confess now I've written about you to dear Momma in adulatory terms. Talked of us being the best of friends. Now she says that if you are so good a friend, then you should come with me.'

For a second the storm outside seemed to still. Astrid's head whirled. Carmel looked at her daughter with wide open eyes. 'Astrid, if you wish . . .'

Astrid allowed herself to wait a full minute before she said anything. Around her she could hear the swirl of clocks and the click of wheels finding their position. Yesterday at this very hour she'd stood in the window at Seland Hall, listening to sycophantic murmurs, watching over-attendant flutters as the King embarked on a morning's shooting. And she had turned to see a little dark-haired maid with golden eyes clearing out the fireplace.

'Well now,' she said, 'what do you think, Mother? Could Honesty Leeming play the lady's maid all the way to America?'

Part Two

The Americans

Colorado
June 1907

May 2 India: Riots break out in Rawalpindi and East Bengal, spreading to the Punjab

May 10 London: Second reading of bill to provide an old-age pension of five shillings a week to people over 65

May 18 London: Women's Labour League holds first conference, chaired by Mrs Ramsay MacDonald

May 30 Glasgow: Launch of King Edward VII's new turbine yacht *Alexandria*

One

Honesty

Well, it seems like it's a special day today. This afternoon there's to be this big party out on the prairie by the General's place. According to my friend Slim, who's the General's driver, it's to celebrate one time when America fought the English and won. It should be in July but he's having it now because he wants to be first. Trust him to shift the calendar. And I could be wrong but I have this suspicion it's because he thinks we – me and Miss Benbow, that is – might be away by July. Anyway, it means everybody who's anybody from this whole district is coming. Some are even coming from as far away as Denver City.

In the afternoon there'll be peaches and champagne by the lake pool that the General made by diverting the creek and blasting out a bit of the red mountain rock. (Just now, this brings to my mind those peaches in Mrs Benbow's peach-house. This time of year when I was just a young thing I'd be up those ladders tying little nets round them to keep them safe so they didn't drop too early. When I think about it, there was nobody to tie a little net round me. To keep me safe.)

Anyway the General's men have got this army tent up already to keep the sun off the dancing platform. The sun here is hard and bright. (I've seen more sun in the months I've been here than I did in five summers at home.) And – best of all – there's to be a circus with an elephant, a tightrope walker and a singer from the big opera in New York to entertain the crowds.

143

Then tonight there'll be this grand dinner where the finest people in the state will dine in the great hall of the castle. That's what they call it, a castle, but it's not really. No comparison to Raby Castle that we see on our way to Appleby Fair. Nor even Seland, that horrible cave of a place. Anyway, the New York tenor will sing again at the dinner.

They wanted me to do some of my contortions and acrobatics as part of the entertainment but I've been a bit stiff of late and was minded to refuse. Anyway, the last time I performed look where that got me. Miss Redoute tried to insist – fulsome, saying how good I was – but this woman here who I like – name of Aunt Beatrice – told her *not to harass the child* and she desisted.

It's strange, isn't it, how things turn out? How long did I have Keziah telling me into my ear that I've nothing of the traveller in me, that all I wanted was to be stuck in one place all the time, to grow roots in my heels? And here's me thousands of miles from her in this hot, high country that butts up to mountain peaks and has a horizon so far away you have to imagine it, for your eyes can hardly make it out. And here's me living in a house tucked into the elbow of one of those mountains; a house that's half castle, half garden shed – a house where the people who serve are so familiar with their masters that it's some kind of paradise.

And I've met these two people – a mother and daughter – who sport the colour of Mrs Benbow's dark plums all over their bodies except for the palms of their hands and the soles of their feet where they are the colour of ripe peaches. These two are wondrous visions with gleaming smiles and sparkling eyes. I nearly fell over when they greeted Miss Redoute with kisses and hugs like she was their sister. Indeed they told me they were called Aunt Beatrice and Cousin Vera, though they were clearly not kin to Miss Redoute.

These two are strange folk; they laugh like music and talk sometimes in a language that I feel I should understand but which baffles me with unfamiliar words. The two of them sing in strange harmonies as they work and the smoothness of their tones makes your skin prickle. And they've been so very kind to me in the months I've been here.

This has been especially so of late. Aunt Beatrice even made me poultices for my bad back and made me put up my feet. She pats my head and strokes my cheek and calls me *honey child* with a look in her eye I can't understand. I've not known such softness, not in all my life. Auntie Edith was kind enough, but she never touched you. And Keziah was not one to pat your cheek. Ha!

So I've been thinking all day how at fifteen years old I've travelled more in this one big jaunt than has Keziah in all her life. And her the great traveller? But she might say how would you count the ship as travel? The *Atlantic Pride* it was called. Like a town on water. All those weeks on the ocean bobbing and whooshing in this tin can whose great size would take in Bishop Auckland main street from the castle to the workhouse.

It takes ages to walk the ship from end to end. Longer, when you have to cling to the rail as the great thing rocks from side to side like an overloaded haywain with the waves dashing against its sides with the force of steam-hammers.

Not that everyone *can* walk from end to end, if you get my meaning. You can't do that if you're travelling steerage, as I was in my first days on that voyage. (The young ladies could only get me a steerage ticket, me being so late aboard, so to speak.) So I could only walk around in the narrow spaces allotted to the lowest travellers. Even so, a lot of the time I was up in the young ladies' cabin, battling with the stewardess for charge of the ladies' clothes. This *brewer* had coal-black eyebrows and big shoulders and, if you want the truth, I shied away from taking her on. One day she was giving me what-for and I was sick, right in front of her, throwing up all over the carpet in the stateroom. She was furious, I can tell you. I hid from her all day after that.

Then, on the third day, when I'd been sick yet again (this time in my own stinking cabin), I stayed in my cot and didn't bother to go up to the big cabin with the portholes. I turned down an offer of bread from the kind woman in the upper bunk, pulled the rag they called a blanket over my head, and turned my face to the wall.

I lie there all day sleeping and dreaming. The bobbing movement of the boat transforms itself to the swaying of the *vardo* as it makes its slow way down that narrow lane on the road from York and Knaresborough, shouldering through heavy branches that whip your face if you're not careful. I'm leaning against Keziah, relishing the smoky, horsy smell of her, the hard thrust of shoulder-muscle under the sleeve of her shirt. Jack's leading the horse by the rein, slashing his way through intrusive branches with this hooked blade he has. Then the way closes off altogether and the horse rears, flinging Jack over its head. He comes crashing on top of us and the whole rig tips over. I bump to the ground and scream out loud.

Of course it's not the rig, it's the ship that's reared up and I'm on the sticky floor of the cabin. Nursing my bruises I clamber back into my bunk, and though I'm ashamed to say it I cry bitter tears under the blanket. I cannot fathom, now, why I agreed to leave Keziah and Jack and come on this weary journey. I think Miss Astrid Benbow's to blame, her adding her urging to that of Keziah. She looked me deep in the eyes and brought to my stomach that lead-heavy feeling I had at Seland Hall, when I told her of the King and all his antics. She'd not told anyone about that and now I was really scared that she would and they would blame me for being bad. So I submitted to their soft words and here I am in a dark hole in the belly of a huge ship, in the middle of a giant sea that stretches to every horizon.

The ship's bell has just sounded three o'clock the next afternoon when Miss Astrid Benbow comes through the narrow door bringing with her the clean salt air mixed with the scent of

146

magnolias. 'Come on, Honesty! This won't do.' She pulls off the blanket and hauls me upright.

I tell her how sick I've been and she wrinkles her nose and says she can tell. 'Get your bag. I want you up there with me,' she says.

'They won't let us up there,' I say. 'Just to work, not to stay.'

'They will if I say so.' She has that soft-hard tone in her voice and she's just like her mother, who has her own way of getting exactly what she wants. Next to Keziah, Mrs Benbow's the hardest woman I know.

So I spend the rest of the voyage in a special little bolted-down bunk behind a screen in the stateroom belonging to Miss Benbow and Miss Redoute. I can't make out whether it's the persuasiveness of the one lady (Miss Benbow) or the gold proffered by the other (Miss Redoute) that has wrought this miracle. Whoever it is I'm mighty grateful. Even in the stateroom the seasickness persists but only in the mornings. By eleven o'clock I'm usually right as rain.

Anyway when Miss Benbow witnesses another spitting row I have with the stewardess she sorts things out. There are new rules. I'm to help both the ladies to dress and keep their things tidy. The black-browed *brewer*'s to supply and clean the cabin and offer extra help where needed. She's none too pleased but a gold sovereign from Miss Redoute smooths the way a little.

The ladies I serve are very different from each other. Miss Redoute likes a lot of help with her toilette and has a weakness for having her hair brushed. She almost hums with delight as you do it. Miss Benbow more or less manages herself and hates having a fuss made around her. When it's too bad up on deck she sits in their little sitting room, turns the pages of her books and looks at pictures of paintings. Sometimes she draws in her sketchbook. She draws a picture of Miss Redoute at her little dressing shelf, she draws me as I brush Miss Redoute's hair.

I have to admit I really like her. She can keep secrets and she treats you with respect. And she's pretty despite being plain, if you see what I mean. I think that in spite of not liking the *gorgio* too much our Jack liked her too. He asked me all kinds of questions about her which is unusual. He usually keeps his own counsel about people.

I look at Miss Benbow's sketchbook when she is out of the cabin. She makes very fair likenesses. Further back in the notebook are drawings of doorways around Benbow Hall. There is a section where the drawings are all from Mrs B's walled garden. The roses in pots on the benches with their little paper hats tied on. The spreading peach tree in the fruit house with three round peaches. There's a portrait of Keziah that I know she didn't sit for. And one of Jack, where he looks much older and quite wicked. I'd never a thought she'd even noticed him but she must of. She's got a very true likeness. Oh dear. How all these images make me ache for home.

In the cabin the young ladies talk as though I'm not there. I am used to this of course. Think of Seland Hall where, if someone passed, you had to turn to the wall and pretend you were invisible. But, stupid though all this is, it has its consolations. They may treat you as though you are deaf but you hear everything.

I learn about Miss Redoute and those she calls her momma and poppa. How Momma was a real beauty from somewhere called Virginia, how in her day she had led something called the *cotillion*. I thought it sounded like a coach but it's a dance for the young beauties, I guess, who are out fishing for a nice rich young man. Well, it seems Mrs R caught Mr R on her hook at this social occasion in New York City. He was handsome, a hero of their own war, and what's more had been a great pioneer, helping the railroad to force its way west into the goldfields and the great fruitful plains. Miss Redoute tells the story many times over, like it was a fairy tale.

Seems like the General was a big feller among his people, somewhat like one of our gypsy kings. And rich. Crazy rich, from the railroad and the silver and gold that came out of the earth. Seems he loved this raw land with its raw people and wide open spaces. So he built a castle for his great Virginian beauty and brought her West, along with Aunt Beatrice and Cousin Vera. But she was too fine a flower for this red earth, for the thin air of the mountains. The poor woman caught what Miss Redoute called 'mountain sickness'. She had headaches, went half blind and was sick all the time.

I can recall all this, listening as I stood there in the stateroom, brushing Miss Redoute's hair while the boat lurched to and fro. Lord, how sick I was on that boat! I was sick also on the endless train journey West even though Mr Redoute's railcar was like a palace on wheels. We were days and days in that railcar, through snowdrifts and hailstorms! I lost count of the days.

So anyway it seems Mrs Redoute left the General and took her daughters to Europe and finally to England for the softer climate. Seems as well that the General was keen for his daughters to mix with fine people in England. But only Miss Redoute got to do that, as her sister and her mother were delicate and could not take the thick London air. They got stuck at the English seaside.

In all this time Miss Benbow spoke very little about herself, even though she seemed keen to enjoy all Miss Redoute's tales. Eager to find out about her host before she landed, I expect. There was much talk about the fact that they would find the General – they always called him 'the General' – on his sickbed. Miss Redoute read out her mother's letter to Miss Benbow. I read it myself when they went up to have dinner at the captain's table. (Good job old Mrs Benbow learned me how to read.) *It seems, dear Constance, that the General went on one of his treks up through Garden of the Gods onto the old Ute trail and beyond that to where no one has been. I declare he will never rest, that man. Well, my dear, there was one of those dreadful lightning storms. Do you remember those? How I had to hide away from them! Well, his horse bolted and he fell, crushing his ankle. He lay out there all through the freezing night. It was a pure miracle that the wolves or bears didn't get him. He was entirely lucky in that his horse wandered back to him. So he hauled himself onto the brute's back and chivvied it to return home. Now the dear man has a broken ankle and has succumbed to pneumonia and Dr Stannington fears for his life. My dear, at sixty-six your father needs to rein himself in. I have begged and begged him to come to us here in England. But he is intoxicated by Colorado and will not leave. Even for me, whom as you know he holds in such high regard . . .*

I've got to admit I was very stirred up by the words in the letter. 'Garden of the Gods', 'the old Ute trail', 'wolves or bears'. And a place 'where no one has been'. I so longed to see this fairy-tale place. But the ladies didn't know I knew all this because, like all maids, I am supposed to be deaf.

I thought the old boy would probably have snuffed it by the time we got here. But still I kept quiet and hugged to myself the dream that I would see this wondrous land. As I stood in that cabin on the high seas, brushing Miss Redoute's long black hair, I relished in my heart the tales I'd to tell Keziah and Jack when I got home.

But now today, so many months later, there are other things to think about, more tales to tell back home. I'm wearing a new red dress that Miss Redoute brought me from Denver and I'm told to enjoy myself at the celebrations this afternoon. I am not to serve! There are plenty of serving people, mostly Irish but there's a sprinkling of purple plum people like Aunt Beatrice and Cousin Vera. There will be miners and railway men coming; bankers and entertainers. Miss Redoute has declared me very *purrty* in my new dress and said this morning it was time I had myself what she calls a *beau*. 'Overlook no one, honey. There is gold galore in this town. Why, the richest man here, Mr Stratton, started out as a carpenter. And Mr Stratton can buy and sell the General five times over.'

I blushed at her teasing. There is always my friend Slim who is the General's driver but he's no millionaire. He's kind of adopted me like a big brother. He's a bit like our Jack but he's lanky as a beanpole and calls you *ma'am* like it's something funny. On his days off he takes off into the mountains by Cripple Creek where he has a little hole in the ground where he digs for gold or something called sylvanite. A kind of silver I suppose. The General surveyed it for him and he said it was as promising as any dig on Battle Mountain. Seems like gold is pouring out of the mountains like there was a tap inside that barren place. There are twenty-five millionaires in this little town and most of that has come from the gold and silver buzzing inside those mountains.

Slim took me up on the train one day to see his mine. The General was away in New York doing business. Slim hired horses from the livery in Cripple Creek there and we rode up to the diggings. (He laughed when I said I would ride bareback and called me a *little Navaho*).

It really wasn't much more than a hole in the ground. I helped him dig and scrape in the earth and I wound his makeshift windlass for him. He put his arm over my shoulder, called me 'little sister' and told me I was as useful as any man.

This afternoon at the party he's to help ferry the guests up here from the Antlers Hotel down in town. After that he'll join the party too. He's told me he'll come looking for me as he wishes to dance with me. He'll not take the blindest notice of my protest that I cannot dance. 'Why, I'll teach you myself, ma'am,' he says. 'You can't get no better teacher.'

There's something about Slim that makes me think I should wait for him to make his million, rather than go fishing for any of the millionaires who'll be here today. They'd not make me laugh, or make my insides go slippery like he does; nor throw their arm about me in that way he has. I'm looking forward to what he will say about my fine new frock; whether, like Miss Redoute, he'll think me *purrty*. I think maybe he will.

Two

Early Morning Ride

9am

'Astrid!' Richard Redoute lifted his crop in salute as he turned his horse to join Astrid on the narrow path that led over the creek away from the castle, through the new fir plantation and towards the high mountain pass. 'I must say that the morning light becomes you, my dear,' he said.

Astrid smiled and nodded. Early morning with its residue of night coolness was the best time to ride like this. By ten the June day would be too hot to ride on narrow rock-strewn paths.

She glanced up at the clear light and the intense blue of the Colorado morning sky and took a very deep breath of pleasure. She said nothing. It had taken some time to get used to the General's easy compliments, just as it had taken some time to get used to the General himself. The first shock had been the sight of him at the railway station. She'd been expecting a doddering old creature, just up from his deathbed. Yet here was a tall slender man, immaculately tailored in a faintly military style. As he swept off his hat to greet them his thick hair, faintly putty-coloured, glinted in the sun. His darker moustache was set neatly above his firm mouth. The only sign of his recent brush with mortality was a silver-headed cane carried for occasional use in taking the weight from his recovering ankle.

He'd walked swiftly to his daughter, brushed aside her silver fox fur and held her close, exclaiming how she was quite the

European lady now and would make the whole of Colorado society blink with her great style. Then he shook Astrid heartily by the hand and welcomed her to his town. (Astrid knew from Constance that it was indeed *his* town. He had built its broad streets, endowed its college, given it parks, even a hospital.)

She watched with some surprise as he shook the hand of Honesty Leeming, which made the girl grin and nod in delight. Then he handed them all goggles and told them to wrap up tight and hold on to their hats as Slim Struder, his driver, would drive them up to the castle in his motor car. Poor Honesty was so overcome she had to go to find a bathroom to be sick in before they set out in the car. Astrid apologised for her, explaining the residual problem with seasickness. Apart from that she was always very well.

They wove their way through slushy streets crowded with wagons and horses, down a narrow road planted with young cedar and ash interplanted with much older and more mature mountain firs. They were windblown and freezing cold when they arrived at the castle. In the echoing hallway a crowd of uniformed servants clapped briefly as they came through the door. A little girl came forward and gave Constance a posy of white roses. Then they were greeted by 'Aunt Beatrice' and 'Cousin Vera' who hugged Constance with murmurs of delight and asked lovingly after the health of Miss Aurelia, Constance's mother now so far away. Constance turned to Astrid. 'This dear person is Aunt Beatrice, who took care of my momma back in Virginia, way before she met the General.'

Aunt Beatrice took Astrid's hand in both of hers and shook it firmly. 'And that there's is my Cousin Vera who don't much use her voice but is a lovin' soul.' Then she greeted Honesty just as warmly.

After this, without asking permission, the woman called Aunt Beatrice turned and removed Constance's hat, furs and heavy-collared coat as though she were a child. She handed these to Cousin Vera. Then she hugged Constance properly, saying, 'Don' I tell the General to tell Miss Aurelia in those letters of his that I miss her and my little girls like the sun coming up?' She laughed a deep gurgling laugh and Astrid did not quite know whether or not she was teasing. It was hard to tell the woman's age: she was tall and graceful in her violet cotton dress with its neat collar. Her soft strong hair was controlled into a large plait that encircled her head like a halo.

All the time she was observing Aunt Beatrice and Cousin Vera, Astrid had felt Richard Redoute's attention on her. She could feel it even when he was looking at and talking to the others. This consciousness made her awkward and uncharacteristically shy and she was glad when at last Cousin Vera showed her to her bedroom: a large room on the second floor within the high wooden turret. Directly above Constance's larger room on the first floor, Astrid's bedroom had windows on two sides that allowed the eye to move round from the snow-topped mountains with their snow-scattered, tree-clad gullies to the ruddy columns of rock which stood proud from the grey ground-rock, strewn about like discarded giant chess pieces, then down to the town, laid out like a toy in the distance. From her window she could see the wisp of steam above the railway station as their train fired up for its return journey. The vapour floated up into the big sky, marking its rise very sharply against the intense blue.

Standing at the window on that first day Astrid had reflected on the magnitude of the achievements of the General and people like him. The familiar towns and cities she'd known in England and Europe had always seemed to her God-given, as permanent as the mountains and the sea. It seemed that England had never been an empty land. But here, despite this town with its brave hotels and the station with its self-important steam engine, despite the scattering of very decent houses, and the avenues of barely grown trees, despite this pretend castle with its strange wood-clad turrets and bizarre sun-blinds – despite all this, it was easy to envision the empty land as it had been before the General and his friends had got here with their railway; their industry and vigour. Now half-closing her eyes she could see the snow-capped peak that dominated the landscape, the broad high plains and the distant endless mountains; with her inner eye she glimpsed a gaggle of figures trudging along, hauling heavy loads, migrating across the land with the seasons, and leaving only the faintest trail.

That first day she was pulled from her reverie by a knock on the bedroom door. It must be Cousin Vera with some part of her luggage. 'Come in,' she called from the window. The door opened to reveal the General himself. She stood up but he gestured her to sit down again.

'I came to see that you were comfortable, Miss Benbow.' He sat down a little stiffly beside her and she avoided looking at him by turning back to look out of the window.

'This is a breathtaking scene, General. I was imagining it very barren and treeless, as it must have been when you first saw it.'

He grinned and shook his head. 'Ah, you should have seen it, Miss Benbow! I was up here with three other fellows on the first survey for this spur of the railroad out of Denver. The work was well ahead. We were somewhat pleased with our progress. Then one fine morning I rode up here and saw those strange pillars of rock and I thought it must be some native holy place. I rode along to this little plateau at the foot of the mountain with the creek running through it and I knew this was the place I would build my house and bring my bride.'

She found herself staring at his hands, lying very still in his lap. The skin was brown and freckled: the hands of a man who spent a good deal of his time out of doors. But his fingers were long and tapered and well manicured: a city man's hand.

She realised he was staring at her. 'This is an enchanting place,' she said hastily.

'I'm real glad you think so.' He looked at her closely. 'There are still routes and passes through the mountains that are unexplored,' he said. 'New wonders to be found. There is no finer feeling, Miss Benbow, than to walk in places unsullied by human tread. It is like being at the beginning of creation. The creatures are tame, the birds sing in your ear.' His voice resonated deeply in his chest. She imagined herself to be one of his soldiers and caught a shred of feeling that she could follow him to the death.

'Was that how you had your accident up there in one of the passes? When your horse ran off?' she said hurriedly, bringing her straying thoughts to heel.

He shrugged. 'Too much was made of that.' He nodded. 'The thunder and lightning storms in the mountains come on with ferocious energy. My horse was freaked by the thunder, threw me, and left me there for a few hours. When I returned somewhat *hors de combat* Aunt Beatrice rode the buggy hell for leather – excuse me, Miss Benbow – down to the Springs and got my lawyer to wire Mrs Redoute. Quite unnecessary.' He looked at her closely. 'But then it would not have brought my daughter and her friend to my side and that would have been a great pity.' He stood up, smiling slightly. 'The best time to see this country, Miss Benbow, is in the early morning. I shall take you with me tomorrow. How do you ride?'

'I ride side-saddle. I'm not quite as brave as Constance.'

'Stable gate.' He made for the door. 'Wear your warmest clothes. It is chilly this time of year. Eight o'clock sharp.' At the door he turned round and looked her in the eyes. She felt a ripple of shock course through her. 'You will find a jug of water on your night table, Miss Benbow. Drink at least three of those each day. We are very high here, more than six thousand feet above sea level. The air is very thin, very pure. It is very good for the chest but has a tendency to attack the unwary with the most devilish headaches and I would not wish such suffering on you.'

The door had clicked behind him and she sat very still for a moment, staring at it and wondering that she'd been so deeply stirred by a man old enough to be her father. She drew her knees up under her chin and looked back at the snow-capped mountains and the columns of striped red rock which seemed to pulse their colour under the clear blue sky.

That early morning ride with Richard Redoute had been the first of many in the months Astrid had been at the castle. Every morning the General was not away on business she rode out with him. He led her onto mountain trails that were barely marked, and some that were not marked at all. He brewed her coffee as they rested on rocks above a rushing river or under trees. He showed her deer and elk among the shivering aspens. They watched sleek black squirrels jump from tree to tree. She once caught a distant glimpse of a bear and saw the dried-up pine-needles move as – so Richard Redoute told her – a mountain lion raced away from their intrusion. She heard the early morning birdsong and savoured the deep silence of the high mountain passes.

Sometimes they did not speak. At other times in response to her tentative questions he told her of his experiences as a very young commander in the Civil War, of his passion for surveying the empty land beyond the civilised cities of America. Of his ambition to forge pathways for all Americans to make their way West so they would claim their country by inhabiting it. He spoke of his principled battle against slavery, which, he said, was still not totally won. Astrid thought that in the mouths of many men these ideas would have seemed grandiose and boastful, but from him they seemed to be plain statements of simple truth.

He questioned her closely about London and Paris, cities he knew quite well. He mentioned names unfamiliar to her: city men, businessmen from another generation. He asked about her home in the north, about her parents and about her ambitions for herself. It was very easy to tell of her father, and her mother with her garden. Of her two brothers, one of them now a young recruit as Richard Redoute had been. 'He's in India at present, learning how to be a proper soldier.' She did not mention that Michael John's army career had had such a precipitate beginning.

Back in April, on one of their rides, she and the General had come upon a family group of Utes sitting by a smouldering fire and a kind of bower hut of sticks and mud. The people in their setting reminded her of one of her father's photographs of the Romanian gypsies. The General slipped down from his horse and talked to the father, a short man with gleaming skin and drooping black hair. The General gave him a packet of tobacco and the man took it, staring at him without smiling. Astrid held her breath. A child sitting by her mother at the fire let out a great wail. The General remounted and they went on their way.

Astrid finally said, 'I was worried back there, when that child cried out. The man looked so fierce.'

'He was fine, dear girl. He looked fierce because that is their customary gaze for strangers. He may have been a little worried. He should be on the reservation down in the south, but in the summer small parties make their way up here to do a little hunting, to remind themselves of the old days, to touch their land again. His ancestors roamed these high plains for hundreds of years.'

'Is he an Apache?' She brought up the only name she knew.

'He's a Ute. They were here for many hundreds of years before we arrived. But they had to be moved when the rush for silver and gold burst on the land. The miners and settlers were afraid of them. There was murder on both sides.'

'It seems such a pity. If it's really their place.'

His big shoulders had moved under his jacket in what she had learned was a characteristic shrug, 'It's progress, ma'am. In the modern world things may never stay the same. These original peoples were in the way of change so they've been swept aside. The way of progress.'

As she rode behind him she watched him sway in the saddle, at one with the horse. Her mind flashed back to Jack Lomas who rode in this same easy fluid way, without even the benefit of the worn military saddle that the General favoured. Astrid thought of the drawings she had made of Jack Lomas, just to exorcise images of him that had lodged themselves inconveniently in her brain. It hadn't really worked but the clarity of the images was fading now. The golden eyes were not so bright.

Then they had started to climb. The trees became more sparse. 'My father was interested in original peoples,' she called forward to Richard Redoute. 'First the race long dead in Mesopotamia. Then he studied the gypsies, the travelling people who go all over Europe. He knew all about them, wrote papers, made photographs. Honesty Leeming is one of their number.'

'Your young maid?' He waited for her to catch up to him on a dry precarious ledge. She pulled back the veil that she was wearing against the inevitable dust, so she could see him properly.

'We have such people as your father here,' he said, 'travelling about taking photographs of the old warriors and medicine men. I cannot see the purpose of such things. The past is gone. Future times should be our concern.'

Now on this June morning, the morning of the great party, the routine of their morning ride seems to be the same. He teases Astrid a little as he helps her to mount, telling her that it is his earnest wish to get her into a more comfortable saddle where she need not sit to one side. 'I've had one made especially for you in Mexico. There are very fine saddlers there.'

'Tomorrow.' She finds herself smiling at his almost youthful urging. 'I'll try it tomorrow.'

He beams. 'Good, good.' He pauses, stretches out and puts a hand on hers, as she holds her reins. 'My dear girl. If I were just twenty years younger, this would be a somewhat difficult situation. As it is we must satisfy ourselves with the simplest of passing pleasures.' He clicks his teeth and sets his horse to walk on ahead. It scrabbles a little on the loose rock, steadies itself and moves on. The loosened rock moves and scuffs its way down the slope.

Following Richard Redoute up through the pines in the clear mountain air Astrid wonders if she's ever been so happy as she is in these moments, in these times. Later as she sits by a smouldering fire of dry wood, and drinks the coffee he has made, she only half listens as he speaks of the plans for this special afternoon and evening. 'It'll be a great party this afternoon, Astrid. I've my army tents to save people from the sun. Entertainers. Music. Everyone will be here. All my people who work on the railroad and in the mines, at the waterworks and in the park. At the hospital and the college. Did you see the circus vans arriving? Wild animals. I'm told they have an Indian elephant. And there is a tightrope walker who will cross the creek a hundred feet in the air on a rope, strung between two rocks.' His voice cuts the high air, keen with excitement.

'Wonderful,' she murmurs, idly stirring the fire with a stick.

'And tonight there'll be the festive dinner for all the fine and fashionable people. You'll like it, my dear.' He refills her coffee from the battered tin pot.

She laughs. 'Dearest Richard, I'm neither fine nor fashionable.' It was on one of their early rides that he asked her to call him Richard and for her permission to call her Astrid. She knows that Constance, rather cross these days, is none too pleased that her father is paying such very close attentions to her friend. Astrid has missed the laughing, naughty companion of their early days and the sea voyage, hardly recognising the sulky hermit that Constance has become since she stepped off the train at the Springs that first day.

As for tonight, Astrid knows she will make a very plain moth among all those visiting butterflies. Ever generous, Richard has tried to persuade her to order a new frock for the occasion. There are one or two better costumiers in Denver. Or perhaps she should try the catalogues of one of the grand emporia in the East who could prove very accommodating with regard to shipping any goods at the gleam of a dollar? She has refused very firmly, saying she would wear what she had brought from England.

But for one second now she wishes she'd said yes, that she would appear tonight in a fine glittering dress and bright jewels;

that Richard Redoute would forget the years between them and treat her as more than just a second daughter, more even than a friend. Unbidden, an image of Jack Lomas comes into her head. He is with Richard, and they are walking towards her side by side down the sweeping stairs of the castle.

She shakes the fantasy from her mind. 'Perhaps we should turn for home, Richard? Constance has urged me to get back in good time. She's sorely put upon by the problem of which of three very fine dresses she should wear this afternoon, and which of three even finer dresses she should wear this evening.' She pulls her horse's head round to lead the way.

Behind her now, he calls, 'I imagine you see Constance as over-indulged and spoiled.'

'She's a dear,' Astrid calls back. 'And she is loving being here for you to indulge, so what harm is there in it?'

But he has hit a tender spot. Again she contemplates the feeling that Constance has changed in the months they've been here. She had more than one tantrum about the early rides but refused to get up and join them. Then she said Astrid should not go without her.

She would often butt into their conversations in a shrill voice, complaining that they were keeping secrets from her. Once, when she came upon her father talking closely with Astrid, instead of playing cards with her as planned, she'd quite flounced out of the drawing room. Astrid hardly recognised this termagant and mourned the Constance she knew.

Back at the castle, Astrid hands the reins of her horse to the Irish groom and as she walks across the fake drawbridge to the great doors she glances up to Constance's wide windows on the first floor to see the white face of her friend staring down at her. Astrid raises her hand in a wave. Constance gives a rather peculiar perfunctory wave in return. When Astrid reaches the door she closes her eyes and sees the gesture again and realises that, far from waving at her, Constance was shaking her fist.

Three

The Cost of Jealousy

'This is the dress, ain't it, Miss Constance? Did you ever see such a beautiful dress?' Aunt Beatrice moved the tissue, lifted the armful of smoky blue muslin out of its box and placed it as gently as a new baby on Constance's bed. 'See the collar here? Sneaky little wires to keep it high? And ain't those pearl hearts neatly stitched?'

Constance, sitting at her carved pear-wood dressing table, barely glanced at the dress. 'I don't know whether I'll be well enough for this affair this afternoon, Aunt Bea.' She leaned forward and stared at her immaculate reflection. 'I did not sleep one second in the night. Not one wink. My head aches and my eyes are like poached eggs.'

Aunt Beatrice knew very well that Constance had slept all through last night. Hadn't she herself slipped into the girl's bedroom in the middle of the night and watched her for a few minutes as she snored gently, her mouth slightly open? Beatrice beamed and picked up a crystal jug and poured fresh lemonade into a crystal glass. 'You're as beautiful as the sunrise, honey, and don't you know it? Here now, you drink this. You don't drink enough. Your momma never drank enough. The General says . . .'

Constance took the glass and sipped. She looked at Aunt Beatrice's face through the mirror. 'So what d'you think of my friend Astrid, Aunt Beatrice?'

162

The other woman's eyes narrowed. 'Why, she's your friend, honey. A ver' nice lady. Now, honey, you just drink that lemonade.'

'But what do you think of her?' Constance persisted.

'Well, Miss Astrid ain't no beauty. Even a friend would have to admit that. But she has a nice shine about her.'

Constance nodded. 'What else?'

'She's very polite, talks to you face to face, eye to eye. I have to say I like that in a person.'

'And . . .'

'Well, honey, I do like the way she draws those pretty pictures of hers. Ain't never seen anything like it. The prairie flowers and the trees by the creek and that picture of the General! Why, I declare he stares out at you like life . . . Drink, honey, drink!'

'So, what about this thing with Astrid and the General?' Constance frowned.

Beatrice leaned over, took the glass from her hand and laid it on the dressing table. 'Sit right back, honey, an' I'll rub your neck. Your momma used to love me to rub her neck. Said it took her headaches clean away.'

Constance allowed herself to be pulled back in her chair. She put her head against the high back cushion and closed her eyes. She relished the soft poke and prod of the other woman's hands into her shoulders and her neck. She shivered when it came to the soft firm strokes. A picture came to her mind of a time when she sat on the bed in this same room, watching her mother submit to these same ministrations. She blinked. 'So what do you think about the General and Astrid, how they . . . Well, these rides, and the way they talk?'

'Well, Miss Constance, ain't I been here in this very room and seen Miss Astrid beg you to come, to ride with them in the early morning? Ain't I heard her say what a great rider you were in England when you were there visiting? Ain't I heard the General beg the same thing at the breakfast table? Ain't I heard you say no to each one in turn, that they should go without you?'

'But that's the headaches, Aunt Bea. How can I go riding with the world splitting in two?'

'Are you saying, honey, that your friend Miss Astrid shouldn't go for her horse ridin'? That she should stay here and hold your hand?'

Constance now was lying further back in her padded chair, her head resting on the top cushion. Beatrice was passing two firm fingers from the centre of her forehead past her temples and down her cheeks, stopping at her chin. She did it again and again and again.

Constance struggled back from the edge of unconsciousness. 'But what about the General, Aunt Beatrice? How can she . . . how can he want to be so close? For they are close, don't deny me that.'

'Well, honey, the General is a human bein' and there ain't no denying that he likes talking with the girl. Ridin' with her. She puts a spring in his step, no question. An' she likes him, no denying that. Don't worry, honey. A little bit of loving friendship ain't gonna do nobody no harm. No how.'

Constance flung Beatrice's hands away from her and sat upright. She shook the fog of relaxation out of her head. Violently she thrust the half-drunk glass towards Beatrice, spilling the contents down the other woman's dress. 'You know nothing, Beatrice,' she said, omitting the courtesy title. 'You're just plain ignorant. How d'you know what *Miss* Astrid thinks, what the General thinks? Get out! Get out!'

Beatrice put the glass carefully on the onyx tray and wiped her sodden dress with hands that looked entirely black against its pale soft surface. At the door she turned back. 'Now you drink that lemonade, honey,' she said softly. 'We want you pretty for the party this afternoon.'

Constance watched the door click quietly behind her and stood up. She went to her bed, picked up the blue muslin dress and threw it onto the floor. She stamped on it, relishing the feeling of the pearls cracking and the corset wires bending beneath her feet. Then she sat cross-legged amongst its folds, closed her eyes and waited for the return of the headache.

It had been such a big adventure when she and Astrid, with Honesty in tow, arrived here in the winter. How relieved she'd been to see the General fit and well! What a pleasure it had been to show off her country and its people to her beloved friend Astrid. In the first few months there'd been a flurry of visits to old friends and social dinners at the castle. There'd been the dedication of the new wing at Redoute College. The great dinner in the grand hall for the survivors of her father's old regiment. She'd sat to the right of the beaming General and Astrid had sat to his left. She felt with him the waves of affection and respect rolling towards him from his soldiers, all old men now.

Their neighbours and friends had been delighted to see the General moving back into society again. Most of them were curious about the English girl; some were disappointed that she was so plain and unassuming, but they put this down to English eccentricity and consulted Constance as to whether it was smart in England to dress so plainly. Constance had assured her closest friends that this was really Miss Benbow's own style, that, though she was delightful, she was a bit of a bluestocking and eschewed the world of fashion. She assured them that she'd met many more fashionable people in London.

In the beginning it had been fun to bask in the interest of the cream of Springs society. It had been an amusing pastime to enjoy the attention of all the eligible bachelors in the district, even despite her natural scepticism when the attention was mediated in a honeyed way through the young men's parents, aware of the high financial and social rewards of an alliance with General Redoute's daughter.

At first she and Astrid had giggled together and made up a running list of the particularities of gaucherie and outright

ugliness of the eager young men who called. How tiresomely
unsophisticated these Westerners were; how large-boned and
strange of speech! How much smarter and more subtle were
the English men they knew, the suave Easterners from Boston
and Virginia.

But then things changed. Astrid started to talk seriously to
the young men and to listen to stories of their adventurous
fathers and their courageous mothers. She had contradicted
Constance's judgements, saying they were verging on the
unkind and the unnecessary. She started to quote the General,
who respected many of these families and was quite fond of
some of the young men.

It now seemed to Constance that not only had the General
replaced her in Astrid's affections, but Astrid had replaced her
in her father's affections. She was left alone outside their bubble
of mutual esteem and it made her bereft and angry. The helpless
fury began to distil in her head and that was when her sick
headaches set in in earnest. She sought out Astrid less and
when they were together was often sulky and rude. She watched
even more gloomily as Astrid and the General set out for their
rides or sat with their heads together in the long sitting room,
looking over one of the General's early survey maps.

Now there was a knock on the door. Constance sat up straight
as with a rush of fresh air Astrid swept into the room, her
cheeks pink and her hair falling from its pins. To her astonishment Constance found herself thinking how pretty she was.

Astrid looked in astonishment at Constance on the floor
amid the wreck of the dress. 'What have you done, dear
Constance? Oh, your pretty dress! Did you fall?' Her hands
were out and she was pulling Constance to her feet. 'What
happened?' She decided not to challenge Constance about the
shaken fist.

Constance scrambled to her feet and watched as Astrid
picked up the dress, shook it out and laid it – a battered, sorry
sight – across the bed.

'I think I must have fainted,' said Constance with a sigh. 'My headache was so bad today.'

'Poor, poor you.' Astrid led her to a high-backed chair by the window and tenderly settled her in it. 'Can I get you a drink? How badly you suffer with these infernal sick heads.'

Constance watched her carefully, coolly. 'It's something about the altitude, the dryness. It drove my mother away from this place and now I fear it will drive me away. We must leave soon, Astrid. We must travel back East or even back to England, and you . . .'

Astrid's cheeks were bright red. 'Of course, dear. In any case it's time we went back, Honesty and I. How very quickly the time has flown.'

'Do you think so?' Constance laid dull eyes on her. 'To me it has dragged infernally.'

Astrid waited a second. 'But you've been so poorly, dear. As you say, this climate . . .'

'Suits me no more than it did my momma. I have to get away from here. Though perhaps not as far as Torquay, England.' She smiled slightly, then winced as another pain hit her just above the eye.

'I have an idea,' said Astrid. 'Why don't we go for a swim in your beautiful pool? That might drive away that naughty headache and your bad feelings. And I rather want to ask you to help me with a matter that has been concerning me. Please, Constance. You can't just sit here and suffer. I won't let you. A swim will be wonderfully cooling.'

The pool house was a long room built of carved elm whose ceiling consisted almost completely of stained glass that, on bright days such as this, created spots of surging colour in the moving water. At one end there were three changing parlours with bathrooms: at the other was a shuttered balcony with wooden lounging benches. Aunt Beatrice, so instructed by a curt Constance, followed them into the pool room with a pile of fresh white towels and two bathing costumes and hats.

Constance lifted the first hat, a striped affair tied with ribbons. 'This is all I need.'

'Miss Constance.' There was rare reproof in Beatrice's voice.

Constance laughed. 'Why, Aunt Bea!' she said. 'I do believe you think me very naughty.' With that she slipped out of her morning gown and every one of her undergarments and took up the hat. 'You were right, dearest Astrid. I feel better already.' As she lifted her arms to tie her hat over her hair there was a pull on her generous breasts that extended the dark aureoles. Astrid blinked at the sight of the shadow under Constance's arms that matched the faint smudge of hair down below.

'Come on, you old sobersides, have a swim,' said Constance. 'I dare you!' She jumped into the water, sank like a stone then rose to the surface, spitting water out of her mouth. 'I dare you,' she spluttered.

Astrid had to smile, relieved at this brief glimpse of the old Constance.

Beatrice, already collecting together Constance's discarded clothes, smiled understandingly at Astrid. 'Miss Constance and her sister Delphine, they swim in the natural way all the time. I keep guard by the door, so don't you worry, Miss Astrid.'

So Astrid found herself divesting herself of her boots and stockings, her riding coat and skirt and all the underpinnings, in a way which rather lacked Constance's panache. Once naked, Astrid was aware of her own small breasts and thin legs, of how her body hair was ridiculously curly, but so light as to be almost invisible.

Aunt Beatrice watched her with open interest. 'Don't you worry now, Miss Astrid. I'll keep guard.' She marched away on heavy feet to drape the clothes over a chair in one of the sitting rooms. She came back carrying a small stool. 'You still here?' She grinned broadly.

Astrid moved away from her and walked down the stone steps into the edge of the pool. The water was tepid and strangely comforting. It smelled faintly of eucalyptus. The waves being created by Constance's gentle backstroke were tipped with purple, green and red, filtered by the church-like coloured glass of the ceiling.

Astrid walked in even deeper and launched quietly into the water. She embarked on a sedate breaststroke, trying to keep her head above water. She swam one length, turned and made her way back. For a time she was aware of Constance somewhere ahead and then she seemed to vanish. She caught a damp glimpse of Beatrice sitting reading by the door, wire-framed spectacles halfway down her nose.

At that end of the pool she clung to the side and looked back down but could not see Constance anywhere. She was just about to swim again when her ankles were gripped and she was hauled underwater, fighting for breath. She reached up to claw her way to the surface, only to be pulled down again. This time she kicked out hard with both feet and Constance swam up into view, spluttering and laughing. 'What fun, Astrid! Don't you think this is great fun?' She was treading water. Her full breasts floated almost weightless to the surface, caught by an edge of purple light from above.

Then she leaned across, pulled Astrid to her and kissed her roundly on the lips. She tasted of eucalyptus. 'There! I have surprised you. Miss calm and cool. I never thought I would surprise you.'

Astrid drew away. 'You're incorrigible, Constance.'

Constance's smile faded. 'I would be careful, Astrid. I know you love my father. I can see it. I have seen it. It's ridiculous.'

'That is not true. I . . .'

'I've seen it,' she said flatly. 'You have tried to take my father away from me. It will not do. So now you must go home, Astrid. You must, must go home.' She swam along to the stone steps and walked up them, the water dripping from her. She

169

turned. 'But I will come with you and everything will be as it was before.'

Beatrice was waiting there at the top of the steps, ready to enfold her charge in a huge white towel. They walked towards the dressing parlours where, Astrid knew, Beatrice would dry Constance and dress her like the child she had once been.

Astrid could not face following Constance tamely out of the pool so she began to swim lengths, surging through the colour-soaked water, creating rainbows with the movement of her body. She was still swimming when Constance, fully clothed now, her head wrapped in a towel, walked along the side and through the wooden doors, followed by a stately Beatrice. Constance neither looked at nor acknowledged the presence of Astrid, who felt her rejection like a blow.

Four

Fair Ground

10.30am

Richard Redoute looked out with pride over the stretch of
scrubland which he'd tamed to a meadow by having his outside
men water it assiduously, root out the Indian paintbrush and wild
yucca and encourage the wild lupins and harebells to grow on in
natural elegance. The acre of land now lay before him like an
embroidered green handkerchief against the grey parched
summer grass and the red rocks which surged upwards at its rim.

The field hummed with suppressed activity like an army
encamped before a battle. The pitched tents had their flaps up to
show the linen-draped trestles now beginning to groan with the
weight of ghostly gauze-draped victuals and fancy eats, all
dreamed up by Philippe le Blanc, the chef brought down
especially from Denver. Bandsmen in flapping shirtsleeves were
fixing their music stands on the dancing platform. Down towards
the creek the painted wagons of the travelling zoo were drawn
round into a defensive circle in true wagon-train tradition. By
the arched gateway stood two low-topped gypsy rigs whose
owners he'd invited to the festivities as a treat for young Honesty
and to honour Astrid Benbow's father's interest in their kind.

Old soldiers in faded uniforms loitered at the entrances of
their tents, wary that a summer storm might whip them up and
batter them down. The General had resisted the temptation to
don his own immaculate uniform, which now hung in the Dutch

elm wardrobe in his bedroom. It would have been less than
tactful to wear that. Several eminent guests had confederacy
blood flowing deep in their veins. The echo of more recent
local histories would hit the wrong note on this day when he
had elected to celebrate his country's liberation from the British.

He smiled slightly. There was irony in that. A good quarter
of his guests this afternoon, and perhaps half his guests tonight,
were either wholly British, recently British, or the children of
Britishers. Had he not raised much of the capital for his railroad
enterprises in Britain, where they had a taste for fruitful
investment and were intrigued by the Western adventure? The
British involvement in the town – especially when they discovered that there were healthful waters at nearby Manitou
Springs – was so complete that locals called it, not without
irony, 'Little London'. The Britishers relished the luxuries of
his Antlers Hotel and never failed to comment on the civilisation
that the General had brought to these wild parts.

It was at the Antlers Hotel that he'd met Lady Parlellum, into
whose tender care he'd placed his daughter for the London
season. Her ladyship was chaperoning two nieces, just out of
New York for a Western adventure. Despite the niceties of the
encounter, and her ladyship's innate grandeur, the General's nose
for business had told him that the Lady was definitely for hire.

And today the guest of honour was to be his daughter,
gratifyingly Britified after her years in England. And alongside
her was her guest, Miss Astrid Benbow, that most English of
creatures: restrained and clever, unworldly in some ways and
mistrustful of show. She was brave and resourceful, enquiring
and humorous.

Richard Redoute sighed. He realised with reluctance that
the days of his surprising friendship with this young woman
were numbered. His daughter Constance, who'd bounced into
town in her velvets and furs like a princess, had as the months
unfolded turned into a tart gremlin, peering out at the world
through belligerent, self-pitying eyes. She slept too long; she

took too little exercise; she shut herself away in darkened rooms. Aunt Beatrice was the only one of all of them she would allow near her.

He had tried to laugh her out of her moods; he had bought her presents; he had set up treats and surprises that fell very flat; he had tried to talk straight with her. All to no avail.

All this was not unfamiliar to Richard Redoute. He'd seen it all before. Had he not endured it with his most dear wife Aurelia? He'd brought her here, built her a palace and set her up as queen of all she surveyed. In those early days Aurelia was a beautiful, elegant, loving woman. But then she too had faded and shrunk, to the point where his – and the children's – only contact with her was notes from her darkened room written in a shaky hand. The notes affirmed her love for them and told them how she bore all this pain for their sake.

He blinked, squeezing away an uncharacteristic tear. How could a country that opened up hearts and minds, that indulged visions and fulfilled dreams, so kill the spirit of such fine, beautiful women? This vile thing. This 'mountain sickness'.

The Utes saw magic in the great peak that dominated the town. He was struck by the fanciful thought that perhaps the Utes' mountain took vengeance on those it wished to reject. While it was a life-giving magnet for him it had wrecked Aurelia. And now it was threatening Constance.

He knew now that Constance, like her mother, would have to leave in order to survive. He'd have to accept that with dignity. He had to admit now that the worst of it was that Constance would sweep away with her his new friend, the girl Astrid Benbow, whom the mountains had enfolded and welcomed. They had not rejected her. They had shown her their magic and made her beautiful in their embrace.

How small was his life, with all its achievements, its public significance, now that this fine late-flowering thing that was just beginning to happen was slipping from his grasp.

Swiftly he turned away from the scene of party preparation, untethered his horse and rode at a canter towards the house. He looked up at Astrid's window, but there was no face, no friendly wave. Constance's window too was blank, like a closed eye. He dismounted at the steps and thrust the reins into the waiting hands of Josey, another of Beatrice's cousins.

In the vestibule he passed the girl Honesty, who had put on weight since she came and was trussed up in an unlikely red dress. He asked how she was and what she wanted. She thanked him and said she was very fine. She also enquired politely about the whereabouts of Slim, his driver.

'He's waiting down at the Antlers Hotel to bring up some guests in the brake.' He stared at her, suddenly sympathetic. 'But after that Slim is his own man, Miss Honesty, and will be free to dance the afternoon away with his sweetheart, whoever she may be.'

She blushed and bobbed a ghost of a curtsy. 'Thank you, sir.'

Inside the house, servants were moving quietly through the rooms, preparing for the evening's indoor festivities. There was no sign of Astrid. He leapt up the stairs and knocked on her bedroom door, but there was no answer. Coming back down he met the accusing gaze of his daughter, trudging up the steps, accompanied by Beatrice.

'Morning, my dear. You're looking very bright,' he said hopefully. In fact she did look well. Her face was shining clean, and her hair, slightly wet, gleamed in the light.

She stared at him coldly for a second. 'And you, Poppa. I declare you look like some young beau comin' courtin'!'

He could feel himself going bright red. He said nothing.

'I declare you got it right, General. Don't our Miss Constance look like a morning rose?' Beatrice cut into the silence. 'Ain't we had the nicest swim with Miss Astrid to cool us down before we put on our pretty dress for the party?' She put herself between Constance and her father and hustled her charge up the stairs.

As he walked the long corridor which led to the swimming pavilion he reflected, not for the first time, on the intelligence of Beatrice Lawler. She'd been his comrade and co-conspirator since she'd first known him, first in his courtship, then in later life with Aurelia. Always a battler against slavery, Richard had calculated Beatrice's wages since she'd been acquired from the Lawlers at the age of seven to be a playmate for young Aurelia. He'd had the amount made up in silver dollars and had given it to Aurelia on their wedding day to pass on to Beatrice. A day later Beatrice handed the chinking bag back into his hands and told him he must take care of it until she was ready. She told him politely that he must also do this with the further wages he was offering.

All this money, properly accounted, he'd invested in his own stock. So, like many others now in this topsy-turvy town, Beatrice Lawler was a rich woman. Each year on the first day of January she came to his study so that he could update her on her investments and ask her if she wanted her money for herself. Each year she said no, she was not ready.

There'd been a serious crisis when Aurelia had finally decamped to England for her health. Aurelia had a tantrum when she realised that Beatrice would not go with her. Beatrice had looked at her beloved with troubled eyes and shaken her head. 'This is my country, Miss Aurelia, and nobody no how's gonna get me to leave. Not even you.'

The goodbyes between those two women had been difficult to watch. Beatrice had stayed on at the castle, thinking that her Aurelia would return. But when Constance turned up without her mother, even when Richard was alleged to be on his deathbed, it had been apparent to both of them that Aurelia would never come back. Now he reflected that Beatrice, like himself, would soon have to face another goodbye to this other beloved, destroyed by the jealous vengeance of the mountain.

When he got to the swimming pavilion Richard could hear the regular splash of water through the half-open door. Silent as a cat, he moved just inside so he could watch Astrid threshing the water with long white arms, the ribbons of her cap floating behind her. Red and blue light streamed through the overhead windows and stroked her white flesh as it moved through the water. The light spread along the edges of the ripples as they surged to the sides of the pool in her wake.

He stood very still and watched. After five more lengths she climbed out of the water at the far end of the pool and made for the little changing parlour. Richard drew back from the doorway into the wide vestibule of the pavilion. He leaned his forehead against the cool green tiles and wondered what on earth he was doing.

Astrid towelled her hair thoroughly with one of the immaculate white towels, brushed it and twisted it into a bun on the top of her head. Then she sat and loosened the side and top hair to make it fuller and less sleekly wet. She turned the wings of the triple mirror so that she could view it from every angle. Fine. When it was topped with her neat flower-laden straw hat this afternoon no one would realise that she'd given her hair a thorough wetting in the General's famous swimming pool.

She had pulled on her drawers and her shift and was just hooking her corset when there was a knock on the door. She glanced at her reflection in the mirror and said quietly, 'Who is it?'

'It's Richard. Can I speak with you?'

'Wait a moment.' She took some minutes pulling on her green lawn dress and fastening its bound buttons, adjusting her sash and making sure her short train fell straight. It was only when she opened the door that she remembered her feet were bare, her slippers and stockings still on the stool behind the screen. 'Richard?' She looked up into his face. 'Is something wrong?'

He walked stiffly into the room. 'Perhaps I might sit down, Astrid?' he said heavily. He waited for her to seat herself on the dressing stool, and then he sat on the small couch by the window.

'What is it . . . Richard?' she said, quite sharply now.

He was gazing at her bare feet, where they peeped from the hem of her gown. She caught the gaze and pulled her feet out of sight.

'Did you enjoy your swim?' he said.

She blinked. Then she went red. 'You saw. I can't think, sir, what . . .'

He did not deny it. 'I came in search of you,' he said simply. 'I saw Constance and Aunt Beatrice and I thought you too would be ready . . . Well, you were still swimming. So I waited.'

She lifted her clear eyes to his. 'Well, Richard?'

'Constance will have to go back East,' he said abruptly. 'Perhaps back to England, to her mother. This sickness will destroy her, else.'

She nodded. 'She and I have talked of this just today. She's not the girl I knew in England. She was so lovely there. Full of life. So funny. So special.'

'Then you will know that she must return, Astrid.'

She kept her eyes on him. 'It will be a sad thing to leave.'

He coughed. 'It wouldn't be necessary for you, Astrid. You could stay here.'

'Richard, you know that's not possible.'

'Not here at the castle, of course. But I would find you a house. I have two on Cascade, a very fine avenue. They are very sound brownstone with cedar trees in the gardens. Then you and I could still ride and talk, and you could do your drawing and painting.' His old friends and colleagues from this town that he had built out of the dust would not have recognised the uncertain, pleading tone in his voice.

She came to stand before him, quite small in her bare feet. He made to get up, but she put a hand on each shoulder and pressed, making him stay seated. 'Why?' she said.

He stared up at her. 'I regret too much the loss of a rare friend,' he said.

'Is that all?'

He coughed. 'Well, cards on the table, Astrid.' He took a very deep breath. 'Ridiculous as it seems, and ancient and married as I am, I fear that I may love you.'

His cheeks were stained red. She kissed one and then the other. He stood up and pulled her to him, his lips hard on hers. After some minutes they subsided back to the couch and the buttons so recently buttoned were undone, and the corset so recently tightened was unhooked. Then for a while Richard Redoute was the young man he had once been, and Astrid Benbow was the woman she'd always wished to become. Once, when he cried out his delight, an image of Jack Lomas glowed before her.

Later, tousled and relaxed, they sat side by side, very close. He smoothed a curl back into her still damp hair, his smile tender and open. 'I'd thought that . . . you . . .'

She shook her head. 'There have been two people in my life who, for a time, meant everything to me.' She smiled. 'But that doesn't make me what they call, in these parts, *a sporting woman*.'

He laughed out loud at this. 'I don't reckon it does.' He took her hand. 'Dear Astrid. The honour overwhelms me. This old man . . .'

She squeezed his hand. 'Never.'

He put a hand to her face. 'Astrid. I know that Constance is aching to be away from here. Like her mother she is choked just about to death by the place I love more than anywhere in the world. But perhaps you would consider staying on close by here, in the Springs? We could ride and talk. Even after . . . this . . . I promise, hand on heart' – he put his hand over his dishevelled shirt – 'I promise you I'll make no demands on you.'

She took his freckled hand, turned it over and kissed his palm. 'And what if I make demands on you?' she said.

178

He groaned and pulled her to him. 'Does that mean you will? You'll stay on?'

She thought of Constance, not just the petulant Constance of recent days, but the woman who was her friend in England, her companion on the voyage. She pulled away, her face more serious now. 'Can we leave it for the moment, Richard? Talk about it tomorrow or the next day?'

His face went blank and his hold on her loosened. The silence that followed was broken suddenly by the crackle of gunshot outside. She jumped. 'What's that?'

He laughed. 'Just the good old boys shootin' at clouds, celebratin' our deliverance from bondage to you British. We do it every July fourth. But this year, knowing you would be gone soon, I changed the date of that celebration.' He disentangled himself from her and stood up. 'Well, Miss Benbow, I'd better attend to my chores on this most special of days.' He rebuckled the leather belt on his immaculately cut trousers, buttoned his shirt and retied his necktie. He put a hand on her head like a benediction. 'We will have that talk tomorrow, Miss Astrid Benbow. I swear it.'

The door clicked behind him and Astrid sat there for a few moments staring at it. In the last hour the world had moved a little on its axis. Life for her would never be the same again. What he spoke of was impossible. Unthinkable. And yet it was as logical as the sun rising in the morning. Perhaps it was her fate to stay here, living each day for itself. Then she could know Richard Redoute for whatever time there was for them. For sure there would be opprobrium, if they made this very much desired decision. Not from her mother whose detachment would allow her to take it in her stride. But there would be others. Again from nowhere came the thought of Jack Lomas. She supposed he would be angry at her keeping Honesty here. But they would make their decision. Tomorrow or the next day. They would make it, for good or ill.

Despite the stuffy heat of the changing parlour Astrid shivered and made her way again to the water.

Five

Dancing Lesson

2pm

By two o'clock the fairground was full of people dressed in their best 'bib and tucker', each outfit showing for all to see from which crack of the land its wearer had emerged. There were women from the city, some of them pure Gibson girl with their single pouter pigeon breasts, their tiny waists and their sweeping hats; some women were heavier, more stiff, hard-corseted despite the heat, their hats redressed by Mademoiselle la Neige, a skilled milliner in the Springs whom everyone went to these days. Others eschewed the corset and wore simpler home-made blouses with skirts in print or calico and wired cotton bonnets or cheeky straw hats, their shoulders covered by pretty shawls, some of these were knitted wool and some elaborately woven in the Indian style.

The men's clothes mirrored those of their women, ranging from subtle London tailoring (not always of the most recent cut) right down to decent canvas or corduroy and thick store-bought shirts with optimistic neckties. Hundreds of buggies, rigs and single horses were hitched in a line that rippled for half a mile from the wide castle gates.

Honesty strolled along, trim in her red dress that today was nearly too small for her. She wandered past the bandstand where the musicians, fully dressed now, fixed keen eyes on their conductor, elbows poised. The first limber of chords crashed behind her but she walked on, half of her relishing the buzz of all the people, the other half looking for Slim. She resisted the caller posted in front of the circus tent who tried to entice her to come in. 'You'll be much surprised, miss. You'll be mighty astonished. See the great monstrous elephant all the way from *the Indees*.' The caller had a tooth missing from the front of his mouth and a neck like one of Keziah's turkeys.

She made her way towards the decorated gateway. Slim would surely bring the brake there to unload his grand visitors from the Antlers.

She was just thinking that the whole set-up reminded her of nothing so much as a parched-dry version of Appleby Fair when she came upon the gypsy rigs just to the left of the gate. There were two of them, crudely painted. The space between them seemed filled with lounging men – perhaps seven in all – and a gaggle of children playing with two mismatched dogs. A woman, her head bound with a coin-dangling kerchief, sat on the back step of one of the rigs. Beside her sat a young girl, perhaps no older than Honesty herself, who was fashioning some children's gew-gaws with feathers and what looked like clay.

An older woman sat away from them on a stool by the buckboard of the other wagon. She sat very still with her hands in her lap, watching the passers-by with placid eyes. In front of her was a very inviting, empty stool. Its polished back, intricately carved in black oak, caught the bright sunlight on its hard edges.

Honesty sat down on the stool, pulling in the wide skirts of her red dress so that they did not spill onto the woman's embroidered dress. The woman leaned across and put a finger on the back of Honesty's hand. 'You are *Rom*?' she said, in their own language.

Honesty shook her head but answered in kind. 'My mother only was of these people. Her name of Keziah Leeming, but her first name was Lomas.'

181

'And thy father? What was he?'

Honesty smiled into the other woman's eyes. 'My father was a *gorgio*, and a scallywag. So says my mother.'

A faint smile visited the old woman's still face. 'You have gold, Honesty Lomas?'

Honesty shook her head. She fiddled with her little velvet *pochette*. 'I have silver.' She palmed a silver dollar.

The other woman took it, held it up so it glittered in the bright sun. 'Dost thou freely offer me this silver dollar, Honesty Lomas?'

'Aye.'

The old woman tucked the coin into a battered leather purse attached to her whipcord belt. Then she took both of Honesty's hands in hers and turned them over and back several times. She put them down and took Honesty's face between both hands. The girl could smell hickory smoke and tobacco and the musty smell of cloves. She sat there quietly, comfortable in the woman's clasp.

'Thy mother is a long way away.'

Awkwardly, Honesty nodded.

'I would be thy mother if thou would have the need.'

Honesty nodded again. The old woman's words reflected a common *romani* courtesy.

'A great thing is to happen to thee. A dark thing it is. But a light thing too. What is that thing?'

Honesty smiled within the urgent press of the woman's fingers. 'No great thing,' she said. 'Unless you count my friend Slim hitting gold at his digging. And that ain't likely,' she added in English.

That ain't likely. Aunt Beatrice's phrase. Honesty had always thought it a very neat expression.

The woman let go of Honesty's face and her own hands dropped in her lap. 'I do not see gold,' she said. 'Thou has something in thee, child. I see people clapping and laughing.'

Honesty grinned. 'I can fly through the air,' she said. 'Twist my body all ways. It has earned me applause.' Her grin faded. 'I have done it before the greatest in the land. England, that is.'

The woman frowned. 'A dark thing happened to thee, child.'

Honesty stared at her.

'But this dark thing will not stay with thee. It will fade from you like the impression of a thumb dipped in a flowing stream.'

Honesty nodded slowly, not understanding at all. She looked away to lift from herself the pressure of the woman's intense gaze. In the distance she could see Slim's tall figure, his shady hat on his head, his ruddy, weather-beaten face. She stood up. The gypsy put a warm dry hand on her arm. 'Come and see me again, child. Come travel with us. My granddaughter needs a sister and there are too few women in our family. Come away with us.'

'Thank you, Auntie.' Honesty pulled away slightly. 'But I have a home here. Friends too.' She started to walk away. 'But thank you,' she said over her shoulder. 'I thank you very much.'

'Child!' the woman called after her. 'Don't forget.'

Slim waited, watching her as she bustled towards him. 'Well, if it ain't Miss Honesty,' he drawled. 'Purrty as a picture.' He pulled her hand through the crook of his arm. 'The gypsy woman was telling your fortune. Don't tell me you crossed her palm with silver?'

She pouted. 'I did cross her palm, if you want to know it. But we were talking, that's all. We were talking in the old language. She reminded me of my mother.'

He strode on, almost pulling her along beside him, her red skirts billowing and slapping against his corduroy-clad legs. 'This old Ute medicine man, he once looked to my future, using stones from this old fire that he'd stamped and sung around?' His voice went up in that characteristic way, making a question where there was none. 'D'you know what he said?'

'No,' she gasped, out of breath now.

'We'el, that old Ute told me that he saw me standin' astride a great mountain with a golden buckle in my belt. I tell you? Don't that keep me goin' in the long nights at the diggings?'

'Stop, will you?' Honesty planted her feet on the ground and hung on to his arm, making him swing round to face her. 'Slow down and stop jawing, will you? What about this dancing? Didn't you say you'd teach me how to dance?'

'Sure did, ma'am. And my guess is you'll take to it right away.'

When they finally walked up the steps to the dance floor the band was sawing away at a merry polka and the platform was full. They stood at the edge waiting for a suitable space to open up.

Honesty turned round and hung over the rail and looked out at the crowd. In the distance she could make out Aunt Beatrice and Cousin Vera, in matching pink lawn dresses whose lace collars glowed against the dark skin of their necks. They were bareheaded and walked with remarkable ease among the white revellers. Honesty knew there were other black people in the Springs but it was rare that one came face to face with them on social occasions. Honesty had heard mutterings, one or two from Slim himself, about the leeway the General allowed his Negro servants. 'Don' get me wrong?' Slim had said. 'Miss Beatrice has a style about her, and a kindness? And Miss Vera is as quiet as a mouse. But really an' truly is it right? Gives 'em all the wrong ideas? It'll be the redskins next.' This last was said with confident disbelief. 'The General's rare to make a mistake but he sure has made one on this one.'

Honesty could see the General now, as he stopped to talk, even laugh, with Miss Beatrice and Miss Vera. He'd changed from his dark grey suit into one in brown worsted, that made him look younger entirely. Why, if you didn't know he was nearly as old as the great mountain that loomed over them all, you'd have sworn he was a much younger man.

Honesty pressed a hand to her back to relieve a twinge of pain brought on by standing too long. 'Can we sit down while we wait?' she asked Slim.

He led her to a row of white-painted chairs set alongside the dancing platform. He watched her sit and arrange her dress then said, 'I'll find you a lemonade, Miss Honesty? I know for sure there is lemonade,' and stalked off like a long-legged bird.

Honesty sat back to watch the parade of passing people. She wriggled her swelling feet in their black kid slippers. Miss Constance, the fluttering cynosure of three eager young escorts, passed by. She was wearing pale green georgette in the latest style and a shady hat in the finest silvery green straw against the invading sun. She didn't notice Honesty. Her face beneath its shady hat was very white. Her jaw was set.

Honesty flexed her back a little to ease the ache. That Miss Constance had grown a bit peculiar lately. A proper cross-patch, she was, whining and whingeing at everyone. Even at Miss Benbow, who was nothing but sweet reason. Miss Constance even – and this was worse – shouted at Miss Beatrice, who was a saint. She was a different Miss Constance from the one who had shared the stateroom on the voyage with Miss Benbow. That one had chattered and sung and had a laugh like gurgling water.

Miss Benbow, trailing six yards behind Miss Constance, caught Honesty's glance and came across to sit beside her. 'So, Honesty. How are you liking all this? Is it as good as Appleby Fair?' She beamed.

No one in their right mind would call Miss Benbow pretty. But there was something about her today that really glowed. A funny thing, her hair beneath her golden straw hat looked dark, even wet. Honesty stretched out her legs in front of her. 'Rum do, this, Miss Benbow.'

'Rum do? That's a funny thing to say. Rum do?'

'Freddy Leeming used to say that when things were out of kilter, didn't quite fit.'

'So why is all this a "rum do"?'

'Well, Miss Benbow, look around you. You and me sitting here side by side. Maids dancing with masters on the dance floor. Miss Beatrice making royal progress through the crowds like she's the Old Queen. Everything topsy-turvy. Sommat to do with the old General, I think.'

Astrid found herself prickling slightly at the word *old*. 'And don't you like this topsy-turvy world, Honesty?'

Honesty frowned. 'Well, truth to tell, that's the worst of it. I guess I do. I like all the things about this place. The sun. The mountains. Miss Beatrice. The General. And Slim. I like him.'

'So why the long face?'

She sighed. 'Sure as night follows day, Miss Benbow, I know we'll have to go back. An' afore long it'll be me bunked in some garret alongside a sniffy parlourmaid in some prison place like Seland Hall.'

Astrid took Honesty's hand and turned her so that they were facing. 'What if we didn't go, Honesty? What if I wrote a letter to my mother and one to Keziah to tell them that we'll stay awhile?'

Honesty's face glowed. 'Well, Miss Benbow, I'd say it was a good thing. A very good thing.'

'Afternoon, Miss Benbow?' Slim was suddenly towering over them with a glass of lemonade in both hands. 'Would y'all excuse Miss Honesty an' me? I spy a space on that there dance floor and I promised her good and faithful that I'd teach her how to dance.' He handed Astrid both of the glasses and hauled Honesty to her feet. 'Shall we dance, Miss Honesty?'

Six

The Little Black Book

3.15pm

Despite the arid brilliance of the afternoon the lofty reception
rooms were shuttered and dark as Richard Redoute made his
way back through his castle. Above him the fans, figured brass
and oiled wood from Philadelphia, stirred the parched air into
some semblance of coolness and life. He opened the door of
the dining salon. Light let in through a crack in the shutters
spilled onto the damasked table, the cooling marble fountain
and the newly acquired Italian tapestries lining its walls.

He walked round the table scanning the neatly calligraphed
place-cards. He wondered how he would survive the evening,
pulled to his left by the petulance of his daughter Constance, to
his right by the compelling charms of Astrid Benbow.

On a whim he took Constance's card in his hand, moved to
the opposite end of the table and placed it so she would be facing
him through the tangle of flowers and glittering crystal. Trans-
posing other cards, he shifted Burleigh Railton, the son of one of
his fellow directors in the railroad company, to her left hand. To
her right he placed the card of a visiting nephew of Elmer Rivas,
who was making such strides in the town. Rivas was a very
competent man sometimes let down by his desire to be sociable.
Still, he was making great strides now with his Grand Hotel.
This palatial building was the epitome of luxury and indulgence;
the very essence of the softer side of the Springs that was to do

with the consumption of luxury rather than the production of the wherewithal to acquire the requisite wealth.

In changing some cards he had disturbed the arrangement of the whole table. He had to move another card, then another. So senators were put beside soldiers' wives, new-rich were placed cheek by jowl with old-rich. In the end he had rearranged them all. Like the general he was, he had changed the battle plan.

His mind flicked momentarily to those early days when he and Aurelia did this task together. What fun they used to have, discussing their guests and where the best deals could be made, the best firecrackers set off. How Aurelia, with her Eastern sensibilities, had loved the game!

In later years, of course, it was impossible for her to attend such events, those necessary festive occasions when they entertained the leading citizens from the Springs, from Denver, from the whole state. Sometimes they had guests from Washington, from Boston, from New York. But by then the mere sound of voices and laughter gave her great pain. She lived her life in a whirlpool of whispers.

Then she went off to find healthier places. She wished him to go with her but he could not leave for good this place he had created. So, he was on his own. Of course there was no need, in the ambiguous world of the elegant, proper Springs and the raffish Cripple Creek, for a man such as General Redoute to lack gentle company. He could have been like Mr Stratton and made use of the entertaining company of sporting women; he could have enjoyed the more mannerly flirtations that occurred in his own Antlers Hotel. But all he had ever wished for was the return of his Aurelia. Until now.

He sighed and pushed the electrical bell beside the great marble fireplace that had been built round a very effective painting of a roaring fire. In a minute John McLachlan, his inside man, charged through the door, his face well scrubbed and his dark livery neatly pressed. He swerved to a stop. 'Yes, General?'

'I've changed the placements, John. I have put Miss Constance at the end, where Mrs Redoute used to sit. And Miss Benbow is here. Now they all need neatenin' off again. Will you have this done? And will you enter the changes in the Dining Book? Can't have the battle record wrong, now can we?'

John, who'd been a boy bugler in the General's company, shook his head, clicked his heels and said, 'No, *sir*!' and made a very passable salute. Then he went to find the book in which they had kept a record of every social occasion since the building of the castle; the purpose of the gathering, the length of its duration, the list of guests, the victuals and drinks consumed — even alcohol, which was only available for private consumption in the puritanical Springs, unlike Cripple Creek and the mining villages where bars and low hotels maintained a ready flow.

The General slipped out of the dining salon onto the long shaded balcony that ran alongside it and the small parlours including, at the end, the sitting room that Aurelia, with her Southern fancy, had called *the boudoir*. He leaned on the carved rail. In the distance he could see the multicoloured swell of the crowds and the bright pennants flying from the cluster of tents.

Drawn by the faintest thread of the scent of cologne he made his way along to the end, to the darkest, shadiest part of the balcony. It was not Aurelia but his daughter Constance who was sitting in the long chair, her dress arranged around her like smoke. Aunt Beatrice was hovering in attendance behind her, placing a cologne-soaked cold compress on her forehead.

He shot a glance at Aunt Beatrice, who picked up her towels and her bowl and glided through the long glass doors into the boudoir.

Constance's nostrils flared at the scent of his cigar but she did not open her eyes. 'Poppa?' she said.

'Honey!' He eased his jacket and sat back in the long chair opposite her. 'Have you been down to the fairground?' he said. He knew the answer. He'd seen her walking in the covey of young men.

189

'Yes, of course. Didn't I walk and nod to this tiresome person, chat with that one? Weren't there smiles in all directions?'

'Well done, honey. Your mother had just that touch with the ordinary folks.'

She shook her head this way then that, her eyes still closed. 'I cannot do all this, Poppa, any more than she could. My head hurts, my sides hurt, I feel really sick. My feet are swollen and my face is up like a puffball. I had to drag Aunt Beatrice from the fair to take care of me. Do you know, for a minute I thought she'd refuse?'

The plaintive tone cut into his nerves like a baby's cry. 'You should get out and about, honey. It's the only cure. Respect this land. Embrace this country. And you can be sure it will embrace you.'

She stayed there very still for a moment, then her eyes snapped open. 'As it has in the case of Astrid Benbow? Is that what you mean?' She closed her eyes again. 'I'm so sorry I cannot be quite as respectful as my friend Astrid,' she drawled. 'It seems to me that she is embracin' everything in this land and being mightily embraced in her turn.'

He stared at her. 'No, my dear, one could never demand such loyalty of Astrid. But this is your home, your home ground. I built it for you. This house and this town. For you and your dear mother and your sister.'

Her laughter echoed along the shuttered veranda. 'That is so untrue, Poppa. So very untrue. The truth is that you built this town and this house for yourself, to show everyone just how grand you are. How you are bigger and grander even than Mr Stratton or Mr Rivas, all on your own. And you didn't even need to try, because you were bigger and grander than either of those before you even started. But not for us, Poppa, not for us.'

The General hauled himself to his feet, grasping his cane. 'I regret to see, my dearest Constance, that your travels in Europe have not quite had the civilising influence your dear mother and I wished. You're becoming arrogant, disrespectful and even vulgar. I cannot recognise you as your mother's daughter. She was never less than a lady, even in her suffering. I so very much regret this.'

For a second there was silence and she resisted the urge to open her eyes again. Then her father's voice came to her like slivers of shredded ice. 'I came to inform you, Constance, that I have changed the placements at the table. You are to sit at the foot of the table in your dear mother's place. No one has taken that place since she departed for Europe. You will have Burleigh Railton to your left and Elmer Rivas's nephew to your right. Perhaps you could dig very deep and talk with them in a mannerly fashion. If you do this I shall be eternally grateful.' He sounded the absolute opposite.

She could hear the crystal door knob turning in his hand. She screwed her eyes tight against the pain like steel pins in the back of her head. 'I will talk to your booted Westerners, Poppa,' she called into the darkness. 'But tomorrow I will make my plans to return East before I die in this place. Don't talk to me about all this embracing. Not your mountains nor any of your dusty Westerners. None of it. I'm goin' back East where the air don't kill you. The air here chokes me, exhausts me. It drives pins through my head and when I look in the mirror I don't recognise myself.' She heard the boudoir door creak wide open. She raised her voice. 'So I'm leavin' this place tomorrow. And my dear friend Astrid will have to come with me. What do you think about that? Now which will make you sadder, Poppa: losing me for ever, or the embraceable Miss Benbow?'

Richard Redoute blundered his way out of the cluttered boudoir with its achingly familiar sights and smells. Aunt Beatrice sat outside the door on a low seat with her towels on her lap. She stood up. 'General, sir?' she said.

He nodded, calming down by the second. 'Beatrice,' he said. 'Perhaps you would be so kind as to use your considerable influence on my daughter to ensure she gets to the grandstand at four o'clock to see this blasted tightrope walker?'

'Yes, sir.' Aunt Beatrice nodded. She relinquished the towels, placing them neatly on the chair. 'And I wondered, General, if I could speak with you about another matter? Right now?'

He glanced around the deserted hall. 'I must return to my guests, Beatrice.' He took out his watch. 'Nearly four o'clock. The tightrope walker will be dicing with death over the ravine at four fifteen precisely. You should come. It seems that he is a very brave man.'

She shook her head. 'No thank you, sir. My place is here with po' suffering Miss Constance.'

He glanced at her sharply but her innocent eye showed no flicker of the snake of irony. 'Well . . .' He strode before her, leading the way to his study opposite.

Inside the shuttered space he sat down on a low velvet chair beside a carved wooden fireplace that boasted another excellent painting of a fire. He nodded towards her and she sat on an upright chair opposite, her hands in her lap. 'So what is it that is so serious, Miss Beatrice?' His use of her proper title reflected his assumption of the seriousness of the encounter.

'Wa'al, General. There is the issue of my money. The money you're very kindly holdin' for me.'

He lit a cigar, drew on it and blew the smoke towards the chimney. 'Yes, Miss Beatrice, it is quite, quite safe.'

'Then I would be mighty grateful, sir, if I could have it right now.'

He looked carefully at the glowing tip of the cigar. 'Of course. It's your money, Miss Beatrice. You can have it any time. You could always have had it any time. May I ask why this particular time?'

'The time has come,' she said. 'Miss Constance, she goin' back East, sure as firecrackers burn. And my Miss Aurelia, seems she ain't never coming back to these parts. So I reckon me and my cousin Vera, it's time we go too.'

He went to the desk and from a lower drawer he pulled out a small black leather-bound book. He handed it to her. She turned it over. The name *Miss Beatrice Lawler* was stamped on the front, in gold tooling. 'Is this my money?' She frowned towards him.

'Look inside, Miss Beatrice, and you will see the original amount I gave you when I married Miss Aurelia, the amount you returned to me for safekeeping. Then subsequently each month you will note your remittance for the work you have done since. And, from the date of Cousin Vera's arrival, you will note her own entries. In the next section you can see how the accumulated amounts were invested in Redoute stock. To the right you will see the yield from this stock. Right at the bottom of the page, d'you see there? The current running total. Eleven thousand, two hundred and eighty dollars.'

Her elegant body sagged a little in her seat. 'Why, General, it cain't be so much.'

His severe face melted into laughter as he relished the moment. 'Well, Miss Beatrice, Redoute stock has been a mighty fine investment in all the years you've been part of this family. Even in bad years it has held its own. Many fortunes have been made in this town, Miss Beatrice, mostly through risk and speculation and cuttin' the other fellow down. I reckon you've made your fortune by loyalty and a loving demeanour and that makes it special.'

She took out her wire-rimmed spectacles from her breast pocket and pored through the figures line by line. Then she returned the spectacles to her pocket, sat up very straight and said, 'I guess I gotta thank you, General, for being the fair man I know you to be. I thank you very much.'

He coughed. 'Every cent here has been worked for, Miss Beatrice, and well deserved. Now then, what're you plannin' to do with your well-earned treasure? Will you invest it again, here in the Springs? I could help you do that. Or perhaps you could buy a little business of your own . . .'

She was already shaking her head. 'I reckon outside of these walls and except for yourself, General, this place ain't no place for no Negro woman.'

'Miss Beatrice . . .'

She put up a hand to stop him. 'Don't you know, General, that there are ghost-men riding even now to keep us coloured folk in our place? And didn't the white folks vote for one of their kind, another ghost-man, a while ago? Saw in him their ideal man? Their government man?'

He was silent. No denying the truth.

'No, sir,' she said composedly. 'And no point going back to Virginia 'cause I hear things ain't no better there. No, I think me and my little cousin Vera is aimed for the big city. I read about it in your paper, Colonel, as I iron it so you don't get the black on your hands. New York is the place. There we'll have us our own little business, Vera and me. A fine laundry, maybe, or some kind of a store. Or flowers. One thing certain, General, we work for our own selves. We'll be grateful to no man for work.'

Richard Redoute was so astonished that his cigar remained unsmoked and was burning to an ash tube as they sat. In all the years he'd lived in this house alongside Beatrice Lawler he'd never heard her say so much. He ventured. 'Even in big cities, Miss Beatrice, there are men . . . and women . . . who—'

'Don't like uppity coloured folk?' She gurgled a laugh. 'That may be so, sir, but in the cities ain't there a likelihood of more of the other kind? More of my kind. More of your kind. Me an' Miss Aurelia, we were up in New York one time and there were thousands of faces all different. Looked to me it was a place you could melt into real easy.'

He sighed and nodded. 'You may be wise, Miss Beatrice.

But it won't be easy.' He shook the ash off his cigar, drew on it and sat back in his chair.

She stood up and looked him in the eye. 'It ain't never been easy, General. It was never easy when the Lawlers give me for a plaything to Miss Aurelia on her birthday. When they put a red ribbon in my hair and took me right away from my mother and my aunt Mima and my brother Solly. And it was never easy when our folks got free and Miss Aurelia kept me tied to her with silver strings of love. How could I leave her? She need me so much. Even when she let my cousin Vera come to stay to keep me company, it was not easy. Then when she leave me but beg me to stay to wait her return, that was never easy. You remember, General, you an' me beached here gasping like fish on a bank when she been gone? It ain't been easy, no sir.' She slipped the black book into her apron pocket. 'This money, sir? This money is owed me.'

He stood up. 'You're right, Miss Beatrice, though there is great pain in saying it.'

'I'll take the money in gold, General. Soon as you're ready. Me and Cousin Vera's like to be on our way.' She glided towards the door. Then she turned. 'Oh, General?'

'Yes, Beatrice?'

'It ain't none of my business, but I think you should ask your friend Miss Astrid about her girl Honesty. There is something not right there. Not right at all.'

He frowned. 'The gypsy girl? What's wrong with her?'

'Like I say, you should talk to Miss Astrid. She know about this. The child's in her care.'

He frowned again at the door as it closed quietly behind her. So what was this business? The child seemed pleasant enough. Obviously adored Astrid. A good child. Young Slim was very fond of her. Treated her like a little sister or a pet puppy dog. He sat down and flicked his ash towards the picture of the fire.

Hard to think what might be the problem there. Not Slim. He was a very good boy. The General knew his men.

Seven

Balancing Act

4.15pm

A large red-bearded man in a Ruritanian uniform clambered to the top of what looked like a racing judge's platform. He put a bullhorn to his mouth. 'And now, ladies and gentlemen,' he bellowed, 'you have seen the great Indian elephant and the tiger from the East. You have watched the fire-eater toast his insides. You have danced the leather orf of your shoes and now we have the highlight of the day. I present to you the one, the only, the Great Mandolio, the Man Who Dances On Air. The Great Mandolio, ladies and gentlemen, will climb to the platform you see to your right. He will take orf his shoes which are right now protecting the precious bones and muscles of his magical feet. And then, ladies and gentlemen . . .' The crowd below him finally hushed their chatter. 'And then he will walk on that high wire you see strung from one side of the gorge to the other. In his bare feet he will walk across that yawning space. One false move and he will crash to the rocks below, to be carried orf on the mighty torrent and never seen again.'

Mandolio started to climb the gantry to the platform on this side of the gorge. There was a murmur among the crowds, who had been kept back for their own safety behind moveable picket fences. The General's honoured guests sat to one side in a small beflagged grandstand. Constance Redoute, escorted by Aunt Beatrice, muffled in gauzy scarves and hidden by a shady hat, was the last to climb up and take her seat. Astrid stayed down below with the crowd behind her, pressed against the picket fence, standing shoulder to shoulder with Honesty and Slim.

She watched as the Great Mandolio reached the platform and put up a hand in response to cheers from the crowd. He bent down to slip off his fine leather boots. Then he shook out and flexed first one bare foot then the other. Then he opened the gate. He reached down to test the hawser on which he would walk across the abyss. Below him the crowd drew a collective breath.

Astrid reflected for a moment on the abyss across which she herself had walked that morning. The abyss between virgin and not-virgin, between knowing and not-knowing, between being loved and being unloved.

There in the swimming pavilion she was sure that Richard Redoute loved her. Surely that heat, the magnetism in the air, could justly be labelled love? She had known there would be pain. Had she not heard as much from Honesty who was now standing beside her, shoulder to shoulder, against the fence? But she'd not reckoned on the sense of opening, the yearning deep in her muscles, in her flesh, to engulf him, to make him part of her. Only now did she put words to that thought. In those moments in the pavilion she'd been all feeling, all sensation. In those moments the flood of emotion had made two parcels of flesh and bone into one. Now she knew, and would never *not-know* again. She knew now about nuns being the bride of Christ. She knew about her own father and mother and what bound them together.

The crowd roared in unison again. The Great Mandolio was now hefting a long pole in the air, testing it on his open hands, tipping it first this way then the other. Finally he put one bare foot on the rope to try it. He tested it with the other foot and drew back again. Then he stood up very straight, balanced his pole and appeared to step into the air.

In the pavilion Richard Redoute had been tentative at first, unsure of his ground. Astrid felt she had to make sure that he knew that she wanted him. She had found a new self, a self that allowed her lifelong reserve to melt away. He had seemed to feel this in her and became tender, loving every part of her, making her even more welcoming. There were broken words of tenderness and gratitude that did not stay in her mind. There was a point beyond pain when it was as though she were in a great echoing cave from whose mouth streamed the light of the universe.

Now Mandolio was making slow, steady progress across the gulf. Before each step he paused a little to allow his audience's nerves to tingle. Then his foot slipped and his pole swung wildly while he regained his balance. A woman on the grandstand fell in a faint and Honesty clutched Astrid's arm. She pulled away instantly, as though she had been burnt. 'Sorry, miss,' she said.

Astrid put her hand on the girl's where it lay on the white picket fence and left it there. 'It's almost too exciting, don't you think?' she said.

At last she understood about Honesty and the awful thing that had happened to her. She knew now that without the hand of love, the furnace heat of mutual attraction, that extreme act must be hateful, like being cleaved in two with a sword. It occurred to her that the King and Richard Redoute must be of an age. Yet they lived in different worlds and there was a world of difference between them.

After that final gesture of benediction Richard had finally left. She had gone back into the pool for a swim, not caring at that point how wet her hair became, or how late she would be for the tightrope walker. That was how she ended up against the rail with Honesty rather than up in the stand with Constance.

The Great Mandolio was halfway across when there was a roll of drums from the distant bandstand and he lost his footing altogether, ending up astride the wire, his pole threshing wildly hundreds of feet above the creek.

People in the crowd were gasping and shouting as Mandolio made a play of struggling to retrieve the situation. He balanced the pole and made a prodigious effort to get one foot back on the wire, then still crouching he brought the other foot behind him and got his instep in place. For a second it seemed as though the whole High Plain was still: even the crickets stopped chirping. Then the Great Mandolio slowly, slowly hauled himself to his feet and pulled himself upright, his pole balanced lightly before him.

The cheers of the crowd rang across the meadow, climbed halfway up the mountain and echoed back. The band set up a brisk march and Mandolio seemed to run across to the platform on the far side of the ravine. He turned to the crowd, took off his velvet cap and raised his arm in a graceful balletic acknowledgement of the cheers. The crowd by the fence went wild. The men threw up their hats and the women threw posies and gloves in the air. Shouts of *Hurrah* and *Bravo* from the grandstand were lost in the cheers from down below.

'A wonderful show, don't you think, Astrid?' Richard's voice was in her ear.

She turned to him, her eyes sparkling. 'Wonderful! What a risk he took! But it all seems fine now.' She felt Honesty slumping against her. 'What is it, Honesty?'

''S all right, miss. Just the heat, I reckon. And the excitement.' The girl gasped and slid to the ground. 'Did you see that man? The Great Mandolio?'

Slim put his arm around her, then lifted her bodily.

'Take her to Aunt Beatrice.' Richard nodded to him. 'She'll know what to do. A cool drink. Some shade from the sun.'

'I'll go,' said Astrid. 'I'll go with her.'

Richard held her back. 'She'll be fine with Aunt Beatrice.'

They watched as Slim joined Aunt Beatrice by the stand and they began to walk towards the castle, Honesty still cradled in the young man's arms.

'Aunt Beatrice thinks there's something amiss with your girl,' said Richard thoughtfully.

'Amiss?' Astrid shook her head. 'She's fine. It seems to me that she's very happy here. The sunshine, and the fresh air. She's put on weight since we arrived. She's as sturdy as a rock. She loves Aunt Beatrice and has made quite a friend of your young driver.'

'Slim's a good boy. Honest and keen,' he murmured. Oblivious of the hundreds of eyes on them, he took her arm. They strolled back towards the bandstand where the final entertainment of the afternoon, a short programme from the Italian tenor, was about to begin.

'How are you?' he said.

'As well as I was this morning. Which is extremely well.'

'No regrets?'

'No.'

'You're sure?'

'I'm twenty-five years old, Richard, not fifteen.'

'Then you must stay here with me. We will find some way.' He nodded absently to a well-corseted lady who passed them carrying her parasol very low, almost like a helmet. 'We will find a way.'

'I have not . . . cannot think clearly about that just now.' She wondered at the justice of it all. Today she'd found something in herself, had touched some depths just because of Richard. The thought of leaving him now gave her physical pain. She wanted to cry out that it wasn't fair, it wasn't fair. She had discovered what he meant to her and now she would have to leave with Constance.

He hugged her arm to his side. 'You must think about it. My poor dear Constance is just about expiring and is talking of leaving tomorrow. And now Aunt Beatrice has taken it into her head to leave us as well. She has plans to go to New York to set up a hattery or a laundry or some such emporium.'

'How could she do that? A servant . . .'

'She is not a slave. She may do as she wishes. You underrate her, my dear. I'm darn proud of her. She's an exceptional person. A discreet person.' He paused. 'More than a servant.'

'Your house will not be the same without her.'

'It will be fine, though, with you here.' His grip on her arm tightened. 'You have to stay, my dear girl. You will stay.' His voice was low, urgent.

'General!' A large man in a shady hat and a cream linen suit stood before them.

'Senator!' The two men shook hands.

Astrid glided away back towards the grandstand nearly empty now as the people who had gasped at Mandolio were making their way to the bandstand to hear the tenor. Constance was still there swathed in gauze under a grey silk parasol. Astrid climbed up and sat beside her. 'Connie!' she said. 'Wasn't the Great Mandolio amazing? Do you imagine he did those falls on purpose? I think perhaps they were some kind of trick.'

'If you tell me so, Astrid, I suppose it must be so,' said Constance wearily. 'If it entertained you, my dear, I suppose we must all be grateful.'

Astrid ignored her friend's waspish tone. 'Connie, dear, I'm so sorry you're in such distress. And so sorry that you seem not to thrive here.'

Constance looked at her carefully. 'It seems that this revolting place has quite the opposite effect on you. Look at you. You are glowing, honey, blooming,' she said coolly.

Astrid found herself blushing. 'The mountain air suits me, perhaps, a little better than you.' How she wished she could talk to Constance about her problem. If it were any other man they would have discussed it at length. Connie would have told her that the man, however charming, was far too old for her and she would have protested that true love could overcome any such barriers. They would have laughed about it.

'I'm sure,' said Constance dryly. 'It could be the mountain air and it could be other things.' She stood up. 'I'm going back to the house to get under cover and see where that naughty Beatrice has got to. Really, she is getting above herself these days. Those eyes of her do look at you so.'

Astrid only just stopped herself telling Connie about Beatrice's plans. She tried to help Constance make her way down the steps only to have her hand smacked away. 'I can manage perfectly well, thank you, dear. Don't think I cannot,' snapped Constance. 'I do need a rest before I come down to dinner. I'm to take my mother's place at the table. I must be at my best.' She hobbled away. 'Dinner will be at seven. I had to battle with my father for it not to be at five. So hard to get these Westerners into anything near civilised habits.'

Astrid stood stock still, her hand still stinging where Constance had slapped it away. To her dismay she felt her eyes welling up with tears. When Constance was ten yards away she looked over her shoulder. 'I'd be grateful, honey, if you'd join me in the boudoir at six thirty? I have something to show you.' When she was thirty feet away she stood up straight. When she was forty feet away she began to walk quite swiftly towards the castle without another backward glance.

Eight

The Picture Album

5pm

'Go away.'

'But Miss Beatrice, I can sit with Honesty.'

'I tell you, sir, go away. Leave the child with me.'

Slim stared at the black woman, reluctant to do her bidding like some small boy. She met his gaze. 'Go!' she said.

Honesty's room was a virtual cupboard at the bottom of a staircase. Slim peered at the white-faced sweating figure on the bed, Vera sitting quietly beside her. 'What's wrong with her?' he said.

Beatrice looked him blandly in the eye. 'Some kind of fever. What they calls heatstroke. Who knows? Now go.' She gave him a little push. For a moment he looked blankly at her hand, then turned on his heel and strode off, his boots clattering on the bare wooden floor.

'Now!' said Beatrice, advancing towards Honesty. 'What have we here, child?'

When Astrid got to the boudoir at six thirty Constance was sitting in front of the wide mirror. She had changed into another georgette dress, this one in forget-me-not blue with intricate pearl stitching in the front panel. Her smooth unlined face glowed white against her undressed hair. She was scowling but at least she was not wincing with pain, which was unusual these days. 'Thank goodness you're here, Astrid. Beatrice is not answering her bell and Honesty's nowhere on the planet. How can they expect me to put up my own hair? So you must do it. Beatrice has laid out the pads and pins. I'll tell you what to do.'

Astrid enjoyed the business of dressing Constance's hair. It was intimate, intensely close, yet somehow neutral. Today it bridged the gap of estrangement that had begun to yawn between her and Constance in these last months. When the coiffure was at last done to her satisfaction Constance moved gracefully to one of the couches. 'Perhaps you would pour the lemonade, Astrid? That Beatrice can sometimes be such a lazy girl. One day I'll dismiss her and where'll she be then?'

Astrid poured the lemonade.

'No matter.' Constance brightened up. 'Astrid. I have made up my mind. We will leave as soon as the journey can be arranged. We'll go back East. First Boston for a little civilisation. Then Europe. What do you say?'

'Constance, I don't know . . .'

Constance put her glass down with a crash on the gold-embossed table. 'Now then, what did I have to show you?' She stood and picked up a very large leather-bound album from one of the side tables then sat down again. She patted the couch beside her. 'Sit here, dear Astrid, and do take a look at this.'

Astrid sat beside her and Constance opened the heavy volume so that half of it was on Astrid's knee. 'Look. Here is my mother as a bride. Do you know she was the beauty of her generation?'

It was very clear to see. The beauty shone from the page.

'And the General,' said Constance. 'So handsome in his uniform.'

And heartbreakingly young. Thick fair hair, luxuriant moustache, smooth young skin. Astrid thought her heart would break. She had missed his youth. But somewhere inside him that young man was there still.

'They were so young. So very well suited. Everyone said so.' Constance turned a page. 'Look here! On honeymoon in Paris! Their lives before them. And here am I as a little girl, with my sister Delphine. They tell us that we both take after our dear mother in our fine looks. It is as though one is an extra ripe peach that everyone wants to pick. In turn one has the pick of one's own generation. It can be so confusing, such choice. How lucky you are, dear Astrid, not to have the problem. Beauty is a burden you have been spared.' She closed the book and raised limpid eyes to meet Astrid's. 'Some people have so little choice, of course, that they are driven to set their cap at a poor sick old man who knows no better.'

Astrid gritted her teeth, then breathed very deeply and slowly. 'It is such a tragedy,' she said quietly.

'Yes, a tragedy. Astrid, honey, I know you do not intend to humiliate yourself, setting your cap at him, making an old fool of my poppa, but—'

'I'm talking about you, Connie. Not about me.'

Constance frowned. 'Me?'

'I've been thinking lately about that gay, brave girl who made me laugh so much in England. That lovely Connie who would take risks and shatter conventions. The girl so wise and genuine who made life such fun.'

'That's not—'

'Where is she? It seems she has changed to a querulous, pouting child who insists on being the centre of her own cramped universe. She is so full of self-pity and vindictiveness that it makes her quite ugly. A tragedy for one so beautiful.'

'But I am sick!' Tears welled up into Constance's eyes. 'This nasty place makes me sick.'

Astrid put a hand on hers, where it lay on the thick leather album. 'I know it does,' she said quietly. 'It makes you feel so low. But I've seen how the sickness has transformed you into someone at whom you'd have laughed in the damp lanes of England. So I think you're right to say you should go back

East, even back to Europe to recover the real Connie. Don't take your sick self there and let her flourish. Peel her off as a snake sloughs its skin. Become yourself again.'

Constance turned over her hand and clutched at Astrid. 'Yes! And you, dear, and you! You come with me.'

Astrid shook her head. 'This place has made changes in me as well as you. It has made me slough my old tired skin. I feel I'm more myself here. More the person I should really be. For me going back would be dangerous. Perhaps I don't want to be the person I once was.'

Suddenly, like a streak of sunlight on a stormy day, Constance laughed. A real echo of her former self. 'Then, dear Astrid, perhaps you should stay. Stay and put a spring in my old father's step.'

Astrid blushed. 'Constance . . .'

Constance put a hand to her mouth. 'How vulgar I am. And how mean, dear Astrid, and lacking in thought.' She sat up very straight. 'D'you know I came here thinking my father was dead or dying? Instead, I find him very much alive and enjoying his life. And then, rather than paying me attention like a beau, he only has eyes for you. And in this horrible place it makes my miserable self even more miserable. And then I see him taking my dearest friend from me. And I wallow in misery like my mother at her worst.'

'Oh, Connie, I would not have that for the world . . .'

Constance let out a peal of laughter. 'Honey, I should be rejoicing. I'm going back East away from this terrible place and I'm leaving my best friend to keep an eye on my poor old poppa.' She stood up and crooked her arm. 'Well, dear old Astrid, perhaps we should go down to dinner and show all those gossiping old harridans that we're sisters under the skin.'

Aunt Beatrice, standing in the deep shadow of a doorway at the other side of the hall, watched the two young women tripping arm in arm across the marble floor and decided not to say anything further to Miss Astrid about the child. Time enough for drama.

Tonight General Richard Redoute was a happy man. His early Independence Day Fair had gone like clockwork. His house was at its very best. At a meeting in the library before dinner he'd brokered a deal for hauling sylvanite and rendering gold for Nathan French, who had just opened the largest seam yet on Battle Mountain. That same Nathan was sitting at the centre of the dining table between the wives of the two senators who were his guests of honour tonight.

To Richard's right hand at the table, talking about London to his senior surveyor, was the very fine young woman who had managed over the last months to melt the steel band of his utter isolation. At the other end of the table, fluttering and flirting with everyone, playing her role to the hilt, was his daughter. Her thunderous mood had vanished and she gave every appearance of enjoying herself. She was the very image of his dear wife at her very peak in those days when she too was her real self, the woman with whom he first fell in love.

A man could ask no more.

Nine

Honesty Confined

10pm
It has spoiled my day, this pain that has been nagging me.
I must have twisted my back riding Slim's horse with no
saddle. That Slim's a good lad. He carried me like a feather
all the way back to the house and if it hadn't been for Aunt
Beatrice shooing him away he'd have still been here. But here
I am with Aunt Beatrice, who's sitting like some dark guardian
at the door with Cousin Vera beside her like an attendant
mouse.

My favourite of all today was the dancing, whirling away on
the dance platform, my skirts wrapping round Slim's legs as we
swirled round and round. I've seen dancing at the fairs but I've
never really done it. When I'm better I'll make Slim take me to
one of those dance halls down at Cripple Creek and we'll dance
the night away.

Ouch! This ache comes back and back. It really hurts. Aunt
Beatrice comes and takes my hand. 'Do you know what this is,
child?' she says.

'It's a great big belly ache, that's what it is.'

'You just let Cousin Vera here feel your belly, honey. She
knows how to feel what's wrong. Then Aunt Beatrice'll know
what medicine'll help.'

I pull my shift right down and hold it tight. 'No. I'm all
right. It'll go away.'

She sighs. 'Then I'll jes' have to get the old General and get him to send for the doctor to come here.'

'No. No. No, no doctor,' I say. 'Just what will Cousin Vera do?'

'All she does is have a feel of your belly, honey. Then she'll know what to do. She'll know what we all should do.'

My hands fall away and Aunt Beatrice pulls up my skirts and settles them round my waist like a pie frill. Then she pulls down my drawers and Cousin Vera lays little hands like bird claws all over my belly. It flips in this queer way as she touches it. Then another pain cuts through and I scream. Aunt Beatrice makes me sit up and the pain stops. Her head is on my shoulder and her voice whispers in my ear. 'Do you know what this is, child?' she asks again.

'A great big belly ache, that's all.' I shout the words because the pain is sawing at my back again. 'I got a belly ache.'

'That ain't so, honey. I gotta tell you there's a baby in there that's bin longing like Jesus to get out into this old world.'

'A baby?' I shout. 'It can't be!' over and over again until she puts her hand, dry as a leaf, over my mouth.

'Hush, honey. Have you been with a man?'

'I was with Slim all day long.' I have to say this through gritted teeth, the pain's so bad again.

'I don't mean now, honey. I mean a while ago. While you were back home. Did some man git inside of you?' Her tone is grim, ugly. 'Maybe nine months ago?'

'I was on a ship nine months ago. Tending the ladies.'

Then I remember that thing that I put right tight into the back of my mind. 'But before. There was the . . . this old man. I didn't want it, what he did, but I couldn't stop it. Ooh.' Then I'm in pain like a dark underground cave. I shut my eyes to bear it. When I open them I see them exchanging glances. Cousin Vera whispers into Aunt Beatrice's ear. I hear something about the first being late. And a young body holding it in. Aunt Beatrice turns to go. I can hear myself shouting then, as if I'm some other person on the other side of the creek. 'Don't go, Aunt Beatrice. I'm not a bad girl. Please don't go.'

She comes back then and pulls up her snowy pinny to wipe the sweat from my forehead. 'I know you ain't no bad girl, honey. But ain't a bad thing been done to you? I'm a-going now to get your Miss Astrid because I know fine she'll want to be here.'

Then the pain becomes so much that the night sky sets around me like a cloak and I shout my mother's name, 'Kezia-ah!' And I want the call to go over this land and right across the sea so she'll hear it in her *vardo*. But I know it won't.

Ten

Late Arrival

Astrid was relieved by what seemed to be a change in Constance's attitude. It had not been easy being a guest in a house where suddenly her hostess had transformed herself into a bitter and distressed stranger. When it had first started she'd kept to her own room, drawing and reading, to be out of Constance's way. Then, as Richard Redoute had demanded her company more and more it had at first seemed a good thing to escape the silent house where even Constance's bedroom door had a forbidding, tearful look.

So it was with a lighter heart that she sat at the Independence Day dinner table and talked easily to the man on her right about the delights of the Natural History Museum and the National Gallery in London. She felt confident in advising him to take a house in the Cotswolds if he wanted a really good season's hunting. She was very conscious of Richard on her left talking to some people about the proposal for yet another new wing on the college and the imperative for a new Faculty of Design so they could attract good artists and designers to the region. Such people would reflect on its beauty and modify the rip-roaring image it had back East. It was the twentieth century, after all. He kept saying this. 'After all, it is the twentieth century.' She listened to his faintly drawling tones with a new pleasure, digging into her memory for the words he'd said as they made love but failing to remember them.

'Perhaps you have a name? Someone you'd recommend?'

She looked blankly at the neighbour to her right then her brow cleared. 'The hunting? Oh, well, I must be honest. Hunting is not to my taste so . . . But Constance, the General's daughter, hunted down there last season. She is sure to know people.' They both looked along the table at Constance, beautiful in a low-necked gown that flattered her full neck and shoulders and the high choker set with small diamonds.

The General's knee just touched Astrid's. She turned to look up into his smiling eyes. 'You are truly wonderful,' he murmured. 'Truly wonderful. You will stay here, you surely will. Constance will go, but promise you will stay?'

She smiled back. 'I . . .' She felt a light touch on her shoulder.

'Miss Astrid?' said Aunt Beatrice.

A shade of anger passed over the General's face. 'What is it?' he whispered fiercely.

Beatrice murmured in his ear. His fair eyebrows shot up. 'I think perhaps you should go with Aunt Beatrice, Astrid. Your girl Honesty appears to need you.'

As she followed Aunt Beatrice out of the glittering room the conversation lulled as the company took note of what looked like some minor drama. Then the charge of talk spattered through the room again and Astrid was forgotten.

As Astrid mounted the third staircase a high-pitched scream made her run the rest of the way along the narrow servants' corridor to the little room at the end. Aunt Beatrice glided beside her, her skirts rustling. At the door she barred the way to Astrid. 'Did you know?' she demanded quietly. 'Did you know that this child in your care was with child herself?'

Astrid staggered a second, then straightened herself. 'No. I did not.'

'Did you know there was a chance that this could happen?' A bit more'n nine months ago. I fear this one's late, her bein' so young an' all.'

'Yes. No. I know little about these things. But something was done to her. I know about that.' She put a hand on Beatrice's arm. 'Let me see her. She's my . . . responsibility.'

Another scream pierced the polished wood of the door.

'Let me see her!'

Inside the room she was greeted by the sight of a red-faced Honesty, squatting above a heap of folded blankets that had been set on the polished floor. The sweating, bulging face that raised itself to Astrid's was almost unrecognisable. Cousin Vera was standing over Honesty, holding the girl's shift twisted up behind her with one hand, and grasping her shoulder with the other. 'Miss Astrid,' wailed Honesty. 'What's happening to me? They say it's a baby.'

'I'm sorry,' said Astrid helplessly. 'So sorry.'.

'Will you take her other arm, Miss Astrid,' whispered Vera. 'The child needs you to help her.' She looked up at Beatrice. 'And you, Auntie. You take this side, and hold the back of her dress here.'

They did as they were told and Cousin Vera went to kneel before Honesty. She took her face in her hands. 'Don' you worry, honey. All your friends is here now. Your lady an' my auntie. Good people. I done this times before in Virginia for other sisters. Once someone did it for me. While ago now.'

Honesty breathed heavily. 'I'm frightened, Cousin Vera. I'm so frightened.'

Cousin Vera chuckled. Her voice crackled with rare use. 'No need at all, honey. You jus' let that baby come. She want to come. She dyin' to come into this world. You jes' help her to fall out when I say. Next time when the big pain come you let her out. Don' you clench up an' keep her in. She ready.'

Astrid spoke into Honesty's ear. 'Cousin Vera's very wise, Honesty dear. Do just as she says.' She felt buzzing with life. Her vision, her world was filled with this straining child beside her.

213

Honesty screamed again, and then let out another tearing scream and Vera's face split into a great smile. 'Ah, here she comes. Look at her, hair like an angel. Good girl. One more push. A little turn. Here we are, child. Here we are.'

Honesty sagged in their arms. Beatrice hauled her back onto a stool that had been placed behind her. Then she put her arm right round her, pulling the child's sobbing face into her shoulder, muttering soft crooning noises which were not words.

Astrid stood up, her back aching, feeling lost. She looked at the small bundle of blood-streaked flesh held in one of Cousin Vera's hands. As she watched, Vera did something with the trailing cord. Then she held the baby up as though it were some kind of offering and juggled it about softly with her hands. A soft cry, more like a kitten's mew than any human cry, bubbled from the tiny mouth. Tears filled Astrid's eyes. Vera grunted with satisfaction and placed the baby on a sheet already prepared beside her. Then she wrapped it expertly, swaddling the baby like a tight parcel. She held it up to Honesty. 'There you are, honey, you see your baby? You see your little girl?'

Beatrice turned Honesty's face so that she could see the baby. Honesty shuddered and buried her face in Beatrice's shoulder again.

Beatrice pulled away from her. 'Come on, honey. Look at your baby.'

Honesty turned her face in the opposite direction. 'I don't wanter see it. It ain't nothing to do with me. I don't wanter see it.'

Beatrice looked at Vera and nodded. Vera lifted the baby, still like an offering, to Astrid. 'Here, ma'am. You take this little scrap. Ain't I got more to do here before I'm finished? This little girl too scared to know her baby.'

Astrid took the bundle and held it gingerly.

Vera turned and tugged at Honesty's arm. 'Now then, child, we've just one more thing to do. I want you to try just one more time to bring the rest away. Come here now.'

Astrid settled the strange bundle in her arms and went to sit on a chair by the window which had its back to the room. She looked down at the head almost obscured now by the binding cloth. The pink face bore snail-trails of blood but was plump and smooth and healthy. There was a sharp little nose and the peak of hair was distinctly blonde, unlike Honesty's own dark locks. She closed her eyes and there flashed into her mind the image of the genial monarch holding court at Lady Seland's dinner table. She cursed her own ignorance at not recognising the changes in Honesty for what they really were. It was not just Honesty who had blossomed in the Colorado sunshine. This little being. She had blossomed.

Then, as she watched the small perfect face, the eyes snapped open and it seemed as though light streamed from them. They were very dark blue. A very distinctive blue. As blue as the ink in a crystal inkwell. Thick fair lashes dropped over the eyes and then the mouth opened and the mew turned into a healthy piercing cry. Suddenly Astrid was flooded with happiness that spread from her heels to the top of her skull. 'Welcome, baby, welcome,' she whispered.

Behind her she could hear the rustling of sheets and the sloshing of water; murmuring, and low protests from Honesty. When Astrid finally stood up Honesty was lying on the high single bed in a clean shift, the sheets pulled up neatly around her. Aunt Beatrice was holding her hand and still crooning to her as though she herself were a baby. Cousin Vera was at the door with a bundle of linen and a package of some sort.

Astrid took a step to the bed, the crying baby in her hands. 'Here, Honesty,' she said humbly. 'See your baby. She is a very fine girl.'

Honesty turned her face to the wall. 'I don't want it. It's nowt to do with me.'

'But Honesty . . .'

Beatrice looked at Astrid. 'Didn't you know either, ma'am? This child didn't even know she was with child.'

215

'Honesty!' said Astrid, more sharply this time.

'I telt you, miss, it's nowt to do with me.' Honesty turned her head and looked Astrid in the eye, without sparing the baby a glance. She said, 'Take it. It's yours. You take it.'

At that second the baby stopped crying and the room was filled with silence.

'There,' said Honesty. 'It's shut up its caterwauling. It's yours.' She turned to Beatrice. 'Aunt Beatrice, will you pass us me bag?' She took the small leather bag and rooted around inside. Then she held up a hand to Astrid. 'Here. Teck this. It's not mine. It never was mine. I never wanted it.' On her flat palm was a gold coin. 'Teck it. It's a sovereign.'

Astrid stared at the coin.

'Teck it, will you?' Honesty sounded tired, weary now. 'That's what he give me. The old man that did it.'

Astrid took the coin. 'I'll keep it for the baby,' she said. 'I'll keep it safe.'

Honesty slid down the bed. 'Now I'm tired. Let us have a sleep, will you?' She closed her eyes and in seconds seemed fast asleep.

Astrid glanced at Aunt Beatrice who put her fingers to her lips and led Astrid from the room. In the corridor she said, 'We should let the child sleep. I declare she nearly died of fright when she realised what was happening. She knew nothing of this. She's had no blood-show. Not ever. So she knew no difference. How about you, Miss Astrid? You knew nothing of this?' Disbelief still threading through her voice, she led the way to the eyrie of two rooms that she shared with Cousin Vera. A sitting room and a double bedroom: they were larger and rather better appointed than Honesty's little room.

'How could I know? I've never had any experience.' Astrid looked helplessly down at the swaddled baby.

Beatrice pushed her gently down into a little chair but didn't offer to take the baby from her. She smiled. 'I reckon you've had a shock yourself, honey. An' now here look! Ain't you got a baby to care for?'

Astrid stared at the tiny rosebud face. 'But I can't . . . I know nothing of babies.'

'We'll help you, Vera and me. You'll soon learn. You have to do this, honey. The child put her into your care.'

'But tomorrow . . . She'll be better, won't she? Honesty? She can take the baby herself.'

'Honesty is in fine shape. That strong young body. But the shock, and getting the babe the way she did, that's some hard knock. Will she want it tomorrow? The next day? She made you the protector of this babe and it's as good as maybe that you'll have to protect that scrap of humanity from Honesty herself. Vera tells a tale of one girl in Virginia whose child was gotten in that way and you believe me, turned round and smothered the new little innocent to death! All lost and hidden now but don't such things happen?' She paused. 'You know how she got this child, Miss Astrid?'

Astrid nodded. 'I know what happened. It was none of Honesty's fault. This man . . .'

Beatrice nodded. 'I know of these men. Don't you think that this even more is a reason for you to protect the babe?'

The baby blanked out any further discussion by starting to scream, a scream that sliced Astrid to the very marrow. 'What is it?' she shouted to Beatrice. 'What can I do?'

Beatrice leaned over and made a knuckle of her little finger and brushed the baby's lips with it. Instantly the screaming stopped and the small mouth closed round it and sucked. Beatrice laughed. 'Miss Constance, she just like this,' she said. 'Weren't she hungry from the first minute of her life?' She pulled her finger away and the baby started to scream again. She nodded at Astrid. 'Now you do it,' she said. 'Just bend your little finger.'

Astrid bent her little finger and the baby clamped onto it and started sucking. The thrill that went through her stopped somewhere at the pit of her stomach. She smiled up at Beatrice, who said, 'Nice, ain't it? But she won't be tricked for long. Cousin Vera's down looking for bottles and rubber teats so we can feed the child proper.'

Five minutes later the baby was just getting restless again when Vera came in carrying a tray. On it were a teapot and three china cups, and, lying on its side like a boat, a baby's bottle half full of watery milk. She placed this on a table beside Astrid. 'I'll go down and see the child Honesty,' she whispered under the screaming of the child. 'To watch her sleeping.'

Beatrice looked at Astrid. 'Now, honey, you take that bottle and feed that babe of yours.'

Astrid wanted to scream at her, 'This baby's nothing to do with me. Nothing.' But those were the words Honesty had used, so she couldn't say them. She picked up the bottle and passed it over the screaming mouth. The noise stopped and the baby turned her head and felt for the teat.

'That's it,' said Beatrice approvingly. 'Keep the teat full and just tease her lips. Let her grab. Sure as eggs, she'll soon git the idea. I tell you, Miss Astrid honey, babes are formidably survivin' kind of creatures.'

They tried it once, twice. The baby screamed again in frustration. Then she latched onto the bottle and sucked energetically. Astrid sat back in the chair, wriggling a little so that the baby was more secure in her lap. She looked up victoriously at Beatrice.

The other woman beamed. 'There now, honey. Ain't it all just fine?'

They watched the baby suck until she twisted her head and spat out the teat. 'Now!' instructed Beatrice. 'Sit her straight up, facing you like a little prairie dog. You look her straight in the eye and tell her to cough up that bubble. Just you tell her.'

Astrid obeyed. She looked the swaddled child in its sleepy eyes and said, 'Come on, baby, cough up that wind.'

Nothing.

'Come on, baby, cough up.'

A small burp presented itself in a little bubble.

'Good!' said Beatrice. 'You ain't half got the touch, honey. There ain't no denying it.' Her eyes were shrewd. 'Now she truly yours. You sing to her and get her over to sleep and she know she's welcome to this old world. I gotta go and see that Honesty, and I got a few things to do.' Before Astrid could protest the door had closed behind her.

Astrid pulled the baby to her and loosened the swaddling a little so that a small hand popped out and settled, like a delicate starfish, on the cotton blanket. Her eyes opened again and her rosebud mouth quivered and she started to cry, softly now. 'Well, Rosebud,' said Astrid. 'I think perhaps we're stuck with each other. For tonight at least.'

Then, rocking from side to side, she started to hum a lullaby that she didn't know she remembered: a lullaby once sung to her by Detta O'Farrell, the Irish woman who rescued her from her own uncaring mother twenty-four years ago.

During the night Aunt Beatrice came to the room three times to say 'the child Honesty' was still asleep. Cousin Vera came in three times with freshly made bottles. Neither woman offered to feed the baby herself, although with the second bottle Cousin Vera brought a bowl and a jug, a baby's gown and soft muslin squares. After Astrid had given the baby her milk Cousin Vera bathed her in the bowl, sponging the film of birth scum from her skin and her hair. In the harsh electric light the hair glowed like spun gold. After the third feed, under the supervision of Beatrice, Astrid went down the stairs and into her own bedroom.

She laid the baby in her bed, undressed herself and took down her hair. She washed her face and arms and pulled on her nightgown and her dressing gown. The baby started to whimper. Astrid turned off the light, picked up the baby and moved to the cane chair by the night-dark window. She settled the baby in her lap and hummed the song again until they both went to sleep.

Eleven

New Dawn

8am

Astrid was woken by the sudden illumination of the eastern sky. She blinked. The baby stirred and settled again. Astrid yawned and opened her eyes wider. She became aware of two people sitting in her bedroom. In the chair at the dressing table sat Constance, her hair down, wearing a pink dressing gown with a swansdown collar. And in the small chair by the door sat Richard, his hands clasping the silver knob of his cane. He was dressed for riding. Astrid had a sudden hysterical thought that perhaps he expected her to go riding with him.

She put a hand to her tumbled hair and sat up in the chair, desperately trying to gather her thoughts. The baby stirred and opened her eyes. Astrid loosened her shawl. Cousin Vera bustled in with yet another bottle on a tray. Astrid put the teat against Rosebud's mouth and she started to suck.

'Well, well,' drawled Constance, smiling slightly. 'Such adventures. I could no-ot believe it when Aunt Bea told her tale.'

Astrid frowned at her over the baby's head. 'Aunt Beatrice was very good. Wonderful.'

'Did you know about this?' said Richard crisply. 'Did you know about the girl Honesty?'

She shook her head, angry at her own blushes. '*Honesty* didn't "know about the girl Honesty"! She and I were equally ignorant of these matters.'

220 –

'You look very knowledgeable now, honey,' said Constance, nodding at the baby.

Astrid wriggled her stiff back. 'It's been a long night learning. Aunt Beatrice and Cousin Vera . . . well, they're good teachers. Aunt Beatrice insisted I look after the baby. Like you,' she glanced directly at Richard, 'she thinks I am somehow responsible.'

'Why aren't they teaching the child herself to do this?' said Richard with asperity. 'This is her baby.'

Astrid shook her head. 'She wants nothing to do with the baby. As I say, she didn't even know she was . . . well . . . until last night. She was very frightened.'

Constance spluttered with laughter.

'It's true! You remember our stay at Lady Seland's?' She stared at Constance. 'The shooting party?'

Constance nodded.

Astrid stared at her for a moment then turned to Richard. The whole truth would be too much. It would always be too much. 'There was a fellow there, a guest. He took advantage, forced himself on her.'

Richard stirred in his seat. 'These young girls! They have their heads turned.'

'It was no romance, sir,' said Astrid. 'No young blade. It was an old man, who should have known better. And she was a child. And the household colluded, from the highest to the lowest.' She paused. 'She was obliged . . . forced, in effect. No blame was attached to the man. Even *I* said nothing, though she told me about it the following morning. I have felt so guilty about that.'

'So much happening under my nose,' said Constance. 'Fancy.'

'It's not some joke, Connie,' said Astrid sharply. 'We're all responsible, all of us. How could we let that happen?' Now she was near to tears. She glanced at Richard Redoute. 'Cousin Vera told me that the same thing happened to her. But they took the baby away from her.'

He raised his fair brows.

'She spoke to you?' said Constance. 'Cousin Vera never speaks.'

'She does. Well, she whispers. But that was why she came here,' said Astrid sharply. '*They* sent her away.'

Richard looked at her coolly. 'I do concede, Astrid, that there was a degree of sanctuary in that arrangement. According to an aunt of my wife, Cousin Vera was in great distress and needed to get away.'

'Don't you see? We're all responsible.' She glared at him and he shrugged slightly.

'We will do all we can for the child Honesty,' he said abruptly. 'You may be sure of that, Astrid.'

Constance yawned and stood up. 'Such excitement! I swear my horrible sickness is liftin' its ugly fist. And this is before I even set foot on the train.'

The baby whimpered and Astrid jiggled her about until she stopped. 'Yes,' she said. 'We should start making arrangements. I should get Honesty back to her family.'

'Astrid!' protested Richard.

'Now, perhaps you would both leave? The baby needs to be changed. And that is a messy business.'

The General got to his feet immediately. Constance walked across and landed a sleepy kiss on Astrid's temple. 'Do you know?' she said. 'You are a most unlikely heroine of this drama?' Then she drifted past her father onto the corridor outside.

He stood in the doorway. 'Astrid . . .' he said.

She stared at him. To her, he looked like a stranger again. Like the distinguished bright-eyed man she'd met on the railway platform at the Springs. A stranger. 'Good morning, Richard,' she said.

His warm smile lit his face for a second. Then he stood up very straight, clicked his heels and gave her a very fine military salute. 'Goodbye, Astrid,' he said.

Later, she had just finished changing the baby on the bed when something rolled off the covers and clattered to the wooden floor. She knelt down and scrabbled for it. It was the gold sovereign.

'Oh, baby.' She climbed onto the bed, and lay beside the softly breathing child. 'How can such a beautiful thing as you come from all that?' Then she laid her head on the pillow beside her charge and fell fast asleep herself.

'Miss Astrid! Miss Astrid! Won't you wake up?'

Astrid clutched her arms but they were empty. Her head threshed wildly, then she saw a wicker bassinet by the bed with the baby in it. 'Is she all right? The babe?'

'She fine.' Aunt Beatrice nodded. 'I went off to the rummage room and found Miss Delphine's old crib. That babe's as snug as a nut in a husk.'

Astrid sat up stiffly. 'I should change. What time is it, Aunt Beatrice?'

'The clock downstairs has just struck half past nine, Miss Astrid. But there's something . . . the child, Miss Astrid. She's gone.'

Astrid glanced at the bassinet. 'But . . .'

'No, the other child. The little mother. Gone with her things in her pillowsack and all her spare shoes.'

Astrid strode past her and made her way down the corridor and up the narrow back staircase. Aunt Beatrice hurried after her. The little room was empty, the bed stripped and the blankets neatly folded and squared. There were no clothes hanging from the hooks beside the bed, no personal things on the chest under the tiny window. On the bare ticking pillow was a sheet of paper which said simply, *Give it to Miss Arstrid. She wil taek car. I am orl right. Honesty Leeming.*

'Go and get the General,' said Astrid. 'We must find her.'

Aunt Beatrice looked at her steadily. 'We can get the General to turn out his searchers, Miss Astrid. But she chose to go. She is very fit. With that young body she might never've had no baby. Had it late and closed up like a bud. She choose to go. What you gonna do? Send men after her with *hounds*?' A shadow of deep distaste crossed her face. 'The child will come back when she ready. Or not, if she not.'

'But Constance and I are going East. We must go now.' Astrid felt like crying, resentful of the solid certainties of the other woman.

'And same time ain't me and Cousin Vera going off East?' said Aunt Beatrice firmly. 'But the General, he keep watch for her here. He do that for you. You know that.'

'But we can't leave the babe with him,' wailed Astrid.

'Oh no, Miss Astrid. You heard what Honesty said, didn't you? You saw what she wrote. You must take the babe. You must take care of her. The child Honesty will take care of herself.'

Down below in Astrid's room the baby herself started to cry with the pure pain of hunger, erupting in wails which penetrated the castle walls. They raced back, and on cue Cousin Vera came along with her tray. Astrid lifted the baby and loosened her swaddling bands to free a single angry, flailing arm. 'Well, Rosebud,' she said. 'It seems that now there is only us, only you and me. Perhaps we'll find your little mama. But for now you'll have to make do with me. We both have such a lot to learn.' She sat in the chair and held the baby up to each window in the panorama. 'See? See that mountain? See those red rocks? No matter where you go, you will always know this is the place of your birth.' She looked up at Cousin Vera. 'Now,' she said. 'I'm all set.'

Twelve

The Nature of Refuge

3.30am

Essa Elliot stirred at the scuffling sound of dogs outside the van. A sharp elbow jammed itself into her ribs. '*See what that is, charver.*' Her mother's voice was numb and slurred with sleep.

She scrambled over her mother and squeezed by the bunk where her grandmother was snoring with her characteristic puppy snuffles. Outside, the residual shine from lamps in other parts of the camp lit on a dark outline at the bottom of the van steps, with a cotton sack at its feet. Essa sniffed. A girl. She smelt sweet, like a flower. 'Warris it?' said Essa in English. 'Whatd'ya want?'

'*The old woman. I want to talk to the old woman. The wise one.*' Honesty spoke in their own language. '*I'm called Honesty Leeming.*'

'*Grandma.*' Essa made her way down the steps. She threw the words behind her. '*A girl here wants you.*'

The van shook and creaked as the two older women came out, their feet bare, shawls clutched tight across their breasts: more a defensive gesture than one seeking warmth. The night, after all, was warm and dry – an enjoyable payback from the bright heat of a busy day. The girl stirred the embers of the fire and threw a stick on it to create more light. She drew three small stools closer to the flames. Then she pulled a shaved spill

225

of wood from the embers of the fire and lit a small lamp which she set beside her on the bottom step of the van.

The women sat on two of the stools. The old woman nodded at Honesty. '*Sit down, will you, child?*'

'She says sit down,' said the girl on the van steps.

'*I know that. I understand . . .*' Honesty pushed at the cotton sack with her foot and sat down. She arranged her wide red skirts around her. Her dress hung too loosely on her now. They all sat in silence and watched as the wood kindled and flickered and flared at the heart of the fire. At last the old woman said. '*So what is it, child?*'

'*You said I could come. You said it.*'

'*Why would a girl like you with a fine dress and leather shoes join poor travellers who have to ducker and trade for a living?*'

'*Those people at the castle are not my kind. And like I said, you remind me of my mother.*'

The woman leaned over and took Honesty's face in her hands. She glanced over at the girl on the steps, who brought across the lantern and held it so that its flickering light shone into Honesty's eyes. She blinked and struggled but could not escape the hard grip.

'*You have lost something. It is gone from you,*' the old woman said. Then she released her grip and Honesty fell back.

Honesty nodded. '*I didn't know. I didn't know about this thing. This thing that came away from me.*' She blinked away the tears that were welling in her eyes, letting them fall free.

A silence settled itself into the dark night.

Then, '*What is it you really want, charver?*'

'*I want to get away from here. The gorgio will come for me. I do not want them to know where I am. They will take me.*'

The men, drawn by the voices, had climbed down from their van and were now standing in a cluster just beyond the light. The old woman placed her hands squarely on her knees and hauled herself to her feet. She went across and spoke into the ear of the oldest man. Honesty's tears dried as she watched. The man grunted and the old woman raised her voice. Then he grunted again. The old woman came back to the fire. She kissed Honesty on the cheek. '*My name is Rodi. This girl here is my granddaughter Essa. This woman is my daughter Margaret. We will set out from here before the dawn. The gorgio will not know you were here.*' She nodded at her daughter, who followed her up the steps of the van.

Honesty stood up and bent to lift her cotton bag. Essa took it from her and hefted it into the van. '*It'll be a real squash,*' she said. Her face was wary, but not unfriendly.

'*I'll sleep under the rig,*' said Honesty. '*As long as I can travel with you.*'

'*No need, charver.*' Rodi's voice came from inside the van. '*Eight slept in here when we first set to travel in America. You come in, girl. Those bones of yours will need to rest after the trials of your day. We will set off before dawn and the gorgio, who did you ill, will be no wiser about you.*'

Honesty stooped to get into the narrow doorway. '*It was not the gorgio in that house that did me ill, Auntie. It was a gorgio in another great house a long time ago. In England. I know this now.*'

Rodi grunted as she settled again on her bunk. '*They are all the same. They steal your youth and your smiles and chain you to the ground with their wily words. It happened to my sister and we saw her no more. They say she is in Canada.*'

In the darkness Honesty took off her dress and her stays and, dressed just in her shift and drawers, squeezed in beside Essa. The space was so tight she was forced to tuck in behind the other girl and loop her arm around her. She closed her eyes and breathed in the thick smoky scent of Essa and the whole cluttered van. She thought of Keziah and Jack. She was tired and sore inside. She was bewildered at what had happened to her, at what had expelled itself from her body. But she felt safe now, and in the right place.

Outside the dogs barked a last chorus and settled down to a rustling silence. Up in the canyon the wild shadows of these domestic dogs howled to the moon. Then even they felt silent.

Honesty opened her eyes and stared across Essa's slumbering body into the darkness. She would not think of them up there in the castle. Those *gorgio*. She would not think of them. Not even Miss Astrid Benbow. Not even her.

Part Three

The Rose

Mid-June 1908

June 9 Russian Waters: King Edward VII of Britain and Czar Nicholas II of Russia, monarchs of the two largest empires on earth, meet on Russian waters off Reval on the Baltic Sea. The friendly family atmosphere is a relief to those accompanying the King. Keir Hardie, the Labour leader, has attacked the government for allowing the visit, claiming that the King is condoning the atrocities of the Czar

June 10 London: Parliament passes the Invalid and Old Aged Pensions Act

June 11 London: The Prince and Princess of Wales join 1,000 children from the slums on a trip to Epping Forest

June 22 America: Six black men accused of murder in Houston, Texas, are lynched

One

A Mission

Noon

'Can I go off now, Mrs Benbow?' Lal Burnip, the youngest garden boy, poked his head round the dusty glasshouse door. 'Joe Harrington says I've to leave messing about with the honeysuckle and gan down and help him free up the stream in Bottom Wood. Says that subsidence's dammed it up right good and proper an' we'll have a new lake down there if we're not careful. He says the watter'll back right up to t'house. More work, he says. We'll be bailing out till Christmas, he says. More work for us. 'S got a paddy on him today has that Joe.'

'Has he now?' Carmel looked up from her potting bench, which she'd dragged to the centre of the round house so that as she worked she'd have a straight view down the garden towards the pond. She always relished the straining brightness of her June garden, the visible order. The promise. 'And have you finished tying back the honeysuckle, Lal? I had to fight it back to get in here this morning. It seems to have grown yards in the night, right down over the gate.'

'That's 'cos a whole section of it fell ower, clean off the wall, missis. It was clinging to itself and fell sheer ower. Outgrowed its own strength. Funny that. Same thing happened to me own little sister. Outgrowed her strength. Flopping all over t'place, she was, until me mam put her on goat's milk.'

'I hope you're not proposing that we should feed the

231

honeysuckle with goat's milk.' Carmel enjoyed the boy's reluctant grin. 'So you think the poor thing needs tying back to the wall?'

'Aye. But Joe says I was to gan down there to help him see to the watter when the church clock struck twelve, finished or not . . .'

'Leave Joe to me.' She made a mental note to tell Jerry Carmedy to move Joe Harrington on to another place. He must be nineteen now. He'd made a good leading boy here since he'd come as a tough little shrimp at thirteen. He'd make a good head gardener somewhere where they would indeed give him his head. For her purposes he had just too much initiative these days; he was just too keen to take charge. She supposed that must be a sign of her success in training him.

Lal Burnip was still standing before her, moving from one leg to the other.

'Go!' she said. 'That poor drooping honeysuckle needs you!'

It was a relief when he closed the door and shut out the gush of crisp June air and with it the low level rage of other people's lives. The day was bright enough, but the air was still recovering from an unseasonal early chill. But it was snug inside the glasshouse and she was cosy in the swathe of air that licked towards her from the inner door into the peach-house.

Her own task today was to make decisions about the crucial selection of bulbs to lay down in the autumn. She had before her a new bulb catalogue from Slomerson's, who got their stock direct from Holland. Some of the new tulips were quite intriguing but she was not really enamoured of them. She thought them very contrived, like a woman too carefully dressed: very engaging, though somewhat cold. Still, they might make a nice show by the house, a splash of welcome.

She smiled as she made out her order. Welcome! She welcomed so few these days. No one wished to call on a recluse. Her refusal to engage made some people very cross. She'd received three tactful letters from her cousin and closest friend Margaret Seland on the subject. A month ago when she actually called in person Margaret had winced with distress at the sight of Carmel barrowing horse manure to some outside planting of her roses. Now this week, a letter in her cousin's immaculate, slightly cramped hand.

I am not sure, my dear Carmel – and never was – whether this is some kind of play-acting on your part or whether, as is whispered, you are entirely mad. Knowing you as the sane person you are I feel it must be the former. Some kind of theatre, perhaps. But even as a child how defiantly you went your own way! You and I both know how Uncle and Aunt quite despaired of getting you off their hands. Only a fellow eccentric such as Rufus could dig down to the pure gold so familiar, dearest Carmel, to those who love you. But then, further disaster! Living with him, God rest his soul, gave you carte blanche *to do what you would. So even marriage emboldened rather than tamed you.*

Now, my dear, the reason for this craven letter is to beg you to emerge from that hermit's cave of yours for once and dine with us on Saturday night. Our dear Gertrude has returned to us from the African wastes sans *the adventurer and, though rather subdued, is complaining about how quiet it is here in the north. Even worse, she complains of how aged everyone seems. And further, it appears now she has been tainted by recent convulsions among those vulgar women who demand the vote. She was arrested after joining them in some antics in London. However, the judge reprimanded her and mentioned her father and, thank God, merely fined her. Thank God also that everyone we know of any consequence is in the south of France. I am only here because of this wretched ankle which is taking so long to heal. (I will never venture into*

233

*the National Gallery again! Those stairs are impossible.
It will be no loss. The paintings are so impossibly
depressing.)*

*Though subdued, I fear that Gertrude still nurtures the
rebellion which is, alas, her second nature. There is talk
of her attending another meeting of those women in
Hyde Park. The place will be crawling with thousands,
hundreds of thousands of the creatures. No civilised
person will be safe. It should not be allowed. I cannot
think where she gets these disgusting ideas. Above all she
should know we should leave these things to wiser heads
than ours. I thank heaven her father is in France.
(Between you and me, he bolted as soon as he heard his
dear daughter would be here.)*

*It is interesting to hear that Michael John is home on
leave and poor Ambrose is home from school, being, as I
am,* hors de combat. *Bring them along! Gertrude's thirst
for youth shall be satisfied. So, my dear, an intimate
informal dinner with old friends to brighten her up! You
can tell us stories of dear Astrid in America. (London
simply drips with young Americans these days, here to
rob our poor girls of our nice young men. The lure of
American wealth is so hard to resist for our impoverished
younger sons.) Such a sensible girl, Astrid. So steady.
Please say yes, dearest Carmel, and lighten my load for
me. A chance for you to remove those terrible boots of
yours!*

Your friend always
Margaret S

*PS A rather boring domestic point. My housekeeper is
looking for a new housemaid. Of course she normally
deals with these things herself but she has persisted in
asking me about the girl who came from you last year. A
rather striking dark girl. Mrs McCoy tells me she was a*

*very hard.worker. She wonders whether she would still
be interested in retrieving her place at Seland?*
*PPS I have asked my man to wait for a response. Do not
hurry. He will wait.*

Carmel wondered why her cousin was concerning herself
with matters as trivial as a housemaid. She replied straight
away, saying that Honesty was no longer available but that she
would be pleased to come to dinner, although unfortunately
the boys were occupied elsewhere and would be unable to
accompany her. It was a relief to get rid of the sullen footman
who had delivered the letter. She continued to be surprised and
occasionally warmed by her cousin's persistence in their
friendship. These days Carmel made a habit of accepting only
one in ten of Margaret's invitations, although she did keep
contact through their fortnightly letters. She was reassured by
the fact that tonight would only be family company. At
Margaret's table she usually found herself between some minor
MP and a coal baron, or, even worse, someone who had known
Rufus and talked about him all evening.

Carmel wondered in passing how Margaret was handling
the social difficulties over Gertrude. Despite her being Lord
Seland's daughter, there were those who would refuse the
Honourable Gertude their table these days. As well as her
flirtation with those terrible suffragist women there was the
question of her ambiguous adventures with this South African.
It was not certain who this man was, whether they had been
married, or what exactly Gertrude's status was now. Lord
Seland himself had run off to France to avoid the embarrass-
ment of meeting his own daughter.

Little of this was to be found in Margaret's letters. Carmel
didn't know whether she was lucky or unlucky to be kept
informed of the details by Melanie Tyler, who on her afternoon
off had tea in Bishop Auckland with one of the housemaids
from Seland.

Carmel smiled wryly and turned over the page of her bulb catalogue. There was a certain irony in Lord Seland's scruples regarding his own daughter. At his coronation his lordship's idol, the King, had reserved a special section of the abbey for his mistresses and ex-mistresses. Margaret, who had been there, said so. She had a soft spot for the King herself, so it was said without rancour.

Jacob Ellenberg took one look at the photograph and held the newspaper to his eyes to read it more carefully. The print loomed into focus, describing the English King's visit to his kinsman the Czar of all the Russias. Apparently the visit was not approved of by some British politicians, one of whom called the Czar a 'common murderer'. In the distant reaches of his mind Jacob heard again the screams of women. He peered more closely at the paper. It seemed that, on being challenged regarding the persecution of the Jews, the Russian Prime Minister Mr Stolypin had said that they were going to make some new laws. Jacob sighed.

He looked up from his desk as the immaculate Melanie Tyler, trim in her afternoon apron, glided into the library bearing the lacquer post tray. She placed it in the centre of the small desk that Mrs Benbow used for her correspondence. She looked across at him. 'Cold luncheon set out for you in the morning room, Mr Ellenberg. Mrs Benbow too, though I doubt she'll get up from the garden for it. Your supper will be in there an' all, seeing as the missis is off to Seland for a grand dinner. Bit of a relief, I can tell you. The kitchen's in chaos with Mrs Mac on a crutch after that fall in the dairy. Mrs Benbow says to get a woman to help her but like I say to her, reliable help don't grow on trees.'

'The young men will not be in to lunch?' said Jacob, trying to keep his voice neutral. The thought of eating lunch opposite Michael John Benbow without the mediating presence of his mother had been haunting him all morning. Last night at dinner

Michael John had ignored him entirely. He was teasingly pleasant with his young brother, asking after people of their mutual acquaintance at school and querying the exact nature of the illness that had necessitated Ambrose's home leave. But he did not spare a glance in Jacob's direction.

Melanie said now, 'The young men are off for the day with Colonel Carmedy. They're to have lunch at the club, and then meet the pit managers, though the pit itself'll be closed, it being Saturday afternoon. Mebbe the Colonel thinks he's learning them the ropes. I don't know about that. It's not as if either of them lads'll ever dirty their hands with such things. Ambrose is too dainty and his nibs is too snooty. Or mebbe too busy shooting at fuzzy-wuzzies. Well, he will be when he gets back out to India.'

Melanie was leaning casually against the desk. These days she had reconciled herself to Jacob's ambiguous status in the house. On the one hand, she treated him with fair civility, and on the other she allowed herself to say bold, indiscreet things she would not have said to anyone of higher standing.

Jacob for his part treated Melanie with grave respect and ignored her indiscretions. He stood up now. 'That is so very kind of you, Mrs Tyler. To take the trouble to make lunch for me.'

He never put a foot wrong. You had to grant him that. 'All Mrs Mac's doing. Only cold meat and some cut beetroot, not pickled,' she added, to reduce the favour.

'Still. It is very kind.'

She nodded towards Mrs Benbow's desk. 'Letter there from Miss Astrid,' she said. 'You can tell from the writing.'

'Mrs Benbow will be pleased. Rare though her letters are, Miss Benbow has written such glowing reports of America. She was quite enamoured.' On some treasured evenings Mrs Benbow sat beside the fire here in the library and read the letters out loud to him. The letters read very well. Miss Astrid had quite a turn of phrase. 'It seems that Miss Benbow enjoyed her time in the Wild West. And now the sophistications of the Eastern seaboard of America?'

'Mebbe she was doing that. But this one's postmarked London. She must be there now.'

Jacob ventured out from behind Rufus's great desk. He took off his glasses and lifted the letter from the lacquer tray to peer at it more closely. 'So it does.'

'Mebbe Miss Astrid's coming back. Mebbe she's on her way right now.'

'Do you think perhaps Mrs Benbow would like to see the letter directly?'

'Wouldn't surprise me.'

'Perhaps someone should take it?' he ventured.

She shook her head firmly. 'My John's down in the cellar checking the racks, seeing as there's no dinner here tonight. After that he's off to put a towel over his head to steam off this cold he swears he has coming on. It's Mrs Mac's afternoon off. Says she's away at eleven thirty, her being not troubled about taking liberties. And I'm off now taking broth down to the Taggarts in Benbow, who've lost their dad in a pit-fall at the Red Daisy Pit. Mrs Benbow's orders. Don't see meself as Lady Bountiful, but there you are. Ten deaths in that pit this year. Mebbe they should do something about that. Stop killing them, mebbe.'

'Shall I take the letter to Mrs Benbow?' ventured Jacob.

She shrugged. 'Suit yourself. But if the letter says Miss Astrid's coming today Mrs Benbow will surely want to know. Me too. There'll be beds to sort.' She glided off, the ribbons on her bonnet flying, her starched apron crackling slightly as she walked.

He shrugged himself into his jacket and put on his outside spectacles. Gingerly he picked up the letter with its graceful writing, peered again to verify the London postmark, and tucked it into his inside pocket. A mission, he thought. How very nice to have a mission!

Two

Bad Business at the Mine

1.30pm

Benbow village: squat houses set round a central square of
tussocky grass, dominated by a very old oak which every spring
proclaimed itself a broad-leaf survivor of the original woodland
from which most of the Benbow estate was carved.

The main square was backed by four blocks of houses set in
a grid pattern, each block having its own patch of grass. These
were called respectively Top Green, Bottom Green, Colliery
Green and Bolter's Green – the latter after a legendary horse
that had bolted and overturned the equipage of a certain
choleric Benbow who had come to read the Riot Act to some
striking miners at the Red Daisy Pit which then, as now,
dominated the village.

The main row – flattered by the name of Main Street – ran
along one side of the main square and boasted (very loudly on
pay-nights) three public houses: the Admiral, the Benbow Arms
and the Oak Tree. Littered between them were three butcher's
shops, a grocer and general dealer, a hardware shop with a
yard, and two draper's shops whose windows glittered with
ornate china on one side and were snowed under by lace and
linen on the other.

The central edifice of this row was a small branch of the
Bishop Auckland Co-operative Society whose ornate frontage
belied its modest size. There was a cobbler's shop and a joiner's

yard, both run by miners who'd been injured early in life at the Red Daisy Pit. The rows on the other three sides of the green were each graced by a temple of worship that rose above the narrow stone cottages on either side. There was a Wesleyan Chapel, a Welsh Baptist Chapel and a Salvation Army Citadel – all sound buildings with hearty and intensely partisan congregations. The more grandiose Church of England, complete with obligatory rectory for its gentleman incumbent, nestled by the Hall at the site of the old village nearly a mile away. Only a few families made their way back along to this elegant building, although the vicar's wife was very keen on the Good Works she did among 'her' mining community of Benbow.

At the corner of the square by the colliery gate was the colliery office, a tall, substantial building with wide double doors. Alongside it was the Reading Room, a narrow building with tall windows and a doorway graced by stone columns. This building was Rufus Benbow's conscience in stone: he'd had it built one year on returning home after delivering a paper in Prague on the persecution of gypsies. In walking the bounds one day he'd ventured into one of the Benbow miners' cottages and blushed at the sight of the overcrowding and the conditions under which his own workers lived. He had the Reading Room built and donated a collection of two hundred books. The estate continued, even today, to add ten books a year to the collection and to pay for improving monthly periodicals. Colonel Carmedy had tried and failed to convince Carmel that this expense was unnecessary in these hard-pressed times.

Before their visit to Benbow village Colonel Carmedy, Michael John and Ambrose had availed themselves of a very good lunch at the Gentleman's Club in Bishop Auckland: a good deal of roast beef and not too many vegetables, washed down with a bottle of claret and topped off with half a bottle of port. The talk was mostly of army matters and India, where Michael

John, now a subaltern, was to return within the fortnight.

Jerry Carmedy, given total charge of Michael John by Mrs Benbow the day he nearly killed his brother, felt paternally proud of the boy's showing with the regiment. By all accounts he'd buckled to in an admirable fashion, and he certainly cut a fine figure in his uniform. It had not been all smooth sailing. There had been a problem in the early days with some other chap who'd taken a dislike to Michael John. In the end, Michael John had been driven to give the fellow a good thrashing. Colonel Carmedy had travelled down to the barracks to endorse the ticking off given to Michael John by his brigadier. But in private the brigadier told Carmedy that it had just been soldierly horseplay. The other chap, quite a weakling, had gone off to lick his wounds on his uncle's farm in Africa. Probably the chap shouldn't have been in the army in the first place. No more was to be said. It seemed the brigadier, like Carmedy, had a soft spot for Michael John Benbow, thought he promised to be a sound regular soldier.

Sentiment aside, the colder, calculating side of Carmedy recognised that keeping in with Michael John had its wisdom. Mrs Benbow would not last for ever and he needed to look after the lucrative free hand he had with the Benbow estate. Michael John was the heir, after all.

The dining room at the club was crowded and the three of them had been obliged to share a table with an acquaintance of Carmedy, a Mr Kilburn, a nail manufacturer who was a leading citizen of the town; also a Liberal and a musician. He was a tall stooping man with a pale face and rather too much silver-grey hair. He ate his way steadily through his heavily laden plate while the Colonel and Michael John discussed the army and Ambrose ploughed through his own substantial meal.

Then, in a lull, Mr Kilburn shot a question at Ambrose. 'You're for the army also, my boy?'

Michael John snorted, then choked over some potato.

Ambrose looked into the man's clear eyes. 'Mr Kilburn, I'd rather nail my hand to a barn door than shoot a sparrow, still less another human being . . . sir,' he said very distinctly.

'Fat lot of good for the Empire if everyone was a shirker like you,' growled Michael John. Colonel Carmedy rumbled heartily in agreement.

Mr Kilburn took a sip of his water and smiled at Ambrose. 'I trust you wouldn't think of using one of my rather well made nails to do the deed, my boy.' He cut a small potato in half and popped it into his mouth. 'What do you do, then, if you don't shoot sparrows?'

'He doesn't play rugby,' said Michael John. 'Not tennis. Not even cricket. Duffer at lessons too. Shirking off school even today, don't you know?'

'So what do you do at school?' said Mr Kilburn.

Ambrose shrugged. 'I play the flute. Not too well. I play chess.' He paused. 'I hate and loathe school. Music and chess are all that make it bearable.'

Mr Kilburn undid his napkin from his shirt-button. 'Well then, my boy! You must think of joining our orchestra. We rehearse on Tuesday and Thursday nights in the town hall.' Mr Kilburn's voice had only the slightest local intonation. He took a card from his card case and put it into Ambrose's hand. 'Come and play for me in the morning. Ten thirty. Just before chapel. We'll see if you may come and join us. We're in desperate need of some young blood.' He stood up, pulled down his waistcoat and fastened his jacket. He nodded to Jerry Carmedy and Michael John. 'Good to meet you again, Colonel, and you, Lieutenant Benbow. You should persuade your brother to join my orchestra, sir. There is discipline in music just as there is in soldiering.' He looked down at Ambrose. 'Join the orchestra and I'll find a job for you at my workshop. Clerking. Nice and clean. Good day to you, gentlemen.' He marched out, a tall, slightly stooping figure who drew looks of recognition and greetings the whole length of the dining room.

'Cheeky fellow!' said Michael John. 'Clerking!'

'Very substantial man,' said the Colonel thoughtfully. 'Good businessman, leading citizen, underwrites this orchestra, don't you know. A Liberal, but no one's perfect. He's friend to a musician feller called Elgar. Has him to stay at his house, don't you know? Can't say whether I'd care for that myself. Musician in the house.' His tone suggested it might be rather like having a rabid cat on your hearth. He drained the last of the port. 'Worst about Kilburn though, he's one of those temperance wallahs. Never touches a drop.'

As it was Saturday and the day was fine and the houses in Benbow were small, the whole of the population seemed to have spilled onto the streets. Carmedy's carriage wove its way through the village under the watchful eyes of both men and women who clustered in separate groups in the doorways and along the walls, attended by children, dogs and poultry, all more or less on free wander.

On Colliery Green (specially rolled and nurtured by the pitmen themselves for the purpose), they saw a full blown game of football in progress. The pitch was complete with home-made posts and line markings of powdered chalk. On Bottom Green three boys were playing King of the Castle on a rusted, abandoned pit wagon that had been turned on its side. On Bolter's Green groups of barefoot children were playing games of tip-cat, chasey and a peculiar brand of slogging cricket. On the central green the oak tree shivered with climbing, swinging bodies.

As this was to be an educational visit, Carmedy drove slowly through the web of streets to point out to his young charges their heritage and their responsibilities. Such a set-up, he said, could only come at a cost. His ultimate destination was the colliery office. The ostensible reason for the visit was to discuss a report on recent injuries underground with the pit manager and his assistant. The death the previous week of one of their miners had not been the first this year. And there were the costly new guidelines on compensation. Their shareholders would not be happy about the implications of those guidelines in the light of the recent accidents. There would be questions at the board meeting next week. Things were slipping. Everyone knew that. That is, except these two boys, of course. And their mother.

The sight of the good-looking young officer at Carmedy's side caused a ripple of interest among the bystanders. Two raucous whistles made Michael John swing round. A wall of innocent faces, male and female, faced him. He flushed, then wrinkled his nose. 'Is there nothing to be done about this ghastly smell, Colonel?'

Carmedy laughed shortly. 'That's the smell of money, dear boy. The smell of the colliery and the coal spilling into those railway wagons; the smell of the train that will take it out to Hartlepool to be shipped to London. It's the smell of the people we need to win the coal for us, people whom we must house at the least cost to the estate.'

'Why must it be so whiffy?' said Michael John, frowning.

'So it's not just the colliery that makes the stink?' said Ambrose quickly. 'It's how we house these people, isn't it?'

'Well, it might well be the people with their privies and their rather malodorous yards. Certain busybodies do blame us for not maintaining the houses like palaces, because the people have no other means to wash themselves beyond a single tap in the yard and a tin bath. We are blamed because they keep their coals in a cupboard. When we tell them there's no money for a tap in each house they whine like pigs.' The Colonel sniffed.

'Shouldn't we make it better?' said Ambrose. 'They're our houses, aren't they?'

Carmedy laughed. 'You may make that suggestion to our shareholders next week at the board meeting, if you wish. It will raise a few smiles. They want their profits. We have to pay them before we pay ourselves. There's little left for such elaborate house maintenance.'

'If there weren't all the shareholders we could make it better, couldn't we? Ourselves?'

Carmedy pulled on the reins and stopped outside the colliery office. 'Probably not. We'd have to give rather more priority to the cost of the new safety measures, the buying of the new safety pump, the cost of shoring up against the moving stone in end galleries. We will certainly have to discuss all that at the shareholders' meeting next week. At Benbow we have always teetered on the edge, Ambrose. There is no great profit in mining these days. The estate owns a good deal of land and many assets, but there is nothing spare to maintain the houses. In my view it's the people's own responsibility to keep their homes up to scratch. We pay their wages. Sometimes there are three wages going into a single house. We give them the house. They should take care of it. A bit of handiwork and organisation wouldn't come amiss instead of loafing around in the sun. Or playing football.'

'If we're that short perhaps I should work in the nail shop,' said Ambrose thoughtfully 'Save the school fees, earn some money.'

'You do talk rot, Amby.' Michael John laughed. 'You're not just a coward, you're insane.'

'Now, boys!' Carmedy jumped down and handed the reins to a child who was standing by the road, cap in hand, ready to hold the horse for a small fee. Carmedy set off up the steps.

Michael John stepped down, pulling down his tunic and smoothing it onto his thighs with his hands.

'Now who's a bonny lad, then!' Three women were standing in the sunshine with their bottoms hooked onto a window sill. The oldest, a woman with pulled-back hair and one tooth missing, nodded and grinned as she spoke. The youngest, a girl with curly hair and a round face, moved in front of them. She winked first at Michael John and then at Ambrose. 'So what they ca'al thee then, kiddah?' she said.

'Get out of my way, will you?' Michael John put out a hand and pushed her violently so she fell onto the dirt path. He strode on through the wide doorway of the colliery office.

Ambrose leaned down to help the girl up. 'I'm sorry,' he said. 'My brother has this foul temper.'

She stood up and brushed down her skirt. 'Nee bother,' she said.

'Our name is Benbow,' he said. 'He is Michael John and I am Ambrose.'

'I know that. Them women telt us that.' She blinked at him. 'I'm called Gwennie Taggart,' she said.

The older woman called across. 'If thy name's Benbow tha wants ter get them netties of ours cleaned out proper, and fix the water taps on Bolter's Green. Nowt but sludge comin' out and them hussies come over here and steal our water.'

'I'm sorry, I . . .'

'Gan on, son, get inside and tell yer betters a'al about it. Tha't nowt but a child thiself.'

The other woman spoke up. 'I don't know. Me own lad's syem age. An' he's down Red Daisy six days and canna get clean watter to wash hisself with.'

The older woman laughed. 'Aye, but they breed'm softer t'other side of the hill.' She nodded calmly at Ambrose. 'Gan on, pet.'

Released at last from the compelling gaze of the women, Ambrose scrambled through the doorway and welcomed the sanity of the bright brass door handles and the smell of beeswax polish. He'd been bored at the thought of this visit, pushed on him by the unholy alliance between his mother and Carmedy. Now he looked forward to the meeting in the colliery office and felt that he might even screw up the courage to ask some questions.

*   *   *

Melanie Tyler caught sight of the Colonel's rig outside the colliery office as she drove Mrs Benbow's governess cart into the square and pulled up at No. 27 where, according to the note in her pocket, the Taggarts lived. The curtains in the narrow windows were drawn, the door was tight shut. Sitting in the next doorway was a woman with a small child at her feet and a baby on her knee. She watched Melanie jump down from the cart. 'You lookin' for Mrs Taggart?' she said.

Melanie stared at the woman and her children. One day, in another world, she'd been such a child, playing barefoot in the dirt by her mother's knee. But she'd lifted herself out of that. For a while at Seland Hall she thought she'd hit the real heights. Then down with a bump at Benbow. But, compared with all this, even Benbow Hall was not so bad. She leaned back into the cart and picked up the heavy basket. 'Yes,' she said.

'She's in a bad way about her man,' said the neighbour. 'She's like a woman off. Never seen a woman like it.'

'She will be,' said Melanie. 'Losing her husband like that.'

'Tell yer what, missis. Lucky, my man was. He was just alongside Bill Taggart at the fall. Missed him by inches.'

Melanie nodded. She knocked on the door. 'Very lucky,' she agreed. She knocked on the door again, and waited. No one came.

'Just go in,' said the woman. 'She'll be there. She's not comin' to the door. Like I said, she's in a bad way. Just go in.'

Melanie lifted the latch and opened the door into a shadowy kitchen. It was empty. A low fire glimmered in the gleaming grate. A neat clipped-wool mat warmed the scrubbed stone floor. A table under the window was littered with piles of baking bowls; another in the centre was covered by a chenille cloth. Four chairs. A worn wooden rocking chair stood still by the fire. An immaculate pair of men's pit boots, highly waxed, were perched on the fender and shone in the light from the fire. On the wall a hanging clock ticked away into the silence.

'Mrs Taggart?' Melanie called softly. 'Are you here?'

Wendy Robertson

There was a stirring in the scullery and a woman came through the pulled curtain. 'Who is it?' She looked at Melanie with blank eyes. Neatly dressed, she might have been any age from twenty to forty. She looked lost, as though she'd wandered into the wrong house.

'I'm Mrs Tyler, sent from the Hall by Mrs Benbow. We are sorry for your loss.' She placed the basket carefully on the table. 'Mrs Benbow sent a few things.'

Mrs Taggart stared at the basket. 'We buried him yesterday, you know. Had to bury him in the graveyard at St Luke's. Bill wouldn't a liked that. Baptist to the bone.'

'We're very sorry for your loss,' repeated Melanie.

'What about the house?' said Mrs Taggart, sharply now. 'Our house here?'

Melanie looked round. 'Looks very nice,' she said. 'Although, the curtains being drawn, it's hard to see everything.'

'No, not that.' Mrs Taggart was impatient now. 'The coll'ry'll tak it from us. We'll be in the workhouse, our Gwennie and me.'

'Well . . .' said Melanie helplessly. She touched the basket. 'There are some things for you in there.'

Mrs Taggart sat down beside the table and stared at the basket. 'Is there a house in there?'

Melanie sat down opposite her. 'Can you cook?' she said.

'Anyone can cook,' said the woman wearily. 'What a daft question.'

'Do you like cooking?'

'Best thing a woman does. Look, what is this?'

'Do you know where Benbow Hall is?'

'Everyone knows that. I seen it through the trees from the Auckland bus.'

Melanie glanced at the clock. 'Come there at five o'clock. Come to the big door at the side. Ring the bell.'

'What for should I do that?'

'Like you say, with your husband gone, the coll'ry'll take this house. This week, next week, next month. Mebbe I can do

248

sommat that might get you some work, somewhere to live, both. Just mebbe.'

'But I'm not . . .'

Melanie stood up and moved closer to her in the gloom. She fixed her with a stern gaze. 'Look, Mrs Taggart. Your man's gone. You've buried him. You have to get on.' She went to the door. 'Five o'clock!' she said over her shoulder. 'Set out at half past four. Come!'

At the meeting Ambrose did pluck up the courage to ask questions about the privies and the water but Mr Neville, the pit manager, smiled kindly and said such things would have to be dealt with at the shareholders' meeting. Then he went through the report on the stone-fall that caused the death of Taggart. The coroner – a good friend of the Colonel – had, fortunately, recorded death by misadventure. However, he did advise a more rigorous report on the cause of the accident than that offered by the company.

Now this new report showed in immaculate detail that Taggart himself, who as drawer was responsible for withdrawing the props and collapsing the face, had made an error of judgement and brought down the roof on himself. The company was not liable. This was clear. There would be no compensation.

Ambrose saw Mr Neville exchange a glance with Carmedy. 'What if we were liable, Colonel?' he said. 'What would happen then?'

The Colonel shrugged. 'We would have to pay compensation. Very unusual, dear boy. Not likely at all. In any case, the colliery has no money for any compensation.'

'But let's hypothesise . . .'

Michael John, who was sitting tapping his boot on the floor with boredom, spluttered. '*Hypothesise!* Steady on, old boy.'

'But how will that family live?' said Ambrose earnestly. 'If we are not liable?'

'Well,' said Carmedy thoughtfully. 'Fortunately, as this report shows, that is not our concern.' He gathered up his thin leather document case and his cane. 'Well, Neville. All prepared for Thursday, then?'

They all stood up and shook hands.

'When will you deal with the water and the privies?' said Ambrose. 'Can I come to that meeting?'

Mr Neville and Carmedy exchanged glances again.

'Your interest, dear boy, is commendable,' said Carmedy. 'But, alas, you will have returned to school on that date.'

When they came out of the colliery office it was raining and the square and the pit-rows were deserted. Carmedy asked Ambrose to pull up the hood and they set off at a brisk trot towards the Hall. Just past the forge they had to pull over to let a rather smart rig manoeuvre its way past them in the other direction. Pulled by two very fine greys it was driven by a tall, broad-shouldered man in fine tweeds. His sharp features were made sharper by a dark beard and side-whiskers. He barely slowed down as he swung past.

When the road was clear Carmedy eased back to the centre. 'Who was that blighter?' said Michael John crossly. 'Cretin thinks he owns the road.'

Carmedy urged his horses back to a steady trot. 'I thought you might recognise him,' he said. 'Name of Jack Lomas. Gypsy feller. Son to the horse woman in whom your dear mother takes such a kind interest. The horse woman must have found him that fine pair of greys.'

'How can he drive a rig like that?' growled Michael John. 'Must have stolen it.'

Carmedy laughed. 'Far from it, dear boy. All above board. The gypsy's an inventive feller. Deals in odd designs that change the way a thing works. Arms manufacturer in Newcastle got wind of a modification he made on a rifle that makes a much faster reload. Invited him up there to develop it. Now they sell it with a royalty to him, I'm told. He has his own workshop up there, developing new ideas, and is subcontracted to the arms man. Owns three ironmongeries in South Durham and has his fingers in a few pies. He wanted to buy shares in our company, but I suggested to your mother that perhaps it would be ill-advised.'

'Cheek,' said Michael John.

'If he did have shares,' said Ambrose thoughtfully, 'perhaps he'd have taken care of the water and the privies. What do you think?'

Three

A World in the Making

1pm

Carmel scanned the letter. 'My daughter! How she keeps us in the dark. Astrid's here, Mr Ellenberg! In England. In fact she's probably in Yorkshire at this very moment steaming towards us on the train. They arrive in Bishop Auckland late this evening. How marvellous these trains are!' Carmel smiled up at Jacob Ellenberg who was standing in the doorway of the glasshouse, still shaking out his large black umbrella. She peered at the letter. Then she frowned. 'She's bringing her friend Miss Redoute . . . my goodness . . . and a baby. A baby!' She turned the paper over as though its reverse side might give her more vital information. 'She says that young Honesty is staying in America, as she's joined some travellers and finds it more to her liking. Her liking! What will Keziah say?' She turned back the paper and peered at the postscript that was scrawled sideways in the margin. 'It seems the baby's mother died and the child was put into my daughter's safe-keeping.' She smacked her potting bench with the flat of her hand, and sent a terracotta pot rolling to the edge. 'Safekeeping!'

Jacob caught the plant pot and set it right on the table.

Carmel went on. 'Problems, problems. It's all so annoying.' At least she'd managed to turn the problem of Michael John over to Colonel Carmedy and he was making quite a good fist of it. The problem of Astrid and this alien baby she'd have to face herself.

Jacob smiled at her. 'So your daughter returns. You are very lucky.'

Carmel looked at him carefully. 'Do you have daughters, Jacob?'

'Once I had a daughter.' He paused. He thought again of the Czar of all the Russias. 'But today we talk only of your daughter who returns to the heart of her family.'

Carmel frowned. 'She has been so rarely here, hasn't she? After Rufus died, not at all. Except for that last time, that single day before she fled again. The day she went off to America with Constance and Honesty in such a hurry. Do you remember? Since then I think I have missed her more than ever before. Isn't that strange?' She laughed shortly. 'I must be getting old.'

He clicked his heels and bowed towards her. 'Mrs Benbow, you are eternal.'

This brought a laugh from her. She stood up. 'I should go and see Keziah, Mr Ellenberg. She'll be sad that the girl Honesty has not returned, though she may not show it. It pains me to say it but she's closer to Honesty than I ever was to Astrid.'

Good companions, they walked together back through the late spring meadow down towards the house. The rain had stopped falling but the wet grass soaked into their boots. The bruised smell of bluebells sat in the air. As they were going through the arch by the side door they came across a rather damp Melanie Tyler jumping down from the governess cart.

Carmel told her about Astrid and Constance, omitting any mention of a baby. Melanie threw up her hands. 'We're short-handed as it is, Mrs Benbow, with Mrs Mac lame as a dog and on her afternoon off, and my John languishing with a cloth over his head convinced he has pneumonia.'

Carmel, who knew of all this, frowned. 'It seems that we need a little extra help.'

Melanie took a deep breath and told her about Mrs Taggart. Carmel beamed. 'What a wonder you are, Melanie. Two matters solved at a stroke! You must take this woman on straight away. I'll be far too busy at five to see her, but you must set her on and see how she goes. There are rooms in Mrs Mac's cottage for the time being.'

Melanie wondered what Mrs Mac would think of that, but said nothing.

'Now then!' Carmel went on. 'Take care that you and Mrs Mac share the woman properly between you, Melanie. At least for today Mrs Mac needs the most help, though of course you'll need help with the beds and the rooms for tonight.' She held out her hand for the reins. 'I'll take the trap and go to see Keziah Leeming. She should know that Honesty won't be coming home.' She climbed up onto the cart, turned the horse with remarkable expertise and made her way back down the lane through the dripping trees.

Jacob and Melanie stood side by side until she vanished from sight. 'Just like that!' said Melanie. 'Just like that.'

'Perhaps, Mrs Tyler, you will tell me why you are so troubled? Has not Mrs Benbow just agreed to your request for some help?' Jacob wondered whether he should tell her about the baby, then abandoned the idea.

'Well, think about it, Mr Ellenberg. I have this poor grieving woman coming at five o'clock, who might or might not take to working with Mrs Mac who will be just coming in from her afternoon off. The woman's husband has just died in the pit and I'm supposed to set her on lighting fires and turning back beds the second she comes through the door.'

Jacob stood back to let her enter the house before him. 'Mrs Tyler, Mrs Benbow is a unique person,' he said. 'She has her own ways. She has put you in charge of affairs, which one might think would be a very fine compliment for you.'

'Put like that . . .' she said. 'But what if this poor widow woman flees?'

'In that case I could light fires or turn back some beds? I am very willing.'

Melanie had to smile at this. 'We would have to be very desperate for that, Mr Ellenberg. You just go in that library and write in your books.' They parted inside the side door. 'But I thank you for your kind thought,' she called over her shoulder.

Carmel stopped at the forge and tethered her pony beside a fine sprung rig with a pair of greys standing quietly between its shafts. Freddy Leeming was leaning on his anvil, drinking water from a long stoneware jug. Despite the brighter afternoon he made a shadowy figure against the hot forge fire that glowed behind him. He wiped his mouth with the back of his hand. 'Keziah's not up in the *vardo*, Mrs Benbow. She's at the cottage. Our Edith's put her in the parlour with young Jack, that's visiting today. High tea.' He nodded at the immaculate rig. 'Only the parlour's good enough for our Jack these days.'

'So he's a very grand visitor?'

'Nowt grand about him. It's our Edith. Her and me went in the train to visit him in his new house in Durham. Our Edith loved it.' He sighed. 'It has four downstairs rooms. She was quite overcome.'

Carmel frowned. 'But Keziah . . .'

'Nah, she didn't go. Too busy to be running after the likes of him. Don't like houses anyway. She's fixed him up with them hosses, though. Fine flesh.' He nodded his head towards the gleaming animals tethered to the rail. 'And got that rig from a housebound gypsy mate of hers. Fine craftsman. Wouldn't take a penny off our Jack for it. Says Jack must test it first. He's gonna drive it back to Durham. He has stables too, close by that house with four downstairs rooms.' He sighed, as though this was a great tragedy.

'Jack's done very well. A changed man.'

'Always was clever, like we know. Then your old library feller taught him proper figuring. He took to that. After that no one'll swindle that lad. The things he makes, all kinds of folks want. You know how it is: they see a simple gypsy lad and they think they can cod him. Well, he meks them think again.'

Carmen laughed. 'Freddy, you're as proud of him as if he were your own son.'

'He's all the son I've ever had and better to me than many sons would be.'

'They're up at the cottage?'

'Like I say, our Edith's made them tea.'

Tea was set in the cluttered cottage parlour. The table was laden with scones and cakes and bread spread thickly with butter. Edith, presiding behind the teapot, stood up quickly when Carmel entered. Jack did the same and as he towered there the small parlour seemed to shrink.

'Sit down, sit down! You look like Samson with all that hair, Jack. Makes you look thirty years old at least.' Carmel flapped her hand and sat down herself. 'My apologies, Edith, for walking straight in but I could hear the laughter and I didn't think you'd hear my knock.'

Edith stayed standing. 'Ah'll get you a cup, Mrs Benbow.' Too quickly to be stopped, she slipped out of the room.

Jack sat down. 'Afternoon, Mrs Benbow.' He nodded.

'What is it, Carmel?' said Keziah. She surveyed her friend. 'An't it something big that would bring you this far on a good Saturday?'

Carmel looked round. 'This looks like something of a celebration,' she said.

'It's poor old Edith,' said Keziah. 'She comes over all strange when our Jack comes home.'

Jack reached for a cake. 'Not fair to Edith, Keziah. She thinks a lot of this family. Give credit.'

'Oh, I give credit,' said Keziah rather crossly. 'I give credit.'

Carmel turned her attention to Jack. 'That's a fine rig out

there, Jack. And Freddy tells me you have a fine house in Durham.'

'A house!' said Keziah in disgust.

'It's handy for the train to Newcastle,' he said. 'An' the train back here's no bother neither. But in a little while I'll get one of them cars with a motor so it'll be more than easy.' His voice was not the liquid gypsy speech of his youth. Spliced into its deep notes now were the quaint rounded vowels of Jacob Ellenberg, and the broad emphatic tones of the northern businessmen with whom Jack spent so much time these days. It was a strange mixture but it gave him articulateness and authority beyond his years.

'What is it, Carmel?' said Keziah sharply. 'You've come on a message, I can tell.'

'My daughter Astrid is on her way home. She arrives tonight.' Carmel put up a hand as though to ward off any optimism. 'But I fear Honesty's not with her.' She took the letter from her pocket. 'It seems Honesty has linked up with a troop of gypsies and is travelling in the western parts of America.'

Edith walked into the parlour with a fresh china cup and saucer and was stopped by the wall of grim silence.

Keziah nodded, granite-faced. 'Well perhaps the *charver* knows her travellin' roots better than some, after all.' She glared malevolently at Jack.

Jack scowled at Carmel. 'Your daughter left our Honesty alone in a foreign country? She shouldn't a done that. She should have brought her back. She's a child, a little'n.'

'She must be sixteen now,' said Carmel lamely. 'And she can't be alone because she made friends with these people. She chose it.'

'What'd you think if it was your daughter and she was sixteen? Adrift in a foreign land, half a world from home? Linking up with foreigners?'

'They're not foreigners. They're *romani* like you.'

257

'You don't know that. It's a foreign land.'

'Jack!' said Edith. 'Don't you talk to Mrs Benbow in that tone. What are you learning up there in Newcastle?'

'Dinnat carp, Jack,' said Keziah. 'Honesty always knew her own mind. Now, Carmel, you'll be having one of our Edith's scones?' She pushed the laden plate towards Carmel and asked, 'How's them new roses comin' on then? It's a week since I was up in that garden of yours. I need some lavender so mebbe I could get up there tomorrow to do a bit of harvesting.'

Carmel stayed talking for half an hour then rose to go. They all stood up. 'I'm going to supper tonight at Seland Hall,' she said, 'and must rouse poor John Tyler up from his sickbed to take me. I suppose I could drive myself. But then he'll still have to go to the station to collect Astrid.'

Keziah glanced at Jack.

'I'll take you,' he said, unsmiling. 'I'll take you up to the Hall and get the travellers from the station. It'll give them new horses of mine a stretch.'

'Aye,' said Keziah, 'our Jack'll take yer.' The matter was settled. 'What time?'

'To get to Seland at six. Half past five, perhaps?'

Jack took a heavy gold watch from his waistcoat pocket and surveyed it. 'Hour and a half. I'll be there. Earlier mebbe, as I need to see Jacob Ellenberg.'

'Good. Good,' said Carmel slowly, hiding her annoyance at his show of confidence. 'Thank you, Jack. I'm sure John Tyler will be eternally grateful.'

As she drove home Carmel contemplated her sudden spurt of anger at Jack Lomas's arrogance. She should be pleased about it, really. It was like putting together two kinds of rose. You went about it carefully, methodically. You were sure of the dominance of one colour, one characteristic. But then came something astonishing, unexpected. Sometimes it was a glorious affect of colour, or an intriguing habit; sometimes it was a fundamental change surprising to the point of ugliness:

regrettable, something to be thrown into the bin at the end of the glasshouse.

So what was Jack Lomas? She'd put him together with Jacob Ellenberg: two unusual specimens, both outsiders, both clever and resourceful. The older one shy and discreet, the younger flamboyant, intensely creative and somehow secret. Thinking further, she saw that the fertile ground in which the new Jack Lomas had grown was her own open household, created by Rufus and then fertilised by her own love of the unusual, her dislike for boundaries.

Now here was this new Jack Lomas, made rich from his royalties on the gun mechanism, inventing new fal-de-fals for the eager and competing arms manufacturers. This Jack had a gold watch, a house in Durham with four downstairs rooms and a stable. His maturity and confidence were at odds with his youth. He had grown up far in excess of her own Michael John, despite the boy's elegant uniform and his swagger stick.

So this was surely a glorious pollination, a new strain to be proud of. So why was she feeling uneasy? Why did she feel that some mark had been overstepped? Perhaps what she'd said to Jacob Ellenberg was right. Perhaps she was getting old.

She whipped the pony on. There were still some tasks to perform. There'd be time to brief the garden boys on the raising of the early potatoes and the delivery of a substantial basket of fruit and vegetables to the house, to feed their visitors. She would gather flowers for Melanie to arrange. The show this spring had been very good.

Then she would review her second year pollinations and complete her daybook in the glasshouse. It was good to hear of Astrid's return but she would not change her routine. She would get back to the house just in time to get changed for Margaret Seland's supper. Everything would be fine. Melanie Tyler was very capable.

She urged the pony on.

* * *

Jack let himself quietly into the library. Jacob Ellenberg was in his usual chair behind the desk but he had dropped off to sleep, his balding head gleaming whitely through his thinning hair. The fire was low, so Jack went and knelt down to rake it out and build it up.

Jacob stirred. 'Home again? Nice to see you, my boy.'

Jack sat back on his heels and watched as the old man came from behind the desk, his hand out in greeting. Jack got to his feet and shook it heartily. 'Nice to see you, Mr Ellenberg. It's been a few months, an't it?'

They sat down by the fireside and surveyed each other. 'You get taller,' said Jacob finally. 'And you are now a hairy man.'

Jack's teeth gleamed through his beard. 'You look no different,' he said. 'Except you're losing a bit of hair.'

'We all change as we grow. Are you here for a purpose, dear boy, or is this merely a social visit?'

'I had to collect a rig and some horses that Keziah found me. A fine pair of greys.'

'No finer judge of a horse. Seb Golightly has always told me this. And you, dear boy. Are you flourishing?'

Jack nodded. 'Those Newcastle men can't get enough of me. I have a royalty on the repeater, which earns me a deal of money each month. They must be making thousands of guns, Jacob. Hundreds of thousands. If there an't no war there will be one soon. So many guns'll need targets.'

'I fear you are right. Fortune and war go hand in hand. The gun-makers will be hungry for it.'

'I benefit meself, Jacob, so cannot complain.'

'And you do other things for these gun men?'

'Aye. They had us up to their works. Told us to look at their method, their guns and cannons. Then I tell'm what they might do better.'

'And they do it?'

'Well, they listen to all my notions. I fake stuff up in my workshop then they say yea or nay.'

'And they pay for each one? If it works or not?'

'Thanks to you I make sure it's all down on paper tied up nice and neat before we start. One sum if they don't take it up. More and a royalty if they do.'

'So it is well that you did not go and work for them directly?' Jack and Jacob had sat and talked long into the night when the gun-maker had offered him a highly paid job in his development department.

'Good job I didn't do that. I make more in a week's royalties than I'd have earned in salary for a month. They knew what they were doing. This way I have all sorts coming. I had some Russians last week. They were drenched in scent. Place stank like a bawdy house. And Germans. They smell of carbolic soap.'

'And will you sell to them? To make guns that may kill your countrymen?'

Jack shrugged. 'I haven't done that yet 'cause the Newcastle men are so keen. I can dangle the Russians before them and they give me a bigger fee, or they up the royalty.'

Jacob sat back in his chair. 'How little we knew those nights when we were sitting in here doing our mathematics. That you would end up an important man. Ayee. A rich man.'

Jack laughed, not worried about being teased by this kindly man. 'Without you, Jacob, I'd be selling horses down the country for my mother.'

Jacob shook his head. 'Not you, Jack. You're bound to succeed. It's your destiny. You are a man of this century, a man who will make his way.'

'Well, old friend, I came today because I want to make my way further.'

'I can't think I can help you further, Jack. So far, now, you have gone from me.'

'Not that far. I want something from you. What I want you to do for me is either sell me your coalmine, or sell me a half share in it.'

'The mine? Oh, I forget about the mine. The Colonel takes care of it and deposits something for me at my bank each year.'

'And you know nothing about it? How it is run? What is its profitability?'

Jacob shrugged. 'Mrs Benbow arranged for the Colonel to do it. It was a kindness. It would be terribly bad manners to question it.'

Jack sighed. 'You're such a good old man. But how d'you know Carmedy's not rooking you? Rooking Mrs Benbow? There's something about that feller . . .'

'Don't say such things, Jack. He is devoted to Mrs Benbow.'

'This is a big estate, Jacob. Three mines, including yours, four farms. Money should be swilling round here. But see the way the house is run down? How the pits fail for lack of investment? Anyone with eyes can see that Carmedy lives in better style than Mrs Benbow. Something's wrong, Jacob. Somebody's pocketing the profits.'

Jacob shook his head. 'This cannot be,' he said.

'If it's not so, then we could prove it by you selling me the Carafay pit and the land around it. Or letting me go halves. Then we can see about its profitability. Whether he's been running it all in a straight up way.'

Jacob stared again at the man before him. What changes in these years. He had grown tall and smooth. He talked as an equal to the Newcastle men. He dressed and talked in their manner. Young as he was, he was a person of consequence. This was possible in this country in these days. That was why this country was great. And now, with the new century, there were to be great changes. And it would not be czars and kings who called the tune. It would be powerful, clever men like Jack Lomas who came from nothing and would see the world as theirs for the making.

'Well, Jacob?' For a second Jack's face looked keen, almost feral in the firelight.

'I had a daughter,' said Jacob. 'But she is gone. My wife and I would have loved a son, but there was no son. Perhaps that is right. The son himself would have been taken too.'

'That was really bad, those things that happened to you.' Through the years Jack had pieced together the history of his friend.

'But you have warmed me and given me the pride that any father may feel.' Jacob paused. 'I will give you the Carafay Pit.'

'You can't give it. I have money, Jacob. More money than—'

'A man does not sell to his son,' said Jacob firmly. 'My life is fine and whether or not the Colonel is efficient or even sly, I have more money in the bank now than I will ever need. I will tell Mrs Benbow to ask the Colonel to have papers prepared. To make a deed of gift.'

'Mrs Benbow may not like this,' said Jack. 'And the Colonel . . .'

'Mrs Benbow is a good woman. Wiser in her own way than anyone I've ever met in a long life. And the Colonel is her servant. There will be no problem.'

'Well, dear old friend,' Jack said fervently. 'If you do this for me I'll never see you wrong or wronged. I promise.' He stood up.

Jacob stood too and looked up at Jack, holding his gaze for many seconds. 'It will be good to give you this, Jack,' he said. 'It passes from my friend and benefactor through me to you.'

'Yes,' said Jack. 'The pit . . .'

Jacob chuckled. 'But it's not just the mine that you want, is it, dear boy? This is your foothold in Benbow. You're making roots deep in this old earth. Things are going forward. I see far-reaching changes.'

'I hadn't thought of it like that. My mother will skelp me if she suspects those deep roots you mention. It was bad enough me buying a house.' Jack winked and shook Jacob heartily by the hand. 'You'll not regret this, Mr Ellenberg. Not for one minute.'

Four

The Child Rose

7pm

Astrid put her head against the plush backrest and felt the steady jerking pull of the train vibrate right through her. The child Rose was asleep on the seat beside her, her perfect round head thrown back and her golden curls escaping from her bonnet.

Astrid was alone in the carriage. She and Constance had been stretching their legs on the platform at York and Constance had spotted an old Cotswold acquaintance, the Honourable Megan Courtney.

'Constance! You ran away. I met Lady Parlellum and she said you had darted off to America because your father . . . Oh dear.' She put one gloved hand delicately to her mouth. 'I do hope the news wasn't the worst.'

Constance laughed heartily. 'Absolutely not. The General just rose from the dead. Is that not so?' She turned to Astrid. 'My dear friend here can affirm it,' she said with more than a mischievous glint in her eye. She introduced them but Astrid was unable to do more than just nod, as she had a sleeping Rose in her arms. The train started to steam up and Astrid turned to climb back into their carriage. Megan bewailed the loss of Constance so soon and Constance agreed to travel with her, so they could get up to date on mutual acquaintances and each other's lives. Constance made a play of helping Astrid and

Rose aboard and said she would rejoin them at Darlington for their onward journey to Bishop Auckland.

The pain at leaving Colorado and the particular pain at leaving the silent Richard Redoute had gnawed at Astrid during the long journey across America and all the way home, despite the fact that she'd enjoyed watching Constance unfurl from the dried-up harridan she'd become in Colorado back into the relaxed, flirtatious, self-confident beauty she'd been when they had first met.

Constance's headaches and general malaise had vanished by the time they reached the East Coast. In their months in New York and Boston Constance had dined and partied among her old friends, whom she represented to Astrid as altogether more intellectual, more cultured than the dullards, she said, whom they had been obliged to meet back West. No matter how Astrid protested at this there was no convincing her. Constance relished being the queen in her own country and wanted to show it off to Astrid. Astrid could not be as social as Constance, with Rose to take care of. She turned down Constance's offer to employ a nursemaid as well as the temporary lady's maid she took on when they were settled even for a short time in each city. Astrid, who had very little spare money, took care of Rose herself as a matter of pride.

Constance brought friends to visit Astrid and Rose so they could admire the cute things they'd bought the baby. Constance had chaffed Astrid for being such a hermit and missing the chance of so much fun. Astrid wondered whether Constance would stay and enjoy herself further when she herself embarked for England. But Constance would have none of that. 'What kind of friend do you think I am, honey? Of course I'll see you safely home. And England in the spring. Who can resist that?'

On the voyage Constance had flirted outrageously with two English brothers, the older one a viscount. She was so engaging that each thought he was the love of his life. In London the brothers had pursued her to Astrid's rooms in Chelsea, and each had proposed to her on the same afternoon. She turned them down gracefully, saying that for the present time her place was with her friend and the child Rose. She was duty bound to see them safely home to the north. 'After that I will return to London and who knows? We will meet again. London is so small, like a village, don't you think?'

Astrid allowed all this to happen around her and focused on the baby. She came to feel that there had never been a time in this world, in her life, without Rose. She went to her on waking, she checked on her before going to sleep. In those earliest days in the Springs she turned down Aunt Beatrice's offer to find her a wet nurse or a nanny. From Cousin Vera she learned how to thin cow's milk so the child could drink it, how to bed her down to sleep, how to boil water for her in the night so she would learn to sleep through. She needed no lessons in how to play with her and talk to her. Once Rose's eyes were open Astrid talked to her non-stop and was rewarded by seeing the child's lips move and bubble in mirror-response to her own. She had no need to learn to love the child, as she had loved her almost from the moment she first saw the tiny rosebud face. The child had talked amazingly early and was now, a year old, just about walking.

Richard Redoute, rather dour in those last days, had nevertheless gone with her to register the child in Denver. They explained to the blank-faced clerk that the mother's name was Honesty Leeming, and the father was 'unknown'. Astrid felt that perhaps the clerk didn't believe them; that he thought they were concealing some indiscretion of their own. She blushed at the idea. Standing there, she reflected on the cataclysm there'd have been if she'd entered the child's true parentage.

Outside the office Richard had finally commented, 'I'm still puzzled, Astrid. To be honest with you I'm still surprised you had no idea of the girl's condition.'

'I told you that I didn't. No more did she. She was so young. But there was something – an occurrence – before we came away. It was one of the reasons I brought her with me.'

'I thought she was such an innocent.'

'That's what she was. An innocent. A terrible thing happened to her.'

'Who was the fellow? Do you know?'

She had shook her head then. 'I know, but I'd never, never say.'

He left it at that. He'd been very good. They'd had little intimate communication since the remarkable events of the early Independence Day. No long rides, no close conversations. No hand touching hand. The drama over the child and the business over Honesty had vibrated through the household, leaving little space for discussions about whether or not Astrid would stay in Colorado after Constance departed.

In the vacuum of not-talking the decision grew that she would indeed go with Constance. If she were to stay in Colorado with Rose, everyone would say the child was the General's and her own. It would be impossible for a man of his standing and difficult for the child herself to live in such a crucible of gossip.

One day Slim went galloping off like a Pinkerton agent to look for Honesty. He wired from Denver to say he'd found her in the outskirts of the city with a troop of gypsies. She was performing acrobatics on the sidewalk for pennies.

Astrid turned down Richard's offer to accompany her and travelled to Denver, with only Rose for company, to see Honesty. She found the girl in a dusty clearing by an unfinished sidewalk. Two round-topped vans were drawn up to make an arena. Honesty, dressed in some kind of Indian breeches and tunic, turned double cartwheels for passers-by who put clinking coins into her tin cup. An old woman sat telling fortunes in front of the largest van. Honesty stopped twirling and went to talk to Astrid. The old woman stopped talking and glanced across at them.

'How are you, Honesty?' said Astrid rather lamely.

Honesty grinned. 'As you see. Well enough to do all this. Among my own. Keziah would be proud of us, out here, travelling. Don't you think so?' She kept her eyes right away from the bundle in Astrid's arms.

'It might not be safe.' Astrid's eye went across to the men lounging around the other van.

Honesty shrugged. 'I was not safe in the great hall of an English lord. I'm among my own people here. I'll be safe.' Her voice trembled for a second with a silver thread of pain. The events were not forgotten.

Astrid held out her bundle. 'Will you look at the child, Honesty?'

Honesty shook her head and did not allow her gaze to drop to the tiny face that was peeping though the lace. 'I gave it to you. It's more your kind. It's yours. That thing that happened was not real. It was a nightmare and now I'm awake.'

Astrid sighed. 'Well then, the General says I must ask you to sign this.' She took out a folded paper from her bag. 'I'll be going back to England in a week or so, and I need papers for her.'

Honesty peered at the looping writing.

Astrid took it from her. 'It says, *I Honesty Leeming, being the mother of the child called Rose Leeming, do give her for adoption by Miss Astrid Benbow for her to love and care for.*'

'You call her Rose? Right.' Honesty went across to the old woman and muttered to her. The woman climbed into the van and brought out a pen and inkwell. Honesty signed the paper, leaning on the steps of the van. The old woman took her arm and shook it, talking fiercely to her in the language they shared.

She came back and handed her the paper. 'You must love and care for it . . . her.'

'What did your friend say?'

'She said the baby could come with us in the van if I wanted her to.'

Astrid took a painful breath. 'You could do this, Honesty. You could have her. Even here. If you really wanted.'

She was surprised at the relief she felt when Honesty shook her head. 'I told her and I tell you. The baby's yours, not mine. Now please will you go?'

'I'm going back East next week, then later on to England. If you need anything, anything at all, Honesty, go to the General. He will always help you.'

'I've already fixed things with Slim. He's keen for me to go back to the Springs. If I need anything I'll go to him.' She paused. 'If you're going home will you say hello to my brother Jack and to Keziah? Tell them I think of them sometimes.' Then she touched Astrid's hand, the one that was clasping the baby. 'But you don't tell them about this. There's be no point in that.'

On the long train journey East, Astrid and Constance had the company and the help of Beatrice and Vera. Constance wept copiously as they all parted company at the terminal in New York but Beatrice was dry-eyed. Astrid gave her a card with her English address, and asked her to write and tell them how they settled in New York. Beatrice and Vera lifted their heavy bags and turned to go.

'But where'll you go in this big city, Aunt Beatrice?' Constance wailed after them. 'Let me take you to one of my friends. I'm sure they'll find you work.'

Beatrice turned and smiled widely. 'Why, thank you, Miss Constance, but I don't think so. Me an' Cousin Vera will find us a little hotel and make our plans. The General has given me the name of a soldier friend of his who might help us find a little shop or somethin'. First thing is a hotel. The General says to be careful as some of them don't like coloured folks.'

Constance still hesitated.

'You go, Miss Constance. Me and Cousin Vera is perfectly fine on our own.'

They were dismissed. Constance stared after the two figures as they bustled away. 'I suppose that's it, then.' She paused. 'Of course, Beatrice was gettin' a bit above herself. I thought of gettin' rid of her more than once. How does she think she can manage on her own? She'll be back with the General in six months.'

'I'm sure they'll be fine, Connie. Aunt Beatrice is an amazing person.' Astrid shifted the heavily swathed baby to the other hip. 'Now. We'll need at least two porters for all this luggage. Will you kindly seek them out?'

And now their English train finally stopped under the high arches of Darlington station. Uniformed porters lifted their bags and boxes out of the guard's van and into the Bishop Auckland train almost as soon as they themselves had alighted from their separate carriages. Constance did not wait to wave off her friend, but hurried across to the other platform with Astrid. When they had settled themselves in the empty carriage the child Rose stood up on Astrid's knee and pointed at the train they had just left, saying, 'Train, Mama, train, Mama. Big train.' She bashed the window with the flat of her hand, her blonde curls bouncing, her blue eyes shining.

Constance lay back against the cushions. 'I swear that child was born walkin' and talkin'. How old is she? A year?' A man opposite put down his paper and looked at her. Nearly two years at home had brought back her distinctive American tones.

The train jerked into motion and Rose's round forehead bounced off the glass and she started to wail. Astrid pulled her onto her lap and Constance watched as, expert in this now, Astrid pacified the child. 'Dearest Astrid, I can't understand why you would not let me get you a nursemaid,' she drawled. 'I had not realised the tedious things one had to do with a child.'

Astrid smiled at her. 'Someone once did them for you, Connie.'

'But not my own mother. Ain't there something quite disgusting about that? Doin' it for yourself?'

Sometimes Astrid felt the same. At other times she blessed the constant attendance required by this demanding child. Only that made her forget for short periods the dull ache she endured at the thought that she'd never see Richard again. At times she felt she could never know that particular closeness again with any other man. Rose was her compensation for all that.

Constance seemed to read her thoughts. 'Do you regret

comin' away, Astrid? Would you rather have stayed behind? With the General?'

Astrid stared at her over Rose's head. 'In many ways yes.'

'Would you have stayed if there were no Rose?'

'Probably.'

Constance nodded. 'Perhaps the great and good people of Colorado would've thought Rose was a bit of a by-blow for you and the General?'

'You can be very crude, Connie,' said Astrid, glancing up at their fellow passenger, who was behind his newspaper again.

'But . . .?'

'But yes, I would have stayed.'

'Then I would have lost a father and a friend.'

Astrid shrugged, bored with always having to reassure Constance, to make things right for her. Perhaps the friend was lost anyway. One part of her hoped not.

Connie blundered on. 'I see you had wires from the General in Southampton and letters in London too. Did you write him? Will you write him?'

'Really, Connie. Can't you mind your own business?'

'It is my business. He is my father, after all.' Constance stared at her perfectly manicured hands, looking very miserable.

Astrid sighed. 'To be honest, Constance, I think not. I shall not write to him.'

'Because . . .?'

'I can't think why you're so curious about this. You hated the General and me being friends when I was there. You hated us riding together, talking together.'

Constance shrugged. 'Well, I've had time to think and the whole thing is immaterial now, honey. I was quite, quite mad in that horrible place with that infernal mountain leering down at me. It drove me out of my head just as it drove my mother out of hers. Now I come to think of it, at this distance it seems very sweet that you and the General had a little *affaire de coeur*. Astonishing, but very sweet.'

Astrid laughed loud at this, making Rose jump in her lap. 'Connie, you're incorrigible.'

The man opposite rattled his newspaper.

'Well, to be honest, honey, back there I was never clear in my crabby little heart whether I was jealous of him or jealous of you. You were my friend and he was stealing you away. He was my father and you were stealing *him* away.'

'It's in the past, Connie. As you say, it is immaterial.' Her heart ached as she said the words. 'Leave it alone now, won't you? It's all in the past.'

Constance stared at her. 'I suppose it is. I suppose it's extra hard for you. I'm leaving behind bad things. And you, you're leaving behind something quite . . . good.' Her glance dropped to Rose. 'And what on earth will you do with the child? Will you give her to the grandmother?'

Astrid shook her head vigorously. 'No. Keziah will never know, and you must say nothing, Connie. Nothing. I promised Honesty.'

Constance shrugged again. 'It's your affair, honey.' She left the subject then and went on to talk about Megan Courtney – the *Honourable* Megan Courtney – who had been on the York train. 'She simply insisted that I go for a week or so to visit her in the Cotswolds. They have a dear place in the middle of the most wonderful huntin' country. You know? When I was there three years ago I dined with them. This time I'm to stay at the house, so that should be fun.' She paused. 'She and her friend were talking about all this fallal over votes for women. Seems they even have sympathy for those viragos. According to them they'll compromise on nothing less than every woman having a vote. Then, they say, the world will change. Women will be in charge of themselves. The idea has its appeal, don't you think?'

Rose muttered and mumbled a little then put her thumb in her mouth and closed her eyes, soothed by the motion of the train.

'To be honest I've always felt in charge of myself,' said Astrid slowly. 'My mother, too, feels no constraint. I can't see that it would make much difference. Not to us. My father was away so much; we always lived in a world of women.'

'But what about the difference to others? To the child Rose here, in these changin' times? Ain't she the century's child?'

Astrid glanced down at Rose. 'D'you really think it'll make a difference?'

'Who would you vote for if you had the vote?'

Astrid frowned. 'Well, my father was always out of the country so he never voted. The Colonel – did you meet the colonel? – he's a stalwart Conservative. But, if you discount the miners who're seduced by ideas of Labour, this area is more of the Liberal persuasion. I once went with my father to the house of Mr Kenmir, the furniture maker, to a reception for Mr Lloyd George, who was speaking in the town.'

'Mr Lloyd George!' said Constance. 'Did you take to the Welsh wizard?'

'Well, he was much smaller than you'd think and had these snapping bright eyes that flickered over you as though you were the next course at dinner. But he talked well. About the strong taking care of the weak, our duty to each other. Usual Liberal stuff.'

'So you would vote Liberal?'

Astrid, who had never addressed the thought before, nodded her head. 'I would think so. I very probably would.'

'And what do you think of the way they're beating these women and clapping them into irons? And forcing food down their noses when they won't eat? And setting them free and then arresting them again? How much they must hate women to do that.'

Astrid grimaced. 'It's terrible. Poor women.'

Constance sat back in her seat. 'There now,' she said contentedly. 'Ain't I clever? I've made you into a good little suffragette.'

Five

A Stranger's Kiss

9pm

At Bishop Auckland Constance and Astrid, with the child Rose between them, stood on Platform Two in the middle of an island of cases, bags and boxes. They watched as, one by one, their fellow passengers melted away into the bright, blustery evening, some of them – including the man with the newspaper – marching across onto another train to continue their way up the dale, others going through the archways to the cabs and brakes waiting outside.

As she looked for the slight figure of John Tyler in his bowler hat and his dark jacket Astrid's gaze slipped past a tall bearded man in tweeds and a soft felt hat. She thought perhaps her letter had not arrived and her mother did not expect her. She contemplated depositing their baggage in the left luggage and hiring a cab to get them out to Benbow.

Rose wriggled up into her arms and settled against her shoulder. 'I tired, Mama.'

'Perhaps they didn't get the letter,' Astrid said to Constance. She beckoned to a porter, who wheeled a creaking sack-barrow in her direction. 'We'll make our own way.'

The tall man moved swiftly towards them and removed his hat. 'I hardly recognised you, Miss Benbow,' he said. 'But for the luggage. I wasn't looking for someone with a baby.' He stared down at Rose, frowning. 'Mrs Benbow didn't mention a baby.'

'Here is a man, Mama. Here is a man, Auntie Connie.'

'Is this your little one?' he said to Astrid.

She flushed as she looked at him. He was a tall, heavy man yet in no way fat; brown-skinned, as though he'd been travelling. Perhaps a colonial acquaintance of the Colonel. 'She is mine, but then she isn't.' She smiled. 'She's my foster child.' She peered behind him. 'I was watching for John Tyler,' she said.

'Can't come, I fear. He is poorly, so they say.'

She smiled again. 'Did the Colonel send you?' she said brightly.

'He did not. It was Mrs Benbow sent me. She has to be at Seland Hall and asked me to take her there first and collect you here. We're to pick her up on the way back.'

She looked at him sharply. There was something. The voice wasn't right. He was no friend of the Colonel. Then she noticed the eyes, with their golden flecks. 'I feel I must know you.'

He smiled at her, very easily. 'So you do, Miss Benbow. Jack Lomas. Son to Keziah Leeming. We met in the road one day when I picked up our Honesty. The day she came back from Seland. And then one time after.'

A shock rippled through her from her heels through her stomach to her head. He put out his hand and she was forced to shake it. 'You know my friend Miss Redoute?' she said faintly. This felt wrong somehow. She had the sense again of the world shifting on its axis.

Jack Lomas shook Constance firmly by the hand. 'And you. I saw you that day in the Seland rig. Now you travel in mine.' He looked at the luggage, then nodded to the porter. 'We can only take the small stuff, friend. Not the trunks. Tek that lot over to the left luggage. You may get it across to Benbow Hall in the morning.' He put sixpence into the man's hand. 'Now, ladies,' he said. 'P'r'aps you'll follow me?'

He helped Constance up first into the gleaming rig. Then he took Rose from Astrid and handed her up to sit on Constance's knee. Then he turned and took Astrid by the elbow. His touch was light but it burned deep. She wrenched her elbow away. 'I can manage perfectly well, Mr Lomas.' She cursed herself for her own bad manners and for the blushes he caused.

He stood back. 'Suit yourself,' he said. He watched her clamber up the steps. Then he leapt up in front, clicked his teeth and set the horses away at a trot down Newgate Street, the busy thoroughfare of this thriving town. He had to make his way through carts and wagons, pony traps and donkey carts. Despite the hour many of the shops were still lit up, their canopies still shading the wide pavement. Jack slowed down as they made their way past the grandiose town hall in the market place. The market stalls were still in business, some with storm lanterns hung high from poles to waylay the encroaching night.

Behind the back of Jack Lomas, Constance exchanged a smiling glance with Astrid. Astrid shrugged her shoulders and drew Rose's attention to a stall covered with birdcages fronted by a man in a bird mask. 'Look, Rose, birdies!'

'Nice birdies, Mama. Nice birdies.'

Jack glanced back at them, then reached under his seat and pulled out two fur-lined blankets and flicked them behind him. Constance caught them awkwardly. 'There's blankets for you, Miss Benbow, should either of you or the child need wrapping,' he said.

'He thinks we're parcels,' whispered Constance.

'Hardly parcels, Miss Redoute.' He threw the words over his shoulder. 'But ye'll feel the chill as the night cuts in. Not so bad if we were goin' straight to Benbow. But it'll be twenty minutes to Seland and another half-hour to Benbow. Ye'll be cold to the marrow without wrapping. Ye don't want the child frozen now, Miss Benbow, even if ye're only its foster mother.'

'I wish he'd shut up,' muttered Constance. 'Too breezy by half.'

'Ye can hardly tell us to shut up in me own rig.' The voice floating back to them was both quiet and amused.

Astrid looked up at his straight easy-set shoulders and the way his dark hair curled under his soft-brimmed hat and suddenly smiled. She thought of the drawing of him in her book, sitting easy on the bare back of a horse. She thought of Richard there in the swimming pool parlour. 'You're right, Mr Lomas. It's your rig after all.'

'Sommat like that.' He pulled on the right rein and swung the horses off the Durham road onto Stockton Road for the long pull up to Seland Hall. 'Now wrap yourselves, will you? If you freeze your ma'll have us for salt on her dinner. I said I'd be there for half after nine and she said she'd be waiting.'

He urged the horses to a trot. Then his voice floated back to them again. 'So, tell me. How's my little sister that you took off to foreign lands and abandoned?'

'Honesty sent her very best wishes to you and Keziah. She's very happy there. She was happy to stay. It was her choice.'

'Well now, Miss Benbow, I only have your word for that now, don't I?'

Carmel was waiting for them under the long porticoed canopy at the entrance to Seland Hall. She was wrapped in her battered cape and clutching her muff. Astrid peered out of the carriage along the broad front of the Hall, at the wide steps and the gravel sweep of the drive. Her heart caught for a second like a finger ripped on a thorn. Here it was the King and his party had gathered that morning, for their shoot. Here it was the child Rose had her savage conception.

Behind Carmel the lights of the great hall streamed onto the gravel. To one side of her stood Lady Margaret; on the other stood Gertrude Seland. She was wearing a slender green velvet gown, which set off her fine tall figure and flattered her pale skin. The drama of her looks went a long way to make up for her long face with its features too exaggerated for beauty. Around their feet loitered three lurcher hounds and a liver and white pointer.

Jack Lomas's carriage skirled on the gravel as it turned and the dogs started to growl and run towards it. Jack pulled to a stop and the dogs began to bark. One of the lurchers jumped up at the carriage. Jack Lomas growled. The dogs cut their barking to a whimper and slunk back into the shadows at the far end of the portico.

'We-ell,' drawled Constance.

Lady Margaret called, 'Astrid! Home from the wilds I see. And Miss Redoute! Come in, my dear. You should come in and warm by the fire.'

'No.' Carmel was moving forward determinedly. An evening's rare society and light chatter had exhausted her. 'I must go, Margaret. The girls may call on you another day.'

Lady Margaret and Gertrude marched forward with her, flanking her like bodyguards. They peered into the carriage. 'So this is the baby,' said her ladyship, staring at Rose, who had slipped into sleep and was just waking again. 'There must be quite a tale there,' she went on, looking at Astrid.

Astrid looked her straight in the eye. 'Yes, Lady Margaret, there's a tale here.' Her tone was icy.

Her ladyship's goodwill dropped from her like a cloak. 'Really, Astrid . . .'

But Gertrude had clambered onto the step and was kissing Astrid on the cheek. 'Dear girl, you look wonderful. Have you fallen in love? I have never seen you so well. You must . . . and *who* is this?' She cocked her head at Constance, half hidden within the carriage.

'This is my friend Constance Redoute, Gertrude. Connie, this is my good friend Gertrude who can be a very naughty girl.'

'Charming!' said Gertrude. 'Positively charming, Astrid.' She ignored Constance's proffered hand and leaned over and kissed her on the mouth. 'Do you ride, Miss Redoute?'

Constance laughed and pulled away, then licked her lips and tasted the residue of port. 'Yes, Miss Seland, I guess I do,' she drawled.

'Gertrude!' said Lady Margaret. 'Will you cease your games and allow Carmel to take her seat? It is a good ride to Benbow.'

The dogs had crawled nearer and were starting to growl again.

Carmel scrambled up beside Constance and squeezed in. 'Right. I think we'd better go, Jack. If we linger any longer either Gertrude will explode or those dogs will bite your horses.'

He clicked his tongue and the greys moved forward. When the passengers turned they could see Lady Margaret and Gertrude framed against the lit entrance to the Hall. They all waved and the carriage picked up pace. Suddenly there was a cry behind them. Gertrude had hiked up her skirts and was racing after them. Jack didn't slacken his pace. As the drive curved they could see her galloping figure. Behind them they could hear her voice. 'Riding!' she bellowed. 'Tomorrow, Miss Constance, we'll go riding.'

'Lady run,' chuckled Rose, now fully awake.

By the time the carriage had made its way down the drive to the wide gates and past the lodge, they all began to relax. 'Sommat wrong with that lass, Mrs Benbow,' said Jack over his shoulder. 'Don't you think?'

Constance suppressed a snort of laughter. Astrid glanced at her mother.

'I fear you're right, Jack,' said Carmel. '*Sommat* very wrong.' She straightened her skirts, righted her hat, then turned to Astrid. 'Now then, let me see this child. And what is this tale that can't be told?'

The child was ahead of her. She'd stood up on the seat and was now busy clambering onto Carmel's lap. 'Nice lady,' she said. Then she did what she'd just seen that strange lady do to her Auntie Connie. She kissed the stranger on the lips. 'I Rose.'

Six

The Flautist

9.30pm

Ambrose pushed the black cat from the stool by the chessboard and sat on it himself. He pondered his move. The game moved on very slowly these days. This week he'd had to pester his mother and Michael John to make their moves, so the game would progress. Even Mr Ellenberg seemed to have lost interest.

Last year the board had not changed between one school holiday and the next. Mr Ellenberg always made his move, of course, but then it might stick for weeks for lack of interest.

Black knight takes white pawn. Done. Now another long wait.

He glanced around. After their visit to the pit offices Colonel Carmedy had invited Ambrose and Michael John to join him and a couple of cronies at the Lodge for a rubber of bridge. Money would be involved. The Colonel enjoyed a wager. Michael John decided to accept the invitation but Ambrose had wriggled out of it and they'd not pressed him.

He'd stood and watched the two of them enter the Lodge through the door held by the turbaned footman and then turned to walk the half-mile home. Michael John got on very well with the Colonel. They saw eye to eye over many things and, of course, had the army in common. Good luck to them, thought Ambrose, who welcomed anything that kept Michael John's eye away from himself.

Even when he was on his better behaviour, as he was on this leave, living with Michael John was like living with a time-bomb. Tick-tick-tick. You were aware of his presence even when he wasn't in the same room. School, dreary as it was, had been so very much better when his brother had finally left. Nevertheless, Ambrose sometimes wondered whether the pain engendered by his brother's presence wasn't partly of his own making. There were times when Michael John would be quite jovial and decent. The trouble was you never knew when his temper would break and the storm would come.

Things had been quiet enough lately, but for Ambrose the chilling memory of torments he'd endured at his brother's hands always sat under the surface of his mind. There were other things from their early childhood that he didn't quite remember. He sometimes thought these events might have transformed themselves to the unremembered dreams that caused him to scream in the night – and made him very unpopular at school.

His eye lit on his flute case on the hallstand. Yes. He'd practise that Irish air. He needed to perfect it before playing for Mr Kilburn in the morning. A little practice would not come amiss. He wondered what his mother would say when he told her he wanted to be a nail-maker's clerk. And to play in the town orchestra. Probably very little. She'd nod and pull on her gardening boots. She'd not commented at all when he arrived home from school, despatched by his housemaster with a note to say how concerned he'd been at Ambrose's choking fits and nightmares, both of which disturbed the other boys.

She still didn't comment when, here at Benbow, he seemed perfectly well, failed to choke and slept long and dreamlessly in his childhood bed. It had been Michael John, when he arrived, who'd kicked up a fuss about his term-time presence, calling him a shirker and a layabed. Anyway, with a bit of luck Michael John would be going back to London, or to his regiment, before the week was out. Then Ambrose would set about the life he wished to lead, playing in the creaking town orchestra and being a nail-maker's clerk. That would do very nicely.

He leapt up and set his feet square on the carpet, wriggled his toes a little to ground himself, then lifted the flute to his mouth. The phrases floated into the air around him, winding themselves lightly into shapes and sequences that did not need words to make sense. The flute did not stammer or blush. It didn't choke with fear at the onslaught of other, bolder flutes; it didn't dream of engulfment and choking fire.

A footfall and a rustle of dress behind him stopped his blowing and he turned, expecting to see Melanie Tyler. But it wasn't Melanie. This was a much shorter, younger figure, leaning to one side to balance the weight of the coal bucket she was carrying. 'That sounds pretty,' she gasped. 'Go on playing, will yer? Shame to stop.'

He kept staring at her: at her round cheeks and her round eyes and her frizzy hair.

'Can yer tell us where this drawing room is?' she said. 'Mrs Tyler telt us to fill the bucket in there.'

'Second door on the right. Stop! Come here where I can see you.'

She struggled into the pool of light cast by the cast bronze lamp on the big mantelpiece.

'You're the girl from this afternoon, in the village,' he said.

She hunched her shoulder, then put down her bucket on the once fine, now worn, Indian carpet. 'So what? It an't a crime.'

'So what are you doing here?'

'Me and my ma are *charity*. My da was killed in one of your pits so we lose our house. So Mrs Tyler comes for my ma to work here and live with that old curmudgeon Mrs Mac-something. I'm part of the package.'

'Yes, well. At least it's a roof over your head.'

'Like you say.' She leaned down to pick up the heavy bucket. 'A roof over our heads. We should be grateful.'

He put his flute on the mantelpiece. 'Here. I'll carry that.'

Leaning somewhat himself to balance the weight, he carried the bucket into the drawing room and filled the fancy coal scuttle. He threw the rest of the coal onto the back of the fire and it flared up, the flames leaping in the wide chimney.

'Good firing. Red Daisy coal,' the girl said. 'My da probably saw that very coal when it was just the coal face. One time a long time ago.' She sniffed.

'I say. Don't cry, will you?'

She sniffed again.

He took a handkerchief from his pocket and handed it to her. She scrubbed her eyes and blew her nose. 'Ta,' she said and made to return it.

He shook his head. 'No. You keep it.'

They stared at each other, neither of them quite clear about what to do next. Then she bent down and picked up the empty bucket. 'Well, I'd better get on back out to the kitchen.' She looked at him, red-eyed.

'Can't I do something for you?' he said helplessly.

She looked at him for a long minute. 'Could you play a bit more of that chirpy music? Very cheery, that was.'

'Yes, yes. Of course I can.' He hurried back into the hall and took down the flute. She was right behind him and when he turned he could smell coal-dust on her and a warm smell like soup.

'Now sit down!' he ordered. 'There!' He pointed to the stool beside the chessboard.

Very carefully she placed the bucket on the marble hearth and sat demurely on the stool, knees together. Then he played for her, all the pieces he knew. He scoured his memory for the jigs, the airs, the soft nursery tunes that lay there like seeds in his head waiting to unfurl into the air again. She pattered applause every time he stopped for breath and joined in, singing softly when he played 'Golden Slumbers'.

He played and she applauded until at last they heard the sound of the carriage outside, followed by the rush and gurgle of female voices.

The girl grabbed her bucket from the hearth and fled through the door that led to the back areas. He watched her go. *Gwennie*, he thought. That was her name. Gwennie. It was the girl Michael John had pushed over. The one he'd hauled to her feet. She had a very nice face. Cheeks like two cherries.

As the carriage came along the meandering drive the house was illuminated like a candelabra, the light streaming from its windows. Melanie had made sure that each room was lit to welcome the Benbow guests. She stood under the side arch waiting for them, her arms folded under her bosom. Somewhere out the back the dogs started to bark.

Melanie watched Mrs Benbow get down awkwardly, a rather large child clinging sleepily round her neck. 'What's this, Mrs Benbow? I knew we were to have visitors, but . . . G'd evening, Miss Benbow. G'd evening, Miss Redoute.' She sketched the very barest of curtsies at the young women as they alighted from the carriage. She watched them bustle into the house and looked up at Jack Lomas who had leapt down and was handing down small cases and bags. 'Now this is a turn up for the books. A child . . .'

Jack put two bags under his arms and grabbed two in each hand. He left one on the ground. 'The child? Some little foundling Miss Benbow picked up in America. Don't go jumping to conclusions, Mrs Tyler.'

'You watch your cheek.' She picked up the last bag and led the way into the house. 'You might be the big man now with your black beard and good suits and fine horses. But you and me both know where you come from, don't we?' she said sharply.

'I'm not sorry where I've come from, Mrs Tyler, even if you are. And how's poor old John?'

'Not very well, seeing as you ask. If he's no better tomorrow I'll ask Mrs Benbow to get the doctor down.'

'No doctor'll come down here on a Sunday.'

'He will if Mrs Benbow sends for him. And he will if you pay him. People do anything if you pay them.'

He put down the bags and looked briefly at the doorway between the back and the front halls, through which the women had just disappeared. Then he turned to go. 'I'll ask my ma to come and look out for him if you like,' he offered. 'She's got some potions.'

Her lip curled. 'Jack Lomas! This is the twentieth century. There's science. Proper medicine. No need for . . . people . . . with spells and potions when we've got doctors and surgeons.'

He laughed. 'You can say *witch* if you want. She wouldn't mind. It's an old and honourable way.'

'Humph!' She looked round. 'Now where's that girl? Gwennie! Gwennie!'

His eye was still on her. 'Well, Mrs Tyler? An't you gonna thank me for bringin' your travellers safely home? Letting your John lie in his sickbed?'

She looked him up and down. 'Not up to me. But I'll give you Mrs Benbow's thanks.'

A girl appeared from the back areas, her round face flushed. 'Yes, Mrs Tyler?'

'Help me get these bags upstairs, will you, Gwennie?' She turned to Jack. 'Are you still here? Can I get you anything?'

He glanced again at the doorway to the front hall. 'No. No. I'll get back. Me *witch* of a mother'll be waiting for us.' He turned and strode off, banging the big side door behind him.

'Good riddance to bad, jumped-up rubbish,' said Melanie, rubbing one hand across her forehead. 'Now, Gwennie. You help me get these upstairs or none of us'll get to bed before midnight.'

Seven

The Chancer

10pm

Just inside the Hall gates Michael John Benbow was forced to leap to one side to avoid the carriage and greys as they thundered past him. He cursed the driver loudly then leaned against the carved stone gatepost until his world stopped spinning.

He thought perhaps he should have refused that last port. The Colonel's servant had been so free with the decanter that in the end Michael John had been obliged to throw in his hand at the second rubber. His partner – an old duffer who'd fought in the Crimea – had been quite understanding. He suggested that the others play *vingt-et-un*. No partners needed there.

Michael John had watched the game for a while, impressed at the size of the sums of money that were changing hands. At first the Colonel seemed to win a good deal, but then he started to lose and had to send his servant for a leather box from the library so he could back his bids with gold sovereigns.

After an hour of this Michael John said he thought perhaps he should go. The Colonel waved his cigar in his direction. 'Goodnight then, old boy. A learning day for you! A learning day, eh?' He peered through the smoke at the cards in his hand: a very promising three of hearts, set up with the four and two of spades. He pushed a sovereign into the centre of the table. 'Now, perhaps, the tide will turn.' He glanced again at Michael

286

John. 'A bit of a walk with the old shotgun tomorrow, old boy? Nine o'clock? Nothing beats a good kill before church.'

In the Colonel's wide hallway Michael John was compelled to clamber over trunks and boxes to get to the front door. More boxes littered the driveway outside, scattered as far as the long station-cart, which was yards away and still being loaded by two men in railway uniform. Late work.

No matter.

Up to the point where that lunatic had nearly knocked him off his feet at the gates, the walk home had just about cleared Michael John's head. Now he was dizzy again. This instant effect of drink was an old problem of his. He considered himself more or less in charge of it. He reflected on how cunningly he'd had to work in the mess to avoid the humiliating reputation for having a weak head. He'd discovered that one way to deal with it was to walk out of the company at the right moment. Ragging some other fellow about not being able to take his juice could also act as a good distraction.

One drank, of course, because that's what one did in a life lived among the charmed ones, the idiots and the fools that made up the army. At least now he had this new Indian tour of duty to look forward to. That promised a bit of excitement over and above the routines of life with the regiment: some good riding; a decent life on his army pay. Apart from that prospect, the army had proved something of a partial success for Michael John so far. It was true that manoeuvres, and the drilling of the men, had their own satisfaction. The extremes one had to go to to lick a body of men into shape were sometimes seen as excessive, but his commanders could not deny that Lieutenant Benbow's men were the sharpest in the whole brigade.

What a bore it had been to come back to Benbow, instead of spending the weekend at the York Races with a couple of his livelier chums! But needs came to the fore when the devil insisted on driving. He had strict orders from his brigadier to clear his substantial debts before he embarked. Then there was that problem of a little informal borrowing that had got him into a scrape. Astonishingly the old boy – who had seemed to have a soft spot for him – seemed to think it a resignation issue.

He had also needed a higher allowance from home to cope with the life of an officer. His mother did not understand. Her estimation was ridiculously low and not at all in keeping with his requirements. Hence his mission this week to focus old Colonel Carmedy, essentially the keeper of his mother's purse.

That box of sovereigns the old boy had brought out at the Lodge tonight had been tempting, but Michael John thought it might be just too close to home. Better lift a few shekels from the safe at Benbow than rob the Colonel. Horsewhips came to mind.

In any case, the Colonel had come up trumps. Took up the bills; signed cheques right left and centre and fired them off with an unctuous letter to the brigadier. All solved. In addition, the old boy had promised to see his mother about a hike-up in the allowance. He had muttered something to the effect that a wife with a few thousand a year might be 'worth a bounce for a handsome feller like you, old boy', but still he'd come up trumps. Now the order was back to the regiment on Monday and then on to India within the week.

But until then he had this godforsaken family of his to endure. His mother was still consorting with vagabonds and talking to her dratted roses; Ambrose was still mooning about the house like a pansy of the first water.

And then today the Colonel had received a message from his mother by the garden boy, regarding the great news of the return from America of his sister Astrid the Earnest. According to the note Astrid was bringing back Constance Redoute, the American. His head cleared. If he remembered rightly that one was quite a stunner. And all that money. He lengthened his step.

The front door at Benbow was wide open, and at the bottom of the sweeping stairs was a jumble of luggage topped by two umbrellas. Michael John sniffed the intriguing sweat-and-perfume smell of women. The drawing room door into the hall was ajar; the floor shone conker-bright in the doorway. He could hear the chirruping burr of voices, and, incredibly, the sound of a child crying. He started up the stairs, his earlier urge to meet the heiress again purged by that single sound.

Astrid, carrying Rose, came out into the hall and glanced up at him, surprised. 'Sneaking in as usual, Mick?' She grinned, raising her voice over the child's whimper.

He stopped on the stairs and looked at her, frowning. 'It's late. Seems that the house's been transformed into a nursery.'

' "*Hello Astrid*," ' she said. ' "*How are you?*" '

He took another step upwards. 'Not a nursery. A madhouse. The woman's talking to herself now.'

'And how are you, Michael John?' she said.

Now they were all streaming out of the drawing room. The American woman, his mother, Melanie Tyler. Even that pervert Ellenberg. He leapt on up the stairs, intending to say nothing more to anyone. He was stopped by the voice of Constance Redoute. 'Oh, Michael John.' She looked up at him with her perfect eyes. 'Do you run away from us?'

He hesitated, then turned to come down again. 'So you found yourself a baby, Astrid? A foundling. Ha?'

'She adopted it,' said Ambrose. 'It's an American foundling.'

'Shut up, Amby.' Michael John reached the bottom of the stairs. 'Speak when you're bid.'

Carmel met his eye. 'The boy can speak in his own house, Michael John.' Around them like a wave swept the common memory of the day when Michael John had shot at Ambrose, the night when Carmel sent him off to the army.

Michael John stood there, swaying a little, still fuzzy from the after-effects of the port. 'In this house, Mama, I suppose we should be thankful that it's not some gypsy's brat.' He held her gaze.

Constance broke the silence. 'I declare, Mr Michael John, you have quite grown up. So smart in your uniform! Won't you come into the drawing room here so I can see you to your boots?'

He stared at her then relaxed into his earlier half-formed plan regarding Miss Constance Redoute. He smiled. 'Good to see you again, Miss Redoute.'

Carmel eyed him as he swung past her, then turned to Melanie. 'Perhaps you'd go into the nursery, Melanie, and wheel the old crib into Astrid's bedroom for the child?'

Rose had stopped crying and was closely observing this exchange, thumb in mouth. Astrid took the thumb out of the mouth. 'The crib is not needed, Mama. Rose will sleep in my bed. She's done so for all these months and we do not need to change this.'

Melanie Tyler wrinkled her nose with distaste. She'd never heard of a lady bringing her child into her bed. Pitmen's and ploughmen's wives, yes. Her own mother in their own crowded house. But ladies?

Michael John turned, obviously agreeing with her. 'It may be no gypsy child,' he said. 'But it's certainly made a gypsy out of you.'

Constance, in the doorway to the drawing room, held out a hand. 'Michael John . . .' she said.

He walked past her, head high, without a single direct glance at the child, who was staring at him round-eyed. She transferred her gaze to Carmel. 'Kiss lady,' she said, opening her arms.

Carmel took her into her arms and kissed her on both cheeks. 'Goodnight, Rose,' she said. She was moved in a way that she found intensely strange. She did not want to let the child go.

Astrid held out her arms and Rose leapt into them. 'I'll take her up now, Mama,' she said. 'She's tired. We're all tired. Perhaps Ambrose could help Melanie bring up the small luggage? Jack Lomas has arranged for the station cart to bring the rest. It was on another errand when we arrived.'

Carmel watched them troop upstairs then turned to Jacob Ellenberg. She glanced at the closed door of the drawing room that did not quite keep in the tinkle of Constance's laughter. 'Jacob! Perhaps you and I could revive the last of the fire in the library? We could go over this new proposal of yours. The matter of the mine and Jack Lomas?'

In the library she poked and prodded the fire while Jacob outlined Jack Lomas's idea. She stood up straight. 'So how do you view this proposal, Jacob? What would you like to do?'

'Though I know nothing of mines, Mrs Benbow, I was proud that Rufus bequeathed it to me. That was a wonderful thing in itself. Since then the royalties I believe have provided me with what you call a nest-egg.' He was shuffling uncomfortably from one leg to another.

The core of the fire had brightened now, so she sat down. He sat opposite her.

'What is your inclination, Jacob?'

He stared at her. The lenses of his spectacles glittered, reflecting the flaring flames of the fire. 'I like and trust the boy. I always have. Like me he is an outsider, but unlike me he has great courage.'

'If you allowed him to have the mine, as a gift, you'd have no income from it. It goes out of your possession.'

'No. This is the strange thing. He tells me my income will be no less.'

'How can that be? How does he know?'

Jacob shrugged. 'Jack says he has visited the pit with a surveyor, an acquaintance of his from Newcastle. They talked to the men as they came up from their shift. An overman showed them round the workings. He said the place was neglected, dangerous. Under-used. But the seam is good.'

'And did Colonel Carmedy know of all this?'

Jacob stroked his thin beard. 'Of this I am not sure. I think perhaps not. Or else the Colonel would have spoken to me. Perhaps, just perhaps, Jack slipped a small remuneration to the overman. But I know nothing of this.'

'And did Jack Lomas *ask* you to give it to him?'

He shrugged his shoulders. 'He offered me a fair price, Mrs Benbow. But then I thought I would like to give it to him. How does an old foreigner who only knows the buying and selling of books and the keeping of records know anything about mines?'

'But you trust Jack?'

'It seems I cannot lose. Yes, I trust him.'

'Well, I suppose in that case you should do it. We have Keziah to keep him in line even though it seems he's broached the gate of the castle.' She stared into the fire. 'There is one consolation, Jacob. Michael John is to go to India. He will be away soon.' She sighed. 'What kind of a mother is it, who would say such a thing?'

Jacob smiled faintly. 'When the young man is home I – what you call it – make myself scarce.'

'And what is your view of Ambrose? What is he doing wandering around here when he should be at school?'

He glanced at her. Usually she had so little interest in what happened in the house, or the people in it. 'The young one seemed quite resolved, happy even. Until . . .'

'Until his brother came home.'

He polished his glasses. 'Ambrose tells me he has left school. It is at an end for him.'

'Left school?' She raised her brows. 'Is this so?'

'We played two moves of chess earlier this evening, just after you went out to Seland Hall. Between moves he tells me he will work in an office in Bishop Auckland, and will play the flute in the town orchestra.'

'He told you this?'

'You were not here,' he said. He let the silence run a little. Then he said, 'That was a very fine child, the child called Rose.'

She stared at him. 'That child moved me, Jacob. In a way that never happened before.' She paused. 'Even with Rufus. But how can that be? She's a stranger.'

He looked at her then looked back into the heart of the fire. 'There is purity in a child. My own daughter moved me,' he said. 'My wife was a fine woman but my marriage was a matter of arrangement, of convenience. But my little daughter, Mrs Benbow, she jolted my heart. The finest thing in my life was to walk along the pavement of my city, her little hand in mine. The finest thing.' He coughed and then stood up. 'But I must go, Mrs Benbow. You must be tired. I will go now.' He hurried out of the room without looking at her. Behind him Carmel reflected how little she knew of this man. He was like an old vine that clung to a wall and brought forth only leaves every season, as though it had forgotten how to flower.

As she climbed upstairs Carmel's mind moved to her present project in the garden: a rose that she'd been working on for years. She'd been crossing the sumptuous *Gloire de Dijon* with more humble second-remove hedge-roses. Some of the cross-pollinations were disasters. Some of them refused to flower. Others produced such shrunken failures that she almost stopped the line.

Then Keziah, back from her travels in the early days of their acquaintance, brought her a tree-rose in a big zinc bucket. It was a domesticated hedge-rose that had flourished in someone's back yard. Keziah had exchanged it for two chickens and brought it back as a present for Carmel. She would take nothing for it.

This tree-rose had thrived in the walled garden and Carmel, on an impulse, used it in her next phase of cross-pollination of the *Gloire de Dijon*. Just now she was nurturing its second generation offspring. These sported a refined cream velvety petal but had a simple open habit which allowed you to know them to the heart. Perfect. When the first bud opened, early this month, she had been reduced to tears. A brand new rose, perfect in every way, that had never before existed. She must be doing something right.

Eight

Romantic Manoeuvres

11pm

In the drawing room Michael John stood with his back to the fireplace. He'd buttoned up his tunic and, despite his muddy boots, was conscious that he cut a fine figure. 'I'd have thought, Miss Redoute, that a lady as fine as you would have more to do than to return to this godforsaken place. County Durham! The boot end of civilisation. Bishop Auckland! The counting house of the dale. This house is falling down, the people who live here are completely mad.'

'And d'you include yourself in that description, Michael John? Mad?' She laughed up at him. 'You should know that I came here especially to deliver my dear friend Astrid safely home, having whipped her away so precipitously – was it only last year? The year before?'

'And will you stay, Miss Redoute? Are you prepared to die of boredom?'

She lifted her shoulders. 'Who can tell?' The long face of Gertrude Seland flashed before her eyes. 'There's fun to be had here, I'm quite sure. I'll ride a little, certainly. But then, of course, I'll go to London, where I'm a tiny fish in a very large pool. And that pool itself is but a puddle in the life of the nation. But my dear friend Lady Parlellum has an idea about a party to launch me again in my own particular stretch of water.'

Michael John sniffed. 'Parlellum? Is she Irish?'

She raised her brows. 'That's very naughty, Michael John.'

He threw himself onto the sofa beside her. 'If only I weren't on my way to India, you and I could have such a fine old time, Miss Redoute. I would visit you in London. We'd drink fine wine. We could dance at Society balls and go to the opera.'

She smiled at him. 'How romantic! But why should I choose you above any of the distinguished types in London, whose only wish is to treat me with such romantic courtesies?'

He leaned towards her and whispered in her ear. 'Because those you speak of are all old roués and pansies and I am a man, Miss Constance. You'd find no better.'

She laughed at this and put a hand on his arm. 'Dear Michael John, you're so young. Such a hothead. Strange, but you remind me of myself. I've had these vanities. I remember them in the deep mists of my young life.'

'Young?' He put his hands on her shoulders, pulled her to him and kissed her hard, very hard, on the mouth. She could taste the stain of port on his full lips. She pulled away, protesting, then removed his hands from her shoulders and placed them carefully in his lap. Then she smiled. 'Perhaps not so young.'

He stared at her. 'We could ride together . . . Tomorrow morning.'

She shook her head. 'I've agreed to ride with Gertrude Seland in the morning. I promised her.'

He clapped his hand on his forehead and groaned. 'Another lunatic!'

'Perhaps Monday. We could ride on Monday? I'd like that.'

'I catch the train south on Monday. By Friday I'll be on the high seas. Away from all this. And I won't be sorry.' He allowed his face to look very sad. 'Except for you.'

She flushed. 'Don't go on so, Michael John. We've only been together minutes. Not even hours.'

'I liked you two years ago. But there was no time. They got rid of me.'

'You'd been a very naughty boy, had you not?'

'That was a mistake. An injustice. As I said to you before, they're mad. That cretin Ellenberg. All of them. My mother. Ambrose. Certainly that gypsy hooligan.'

'Poor baby.' She put her fingers on the side of his face. The skin under her hand was quite rough. This was no child. Much less of a child than Astrid was to the General. It occurred to her now that, perhaps, sauce for the goose would be good fare.

He turned his cheek and kissed her palm. He picked up the other hand and kissed it too. 'Please,' he said. 'Please, Constance. I go away on Monday and that will be that. For always.'

Now it was her turn to pull him to her. She whispered in his ear, 'You know my room?' She could feel him nod. 'Twenty minutes. Come and see me in twenty minutes. We can't have you going away across to the other side of the world so unhappy now, can we?'

Upstairs on the first floor Melanie Tyler was sharing with Astrid the task of settling Rose down for the night. Melanie unpacked the bags and put all of Rose's things into the small rosewood chest of drawers by the door. Astrid stripped the sleepy child and washed her hands and face with warm water from the jug on the washstand. Melanie stood holding the towel and stared at Rose. 'It's a very fit child,' she said.

'Her name is Rose, Mrs Tyler. She's a she.'

'I was wondering, Miss Benbow, why you gave her such a name?'

'Because when she was born her face was like a little tight rosebud.'

Melanie looked at her sharply. 'You were there when the child was born?'

'I was.'

'So you would know the mother?'

'Only a very little.' She paused. 'The poor woman died and

there was no one to take care of the babe.' Apart from the time in the registrar's office at Denver it was the first time in her life that she'd been called on to make a deliberate and important lie. Perhaps it wouldn't be the last.

'Poor little soul,' said Melanie.

Astrid pulled the embroidered lawn nightdress over the head of the protesting Rose. Then she removed the pillows from one side of the bed and settled her in the un-pillowed space. She pulled the blankets up tightly around her and tucked her in.

'You certainly have a way with the child, miss. I'd not have thought . . .'

Astrid smiled. 'I've had a year to practise, Mrs Tyler. Now, I think we're done here. Thank you for your help.'

Melanie moved to the door.

'And how's John, Mrs Tyler? My mother said he was not well?'

Melanie clasped her hands tightly together. 'Well, he's quite poorly, or he thinks he is. There's not a mark on him, and he's cold rather than hot. Either case we'll have to do something about him. I'll get the doctor in the morning.'

'You must do that,' said Astrid. 'He was always such a fit man, John.'

Melanie looked at her and did not say what was in her mind. How would Miss Benbow know what John was like? She was never at home.

Rose whimpered and Astrid turned to check on her. When she turned back Melanie had gone.

Nine

Dancing The Jig

11.15pm

Ambrose made his way down the back stairs in his dressing gown. As he emerged at the bottom of the kitchen staircase the two people standing shoulder to shoulder at the sink turned and looked up at him. Their round eyes and round rosy cheeks made them look remarkably alike, although one was considerably older than the other. The younger one was certainly Gwennie Taggart. So the older one must be her mother.

'I thought I'd get a cup of milk,' he said.

Gwennie's mother lifted her hands wearily out of the washing-up water. They were chapped and red.

'Don't worry,' he said. 'I'll get it. Mrs Mac keeps it in the long pantry. It's like the North Pole down there.'

When he came back into the kitchen with three foaming mugs of milk in his hands they'd finished the dishes and were shaking out the wrung cloths and hanging them beside others on the rail over the fireplace. 'I thought you might want some,' he said.

Gwennie's mother sat down. 'Good of you, son . . . sir . . . mister.'

Gwennie slid onto the bench beside her. 'They call him Ambrose,' she said. 'He plays the flute.'

'Now there's a talent,' said Mrs Taggart. 'My man could play the squeezebox like a good'n. Learned off his uncle, his mother's brother. That one came from Poland where they all play such things. He was very popular, my man. You're never short of friends when you can make music.'

'That's a comfort,' said Ambrose.

'Why don't you play it for us now?' said Gwennie. 'Go on, show me mam how you can play.'

He stared at her then said, 'Wait here.' In a minute he was back, flute in hand. In three minutes he was playing jigs for them. At first Mrs Taggart tapped the edge of her empty cup with a spoon. Then her toes started tapping. Then she stood up and moved to the space by the window, her feet kicking forward and backwards to the music. Then she gasped, 'Hey, our Gwennie, come here and dance with us. Nowt like a bit of a jig to cheer yourself up.'

Then they were all there: mother and daughter clicking and stepping in time on the stone floor, and Ambrose capering around them, his flute to his lips. They were making so much noise they failed to hear the door opening. Ambrose caught sight of the intruder and stopped playing. When the music died Gwennie and her mother stopped jigging and looked across to the door to see Melanie Tyler, a lamp in her hands, the darkened corridor behind her.

Mrs Taggart started to gather up the cups that had held the milk. She turned on the cold tap so the water gushed over them. 'Sorry, Mrs Tyler,' she said over her shoulder. 'We were just . . .'

'Cheering yourselves up, I suppose?' Melanie glanced round. 'I see you've finished here. We don't usually work this late, Mrs Taggart. But with all these comings and goings it's like a madhouse here.' She glared at Ambrose.

He pocketed his flute. 'Well, ladies,' he said cheerfully. 'Bedtime for me.'

'And for you two as well,' said Mrs Tyler. 'I doubt if Mrs Mac'll be that happy, waiting up this late for you.'

Mrs Taggart dried the cups and left them on the draining board. 'Mrs Tyler . . .' she began.

'Back here in the morning, if you please,' she said. 'Seven sharp, tomorrow and always. It's going to be a busy day.'

John Tyler had had a very unpleasant day. He'd taken all Melanie's potions. He'd sat with his head over a steaming bowl of saturated balsam. He'd slept now and then, waking up several times in the middle of dreams of drowning and choking.

'Well then, love, how're you feeling?' Melanie inspected herself in the crazed mirror above the fireplace. She removed her cap and began to loosen her apron. 'There's been such a to-do down there, John. Miss Benbow turned up with a baby! Think of it. Not hers. Well, not as far as you can tell. Seems it's a foundling. Can you credit it? And that Michael John came back from the Colonel's reeking of port. Don't you think the Colonel should know better? Haven't I always said there's something not quite right about that man? Gives us the creeps. Anyway, that soldier boy's laying about him left right and centre, so to speak. A cruel streak, he has. Soft soaping the American lady, of course. And then just now I've broken up a cosy little dance in the kitchen with Ambrose being the dance-master and that Mrs Taggart and her daughter dancing jigs. And her in mourning! I tell you, people have no idea how to behave . . .' She turned to look at the supine figure on the bed. 'John, old boy? How are you?'

He groaned.

'What is it?' she said sharply. 'Where does it hurt?'

'My neck hurts. My arms ache. I feel awful, Mel. Awful.'

'Did you take my medicine?'

'Every drop.'

'Well, if you an't better tomorrow I'm most definitely gunna get that doctor whatever you say.'

'No need for that. A night's sleep. A good night's sleep is all I need,' he mumbled.

She stripped off to her shift, lifted the eiderdown and climbed in beside his chill, twitching body. 'Mind you, this has been a long day,' she said. 'A very long day.' She put an arm round his waist and spooned herself around him. For all their differences she and John were close. Unaware as he was, she knew that in this island of strangers he cared only for her.

His voice was muffled by the blankets. 'Longest day of my life, Mel, I'll tell you that. Roll on morning.'

There was something stoical about her John. Despite the fact that she had to live in this shabby house and not in a grand place like Seland, she'd rather be here with John than anywhere else without him. She'd been pleased when no children had come their way. All they needed was each other. Melanie closed her eyes. She supposed that was what people called love.

Ten

Riding the Bounds

6am

Since she'd become responsible for Rose, Astrid was used to rising early. The child was neither noisy nor complaining but she was persistent. Without fail she woke up entirely at five thirty and, with great good humour, talked and chattered, clambered over Astrid and lifted her eyelids to see if she was awake.

The first morning at Benbow was no different. But this morning Astrid's eyes were already open. She was wondering what kind of trouble might lie in store for her. Perhaps she should have stayed in Chelsea and made Rose a London child, a child of the city. She had considered that, but there had been a peculiar inevitability about bringing Rose to Benbow. An instinct inside her. She had given in to it. Something about bringing the child home, perhaps.

Her first inkling that it may have been a mistake was when they were met yesterday at the station by the transformed Jack Lomas. Here in the privacy of her bedroom with only Rose to see, she could admit that the glitter in his eyes had brought to her mind thoughts of Richard Redoute and the swimming pool parlour and the way she had thought of him there. Then there were the drawings in her notebook. In an instant he'd made her a creature of feeling rather than thought, just as he had two years earlier when he had challenged her over Honesty. There was so

302

much between them now. Yesterday she'd had to hold her breath when he stared too hard at the child Rose. How could he not realise? If he didn't guess, then the witch-like Keziah Leeming might spot it. You never knew, with that woman. Perhaps Benbow was the last place she should have come. Perhaps she would lose Rose, who'd become so much the centre of her life in this last year.

Rose pulled at her long hair as it lay on the pillow. 'Mama up!' she commanded.

Astrid sat up, bringing the sheets and the blankets with her. She took hold of Rose and planted her on the floor. Then she swung her own feet to the chilly boards. She glanced at the fireplace with its dusty adornment, a fan of folded newspaper. Her mind went back (as periodically it did) to that first morning at Seland, and Honesty Leeming clearing out her fireplace. When Rose, it occurred to her now, was already a tiny speck in the universe.

She shivered. How extraordinary it all was. 'We'll put our clothes on, Rosie, then we'll have some breakfast and go out and walk the bounds.'

'Bounds,' repeated Rose, tucking the word away in her magpie mind.

Astrid dressed her and brushed her hair. Then she brushed her own hair, pulled the sides up with combs and wove the back into one long plait which she tied with a ribbon from her own childhood box. No corset. A green linen dress with flowing skirts, and a long knitted jacket against the cold. Sufficient for a dawn walk where no one would see her. On an impulse she picked up a silk shawl. It would be a long walk. She would make some kind of sling to carry Rose, just in case she flagged. The child could totter but she could hardly walk the distance Astrid was contemplating.

Out on the corridor Astrid caught sight of her brother. She put a finger on Rose's lips. Michael John was in his shirtsleeves and his tunic was thrown over his shoulder. His boots were in his hand. He was stealing away from Constance's door, which was still slightly ajar.

Astrid waited a moment until he turned the corner onto his own corridor. Then she took her hand from Rose's mouth and proceeded to the narrow door that led to the back staircase.

Down in the kitchen Mrs Mac was sitting on her fireside chair drinking her early cup of tea. The new woman and her daughter were loading the crockery baskets for the dining room breakfast.

Mrs Mac leapt to her feet. 'Miss Benbow, you did give me a fright . . . and this is the little one they were talking about? Mrs Tyler was full of it. Said it was a fine child . . .'

Astrid sat Rose on the bench by the long table. 'Milk and some bread if you please, Mrs Mac. We're off for a walk but need some fuel first.' She glanced across at the mother and daughter.

'This is Mrs Taggart and her daughter Gwennie.' The two of them bobbed curtsies. 'Mrs Taggart was brought in by Mrs Tyler for extra help. And her daughter's just keeping her company. Poor Mrs Tyler. Upstairs now she is, with poor John. Real poorly, he is.' Mrs Mac held a loaf to her aproned, downhanging bosom and lopped off a slice of bread. 'Get us the milk from the long pantry, will you, Mrs Taggart?' She took down the butter pot.

After twenty minutes of Mrs Mac's invasive benevolence, Astrid set out to walk the bounds. After five minutes she had to put Rose into the sling. After ten minutes she was flagging herself so she was pleased to catch sight of the forge. Edith Leeming was outside the door with a chipped enamel bowl, scattering feed for her hens. Putting up her hand to shade her eyes from the flat rays of the early morning sun, she still had to squeeze her eyelids to see who it was, this girl with the child standing at her gate. She blinked and peered again, not quite believing her senses.

'Gracious, it's Miss Benbow! I'd not have believed it. I thought it was some lass from the village with a bairn.' There was the faintest note of reproof in her voice. Edith liked things as they should be. Miss Benbow was not even wearing a hat! 'Will you have a cup of tea, now?' she said.

'That would be so welcome,' said Astrid. She sat down on the wall and lifted Rose out of the sling and set her on the dusty ground. The child wobbled towards a pair of hens that were pecking at the newly scattered seed.

Edith stared at her. 'A fine child,' she said cautiously, wondering what exactly Miss Benbow had brought home to roost. What was she supposed to say?

'Rose is from America,' said Astrid. 'I adopted her when her mother died.' The lie got easier every time she said it.

'I see,' said Edith. 'Will the child have lemon cordial? Honesty always used to love my lemon cordial.'

Astrid looked at Edith sharply but the offer was made in innocence. 'She's just had milk, Edith. Perhaps she's too young for cordial.'

Edith went away, bowl in hand, and Astrid looked around. There was no sign of Freddy. She could hear the ringing of the anvil so he must be at work already. Sunday morning! Perhaps blacksmiths were allowed to break the rules. Keziah was not around, but you might expect that. She could be on the road, or up at her caravan.

Edith returned, and Astrid took the cup from her. 'Keziah's not around?' she said.

Edith shook her head. 'Called in just on daylight. She's off up your ma's garden gathering some of those herbs of hers with the dew on'm.'

Astrid drank her tea quickly and called Rose to be lifted into her sling. 'And Jack Lomas?' she ventured.

'Aye, he's home just now. He's off trying out a chestnut for Keziah. Freddy's just shod her. The poor thing had this bad action on her hind leg. Our Freddy can do miracles with a well-made shoe. And Jack has a feel for horses not much less than his ma, even though machines are more his delight these days.'

She raised her eyes to the lane. 'Talk of the devil,' she said fondly.

Astrid's blood was racing as she saw Jack coming through the trees on the chestnut mare. He was wearing a white cotton shirt and fustian breeches but his feet were bare. He was riding bareback, his heels out, free of the belly of the mare. The finely dressed man of yesterday evening had become a little more like the boy he once was. As she looked at him Astrid fumbled with the need not to admit even to herself how very glad and worried she was, how fearful and happy all in the same moment.

'See here, Jack,' called Edith. 'Here's Miss Benbow walkin' the bounds with a bairn in tow.'

He jumped down lightly. 'That'll be a long haul,' he said. 'With a bairn on your back.'

'We'll get as far as we can, then turn back.' Astrid put Rose down. She tried to keep her voice light.

'Pity to miss the whole thing, like, as that's a grand walk,' he said. 'The land's all a-sparkle this day. It's a rare morning when the east wind doesn't cut in.' He picked up Rose and held her face close to his. 'How about a ride, *charver*? D'you like a ride on my horse?'

Rose beamed. 'Ride horsey,' she said.

'But . . .' Astrid said. She watched as Jack leapt back on the mare and set the child in front of him. He looked down at her. 'It'll be easier to *ride* the bounds,' he said. 'You ride pillion with me.' He stepped the horse across to the wall where she sat. 'One foot on the wall and you're on,' he said. He put down an arm for her to grasp.

'Jack!' Edith's tone was disbelieving, almost despairing. It was not dissimilar to the look in her eye when she saw Astrid with her pigtail and her shawl.

It was this very kindly, disapproving tone of Edith's that made Astrid clamber onto the wall, take Jack's arm and launch herself onto the broad back of the mare behind him. She left one foot dangling and brought another across in front of her.

This was adventure enough, without riding astride. She grasped his belt loosely and as the horse moved to a sprightly trot she felt safe and steady; open for anything.

As they moved down the road towards Benbow village she turned to catch sight of Edith Leeming standing with her hands on her hips, staring at them with a rare frown on her open, pleasant face.

Eleven

The Benbow Rose

8am

This Sunday of all Sundays it was important for Carmel to
make her way to her garden. This morning her house seemed to
be teeming with bodies – sons, daughter, friend, the new woman
and her daughter in the kitchen. And now a child of dubious
parentage who seemed to have clambered into the heart of her
family.

The feeling she had towards this child was strange. She'd
always been quite in sympathy with the relief that Rufus felt
when he got away from the house and the family. He'd never
been able to tolerate the mundane ties of those who by blood or
affection had a right to call on his resources. She learned very
early that this even included herself. Among strangers he was
free to be solitary. For a time she had shared that solitariness
with him.

Then, sensing his rejection, she knew that she had replicated
that comfortable escape into her garden with its undemanding
plants and its compliant roses. But the kiss bestowed on her by
that child had snagged at her feelings, just as a rose occasionally
snags your fingers when you prune it, reminding you that it is
not always so compliant.

Followed by Susannah the cat she went straight through to
her rose-house with its open roof and its skeletal framework.
Some of the buds still enfolded the dew in their petals. She

examined the dozen low bushes that had adopted her new hybrid. Each one was consistent. A hundred blooms. The yellow velvet aristocracy of the French rose joined with the pink open-hearted simplicity of the hedgerow variety. A pale cream petal just tinged with pink. The scent was very faint: the musky scent of old rose cut by a lemon freshness of country lanes. It was a very fine rose.

She led the way back to the round glasshouse. The cat Susannah leapt up on the table, turned round twice and sat on a pile of catalogues. Carmel sat in her wicker chair and picked up the forms from the table. She'd filled in most of the pages. She unscrewed her ink bottle and picked up her pen. In the space provided for the name she wrote *Benbow*. She'd been pondering on the name for weeks, coming up with all kinds of possibilities. But, in the end, she knew the simplest ways are always the best. *The Benbow Rose*. It would always be known as the Benbow Rose. The world would know it as the Benbow Rose.

There was a rustle at the door and Keziah came in, a shallow basket in her hand. Susannah leapt from the table and scampered through the door, taking a sentinel's position on the low wall outside. Cats didn't care for Keziah any more than she cared for them. She preferred her dogs, who were more obedient and could work for their living.

Keziah placed her long basket on the floor. 'G'day, Carmel,' she said, taking a seat beside her friend. 'Just caught the dew. Near burned off now.'

'It's a fine day. June days have that very special feeling.' Carmel paused. 'I just decided on the name for the new rose,' she said.

'A new name? These days it's always new names for new things. So many new things. Jack with his guns and you with your roses.'

Carmel looked at her. Keziah was unusually sharp. 'Your Jack's looking very well these days.' She said the words placatingly, as though she would ward off a storm. 'Such beautiful clothes. Very fine. He seems to be doing very well.' She paused. 'And that's a high-toned rig of his. We were in very fine fettle, coming home last night.'

'Made by Gerry Mulligan. Ferryhill. Best builder all round. Drives a hard bargain.'

'Like you, Keziah? I imagine you drove a hard bargain with him.' She was still placating the storm. There was a timid side to her that hated trouble: another reason for the refuge in the garden.

'Oh aye,' said Keziah. 'Favours to call in. Always favours to call in.'

'It seems your Jack's quite the businessman these days.'

'Aye,' said Keziah gloomily. 'And has bought a house in Durham city too. A house! Them Newcastle *gadgies* has too much say over him.'

'They must respect him. He's very successful.'

'And'll be more. *Es*'ll not stop till he rules the world. Thinks he can do owt he chooses.'

'And can he?' said Carmel, half teasing.

Keziah cocked an eye at her. 'Only time'll tell. Plenty folks around'll stop a *romani* lad if they can. But as long as he has sommat they want he's all right. We'll have ter see, won't we?'

'He's very clever.'

Keziah was bored with this talk of Jack. 'He tells us that your Astrid brought home a bairn. Says she had a bairn with her that seemed like her own.'

Carmel raised her eyebrows. 'I think you might be thinking what others will think, Keziah. But it's not Astrid's child, though she's adopted her for her own. The mother died, poor soul. So Astrid took responsibility for the child.' She laughed. 'Strangely enough she has called her Rose. You should see her, Keziah. She's very beautiful.'

'Seems like you took to her yourself,' said Keziah.

Carmel nodded. 'She's very appealing.'

'So it seems.' Keziah stood up. 'I suppose I'd better be getting on. I s'll go down the far end and tie the lavender.' She picked up her basket. 'You tell your Astrid to get down to see us. I s'll want to hear about our Honesty. Edith was right cut up that she didn't come back with Astrid.'

'Edith . . .?'

'Aye. Me too, seeing as you say that. I'm hoping that child of mine's come to no harm.'

'Astrid said she was fine. She insisted that she'd chosen not to come home. She's with *romani* people.'

'Mebbe that's right but I'd like your Astrid to say it to me face. Tell her to get down to see us,' Keziah said sourly, then stumped out and clashed the door behind her. Susannah pushed it with her paw and sneaked back into the glasshouse. She jumped onto the table beside Carmel, who put a hand out to stroke her.

'I've never seen Keziah so cross, Susannah, have you? Not ever.'

Then she shook out the form to check that the ink had dried and put it in its envelope. Carefully she wrote the address of the society. *The Benbow Rose*. Beautiful, tender, new. What satisfaction there was in that!

Twelve

Making Moves

8.45am

Michael John moved the white knight to threaten the black bishop. Then he moved the white bishop to put the black king in check. He was breaking the rules but at least this sludgy old game was moving on. He turned to see Constance come down the stairs. He'd been loitering in the hallway for ten minutes just so that he would not miss her.

Constance looked very distinguished in her riding boots, her dark green riding dress and her close hat with its swathe of veil ready to pull down. She was rather more tied up and tied in than when he'd last seen her. He stood up straight and saluted her. 'Morning, Miss Redoute.' He walked towards her.

She smiled and put up her riding crop to keep him at a distance. 'Good morning, Lieutenant Benbow. Ain't it just a very fine morning?'

'It was a very fine night,' he said, too eagerly.

A small frown marred her white brow. 'I have to say, sir, that a gentleman never brings up in the mornin' the events of the evenin' before.'

'I'm sorry, Connie. I . . .' He put out his hand to move aside the barrier of the riding crop.

There was a thundering knock on the door.

'Do open it, Michael John,' drawled Constance. 'Even I

know that in this very quaint house there'll be no one to open the door at this time of day.'

Michael opened the door and was almost bowled over by Gertrude Seland, magnificent in a black skirt and breeches and a severely tailored black riding jacket as she marched in. 'Morning, Michael John. I've come to collect your guest for a gallop. Ah, Miss Redoute! Dressed for it I see. I do hope you're not joining us, Michael John. This is most distinctly a ladies' *tête à tête*.'

Michael John went red and wished in a cool part of his brain that he might kill her. 'Gertrude, I—'

'Ah! Now then!' Gertrude beamed at Constance. 'Are you ready for the gallop of your life?'

Michael John said through gritted teeth, 'I was trying to tell you, Gertrude, that there's nothing in our stable worth riding except my mount and I'm riding down to the Lodge. The Colonel and I are going out to shoot this morning.'

'Thought of it! Thought of it!' said Gertrude. 'I remembered that there never was anything worth riding in the Benbow stables.' She took Constance's arm. 'Come and see what I've brought you, my dear. You will absolutely love them.' She dragged her through the door and Michael John followed.

Standing on the gravel by the mounting block, held by a Seland footman in outdoor livery, were two saddled horses: a showy black and a more sturdy mare whose polished coat shone in the sun like hot toffee. Constance turned to Gertrude, smiling widely. 'Which one for me?'

Pleased at her pleasure Gertrude said, 'You choose.'

Constance went to the black horse, took the reins in one hand, climbed the block and leapt lightly onto his back. The horse pawed restlessly on the gravel for a moment and then stood still. Constance looked from Gertrude to Michael John and back. 'Well then? Where do we go?'

Gertrude mounted the bay. 'A gentle trot, then a gallop into paradise. Then back to Seland for lunch.' She looked down at

Michael John. 'Tell them Miss Redoute has been kidnapped and has been taken you know not where.' The women laughed at his look of angry dismay, turned their horses' heads and headed down the drive.

Michael John watched them go, grinding his teeth with fury. He'd planned to get Constance to come shooting with him then persuade her to dally with him on the way back. He knew a place in the Bottom Wood which was entirely private. Now he'd have to make do with the Colonel. While the killing would be good, the company would be less interesting than he'd hoped.

He was just turning to walk back to the house to collect his guns when he caught sight of the knowing smile on the Seland footman's face. He marched across and said, 'What are you smiling at, you oaf?'

The man shrugged but still grinned. 'I was thinking, sir, that a man never knows, with the ladies.' He'd hardly got the words out of his mouth when Michael John landed a closed fist on his cheekbone and felled him at a blow. Then he leapt and sat on the man's chest, landing blow after blow, this way and that, on the footman's face. The man started screaming and bellowing in protest. 'I'll tell her ladyship . . .'

Through the angry mists in his head Michael John could hear someone calling. He paused in his attack and looked up as far as the second floor. Melanie Tyler was hanging half out of the sash window. 'Will you stop that? The man is in Seland livery. Your mother wouldn't like it. Anyway, my husband is here quite ill. The noise is just too much for him. Stop it, I tell you!'

Michael John stood up and brushed down his uniform. He kicked the curled up figure once for luck and stormed off towards the side of the house. The footman stood up, shook his head hard, brushed himself down and set off round the corner to the Benbow kitchen. There, he hoped, the cook would provide him with some refreshment, and butter for his bruises, before he set off on his own hack back to Seland. What her ladyship would think of his battered face he shuddered to think. As one of a matched pair he had to keep himself looking good. Men had been fired for less.

Ambrose, on his way down to breakfast, had seen the drama through the hall window. He was glad that he'd not been in Michael John's way when those women laughed at him. Even the footman had had a close shave and he was a big man.

Ambrose went across the hall to make another move in the chess. His king was in check. He frowned. That shouldn't have happened.

He made his way to the dining room with its very inviting smells of kedgeree, kidneys, eggs, bacon and sausage wafting from their silver dishes on the sideboard. The laid table was untouched. He wondered where everyone was. It looked as though he'd have breakfast in solitary splendour. He didn't mind that. As long as he didn't have to share the table with Michael John he could sit down and eat with satisfaction,

He had almost finished when his mother came in. She was wearing her gardening clothes and carried with her the scent of manured soil and cut greenery. 'Ah, Ambrose,' she said, as she sat down to a plate of kidney and scrambled egg. 'I understand from Jacob Ellenberg that you seem to have left school and set out on a career in industry. Or, as Mrs Tyler tells me, perhaps you may try your luck as an entertainer.'

He flushed. 'I . . . well, Mama, I must tell you that school's not for me. I am a dunce and I am not well liked. That's always been clear. And I met this Mr Kilburn yesterday when I was with the Colonel. Seemed a decent chap. I'm visiting him this morning, in his house in Bishop Auckland, to play the flute for him.'

'I know this man,' she said, tucking into her eggs. 'He is a decent chap, as you put it. Your father and I once went to a concert of his at the town hall. I know nothing of music but it seemed a jolly affair. He seems to be quite a sound man. I have heard from Melanie that not only does he entertain Mr Elgar in his own house, but he actually writes music himself! A strange thing for an industrialist, a nail-maker, don't you think?'

He looked at her innocently. 'Perhaps as strange as a lady being her own gardener?'

She put down her fork and smiled slightly. 'You are no dunce, my dear. What is it, Ambrose, that you'd like to do?'

'Well, Mr Kilburn said he needed a flautist in his orchestra and he would give me a clerk's job so I could have some work.'

'Could he not pay you for playing in his orchestra so you don't have to work in his dirty nail manufactury?'

Ambrose shook his head. 'I don't know whether that's quite the way in which Mr Kilburn sees his orchestra. I think you have to be gainfully employed and then you're allowed to be a musician. It's the Liberal way.'

'How quaint.' She wandered across to the sideboard to find the coffee pot. 'Is this really what you want to do, Ambrose?'

'For the present, I think it is.'

She stared at him. 'Do you know, Ambrose, sometimes I think you are very sensible. The school fees are saved, I suppose. The Colonel says we need to look to every penny at present.'

'I'll have a wage, as well. You can have that.'

She laughed out loud. 'How very kind of you. But it will be a pittance, I promise you. Perhaps you could save the money to launch yourself on the next part of this career of yours. Perhaps you'll be a nail-maker, or even a composer?'

He flushed. 'There is no need to be sarcastic, Ma. No need at all.'

'I'm sorry.' She reached for the rather cool toast. 'But really it will be rather nice to hear you play in an orchestra, Amby.'

'I played in the school orchestra, if you remember. You could have heard me play there. But you never came.'

She frowned and laid on the butter very thickly. 'Could I? Do you know, dear, I never quite realised that. It all seems so far away. Such a very long way to go.'

He looked at her. 'Do you know, Mama, I think you make a very fine model in life? You have always followed your own ways, not done this and that because that's what you ought to do. This is what made me think I might work for Mr Kilburn and play in his orchestra.'

'I'm sure I must take that as a compliment.' She pointed her butter knife towards the sideboard. 'Did you have coffee, dear? It's very good. Very good indeed.'

Thirteen

Commitments

'You call it walking the bounds.' Jack Lomas broke the silence. His tone was soft, polite. 'That's a strange thing. I did wonder why that was, like?'

The big chestnut mare moved steadily along the narrow gully beyond the cluster of houses around the forge. They skirted the village and went left up towards the woods.

Astrid spoke into his ear. 'On the rare times he came home from his travels my father used to take me to walk the bounds. You'd have liked my father, I think.'

'Aye, my mother tells me he was a *rai*. Feller that takes up with gypsies. I said to her, were we supposed to be honoured?'

'I don't think he saw it like that. I feel he might have envied you, rather than feel that he honoured you. In a letter once he told me that we are tied down by more than houses.'

'Keziah thinks I'm going that way. Going all *gorgio*.'

The horse stumbled and Rose cried out. Astrid put an arm round Jack to hang on to the child and her hand met Jack's. He clasped it tight. She let it lie there a minute then pulled back again to hold only to the neutrality of his leather belt. She spoke now more closely into his back. 'You have a choice. You can be one, or the other.'

'Me, I think that you can be both. We're all mixtures. Who knows what mixtures we are?'

Astrid thought of Rose. 'Who knows?' she said.

'Duck!' he said.

She ducked into his back to miss an overhanging bough. 'Do you know my father was away from here almost all of my life? Walking the bounds might be my only clear memory of him. I remember him walking with me and his hand was so big that he had to tuck his little finger up my sleeve. His father walked the bounds with him and his grandfather before that . . .'

'Some kind of old magic, was it? So long as you could walk round it you owned it?'

She smiled into his back and wondered if he could feel her smile. 'That thought hadn't occurred to me. Perhaps his ancestors *rode* the bounds, just as we ride them now. But my father never actually rode a horse. He was happy enough to have them pull his van, of course. He had great respect for horses, but would not get on the back of one.'

The land began to rise and the mare made a bit of heavy weather of getting up a bank. For a second she had to tighten her arms around Jack to save herself from falling backwards. Then she returned to the safe harbour of his belt again. They jogged on. He turned his head so he could glance at her face. 'You have a very nice voice,' he said. 'Soft.'

She didn't know what to say. His own voice was very deep. She could feel it resonating through his back as far as her knuckles where they were clutched round his belt. They had to sway together, side to side, to avoid the reaching branches with their fresh spring green. She found herself breathing more and more deeply in the crisp morning air.

'Do you ride yourself?' he said, taking up their legitimate conversation again.

'I used to ride a good deal when I was young. Mostly with Gertrude Seland, the woman who ran after the carriage last night. She's a very good horsewoman. And in Colorado in America I used to ride with . . . Constance's father. I liked riding with him. He was a wonderful man. You had to ride there. It was the only way to see that amazing country. But now if I'm home I'll use the trap. And in London I have no need to ride. There are the buses and the underground railway. And the cabs. Some of them are motors, of course, these days.'

She felt his grunt of satisfaction. 'Of course, motors are the future. I know two men in Newcastle who have motor cars. I'm gunna have one myself soon.'

'Your mother won't be too pleased. She's a great one for her horses, I believe.'

She could feel him shrug. 'It's not Keziah's life, it's mine.' He paused. 'One day, Astrid, I'll buy you a motor car of your own.'

It was so clearly a declaration, a commitment, that she didn't know what to say and again she stayed silent. She was pleased he couldn't see her face which was burning, and, she imagined, fiery red. They emerged from the trees onto a piece of high ground overlooking Low Wood. 'Now, look around you,' he said.

She looked around. Behind them was the dense belt of trees that entirely masked the Hall from the surrounding district. Ahead the Durham landscape swept upwards to the horizon. The old landscape that had been hilly and verdant with a scattering of cottages and farmhouses now only survived in patches. These days the whole panorama was scratched in here and there, like a steel engraving, with the headgear and industrial buildings of a dozen or so mines, each with its attendant village thrown up for the shipped-in workers. Early on the morning of the Sabbath it was all eerily quiet; the only sign of humanity was the smoke from hundreds of chimneys which wove into the air and joined to sit like a dark crown over each village.

Just before them were their own Benbow pits: the Red Daisy, the Benbow and, way to the left in the hollow, Carafay, which her father had bequeathed to Jacob Ellenberg.

Jack Lomas raised a hand and pointed to the horizon. 'See there?' Right on the tip of the horizon sat Durham cathedral, at this distance an almost childlike block-on-block. 'I have a house in that city,' he said. 'From my house you can see that church and the castle beside it. A river winds round them like a snake.' He paused. 'Now's the time for you to tell me that my mother won't like it, me with a house.'

'Your mother won't like it,' she said. They both laughed. Rose, sitting in front of Jack, laughed too.

Up there, with the Hall enclosed entirely by its belt of trees behind her, and the raggle-taggle of pitheads and cottages in front of her, Astrid knew without thinking that she was on the very cusp of something and was comfortable with it. Perhaps she should tell Jack Lomas now that she wanted to go back to the safety of the Hall; that it was a mistake to ride the Benbow bounds with him: a man who rode without a saddle and guided the horse with his thighs. Then, perhaps she wouldn't.

'Shall we go on?' he said.

'Yes. Yes, of course.' She took her clutching hands from his belt and put them lightly round his waist. This was her declaration. He made no comment, but raised his hand and pointed again.

'Do you know that place?' he said.

Of course she knew it. It was a straggle of buildings by a stream: a seventy-acre farmholding called Low Bent Riggs. Its lower fields backed onto the forge. The Benbow tenant was a crotchety man called Jacky Redrigg. 'Low Bent Riggs,' she said.

'It's mine,' he said. 'I bought it last month outright, from Colonel Carmedy. I paid cash.'

She frowned. 'My mother said nothing of that,' she said. But then her mother hadn't had time to tell her anything. She and Rose had come out too early on their walk. By now her mother was probably in her garden.

'I'm not all that sure your mother knows. And me own mother, part of whose money has gone into the farm, she certainly doesn't know. But she trusts us with her money. I've never done wrong by her.'

'So why d'you tell me all this?'

'You should know it. You should know everything I do. Everything about me.' He made kissing noises with his mouth and told the horse to 'walk on!'

Up in front, the child Rose made kissing noises and said, 'Horsey, horsey!'

At the back Astrid clung on to Jack Lomas' waist and chanted the nursery song:

> *Just let your heels go clippety clop*
> *The tail go swish and the wheels go round*
> *Giddy up we're homeward bound!*

Jack urged the horse on and they moved to a trot, then a canter. Without a saddle they were bouncing all over the place and Astrid had to cling on for dear life. 'Stop, stop, will you?' she shouted. 'Slow down!'

Obediently he slowed down. He turned to look at her. She could see the strong planes of his face above his beard and the downward shadow cast by his thick lashes.

'Me, I only do what I'm told,' he said, grinning.

She beat his back with the flat of her hand. 'Don't tease,' she said.

'Tell me about America,' he said.

She found herself telling Jack about riding the dusty passes of Colorado with Richard Redoute. 'We always went in the early morning. It was much too hot later in the day. Sometimes we rode gullies where no one had ever been before.'

'Not like hereabouts,' he said. 'Every path's been trod a thousand times. This is a crowded island. Ireland's more empty. I was there once buying horses. There are villages with no people.'

They were skirting their way round the Low Wood now,

across the stream at its shallowest point. Rose laughed as the water splashed onto her boots and the hem of her dress. Ahead of them a haze of bluebells shimmered in the green shade of the oaks and beech that made up the wood.

They emerged from the trees almost into the yard of the Carafay. The colliery buildings were scattered in a random fashion around the wheelhouse. Rusty, discarded machinery lay against a stack of new pit props. The wooden walkways were sagging and in need of repair.

'So what do you think of this, Miss Benbow?' he said.

'Is it still working?' she said, puzzled. After the sweetness of the bluebells and the wood and the trickling stream this was a very ugly place.

'Aye. It's supposed to be working.'

'But this is a Benbow pit. Well, the one that my father left to Jacob.'

'So it is.'

'From here it looks like a very dismal inheritance.'

'So it is.'

She was silent. The Colonel had made so little of his stewardship here. She sighed.

'Don't you worry yourself. This place'll be fine soon. Neat and trim. Brought up to scratch. Coal surging to the surface.'

'Someone has seen Colonel Carmedy about this?'

'No. It's changed hands. From today it belongs to me. Jacob has given it to me. It was little profit to him. I'll make him money out of it.'

The farm. The pit. What next? Benbow?' She thought she was silent, but she'd actually said the words.

'I have my way, that could be it.' He turned round. 'We need to get down,' he said. 'I'll hold you.' He held her hand tightly as she jumped down. Then he held it a second too long before taking Rose and lifting her into Astrid's arms. Then he grasped the horse's mane and leapt off lightly himself. She looked at his bare feet in the dirt. His toes were long and his feet were brown and well formed. He followed her gaze, then looked her straight in the eye. 'Gypsy's feet?'

She flushed. 'I wasn't thinking anything like that.'

'Well you should, because it's true. This is who I am, but I'm also the man I've become. The man I made myself into. This is what you can do in these modern times. You can make yourself into what you want to be. Even you.'

Slowly she shook her head. 'It can't be as easy as that.' Then she faltered. 'But where I was in Colorado people were making themselves all the time. One day a poor miner or carpenter, next day the richest man in the state. It all seemed possible there.'

'Why not here?' he said. 'Why not us here?' Then he put out his arms and encompassed both her and Rose. He pulled them to him and kissed Astrid lightly on the lips. Then he rolled his cheeks first one way, then the other, pressing his cheek to hers. His beard was silky against her skin. Then he kissed her again, his tongue flickering against her lips. She shuddered and pressed closer.

'Mama!' Rose's protest was in her ear. 'I squashing!'

They laughed and drew away from each other. He kept his hands on her elbows so the circle was still complete. 'How did this happen?' she said.

'It started that first time two years ago when I saw you in the road. I saw you and I knew I'd do anything, anything to have you, to be with you. So with Jacob's help I made my way, into shoes, into houses, into making things, into businesses. I'm good at all that. People want my ideas. It's no fine science, like. I would have waited. Years, even. But then when I saw you yesterday with this child I knew I must have you now. Or you'll be away in a day, like last time. But now I know I'll have you both.'

Astrid drew away a little and looked down at Rose. She wondered if he suspected the truth about her. Then she looked back at him and saw nothing of that in his golden eyes. 'You like Rose?' she said.

'Seems to me she's a little mirror of you and that's why I want her.'

Astrid blushed. 'She is not my own,' she said. 'Don't think that. I did adopt her.'

He put a hand up and stroked her cheek. 'And now all I ask is that you adopt this poor gypsy lad.'

She turned her head to kiss the hand. 'You're not a child to me,' she said.

He laughed. 'Well then! We should finish riding the bounds and then we can speak of how we'll bind ourselves together. Hold tight on the child.' He lifted both her and Rose back onto the horse. She found herself astride, her skirt riding well above her ankles. He jumped up, behind her this time, and put his arms right round her and the child to pick up the reins. He dropped his head on her shoulder and spoke. His breath was warm on her neck. 'I'll not let you get away this time,' he said. 'You must know that.'

Fourteen

Now Here is a Good Man

10am

Ambrose asked permission to use his mother's pony and trap to get into town to see Mr Kilburn. He combed his hair carefully to one side and wore his best Norfolk jacket. He went to the back kitchen to borrow a cloth from Gwennie Taggart so that he could shine his shoes but she insisted on doing it for him. They did the job in the washhouse by the back scullery. 'What for d'you go and see this man?' she asked. She spat on the shoe and rubbed harder.

'Well, I'm to play my flute for him, so he can tell me whether I can play in his orchestra. And if he wants me in his orchestra he's gunna give me a job.'

'A job? What kind of job could someone like you do?'

'A pen pusher. I can read and write and do mathematics.'

'A pen pusher? Is that what you call it?' She hitched herself up on the mangle. 'Me. I can be a pen pusher. I can read and write and do sums. I was at the top of the class before I left school. My teacher said I could have "Gone Further".'

'Anyone could tell you were clever.' He bent down to lace up his shoes. 'I could tell that.'

'So how're you getting down into Bishop?'

'I'm taking my mother's trap.'

'Well then, can I come with you? It seems ages since I've been into Bishop. A market day that was. My ma took me in for a treat. The last Thursday before my dad was killed. Seems it was the last good time.'

'It was our pit, you know,' he said. 'The one where he was killed.'

'Think I don't know that? My mam was in for compensation but she had a letter from the union saying "Nothing Was Forthcoming". That my dad's death was his own fault.'

Ambrose felt ashamed. He thought of yesterday's meeting where that very blame was discussed. 'Well, you're certainly welcome to a ride in to Bishop. But you can't come into Mr Kilburn's with me. You can't play anything, can you? Not the banjo or something?'

She grinned, showing her small, even teeth. 'I can play war, like.'

' "Play war"? What does that mean?'

'Get mad. Fight you. All that.'

'Well, you still can't go to Mr Kilburn's.'

'I could ask him for a job as a pen pusher. I could do with a job.' She brushed some hair from his collar and patted the back of his Norfolk jacket.

'They wouldn't have girls in there. Not in a nail manufactory.'

She jumped down from her perch. 'All right then. I'll wait outside. Or stay in the market place and watch people.'

'Well. Go down and tell your mother then.'

'Nah. She'll stop us. She winnet let us do nowt. Never let us out of her sight since that happened to me dad. She'll clip us round the ear when I get back but it'll be worth it.'

They slipped round the back of the kitchens to the stables and Gwennie helped Ambrose with the pony. They set off at a trot round the back of the house and down Benbow Lane onto the main Bishop Auckland road.

As they drove across the market place, it was bustling with people arriving on foot and by carriage for morning service at St Anne's, a strange high-spired church attached like a limpet on to the side of the magisterial town hall. They went on to pick their

Wendy Robertson

way through flurries of people in the narrow streets off the market place. Here the public houses were already plying their Sunday trade. Finally they turned on to the wider, more generous roads on the edge of town, where the masters of trade and commerce in the town had built their fine houses. Ambrose pulled the pony to a halt in front of a well-built stone house with a neat garden and great stone window frames. 'Here we are,' Ambrose said. 'Now wait here,' he went on severely. 'Don't run away.'

'Can't see why you won't let us come in with you.'

'Wait here.'

The wide front door of the house was already open, and the morning light fell on the gleaming black and white tiles, fizzing through the red and blue glazing on to the vestibule floor. He rang the bell. A short woman with a face the colour and consistency of pie-crust came to the door.

'I'm Ambrose Benbow,' he said. 'Here to see Mr Kilburn.'

'Aye. Come on in,' she said. She led the way past an open door through which came the sound of laughter and the clink of teacups, to a narrow door in the back hall. This led to a long room lined with bookselves. A big desk cluttered with books and music stood at the far end under a window. Pushed against one wall was a piano; standing beside it was a finely polished cello, fronted by two music stands. 'You wait here!' she said severely. 'Don't touch anything.'

After just a few minutes Mr Kilburn came in and greeted him heartily. He shook his hand. 'You came? How very gratifying, dear boy. I had an idea that Jerry Carmedy might talk you out of it. He has little time for things musical, has Colonel Carmedy. Did you bring your flute? Ha!' He chuckled at the joke against himself. 'Of course you brought your flute.'

Ambrose took his flute from the case. 'What would you like me to play?'

'What music did you bring?'

Ambrose looked blank. 'I brought no music. I do read music, but . . . well . . . really, I just play.'

328

Mr Kilburn sat on a well-padded chair by the fire and folded his arms. 'Well, my dear, play.'

Ambrose settled his feet in his usual manner, raised his flute to his lips and began to play the jigs and airs that had so entertained Gwennie and her mother the night before. They were all fresh in his mind and the sets came easily to his fingers. He played on. His nerves would not let him pause. He went from one tune to the next without a break. Then his fingers fumbled and he was forced to stop. 'I'm sorry, Mr Kilburn. I just lost that fingering.'

Mr Kilburn scratched into his beard. 'That was quite enough. Now then . . .' He went to the piano stool, took out some music and placed it carefully on the music stand. 'Why don't we see if you really can read music? This one is called "An Irish Air" so you'll perhaps feel quite comfortable with it.'

Ambrose walked across to look at the music. It wasn't simple. 'If you bear with me, sir. I need a few moments to try some of the fingering.'

Mr Kilburn waved a hand in agreement and took up his position by the fire. Ambrose made two false starts and then the patterns of notes started to flow from the page to his fingers and he didn't even have to think. When he had finished Mr Kilburn left a short silence then applauded lightly. 'Well done, Ambrose. May I call you Ambrose? I feel certain you'll be a fine addition to our little musical family.'

'I really do need that job you mentioned, Mr Kilburn.'

Mr Kilburn stood up. 'On reflection this morning I realised that you must be son to the late and very eminent Rufus Benbow.'

'That's true,' said Ambrose, his heart sinking.

'So why would Rufus Benbow's son want to work in my manufactory?'

Ambrose thought for a moment. 'Well, sir, I've just left school, which I dislike, and I've no wish in the world to join the army. I don't hunt or shoot or fish. So this is my break for independence.'

'Bravo! An independent spirit.' Mr Kilburn shook him again by the hand. 'We'll test that spirit, my dear. Seven thirty sharp in the morning. Be at my works off Railway Street. We have orchestra on Tuesday and Thursday nights so you may join us here for tea before coming on to the practice.' He went to the desk. 'I will write a letter to your mother to assure her that this is a firm and fair agreement. I guarantee that you will gain much from your working life and that you'll be a welcome member of the orchestra. No better introduction to the values of living in society than to be a member of an orchestra. That is my view, of course.' As he spoke he was writing on fine vellum. He sealed the sheet in an envelope, addressed it with a flourish and handed it to Ambrose. 'So what is your political persuasion, Ambrose?'

'I'm not interested in such things, sir.'

'Ah, but you will be. You should be. It's your world and you must make it. We are Liberals in this house. Perhaps we will bring you into that fold too.'

'Yes, sir.' The boy stood, hesitating, before him.

'Is there something else, Ambrose?'

'I have this young acquaintance, Mr Kilburn. She's quick and clever and a very good reader and writer.' He crossed his fingers behind his back. 'I wondered whether there would be a post for her at the manufactory?'

Mr Kilburn was already shaking his head. 'Only men, dear boy. We only have men at the foundry. Did you say this was a friend of yours?'

Ambrose coloured. 'Not exactly. To be honest I hardly know her. But I feel bad about her. Her father worked in one of our mines and was killed. It seems they're not due any compensation. They say it was the man's own fault. She's lodging near us and she really needs some kind of work. But . . . well, she's not the sort that should go into service. Just not the type.'

Mr Kilburn stared at him and rubbed his beard again. 'A good conscience. I like that in a man. We will make a little

Liberal of you yet. There is one thing I might be able to do. We have a shop, an ironmongery on Newgate Street. A number of young women there. Bring her with you tomorrow and we could try her out for a week there.'

Ambrose beamed. 'That's very kind of you, sir.'

Mr Kilburn led the way to the front door. 'We must hope she's as fine and talented as you say, Ambrose, or my manager-ess – something of a tigress as far as women are concerned; she even campaigns for women's votes – will accuse me of all sorts of indulgences.'

Outside, the trap was still there but Gwennie was nowhere to be seen. Ambrose made his way along the road to find her sitting on a high wall watching the steady trickle of the faithful making their way into the Catholic church. When she saw him she jumped down from her perch. Her skirt ballooned out and her bonnet fell off.

He picked up the bonnet. 'I thought you'd run away,' he said.

'Me? Never. You don't get rid of me that easy,' she said. 'Well?' She bounced along beside him. 'How did it all go? Does the old boy think you are a genius?'

'He couldn't do that because we both know I'm not a genius. But he did like my playing. I am in his orchestra and I do have a job as a pen pusher to the nail-maker and am to be made into a good little Liberal.' He handed her up into the trap, then settled himself down beside her. He took up the reins. 'And I hope you're as good a pen pusher as you said. Because I got you a job in his ironmonger's shop.'

She began to shriek and *halloo!* and pulled him round and gave him a smacking kiss on the cheek. 'You are a genius,' she crowed. 'You are a blinking genius. I tell you.'

Around them the good Catholics of Bishop Auckland averted their gaze from the smart young man in the pony and trap embracing a girl who, from all the evidence, was a Proddy and no better than she ought to be.

Fifteen

Odd Pairings

9.30am

After lingering at the Lodge gates for half an hour Michael John rode up to the house in search of the Colonel. The front door was ajar. He knocked hard, then walked straight in. The motes of dust danced in the sunlight that streamed through the doorway and darted around his own shadow on the floor. The boxes and cases of the night before had gone. There were no silver-topped canes in the umbrella stand, no collection of hats on the hat stand. On the wall a stain of light paper betrayed the space formerly occupied by the Rossetti painting.

The drawing room, dining room and library were stripped bare of the casual artefacts that identify a place as belonging to this person rather than that. Michael John went back to the hall, through the baize door and down the steps to the kitchen. The fire was cleared out and dead, the surfaces were scrubbed and the pots and pans were in their places on the dressers. The pantries and dairy closets were chill and empty of food. He peered through the pantry window towards the stable yards. No groom in black baize apron was currying the Colonel's hunter, or swilling down the cobbles. No dogs leapt around in their anxiety to be pointed towards game.

Michael John returned to the bleak kitchen. Why on earth had the Colonel not said he was going off? The old boy did venture down to London from time to time for regimental dinners and such things. Sometimes he lit off to Scotland to do some stalking. But to go off like this! Sneaking away like a thief in the night. What was the old devil up to?

Michael John made his way up the servants' stairs, along the mean servants' corridor. Each servant's room was stripped and immaculate. It dawned slowly on Michael John that this whole thing had been planned like a military campaign. No one had been left to tell the tale. No prisoners had been taken.

He went back through another green baize door to the central hall on the first floor. In the Colonel's bedroom and dressing room it was the same story. The only sign here of the room's former occupier was the lingering smell of consumed and exhaled tobacco. Michael John was not unfamiliar with this graceful room with its tall windows allowing a view back towards the Hall. More than once when the old boy was rather incapacitated by drink Michael John had helped him to make his way up here. On such occasions the Colonel would be very sentimental, throwing his arms round Michael John and babbling about his being the son he'd never had and how much the boy reminded him of himself when young.

Michael John had always played up to this, appreciating that it was the price of the deep tolerance shown by the Colonel to his own excesses, financial and otherwise. Hadn't the Colonel come up trumps last year when that dratted woman at Cheltenham had claimed that her daughter had not only wed Lieutenant Benbow, but been beaten by him? The Colonel had paid the woman off and the girl had signed a note of guilt regarding perjury. And, even better, the Colonel had ensured that Michael John's own mother had never heard a whisper of it.

He made his way down the main stairs back to the library. On the desk was a pile of green ledgers. He flicked open the top one and there lay an unsealed envelope in cream vellum, addressed to *Mrs Carmel Benbow* in the Colonel's flowing hand. Michael John opened and read it.

Dear Mrs Benbow,

It is with enormous regret that I find I must terminate my engagement in your service. I have family affairs in Belgium that need my very urgent attention. These matters will take a good deal of time to disentangle, and I am obliged to resign my position with you in order to expedite these matters.

I hope that my good and faithful service through these years which I consider to be something of a tribute to my old comrade in arms, your dear late husband Rufus, has met with your satisfaction.

In recent months – nay, years – I have tried to protect you from the decay into which the financial affairs of the estate have been sinking. I have made, on your behalf, investments to ward off the worst of this depredation. Alas, these efforts have come to naught. The ledgers I leave here with you will, to my sorrow, tell their own dismal tale.

My most heartfelt wish is that I could have left Benbow in the light of much better news. I have been honoured and had great joy in being here and being of service to you and your delightful family. It has been a privilege for
  Your obedient servant,
  Gerald Eberhardt Carmedy, Col. (retd)

Michael John stuffed the letter back in the envelope and sat down on a chair. 'Bolter! The bastard,' he said. 'The swindling, cowardly bastard.' He sat there for a further ten minutes to absorb what had really happened, then he set out for a further rummage right through the house to see if there was anything left of value that he might himself pocket. The only thing he found in the stripped-clean house was a just-opened bottle of port in one of the servant's rooms. He took out the cork, and as he went through the rest of the rooms he drank steadily, allowing his temper against the Colonel to flower as he kicked

cupboards and beds and threw chairs against mirrors and glass
cabinets. He pulled up rugs and heaped them in the middle of
floors. He scattered papers and books. In the kitchen and the
bathrooms he turned on taps and left them running. He looked
around for matches, or even flints, but there were none. Outside
he mounted his horse with some difficulty, reflecting that the
whole thing would have made a fine bonfire.

As he clattered down the lane, reins in one hand and bottle
in the other, a further thought occurred to him. No wonder the
old crook had signed those cheques for him so readily. They
would be bouncing to Timbuctoo just as the Colonel crossed
the Channel in his cowardly flight.

'Bastard! That's my army career down the drain,' muttered
Michael John, digging his heels in his horse. 'Nothing but an
old crook.' He drank the last of the port then threw the empty
bottle into a flourishing hedge of may blossom on Benbow
Lane. In the distance, the bells of St Anne's rang the twelve
tones of midday and the parishioners streamed out into the
town in search of their Sunday dinners.

As promised, Gertrude Seland had taken Constance on a very
fair gallop across the countryside. They had raced across
farmers' fields and jumped low hedges and deceptive dykes.
They had cantered down lanes dappled with sunlight, talking
and squabbling as though they'd known each other for years.
Gertrude talked of her childhood friendship with Astrid, and as
she talked she seemed to transpose that friendship to Constance,
saying occasionally, 'Do you remember when . . .'

Constance was happy to let all of this flow over her, relishing
the admiration, the close attention that was clearly surging
towards her. She'd experienced this attention – some other's
intoxication with her own very self – several times in her life.
This was one thing she had sorely missed in the arid months in
Colorado. It was always so very enjoyable. There is a lover and
a beloved and she had always been the beloved.

However, in her previous experience the lover had always been a boy, or a man. Women, in general, were more wary of her; all except dear Astrid who in her otherworldly way had shown a quieter affection that was very compelling and demanded a peculiar loyalty in return. After all, wasn't that why she herself was here with her now, despite Astrid's just about betraying her with her own father?

Gertrude led the way up over a bridge to high wooded plains that, she told Constance, were part of the Bishop's Park. 'See? Through the trees? There is his castle. And just over the bridge and down through those trees is the sweetest place where we can rest awhile before we set out for Seland. There we'll take lunch and decide what we should do with the rest of our day.'

Constance decided to call a halt. 'Gertrude dear,' she drawled, 'this has been the most wonderful ride and you are the sweetest company. Such a surprise. It's very dear of you to take me on this wonderful adventure. But I must not come up to Seland. I have just arrived at Benbow and I am their guest. It would be the worst of manners . . .'

'Bad manners? Bad manners? The Benbows, my dear Constance, left manners behind a generation ago.' Gertrude moved up so that they were riding thigh to thigh. 'My sweet Auntie Carmel is the most delicious creature, the most darling woman, but she's as mad as a hatter. Manners? She has abandoned every social nicety. She keeps almost no staff. She never crosses the threshold of a church. She doesn't call, she doesn't receive. My ma once came here for afternoon tea and Auntie had forgotten to take off her garden boots. They were there! Peeping under the velvet. Once when my mother called she was accosted at the gate by a mad gypsy woman who wanted to buy her horse. Or something. I'm not quite sure what. Of course her groom saw the woman off, but she laid a curse on him. Can you imagine? He broke his leg the next day falling down the stone steps at the stable. Dear Ma was quite shaken.'

Constance moved on, to put some space between them. 'In the matter of manners,' she said over her shoulder, 'in my view the marker is what *I* feel are good manners, not what Astrid's poor mother has forgotten.'

'Ouch! Now you've hit me where it hurts.' Gertrude caught up with her and they rode on awhile in silence.

Then Constance spoke. 'In any case, if you see Mrs Benbow as so unconventional, then it is no more than your own strange view of convention. Astrid tells me that you eloped to South Africa with a diamond hunter and set all the county a-chatter.'

Gertrude moved on and led the way over a stone bridge. 'Little did the county know!' she called. 'It was not the diamond hunter whom I pursued to Jo'burg, but his sister. She was the most darling girl. Brave and elegant. Terribly modern. You'd have loved her, Constance. She was intrepid. We hunted lion. We had such adventures.'

'So why are you not still there on your African adventure? Having a jolly time with this paragon?'

Gertrude stopped beside a stone wall. 'Unfortunately, the naughty girl went and married a Dutchman, a terrible man with a long face and hands like hams. Ugh!' She shuddered. 'One could not have been more repelled.'

Constance reined in and stopped beside her. She laughed. 'Why should you be repelled? It wasn't you who married this ham-fisted Dutchman.' She looked at the wall that reared up behind Gertrude. 'So, what's this?'

The wall was one of four that stood round a hollow unroofed square. On the outside of the square was a peculiar kind of colonnade. In the middle of the fourth wall was a low tower, rather like a jewel set in a ring.

Gertrude put her hand on the wall. 'It's a fairy castle, do you see? All set for you atop this little hill.'

'Don't be silly, Gertrude.' Constance was genuinely puzzled. 'What is it?'

'It's the Bishop's Deer House. The deer shelter here in the winter; the bishop's keeper counts them and feeds them when the frost blights the pasture. Then decides how many they can cull in the hunt.'

'I see.' Constance nodded. 'Deers to the slaughter.'

'Only the bishop can hunt them. But I don't think he ever really does. I've not heard of it.' Gertrude slipped down from her horse, and put up her arms to help Constance down. The other girl did not need the help but she accepted it just the same. Gertrude's hands stayed on her small waist and she pulled her closer. She kissed her first on the cheek, then on the mouth. Then she took hold of Constance's hand. 'Come. See this,' she said. She led her to the tower in the middle of the fourth wall. Then she reached under her skirts into her breeches pocket and brought out a key. She grinned at Constance. 'My father is a friend of the bishop's,' she said as she put the key into the lock. 'Of course.'

Constance followed her up a narrow staircase to a square dusty room that had a scattering of chairs and a narrow table against a wall. 'This is where the bishop used to entertain his fellow huntsmen,' she said. 'See, there's his castle.'

Constance peered through the narrow window at the castle set on rising land to her left. Gertrude was standing close behind her. Her voice was in her ear. 'Rapunzel, Rapunzel, let down your hair,' she whispered. Then Constance could feel her hat and veil being removed. Soft hands began busying about her hair removing pin after pin. Then she felt the welcome feeling of lightness as her hair tumbled over her shoulders and down her back. Then the fingers were combing through her hair, feeling their way through the tangles, smoothing down the massy clumps.

She kept on staring out of the window, quite enjoying what was happening and not quite sure what to do about it.

Gertrude's lips were on her ear again. 'You are such a lovely creature. I am your slave. All I want to do is kiss you.'

Constance turned and Gertrude's soft lips moved all over her face: on her cheeks, on her brow, on her closing eyes. Then they were on her lips and licking and touching until Constance almost howled. 'Stop, stop it.'

Gertrude stopped instantly, but took Constance's face in her hands. She said, 'What a wonderful thing it is, to kiss one's own beloved.'

Constance finally pulled away. 'Gertrude!' she protested too weakly. 'You are a disgrace.'

'Where have you been?' Gertrude stood now with her hands slackly at her sides. 'It's no disgrace to show someone you care for them.' She pouted. 'Are you not my friend?'

Constance laughed out loud at Gertrude's game of false naiveté. She took her hands and shook them, and in doing so shook the languor out of her own bones. 'Dearest Gertrude. Of course I'm your friend. Now, we must get back.' She moved her head from side to side and her dark hair lifted and fell like skeins of silk in the light from the narrow window. 'Now look what you've done. How am I to pin my hair back up again?'

Gertrude dragged a chair across and dusted it with the hem of her riding skirt. 'You sit here, my lady, and I'll dress your hair for you.' She scrambled in the dust for the discarded pins and thrust them into Constance's hand. 'You hold them, my darling, and I will be your lady's maid.' Then, using her fingers as a comb, she coiled the thick mass of hair into a rope and started to pin it up. She nearly managed it once but it sagged to one side and they both laughed rather too much. So they unpinned it and started all over again. This time Constance instructed Gertrude step by step and between them they recreated Constance's coiffure. When they had finished Gertrude kissed the nape of her neck and carefully placed the hat and veil atop the creation.

Constance stood up. 'Now!' she said severely. 'All games are over and we must return.'

On the long ride back they rode together very easily, quite at peace with each other: Gertrude was not so anxious to gain Constance's attention; Constance was not wondering what it was all about. She knew what it was all about. It was not an unfamiliar phenomenon. She'd made many conquests in her life but this one was rather unusual.

They had just got back onto the Benbow Lane when they spied, coming through the trees, a very fine chestnut horse carrying a father, a mother and a child.

'The flight from Bethlehem,' muttered Gertrude.

It was only when they drew nearer that they realised who it was. 'Glory be,' said Constance.

'Cripes,' said Gertrude.

Astrid waved at them and the child Rose did too, calling, 'Connie! See horsey.' Jack Lomas kept one arm round the two of them and the other firmly on the reins.

'Did you have a lovely ride?' Astrid asked.

'Beautiful,' said Constance. 'We had a wonderful ride. Gertrude showed me the Deer House.'

Astrid shook her head. 'I hope you behaved yourself, Gertrude.' She turned her head back to include Jack in her comment. 'Once, when we were young, Jack, Gertrude left me locked in the Deer House for five hours. In the end I had to climb out of the window and onto the wall before I could get down.'

'Your mother must have been so worried,' said Constance.

Astrid laughed. 'She didn't notice.'

'So where've you been, Astrid? I declare, you look just like a dairymaid,' said Constance, frowning ungraciously now at Jack. 'That braid down your back!'

'We didn't realise it was so late, did we, Jack? We've been out for ages, riding the bounds. Jack has been showing me his farm and his mine. Quite the man of property nowadays . . .'

'We'll ride on,' said Jack suddenly. 'Get you back home, Astrid. We need to see your mother and I need to see Jacob

Ellenberg and mebbe you need to get out of that dairymaid's kit so's these friends of yours don't look down their long noses at you.' He set off at a brisk trot and Rose squealed with delight. Astrid waved back at Constance and Gertrude, a wide smile on her face.

The other two women rode after them at a more sedate pace. 'So! The handsome coachman turns gypsy turns man of property. Quite the fairy tale,' said Gertrude thoughtfully. 'I love her dearly but Astrid does make the most bizarre choices. She truly is her mother's daughter.'

Constance thought of her own father, then she laughed. 'Gertrude, honey,' she said softly, 'who are you to talk of bizarre choices?'

They caught up with the others at the side doorway. Melanie Tyler was just showing a man, who by the size and shape of his case was the doctor, to his trap and seeing him off.

'How is John?' said Astrid.

Even in the middle of her own distress, Melanie looked in scowling disapproval at Miss Astrid Benbow (with her hair down in a braid) being grasped round the waist by a gypsy. 'According to the doctor he's in a very poor way, Miss Benbow. I'm to keep him warm and keep him still.' She watched Constance and Gertrude walk their horses round towards the stable. 'Shall I set a place at luncheon for Miss Seland?' she called after them.

Constance looked back at Astrid. 'Is that in order, honey?'

'Of course Gertrude is welcome to join us. It won't be the first time and it won't be the last.' She turned back to Melanie. 'Is my mother here?'

'She's over in the garden, miss. Likes a quiet moment there on a Sunday morning with no boys to boss about. You may tell her we'll have the luncheon on the table at twelve, as usual.'

'I'll do that, Mrs Tyler. We need a word with her.' She nodded at Melanie, and Jack turned the horse.

Melanie stood and watched as the strange mounted trio made their way across the meadow. Her head was whirling. Things

341

were not right, not right at all. The whole place was like a house of cards that was trembling before it fell. Then her worry about John surged through her again. He'd always been so full of energy and fun, pulling her leg about how seriously she saw everything, how keen she was to do things right. His smile acknowledged what an ambition that was, in this subversively chaotic household.

John was a calm man, sometimes too calm for her. But now, today, he'd become this drooping creature, sometimes vacant, sometimes very afraid. How he'd hung on to her just now, resisting the doctor's urging that he should go to hospital. The doctor insisted that his heartbeat was dangerously erratic. But John had clung on to her. 'Don't let me go there, Mel. I'll die there. Me father died there and so will I.'

Well, thought Melanie, at least the doctor had done his bit and had not complained about coming out on a Sunday. Neither should he, as he was well paid for his trouble.

She should have gone straight back to John but she turned towards the kitchens. Mrs Mac needed to know that there would be one extra for luncheon, and she would get the new woman Mrs Taggart to change the place settings. Then she would go up to see him.

But when she got to the kitchen Mrs Taggart was striding around wringing her hands, bewailing the fact that her daughter Gwennie had gone missing and that she couldn't find her anywhere. She was in no fit state to change the settings, so Melanie changed them herself.

When she went back upstairs John was fast asleep. She straightened his eiderdown and twitched the curtains and returned downstairs. One side of her bemoaned the way this household depended on her. The other felt relieved to have purposeful things to occupy her. The last thing she wanted to do was to sit wringing her hands at John's bedside. The very last thing.

Sixteen

Carmel's Version

11am

It might be expected, perhaps, that I should stay up at the house, with my visitors there, this new servant to deal with. There is even this small child, this child from nowhere who disturbs me more than she should. Perhaps only she would have kept me close, but the busy jostling presences, their neediness and urgencies down there have driven me out.

Normally it is not like this. Jacob Ellenberg is an easy presence, light-footed and clear-spirited, leaving little imprint on the air. The melancholy feeling he sometimes evokes does not impinge on me, for it comes from other times, other places, and all I feel is this cool abstraction, this sympathy for him. Mrs Mac stays in her kitchen and the Tylers lurk behind their veil of knowing that renders them invisible.

But Astrid and the boys, her friend Constance and this strange baby all demand to be *seen*. The air is furry with their need. So I thought I'd start this day in the garden, which is especially nice on a Sunday morning. There are no boys here to impede my orders, no organising to be done. The garden can breathe and be itself.

Keziah has turned up again after breakfast but demands no more notice than the bark of an oak, or the large finch perching on a wall. I watch her as she goes down towards the north end of the garden picking armfuls of early lavender as she goes. I watch her from the rising heat of the greenhouse for a while, then make my own way down towards her, picking lavender for her. Her presence draws me.

I join her on the long bench under the north wall and we sit side by side, tying the lavender into bunches of seventeen strands with wisps of strong grass. We do this for a while, then I tell her about Ambrose and his new notion of life. She says nothing about this. Then I go on to tell her about the baby, the child Rose.

She nods her head and says, 'Do you speak of a child or a flower?'

I am just constructing an answer to this when my attention is distracted by a glimpse through the gateway of a horse and rider. No, a horse and two riders and a child that sits on the woman's knee. Travellers, I think. I know there is a rule of welcome in the house but I very much hope they don't bring that horse into my garden. No animals are allowed here except Susannah, who would insinuate herself into any place whether one allowed it or not.

The woman jumps down from the horse. She shakes down her skirts and then takes the child from the man. He looks down at her. His deep voice reaches us across the still Sunday garden. 'I like your little button boots,' he says. My heavens. It's Jack Lomas. I'd forgotten his beard.

'Why, thank you, kind sir,' says the woman, the child still in her arms. My goodness. It's Astrid, a braid down her back and a shawl round her shoulders. She sketches the man a curtsy. He leans across now and kisses her very hard. I take a step forward to get a clearer view of all this.

The child Rose is between them. 'Stop! Stop!' says Rose. 'I squashin'!'

They both laugh at this and Jack leaps down from the horse and swings Rose up onto his shoulders. 'I ride horsey,' she says, very pleased with herself.

HONESTY'S DAUGHTER

I sit down again beside Keziah, who has also been watching the little scene, hands still busy.

The three of them move into the dense, rustling quiet of my garden, leaving the horse tethered outside. They peer into the round glasshouse then glance down the central pathway through the archways of entwined roses and jasmine, to the long battered seat under the north wall where Keziah and I sit tying our lavender into bunches of seventeen stalks.

Keziah's head goes up. Her hands stop moving. I shade my eyes against the sun and peer towards my visitors. Jack puts the child Rose down and she runs on towards me and climbs into my lap and starts to play with the strings on my straw hat.

By the time Jack and Astrid reach us their hands are linked and they are shoulder to shoulder. I look at the two of them over Rose's head. 'So what's this?' I say. I can see 'this' is very much something.

'We rode the bounds with Rose,' says Astrid. 'And it was on the ride that we sort of found each other, Jack and I.'

Keziah ignores them. She stares at Rose. 'Is this the American child you found, Astrid? Carmel telt us there was a child.'

Astrid goes quite red. I hope against hope it's not the stain of guilt. Then her chin tilts. 'Yes. This is Rose. She's my child now.'

In the silence that follows I feel a twinge of pride in her. Keziah is a hard one to challenge and this is what my daughter has done.

'And now the child will be mine, Keziah,' says Jack. He turns to me. 'I have much to offer Astrid, Mrs Benbow. I've the thriving business in Newcastle, the gun royalties that bring in the money. I have a farm, and I've got a pit now, across the hill, the—'

'I heard,' I say. 'Carafay. You took it off Jacob's hands.'

'I've not swindled him, if that's what you think. Jacob is

345

my good friend, my teacher,' says Jack. 'He'll get no less interest off the share he has from me, than when he owned it himself.'

'That's a great relief,' I say. I have to say I'm rather wrong-footed at the calmness, the surface ordinariness of it all. There is no mention of how sudden this all is. Astrid only came home from America yesterday.

Jack glances at his mother, who is tickling Rose's forearm with a particularly long stalk of lavender. 'And I've bought Low Bent Riggs farm, the one at the back of the forge,' he goes on. 'I showed Astrid that as well this morning.'

This surprises me. 'But that's one of ours.'

'It was. I bought it from the Colonel five months ago.' He glances at his mother and I wonder if some of her horse-trade money is in this transaction.

I'm still frowning. 'But the Colonel has said nothing . . .'

'I have the papers, Mrs Benbow.' He says this quietly, without force.

I turn to Keziah. 'Did you know of this?'

Keziah, still staring at Rose, shrugs. 'Our Jack plays close to his chest. He teks care of some of my money for me. He knows a good deal. Still, I felt sommat else was in the wind. What for did he need them horses, that rig? Bricks and mortar, workshops, factories, farms. Not my kind of thing. Diggin' roots deep. I could see this but there was no talk of it at all. But I have ter say I hadn't fixed on your Astrid. I thought some Newcastle lass . . .'

'We'll get married,' says Jack quickly. 'Soon as we can. I'll tek care of Astrid and the child.'

'I can take care of myself, Mother, as I always have,' says Astrid. 'But I'll marry Jack. That is certain.'

'So sudden.' I'm feeling just a little faint.

She glances at him. 'I think it started before, when I was last here. And I thought about him so much while I was away.'

'It's no bad thing, Carmel.' Keziah glares at me with her beady eyes. 'Is it?'

I blush. Margaret Seland and all my old half-forgotten cronies start to make a hobbling promenade through my thoughts, wagging their fingers at me. There'll be no going back for any of us if I let this thing start. Truth to tell, I couldn't stop it even if I wanted to. Every door will be closed to me. So what? I've not walked through many of those doors in twenty years. Then I think about myself and Rufus. We knew in an instant, even though it took us five whole days to acknowledge it. 'You're quite sure about this?' I look directly at Astrid and now take in the fact that she's dressed just as I used to dress when I went travelling with Rufus. Braided hair, simple skirts. So many parallels. 'You're quite sure?' I say.

I can see that he's squeezing her hand hard.

'Never so sure,' says Astrid. (She will tell me much later that she wondered whether she'd have been quite so sure if she'd not travelled to Colorado, if she had not unravelled herself in that heat, had not been so close with that General Redoute.) 'I'm very sure, Mama.'

They are both looking at me.

I smile and detach Rose's warm paw from my hair. 'Well then, you must do as you wish. I am certain your father would have been delighted.'

Astrid looks at me. 'Don't you think perhaps that this might have been a great test even for him?'

She's very perceptive. 'I hope he would have passed such a test with success.' I glance now at Keziah. 'And as for me, I'm delighted you have found someone who . . . so suits you, whatever the world might think. Jack's a man of the future and if you're to take care of this young one . . .' I am trying to say the right thing. Rose is trying to put her fingers in my mouth. '. . . then you'll need all the help you can get.'

We all laugh then. Even Keziah smiles. Then all of our laughter fades at the sight of my son Michael John coming down one of my garden paths *on his horse*! He urges his mount down the path until he is really close to us, allowing its shoulder to lean into Jack. He bends over and bellows at him. 'Get your hands off my sister, sir.'

I can smell port even from where I am sitting.

'Ah think not. Ah have a right, sir.' Jack shakes his head. 'Me and Astrid are together. We'll marry. That's all there is.'

'You gyppo. You dirty scum . . .' Michael John's handsome face is red. His eyes are too bright.

I stand Rose on her feet and rise to my own feet. 'Your horse has no place in my garden, Michael John,' I say quite mildly, keeping my voice down low.

He ignores me and keeps staring at Jack. Then he leaps from his horse, staggering a little. The sour digested perfumes of wine invade the delicate scents of my garden. 'If that's so, then the world has gone quite, quite mad.' His whole body slumps a little then with great deliberation he turns to face me. 'I've just come from the Lodge, Mama. The Colonel and I were going shooting this morning. Good kill before church, d'you know? I went to call for him at the Lodge and he's not there. There's nothing there, Mama. Not a hide nor hair of him. Not a scrap or scrape. I have to tell you the old boy's cleaned you out and done a bunk. He's bolted.'

Rose slips her hand in mine which is now very cold.

'Michael John, this can't be . . .' What is he saying?

Jack puts a hand on his shoulder. 'You're drunk . . .'

Michael John whirls round and thrusts the hand away. 'Don't you touch me, gypsy.' His voice has snakes in it.

'Leave him.' Astrid puts a restraining hand on Jack's arm.

Michael John turns back to me. 'It is true,' he says sulkily. 'The house is stripped. He's taken the Rossetti from the hall and I can't think what other Benbow treasure.' His hand goes inside his tunic and he brings out a battered letter. 'Read it, Mama. Read his weasel words.'

I read the letter then hand it to Astrid. 'Is that how it seems to you, Astrid? Has he gone with everything?'

348

HONESTY'S DAUGHTER

Astrid reads it carefully, then nods and places it back in my
hand. 'Weasel words sounds quite accurate to me, Mother.'

I look down the garden, to my glasshouse, my sanctuary. All
of it is now under siege. I am driven now to take some action.
At last there is only me. I tell Astrid and Jack to go to the
Lodge and check that things are as Michael John says. He's so
drunk he might be wrong. The truth of it will be in the
accounting books, unless Jerry Carmedy has taken them as
well. 'Are the books there?' I say to Michael John. 'At the
Lodge?'

'Where they always are,' he says. 'On the library table.'

I turn to Astrid. 'I'll need Jacob to look at those books. I'll
send him down after you.'

'No, Mother.' Astrid's eye is very stern. 'You must bring
him down. Come down to the Lodge yourself. You cannot hide
here in your garden in this crisis.' She is quite reproving. I
never thought Astrid troubled herself about me and my ways.

She leans down to pick Rose from my arms.

'No,' I say. 'Leave the child with me.'

Keziah glances at Michael John and stands up. 'Here,
Carmel. Give us that bairn. I'm sure our Edith and Freddy'd
like to take a look at her. And she'll like the chickens.'

Reluctantly I hand over Rose and wave as Keziah goes
through the garden, talking away, her hawk-like face held close
to that of the child. Astrid stands almost too still, watching
them until they are through the gate and out of sight.

'Go on,' I say to her. 'Go to the Lodge and see whether
Michael John is mistaken.'

'I'm not mistaken,' he says sulkily. 'I told you what I saw. It
looks as though the Colonel's made off with everything of
worth from the Lodge and who knows what else?'

So they go, Astrid and Jack, his arm round her as though
he'll never let her go.

'What a sight. Don't it make you want to weep?' Michael
John flops down on the seat beside me. 'We're in trouble, Ma.

349

I do really think the Colonel's done a bunk. We're finished. All of us.'

I read the Colonel's letter again. Then I hold it up to the light, flip it over. There's something on the other side. *PS You may tell Michael John that the cheques payable to the brigadier and to him are good and sound so he has a clear start to India.* I read it out. 'What's this, Michael John? The brigadier?'

Michael John sits up straight, the faintest of smiles cracking his glum face. 'Well. That's something. There was this little problem.' He coughs. 'This fellow in the regiment stole mess money from me and I had to replace it. The Colonel told me he'd take care of it. He said he would deal with the brigadier for me.'

'Well, it seems at least he's done that.' I say. 'You're honoured. You have come in for special treatment from this old chancer, Michael John.'

He stands up and straightens his tunic. Then he takes hold of his horse's reins.

'Where are you going?' I say sharply. Suspicion becomes one's first reaction with Michael John. He does not change.

'Back down to Cheltenham,' he says, taking off his cap and pushing his hands through his hair to straighten it. 'We embark at the end of the week, don't you know?'

I stand up quite close to him. 'You'd leave me, Michael John? Leave me to face all this?'

He shrugs. 'Best thing I can do, Ma. You know there'll be nothing left. The Colonel was too shrewd and selfish, too greedy. You have your gypsy and your old Jew. See what they can make of the mess.' He mounts his horse, straightens his back and lifts his chin. He sits there almost posing for a second. As though he wants me to admire his very good seat. Then he looks down at me, his lips held tight back on his teeth. He says very deliberately, 'Do you know a strange thing, Ma? Rogue that he was, old Carmedy was more father to me than my own father. In fact, to be perfectly honest, he's been more of a mother than you ever have.' Then he turns and sets his horse diagonally towards the gate, walking it straight through the soft earth and the tender cuttings in my new rose bed. The cuttings that had been doing so well.

I watch him plough his way to the gate then I sit down hard on the bench. I'm driven to wonder now whether all this might be – even marginally – my fault. I leave my affairs to a flattering rogue whom I've been too self-centred to supervise. My daughter is a fey creature who wanders the earth, returns with a motherless and fatherless child in tow, and is now attached to a gypsy boy years younger than herself. One son accuses me of neglect as an excuse for his own violence and selfishness. The other son is a timid coward whose highest ambition is to work for an ironmonger.

I shake my head clear of these thoughts and go in search of a trowel and a fork to restore the bed over which Michael John has ridden in such a roughshod manner. I'll just do that now, before I go to find Jacob and take him to the Lodge and all the bad news there. That will have to wait. My cuttings are in mortal danger.

Seventeen

A New Strain

11.15am

On the way to the Lodge Jack and Astrid made a detour to the forge cottage. Edith and Keziah were out in front watching the child Rose as she stumbled about, scattering the chickens and squealing with laughter. Jack helped Astrid down from the horse and said, 'Wait here! I'll be five minutes,' and dashed inside.

Astrid sat down again on the wall. Rose played on, hardly noticing her at all. Edith was leaning against the doorjamb, arms folded under her bosom. 'The child Rose is quite at home,' she said. 'If it wasn't for that sharp little face and the blonde curls, I'd say she had a look of our Honesty. Something about the set of the shoulders. But what do I know? All children look alike, don't you think so?'

Astrid forced herself to smile easily at Edith and kept her gaze strictly away from Keziah. 'I can't say, Edith. Rose is the only child I've ever known. To me she just looks like herself.'

Edith stared at the child. 'But then I'd say her smile, and that way she cocks her head, well, she's the pot-model of you, Miss Benbow.'

Astrid laughed. 'I take that as a compliment, but really it's only a coincidence.'

'You knew the ma?' said Keziah abruptly.

'Yes, Keziah. Very briefly. I just happened to be there.'

'And what sort was she?'

Astrid frowned. 'Well, she was a nice girl. Very pretty.'

'Was she English?' the catechism continued.

'Well, she'd been English, but she was American at that point.'

Keziah's power drew Astrid's gaze at last to her. 'And the father? What kind of *gadgie* was he? Was he there?'

'Well, he wasn't there. I think he had gone away,' she said lamely. 'He'd run away.'

'But what kind of feller was he? Did they say?' pursued Keziah.

'They said he was a very big man,' said Astrid slowly. 'An important man. A clever man, perhaps.'

'A man with no conscience, mebbe,' put in Edith. 'There's plenty of them around.'

Astrid dragged her eyes away from Keziah. 'Perhaps he was,' she said.

She could feel the heavy silence from Keziah like a dark blanket lying against her left side. She smiled brightly. 'But none of this matters now, does it? She's mine now and she will grow up with me.'

'No bad thing, that,' grunted Keziah. 'Ye've made a good job of the young'n already. Look at her. Happy as a tick in a bed.'

At that point Rose fell over a tussock of grass and started bawling. Keziah picked her up, said something to her in *romani*, began to throw her in the air in the way that men do. Instantly she was chuckling and laughing. Edith, in the doorway, nodded and smiled. The thought occurred to Astrid that she'd brought Rose home to three grandmothers. And that was no bad thing, as Keziah might have said.

There was a jingle of harness and Jack's rig emerged from the back of the forge pulled by the two fine greys in harness. He was driving, dressed again in his fine coat and breeches, his thick hair brushed back, his beard combed. His feet were encased in highly polished riding boots. 'Now then, Astrid,' he said. 'We'll get up to the Lodge and see what's what.' He held out a hand to help her up.

Edith and Keziah watched them drive away on the hard-packed road. 'Hard to tell who's the gypsy and who's the gentry in them two,' said Edith. 'This has been a queer morning, Keziah. Don't you think so?'

Astrid and Jack wandered through the rooms at the Lodge, their astonishment bubbling and expanding as they went. Smashed glasses and mirrors glittered in the dark spaces. Churned up carpets and broken furniture met them in every room. Curtains had been wrenched off rails, books had been swept off shelves.

'Whatever that weasel has done, there's no need to leave the place like this. He might have tecken your mother's money,' muttered Jack, restoring a fat Chinese spice jar to the drawing room chiffonier, 'but there's hate in all this. Murder.'

Astrid looked around, frowning. 'Really, it's very strange, Jack. The house was always immaculate. Colonel Carmedy had six servants, three of them men. And this Indian major-domo fellow. They kept this place like a museum. I always liked it, with its high rooms and its wide windows over towards the Hall. A much better house than ours, always. And the Colonel loved it. You could tell. He wouldn't spoil it like this. Where is the gain?'

The trail of damage continued all the way upstairs. They went into the main bedroom. Jack picked his way through the chaos and went to the window. 'Why, man, I do see what you mean about the outlook. Look at it. The land all a-sparkle.'

She went to stand beside him. 'I'd never been up here. Not up here. I saw this from downstairs. But from here you might own the world.'

She felt his hand slip into hers and grasp it tightly. 'We'll marry,' he said softly. 'Get this sorted and we'll get married.

And we'll have no big house wedding nor any gypsy carnival. We'll go off somewhere quiet, you, me and Rose, and get ourselves married and come back to this house. And every day you'll get out of your bed in this room and look out of this window. And our children'll come here in their bare feet and clamber on the sill. And Rose'll look on with pride in the way big sisters can.'

She clung on to his hand. 'And how d'you know this?' she said, half laughing.

'I know it because I know and because I'm son to one who always knows.'

She thought of Keziah and her words about Rose. And she thought about Honesty and wondered if, before her own children tumbled on this wide sill, Honesty would have come here to claim Rose for her own. And she wondered where the King might be now and how many other Roses there were sprinkled around the country like some seigneurial mulch. She shuddered.

He put his hands round her uncorseted waist and pulled her towards him. 'You feel very soft,' he whispered. 'Like a good gypsy maid.'

She turned her face to kiss him on the roughened skin of his cheekbone, and put her hand on the nape of his neck to press him towards her. Then they pulled apart as below them in the courtyard Carmel's trap skirled to a halt. 'Mayhap we'll leave this till we're wed,' he said, rubbing the cheek she had kissed as though there were a fine bruise there. 'As we'll always be leaping apart like this and it sets my nerves a-jingle.'

Downstairs Carmel and Jacob were starting their own odyssey through the debris. Astrid explained that it was like this throughout the house.

'This is so very, very odd,' said Carmel. 'The Colonel was such an immaculate man. He shuddered at disorder . . .'

'I said as much to Jack.' Astrid looked round again, and her nose wrinkled at a certain acrid smell. Her gaze met that

355

of Jacob Ellenberg. He nodded slightly. They'd been here before.

'Perhaps all this wasn't the colonel,' said Astrid slowly. 'It looks to me more like the manifestation of my dear brother's evil temper.'

'The books!' said Jacob. 'Did he tear up the books? The books for the estate.'

Jack shook his head. 'No. They're on the table in the library.'

'Well, Jack, you and I should take a good look at Mrs Benbow's accounting ledgers,' said Jacob with unusual briskness. 'They are what is important here. Come!' He led Jack towards the library.

'Did Michael John do this? Did he wreak this destruction?' said Carmel.

'Mama, it looks and smells just like Mr Ellenberg's cottage that night when he wrecked it. Only on a much larger scale. He must have been very cross indeed with Colonel Carmedy.'

'Well, dear.' Carmel frowned. 'He has just told me he saw the Colonel as his best ally in a family . . . especially a mother . . . that had no time for him. Then today even the Colonel let him down. That made him so angry. He didn't even have the Colonel on his side. Or so he thought. But it now seems that Michael John was the only one that chancer Jerry Carmedy saved in the middle of this debacle. He rescued him from some scrape he got into in the army. So even if we lose the house, even if I lose my garden, Michael John will be all right.' Carmel's voice was bleak.

'Where is he? Michael John?'

'He's packed his bags and gone to Darlington for a train south. Then off to India. Away from us all. He cannot get away quickly enough.'

'Don't you think he could have stayed, to try to help with all this?'

Carmel shook her head. 'We know Michael John. He'd not lift a finger to help anyone if there was naught in it for him.

He's off and he mayn't ever come back. He sees the army as his home.' In the silence they each dropped into private contemplation as to whether they really cared whether Michael John came back or not. 'Perhaps, if your father had been home more, taken more note of him . . . Perhaps I . . .' Carmel left the rare, regretful question trailing.

Fighting back her irritation at her mother's inevitable self-absorption Astrid looked round. 'We need some help here. Why don't you go back to the house, Mother, and ask Melanie and Mrs Mac and that new woman to come along? Between us we'll get it back to something like order. We might be sliding swiftly towards the poorhouse but we don't want to look it.'

Carmel stared at the half-open door of the library. They could hear the companionable rumble of voices as Jack and Jacob got their heads down over the books. She looked at Astrid. 'Perhaps the Benbow line has bred itself out,' she said. 'Do you think it could be that only new strains will help it survive? That thought occurred to me yesterday when I met the child Rose. Then, when you came into the garden with her and Jack Lomas it seemed some kind of personification of my thought.' Not waiting for an answer she glided out of the front door. Minutes later Astrid heard the grind of wheels on gravel. She let out a sigh of relief and set about returning the unbroken ornaments to the narrow hall dresser that reflected the garden in its long mirror.

Eighteen

No Picnic

1pm

Ambrose looked across the wide stretch of lawn in front of the Lodge. 'It looks like nothing less than a battlefield.' He was shoulder to shoulder with Gwennie, who was leaning against the oak tree beside him.

'More like a picnic,' she said. 'Mrs Mac packed a lovely picnic.'

'It's no picnic,' he said.

Still, everyone had eaten their fill. It seemed no time since they'd bumped into his mother, racing down to the Hall, gathering people to help with the restitution of the vandalised Lodge. She'd swept them up in her wake. He'd never seen her so brisk. She'd bustled around insisting that Mrs Mac pack their 'wasted' luncheon into baskets and bring them with her in the governess cart. She'd sent Gertrude and Constance on ahead on their horses, to check that none of the Colonel's poor animals had been abandoned. Then she'd careered off to the forge to get Edith and Rose. It was such a strange thing, to see her so active, so present.

Keziah remained behind; a domestic emergency was the last thing she could, or would, help with. Edith observed the uncharacteristic struggle between Mrs Benbow and Keziah over the child Rose. Keziah had said she'd hang on to Rose, to 'keep the bairn out of the way'. Mrs Benbow had insisted that Rose should come with her as it was *her* family's emergency. This time Mrs Benbow had prevailed.

While Jack and Jacob pored over the books, the rest of them had worked together and straightened the house into some sort of order. By that time the whole place smelled so much of lye and cleaning bleach that they were driven outside to eat their basket luncheon in the open air.

It was very hot. Bees were buzzing round the ceanothus that sprawled up against the front wall, and a regiment of Red Admiral butterflies were in formation over the buddleia.

Replete now, Constance and Gertrude were lying close together under the weeping willow, Gertrude's arm carelessly round Constance's waist. Astrid was lying at right angles to them, her braided head in Constance's lap, her shawl draped across her face. Her hand reached out and clasped that of Jack Lomas who was sitting in shirtsleeves against the peeling bark of the willow. His eye met Ambrose's over the sleepy recumbent bodies. He winked.

On the Colonel's long garden bench beside the French window Edith, Mrs Mac and Mrs Taggart sat in a prim row, knees together. Mrs Mac's head jerked now and then, as she resisted the lure of sleep.

The strangest sight to Ambrose was his mother sitting just on the edge of the lawn, back supporting back with Mr Ellenberg. Rose was sprawled across her knee, fast asleep. His mother's voice floated towards Ambrose in the still noon air. 'So what's the truth of it, Jacob?'

Mr Ellenberg took off his hat and mopped his high forehead with a spotted silk handkerchief. 'There is disaster, it is true, dear lady. The graphs slide and slide. The neglect is manifest.'

'So that's it then? We're . . . has it all gone? Have we lost the house? My lovely garden?'

Jacob laughed comfortably. 'It is a big, big crisis. But the benefit of crisis is that it forces change – a change that was, perhaps, overdue. It can be a good thing.'

'And in our case?'

'Well, in our – in your – case, much has been converted to money and much of the money has vanished. But Jack Lomas has a good instinct and many ideas. He tells me that your assets, his assets, all can be used to preserve something. And build. He has many ideas and good friends. He talks of a Newcastle accountant . . .'

Carmel yawned. 'It hasn't been the greatest of days, has it, Jacob?'

'It's been a great day for me,' called Ambrose.

'And me,' said Astrid from under her hat.

'And me,' growled Jack Lomas.

'And me . . . And me,' chorused Constance and Gertrude together.

A Red Admiral set itself in Gwennie's bouncy hair. Ambrose blew it away. 'I think I shall teach you how to play chess, Gwennie Taggart,' he said. 'If you're as good at reading and writing and sums as you say, I think you'll make a good hand of chess.'

Gwennie sat forward suddenly. 'Hey, look at this, Ambrose. It's that Mrs Tyler and she's in some kind of state. Just look at her.'

Melanie Tyler was running down the long gravelled drive with a strange hopping gait, aiming for Carmel. Her white cap was hanging down the back of her loosened hair and there was blood on the shoulder strap of her white apron.

Carmel stood up. 'What is it, Melanie? What on earth . . .'

Melanie stood stock still in front of her, one shoulder up at an awkward angle as though it was causing her great pain. 'It's John, Mrs Benbow. I think he might be dead. The blood was coming right out of his mouth. I think he's dead. My own John.'

Then, hands loose at her sides, she started to cry.

Part Four

The Soldiers

11 November 1918

November 9 Germany: Kaiser Wilhelm abdicates

November 10 North Sea: British minesweeper HMS *Ascot* torpedoed off northeast England by a German submarine and 53 crewmen drowned

November 11 Russia: Birth of Alexander Solzhenitsyn

November 19 London: UK said to have suffered over 3 million casualties, including nearly a million dead

November 25 London: Parliament is dissolved prior to a general election where women will vote for the first time

One

Stand-To

Captain M. J. Benbow stirred in his bunk, twisting away petulantly as his servant Gooding pulled him by the shoulder. 'Five fifteen, sir? Stand-to. The men are stirring to action,' he said in a soft voice made extra hoarse by a lifelong weakness for cigarettes.

Michael John had been dreaming of India and the heat that burnt you to the bone; of rich smells and hard rides and the savouring of pink gins on a certain veranda cooled by the non-stop efforts of the *punkah-wallah*. Before being so rudely interrupted he'd been just lifting his long glass in a toast to Garrard Comstock Myers, known to his friends as Commers, congratulating him on a stunning run on his new filly in the Regimental Cup.

'Wassat, Gooding?' he said groggily, throwing his legs out of the makeshift bunk, dug into the chalky wall of the trench by some hearty newly-out private, and lined with planks which drew water into the dugout like a farm drain.

Gooding thrust a cup of hot tea into the hand that, seconds ago in Michael John's dream, had held a glass of gin. 'Stand-to, sir,' repeated Gooding. 'Five minutes to half past five and the chaps is standing-to and waitin' for you to take a dekko at their rifles.'

Michael John shrugged off the discarded greatcoat he'd adopted as a blanket and gulped the tea very quickly. That coat had survived the war longer than its owner, who had not returned to claim it. When they took up their billet in the deserted dugout Gooding had discovered that its owner-chap had failed to return from some kind of raid on the previous night. He'd ended up 'Dead in no man's land', like many thousands of others. So the greatcoat was anybody's. In this war, after truth, finer feelings had been the first casualty. Even Michael John, not known himself for finer feelings, had at first been shocked by the sight of honourable men taking gloves and boots from dead men without a qualm.

So, the greatcoat came in handy as a blanket; it gave Michael John's own greatcoat time to dry out a bit and to take a rest from the shape of its owner's weary body.

Gooding stood quietly beside the makeshift table, ready to hand Captain Benbow his trousers and tunic as soon as he'd finished the tea. 'I got your greatcoat mostly dried, sir,' he said. 'And the mud nearly all off. This white French mud's a bugger to get off, 'scuse me sir.'

Michael John pulled on his trousers and buttoned them over his still damp vest and under-drawers. As he buttoned up, he looked into the narrow, moley face of Gooding. His servant (in real life a tailor's assistant from a shop in the West End of London) was rather too old to be at the front and had been called up in the very last draft. Once in the army he'd only just survived his basic training, having nearly killed himself in rifle practice. This led his NCO to recommend him as admirable material for a soldier-servant, being deferential, efficient and good indoors. This suited Ralph Gooding, who'd always directed his life on the principle of a neat balance between discretion and gossip. Here, as at home, he could always be relied on to find out what was going on. When necessary, he could keep a secret. In this way he made useful acquaintances and reduced his enemies to a minimum.

'So, Gooding,' said Michael John, buttoning his tunic. 'Is this it, d'you think?'

Ralph handed over the Sam Browne belt he'd polished with

the heel of his hand until the leather shone like freshly peeled conkers. 'So they say, sir. Things are slowing down nicely. They say we blew up all their ammunition on the Metz train. Fireworks, that was. Bang on for Guy Fawkes, one might think. So they've no more reserves, nothing to fire. They're walking away. If it's not today, it'll be tomorrow. One thing for certain, though. It's in my bones. We'll be home by Christmas.'

Michael John pushed his hand up his face and through his hair, then pulled his forefinger first one way then the other across his mouth to tidy his moustache. 'How many times have we said that, Gooding?'

'I imagine that I haven't said it as many times as you, sir, not being out here so long. Truth to tell they only got me into the army kicking and screaming. My old lady would've stuck a knife in Lord Kitchener's gullet for taking me. Have to say, sir, that my old lady, she's no patriot. I was offered quite a few white feathers from them patriotic ladies in Piccadilly, I can tell you. Couldn't persuade them that I was doing my bit keeping those office wallahs in Whitehall all nice and tidy.' He took Michael John's cup from his rigid hand. 'I was sorry to hear of Mr Myers's bad luck, sir. So late in the day, if I may say those words. Don't seem fair.'

Michael John pulled on his greatcoat and busied himself with his buttons. His mind was furred up with impressions and events from the last few days: events that had not quite clarified into any kind of clear shape. Out of this inchoate mist he contemplated the thought that now again, apart from Ralph Gooding, he was alone in this war. He'd had a lucky war, no question about it. He was still alive, after all, and was still in possession of all his limbs.

He'd lost fellow officers: friends of a sort. And many men who'd fought under him had died: men who had irritated and reviled him but whose courage, in the end, he'd had to acknowledge. He had even lost – *lost*, what a word! – even *lost* two servants. When further bodies were needed, these unskilled men had been killed, recruited to support or mop up in the muddy, finally ruined-landscapes that seemed to define this war.

But Michael John had never lost his whole company before.

It was only three days ago in their old dugout that his friend Commers had lounged back and said that, sure as shot, they'd see this lot out now. 'We're fated to live on, old boy, to be crusty old bachelors at the club. Jawing away about India and the good times.'

That dugout had been a good one, a step up from the latrine he was obliged to occupy now. It was ex-German, with panelled walls and six man-size bunks. Commers had wangled a bottle of whisky somewhere and six of them had downed the whole lot, rolling optimism like a ball between them and savouring it like the fine liquor that was slipping so well down their parched throats.

Once the bottle was empty, the others had turned in. Commers and Michael John had stayed up, crouched over the last candle and a nursery mug of cocoa, talking over old times in India, telling each other tales they had already heard: weaving safety from past certainties. They exchanged new tales of more recent times, when the war had separated them and they'd been obliged to fight in different regiments. And then they reflected on the fact that at last, by the bad luck of others and wartime attrition, they were together again in what looked to be the last battle.

Michael John had warmed to the thought of Commers and himself in the role of crusty old bachelors sharing reminiscences at their club. This in turn brought to his mind the thought of his early life at Benbow Hall: old Colonel Carmedy and his cronies crouched over their whisky and gambling to extinction. How he'd enjoyed those evenings at the Lodge. Crook he might have been; embezzler he certainly was, but still the old Colonel had shown him more attention and understanding than his own father, more affection than his mother. Somehow he and the Colonel had recognised a like quality in each other.

HONESTY'S DAUGHTER

After the debacle of 1908, Michael John had learned his lesson. His behaviour was exemplary thereafter, and his army career had flourished. Army life used up his energy; it expiated in its various processes the instinct to cruelty that was born in him. India had made him. Service there was easier on the pocket and offered a fine life at negligible expense. He'd relished the detached bonhomie of the mess with its spice of drama and brief scandal. He loved the dry climate and the sharp light. He enjoyed and just occasionally abused the power he had over his men. However, not being a lazy officer, he earned grudging respect from them for being 'a bit of a tryer'. His immature cruelty faded into an occasional belligerence, a tendency to lash out.

His men learned when and how to lay low. To his surprise he found that he actually came to like them. In time he discovered it was easier to manage them than punish them. Still, the old ways and that flashing temper flared up now and then and stopped him from getting higher promotions he might otherwise have earned.

But then Garrard Comstock Myers arrived in India and became his friend. He was a big blowzy man, very confident and slightly overweight. He was a wonder on a horse if he could get one strong enough to carry him and had a sweet attitude to life. He laughed and teased Michael John out of his tempers and offered his admiration and friendship without guile. It seemed that for the first time in his life Michael John relaxed and even began to like himself a little.

When the war came and the regiment had to move back to Europe, the two friends had been parted, assigned to different theatres of the conflict. Then in this last move forward to their mutual delight the army had brought them together. Michael John, whose organisation, authority and occasional cruelty had served him well in this maelstrom of a war, had finally managed a bit of promotion, so he was senior to Commers. This was a source of great amusement to the big man. On the ground, their joshing friendship was observed and rather dented Michael John's reputation as a hard man.

The day after the whisky celebration, the order at that day's dawn stand-to was to work forward against the retreating Germans. As the men clambered over the parapet and started to walk forward, a thick fog dropped like a veil over the trench. Every man, including Commers, had leapt out, the rumours of the peace negotiations giving them a new eagerness, a new confidence. Michael John had walked the length of the trench prepared to do his usual chivvying and harrying of the stragglers. (He once shot a straggler dead; his men didn't usually linger.) Today they had all gone. The trench was empty, except for the stinking detritus of a long war.

Michael John climbed the fire-step. The fog muffled not only the sight of the men in the forward thrust but the sounds as well: shouts and calls, whistles and the crackle of gunfire were all damped down under the blanket of fog.

He'd lost them. It seemed that they had spun themselves up into the fog and vanished. He followed the hedge at the side of a field and worked his way through the stumpy ghost-trees of an orchard. A skein of fog lifted and against the pale sky he saw a German machine-gun post. He pulled back behind the ruin of a tree but emerged again as he heard the word *Kamerad*. Three men, two of them very young, emerged with their hands up. Their faces were blackened and weary, their eyes dark-ringed. Michael John looked behind him to see which great force had impelled this surrender. There was no one. Just himself. He moved forward, his pistol at the ready.

The oldest soldier, a man of perhaps twenty-five, repeated, '*Kamerad*,' looked Michael John in the eye and shrugged his shoulders. The younger ones were crying. That was when Michael John knew for certain that this war was over, and that he would indeed be drinking at his club with Commers by Christmas.

But it was not to be. Commers had gone forward with the

company and come up against a much less pessimistic machine-gunner's post and he'd been wiped out with every man-jack of them: Michael John's company of fifteen. *Lost.*

So, despite the praise and the promised commendation *for his single-handed capture of enemy soldiers and a machine-gun post,* here was Michael John Benbow in an alien dugout among strangers, fighting what allegedly would be the last phase of the war. And the only person who knew him or at this point cared whether he lived or died was this unwilling soldier-servant who, back home, measured gentlemen for suits for a living.

'Well, Gooding,' he said now. 'Perhaps you're right. Perhaps we will be home before Christmas.'

'Will you go north, sir, when it's over?'

He couldn't go and sit in a club and watch the other soldiers talk their war. Not now. 'Perhaps I will,' he said.

'You have family there, I believe, sir?'

'Well, my sister and mother are there. My brother's out here in this mess somewhere but we're not in touch. He's not killed, though, as I'm sure I'd have heard of that.'

His mother did write to him once a month, offering him rather stilted reports of affairs at Benbow: about the garden (inevitably) and the doings and alleged brilliance of that brat picked up by Astrid in America, as well as the twins she'd spawned with that scoundrel of a husband of hers. Husband! The fellow was one of the rats who was profiteering out of this war. He'd ended up buying Benbow to save it from ruin, of course. Curried favour all round. But still Michael John comforted himself with the thought that Jack Lomas was a rotter of the first water. Gypsy he might be, but there was something of the Jew in him for sure.

There was comfort in the fellow's evident cowardice when he didn't volunteer straight away like any decent man. But then the blighter had spoiled even that agreeable thought. According to Carmel, Jack Lomas was now in the army. And with a grace and favour commission as well! Probably bought it. Something to do with guns, of course.

Perhaps Astrid had offered him a white feather. Reading between the lines in his mother's letters, it seemed that, true to family form, Astrid had now dumped her own children to sink or swim at Benbow so she could play the nurse to recovering soldiers in some makeshift hospital at Seland Hall. How like her own mother, who'd left them all long ago to travel with their father, and in later years neglected them to consort with her flowers in her wretched garden. Somewhere in his soul Michael John felt sorry for those Lomas children – all three of them. They would learn that the tight world of Benbow was no real haven.

His mother's letters were always tucked into a parcel packed with fruit and cigarettes, socks and scarves, and copies of the *Horse and Hound* magazine, Commers's favourite journal. Sometimes she'd include a tin containing a cherry or fruit cake made by this Mrs Taggart who had replaced old Mrs Mac. One time his mother had sent him a wooden box carefully packed with the roses she had bred herself, called the Benbow Rose. When they arrived the flowers had almost disintegrated, their scent distilled to a sawdusty-sweet smell that was quite unpleasant. He'd written to tell her of this and that, really, she should not bother. *Away from the battle here there are many flowers which one can pick, Mother, in the ruined towns and villages. Cornflowers and poppies and hedgerow flowers. But there are some cultivated flowers, even roses, growing in wild abundance among the ruins. There is a jar of them on the table in the dugout as I write.*

He pulled on his boots and buckled his puttees.

After that letter it was two months before his mother wrote again. This time she sent four tins of salmon and three pairs of fingerless gloves. And a very short note saying that all at Benbow were thinking of him and he was to take great care.

'Mr Benbow? Sir?' Ralph Gooding never alluded to his

army rank. He just treated him as though he was one of his customers in the shop. 'Mr Benbow?' His servant plucked him out of his daydream and handed him his tin hat. 'The men'll be waiting. Stand-to, remember? Can't think there'll be much doing today, sir, if the news we hear is right. Like we say, it's been easing off for days, hasn't it? We just have to get it over with. These last events. And when you stand down, sir, I'll have your shaving water nice and hot and some bacon sizzling on the old spirit stove. That'll help you face the day.'

Michael John jammed his tin hat on his head then reached out and shook his servant by the hand. 'Thank you, Gooding. You're a good fellow. I always thought you were a good fellow.' He picked up his swagger stick, slapped it under his arm and marched off.

Ralph Gooding frowned as he watched his officer lift the leather door curtain and step out of the malodorous dugout. Pity about that Mr Myers. He and Mr Benbow'd had something going between'm when they were together. Close friendship. Closer than was proper to mention, perhaps. But it kept them both afloat, it did. People found comfort where they could. But the death of his friend had struck Mr Benbow just too hard. Now all this uncharacteristic gratitude! Ralph didn't like it. He didn't like it at all. It wasn't like Mr Benbow. These things could be the first crack in the wall. And you know where that could lead to, in this war.

Still, he'd be away now for a while. Just enough time for a little break, before the business with the hot water and the bacon. Ralph settled down before the packing case that served them as a table and took out a cigarette, the last of a packet given to him by Mr Myers. The stand-to wouldn't last more than half an hour, unless there was another flare-up. Time enough, though, to write a note to his old girl to tell her that things were on the mend here and he'd be back behind his counter in Jermyn Street in time for Christmas. And then they *would* – he underlined it three times – have a jolly time!

371

Two

Early Shift

6.45am

The rain picked its way into Astrid as she pedalled down Benbow Lane. It penetrated her thick cloak and poked its insinuating fingers into her face beneath its hood. Not for the first time she wondered why she'd committed herself to this daily ride across to Seland instead of staying at the Hall in the snug dormitory Lady Margaret had organised for her volunteers. 'You should really stay, my dear,' her mother had said. 'In the company of the other ladies. So much more convenient. So good for the dear boys.'

Lady M's own effort for the dear boys had been to persuade her husband to offer the vast ballroom and a whole wing of the Hall as a military convalescent hospital. On behalf of this particular end of the county she'd promised to raise sufficient voluntary auxiliary nurses to support the core professional staff which the military authorities would provide. This core included the formidable Mrs Conigscliffe-Rudby, a lady who'd had herself professionally trained to nurse in the South African wars. She had great personal authority at Seland but still had the tact to allow Lady M to swan around in a slightly glamorised matron's uniform while running the place herself. It was an admirable arrangement.

Lady M's promise of finding sufficient ladies for the task nearly came unstuck as many of the younger women had gone to war service further afield – perhaps nearer the bright lights of London or more daringly in France. Some of the married women had actually travelled to France and rented houses behind the lines, to be closer at hand to the travails of their officer husbands. Indeed, had not her own daughter Gertrude ended up in Paris, working with her bosom friend Miss Redoute in an American military hospital?

So her ladyship had been reduced to visiting friends who had daughters still at home to persuade these young women of their patriotic duty. Her visit to Benbow had been surprisingly fruitful, as her cousin Carmel had joined her in urging Astrid to lend a hand. Astrid's boys, four years old now, were very independent, and behaved very well for Mrs Taggart's widowed aunt, who'd come in to help when Melanie Tyler had fallen by the wayside. The aunt was rather ancient but she had quite a way with her.

Astrid's daughter, the child Rose, had become Carmel's treasure. At eleven she was as good as any of Carmel's 'lost boys' with spade and pruning tool, and she had a rare feeling for plants. All the garden boys had gone when conscription came in in 1916. Poor Lal Burnip and Joe Harrington were dead now, one blown up by British shells on the Marne, the other killed by sniper fire on the Somme. Carmel didn't know the fate of the others. They were not the kind, or they did not have the skills, to write more than a scrawled card home. Some did not even do that. This had, perversely, made Carmel rather more assiduous about writing to Michael John despite the fact that, as she murmured sometimes to Astrid, writing to him was a somewhat unrewarding exercise.

The walled garden was no longer the exquisite retreat it had been. It was reduced to something of a wilderness these days. The 'lost boys' had contributed more than anyone realised to its perfection. Even they had always put that down to Mrs Benbow's magical touch. Carmel's own contribution to the war had been to allow three old grandfathers from the village to come to Benbow and convert the bottom half of the garden to allotments to help to feed their fatherless Benbow families and to supplement the wartime rations of the rest.

In 1916, when her husband Jack Lomas had finally – against all advice and her own pleading – gone to war, Astrid had closed down the Lodge where they'd made their home since their marriage and gone to stay with her mother at Benbow. Rose and the twins spent much of their time there anyway and the Lodge echoed hollowly without their young piercing voices.

So Astrid was at home when her mother's cousin Lady Margaret came fishing for volunteer nurses. To her own surprise, Astrid agreed. To her greater surprise, she came to enjoy the routines and disciplines of the somewhat makeshift hospital. Their patients were convalescent rather than critically ill, having been sent there for the last stages of their recovery. The main ward was located in the great ballroom, with its silk-lined walls, intricate Italian moulding protected by custom-made linen-covered battens. Portraits of generations of Selands, some of them in military uniform, still looked down on the men in the iron beds that lined the walls and ran down the middle of the long room, their blind eyes not acknowledging these survivors from another, more terrible war.

During the summer Lady Seland had ordered that the casement windows onto the long terrace should be opened so that the bedridden could be wheeled out there into the sunshine. Not that there were many men still confined to beds. Most of the convalescing patients were fit enough – at least physically – to walk the grounds in their hospital blues and admire the breathtaking views designed for the delectation of some ancestor of Lord Seland.

Astrid's tasks were easy enough but she found them weary-ing as the hours went on. She fed the patients who needed feeding; she helped with making the beds and with bed-baths for the few still bedridden; she talked to the restless and confined, she wheeled basket chairs round the difficult gravel paths. A Captain Arthur, who now had a blanket covering the space where his legs had been, often persuaded her to push him right down the road behind the house and through the great arch of the stable block. There he petted the three remaining horses that were being cared for by the one remaining elderly groom, a man who had worked in Lord Seland's stables since he was a boy of nine. The rest of the horses, and the other grooms, under grooms, horse boys and odd men, had been sucked away by the war, as had most of the male indoor servants including the prized pair of matching footmen. Out of eighteen men and thirty-one horses only two men and three horses remained at their post.

The long walkway of the main stable rang hollow and smelled dusty. Captain Arthur would offer his saved apples to the surviving horses and murmur to Astrid tales of the races he had run and the hedges he had jumped in his youth, all of which made her feel like crying.

On this morning on her way to Seland, Astrid's legs were aching with pushing the pedals of her heavy bicycle. The rain had lessened now and the dark of night was thinning to a more friendly grey mist. She put her feet down and stopped the bicycle for a moment to lean over to turn off the wavering spirit lamp that had lit her way. In the twilight of morning its weak flicker was making no difference.

Jack had been none too pleased to learn of her decision about the nursing. He wrote to her in his neat schoolboy script that the army had one of them in its clutches and that was enough. She'd chuckled at his offended tone. How eager he'd been to leap into the clutches of the army. He'd been keen to volunteer in 1914 but his work with the Tyneside armourer was seen as much more crucial to the war effort than the difference a single puny volunteer might make on the front line. He'd started to work with the Tyneside men on the newly developed armoured vehicles called tanks, where the problems with balance and mobility were still not resolved. And some new ideas were needed for tanks which would cut the enemy wire to let the infantry through. When these tanks were finally sent into the field he went with them, accompanying the army engineers, so that he could continue his problem-solving on the spot.

At the front, the tanks at last showing themselves to be efficient, he'd detached himself from them and their lumbering problems and obtained for himself a roaming commission to examine captured enemy armour. There was so much of it lying about after more than two years of fighting that the men were being paid a tally for recovering scrap and did so in scavenging groups. He preferred to work on his own, specialising in guns found on or just behind the front line.

Astrid had heard all about this when he had come home once on leave, in 1917. He marched down the drive looking handsome in his well-cut officer's uniform, his cap set rakishly over his shorn curls. The boys climbed onto his shoulders and the child Rose clung to his hand. He looked at Astrid with the familiar sparkling laughter and confidence in his golden eyes but there were dark rings under them and his face was pallid and strained.

Apart from explaining just what he had done with the tanks he said very little about the human aspects of the war. When she asked questions he simply held her very tightly and nuzzled her cheek or stroked her hair. He smoked a pipe with his mother Keziah and sympathised with her grumbles that the army had taken all her best horses and even now had their greedy eyes on her yearlings. He took the boys and Rose for long walks in Low Wood and showed them how to find the badgers and watch them play. He spent some time with Jacob in the library, the black head and the grey close together over the big leather-bound estate books.

In the last year affairs at Benbow were most definitely looking up again. As the war proceeded the profits from the coal and the remaining farms were up, as were the revenues from Jack's patents. The mortgages with which Jack had saved the Benbow estate were being gradually paid off. Jacob Ellenberg's war effort was to keep a tight hand on all these financial affairs until Jack returned for good.

One day on that leave, Jack and Astrid retraced their first 'riding the bounds', on bicycles this time instead of a single horse. They bumped along down through Low Wood and up to the Carafay pit. Like the others, this pit was in full wartime production now, and though still very much a place of tangled machinery, coal and black dirt it now looked much more orderly and efficient. Jack squinted up at the big wheel as it creaked round. 'D'you know there are pits where we have been, out in France?' he said. 'And working pit men just like these fellers here. Right by the front line. Frenchmen. Shells blasting over them.'

As they pushed their bicycles back to the house he told her about a place called Messines where pit men from Wales and Durham had been drafted to dig deep mines under the German lines and blow them up. 'It blasted the skies, made a mountain of smoke and ash. You should have seen it, Astrid. Lots of dead, English and German. Prisoners flowing out down the lanes. They say it changed the way the war would go.'

She shuddered.

He grinned at her. 'Them little pit men wasn't much liked by some officers. Untidy beggars and not respectful of rank. That kind of appealed to me when I heard that.'

The next day Jack had returned to the front, leaving her to ache for him as she'd done when he first went. They had more or less never been parted since the day the embezzling Colonel Carmedy had pulled his final trick. The day of the picnic. Looking back she was still amazed at how simple life had seemed that day. They just knew they would always be together. The certainties she'd felt with Richard Redoute in the swimming pavilion were mirrored and deepened for her with Jack from the first time he really touched her. It had been such a straightforward thing. Within a month they were married and within six weeks they were set up *en famille* with the child Rose at the Lodge.

She was pregnant when, in 1913, she and Rose went with him to sort out and set up for sale his house in Durham City. He took them on to Newcastle to show them his neat laboratory in the clattering, pulsing mass of the armaments factory on the Tyne. There he put Rose's hand into that of his assistant and told her to take the child for a walk by the coaly river. Then he set about eagerly showing Astrid what he was about up here; how his modifications were adding in their small but important way to the efficiency of the guns that were sent to him.

She fingered the cold metal. 'These are terrible things, Jack. Awful.'

He met her gaze briefly and then shrugged. 'You're right, sweetheart. Very right. But when I made snares as a boy I made them so they would hurt least. And the things I do here make the weapons safer to use. One old *gadgie* here told me that in the Crimea and in the South African wars lots of our men were killed because their own weapons were bad lots. That's a terrible thing. And in the next war we can't have that happening.'

'The next war? Don't say that.' She had shuddered again. 'There will be no war.'

He nodded towards the high ceiling of the room in which they stood. 'The big fellers here know there'll be a war. They're counting on it. Patriots all. And businessmen all.' He'd picked up her hand then and kissed her palm, there in the laboratory where a clean death was the best of business. 'I have to admit that my patents are profiting from their patriotism and their business sense. And this way we'll hang on to Benbow for your ma and she won't lose everything just because she gave her trust to such a bad old *gadgie*.'

She smiled at this, amused as always when he slipped in the odd gypsy word, a thing that happened less and less.

There was little of the gypsy in him these days except when he talked with his mother or Freddy Leeming. Or, she had noted with interest, when he spoke in low tones to the child Rose, schooling her in *romani* words for everyday things. She wondered privately whether his instinct had told him who Rose really was and this was his way of showing it. Or perhaps in adopting her as his daughter he was just making sure she was really sharing his heritage.

In fact, anyone looking at the child, who did not know her history, would have taken Rose for Jack Lomas's daughter. Her hair was blonde, but it was thick and curly like Honesty's. And she had Honesty's delicate gazelle walk. And like Jack and Honesty, she had high points of colour on her cheeks.

Whatever made Jack behave in this way, Astrid was content. Not that she herself saw a great deal of Rose as the years went on. The child spent nearly all her free time in the garden with her grandmother Carmel, digging or tying or picking, wrapped in a canvas apron of Carmel's that was far too big for her. Something which had started as an instinctive desire to be with Carmel had matured into the role of a genuine helper as one by one the garden boys went off to war.

As well as the time spent with Jacob for her lessons, Rose spent hours up at the forge with Keziah and Edith, learning hedge-lore from one and the art of making perfect fairy cakes from the other. It was only at night that Astrid had her to herself. Since Jack had been away Rose shared her big bed again, while the boys slept in another bed, dragged into Astrid's bedroom because they didn't like to sleep away from their mother now that their father was at the war. This was all very convenient, now there was no one to do the fires. Melanie Tyler, though still in her eyrie at the top of the house, had never recovered properly from John Tyler's sudden death. She was getting stranger and less competent by the week. Astrid reflected that, of the two of them, Melanie had always appeared to be the dominant one, the manager: John had seemed to be the weakling who always followed her orders. But Astrid saw now that the balance of dependence may really have been the other way. Without John, Melanie was distraught, a lost soul who forgot to wash and sometimes did not rise from her bed for days.

Mrs Taggart, Gwennie's mother, tended Melanie lovingly. She told anyone who would listen how Melanie Tyler had come to her aid when her own husband died. 'You get what you give in life,' was one of her frequent sayings. She took over much that Melanie had done in the house, except attending to Carmel, who could attend to herself as she never dressed, except for the garden, and made no calls.

Mrs Taggart's daughter Gwennie occasionally visited Benbow, stepping down from her high manageress's stool at Kilburn's ironmongery and onto the bus that brought her to the end of Benbow Lane. For convenience she had taken rooms in Bishop Auckland to be near her work. She had visited much less since Ambrose was finally and unwillingly conscripted to the colours in 1916.

Astrid had speculated on but never quite understood her brother's relationship with this girl. Gwennie was very smart now, wearing the best that the milliners and costumiers and furriers of Newgate Street could offer. She knew that Ambrose visited Gwennie in her rooms on Princes Street, but generally Ambrose was his usual self, dreaming his way through life, less involved with the making of nails for Mr Kilburn than the making of music. Mr Kilburn was fond of him and considered his ineffectiveness in the office to be well balanced by his eagerness in orchestra rehearsals. It appeared to Astrid that Ambrose and the increasingly smart Gwennie were the best of friends, but it was hard to tell whether anything further was in the wind.

Then the evening before Ambrose went off to the army the two of them turned up at Benbow arm in arm and Gwennie showed off the engagement ring on her finger. Carmel sent the child Rose to get Mrs Taggart, saying that she should come up to the drawing room and join them to mark this special occasion.

Gwennie showed off the ring to each of them, one by one. Little Rufus tried to grab it but Kenneth, always quieter, sucked his thumb and kept watch. Carmel asked Mrs Taggart to sit down and told Ambrose to pour them each a celebratory glass of sherry. Then Mrs Taggart asked Ambrose to get his flute and play them some Irish jigs, as he'd done on the first night she met him. It had ended up as quite a party. Tapping her feet and smiling at the dancing Rose, Astrid thought that this event could only have happened at Benbow. Lady Margaret would have been shocked and spoken of the Bolsheviks and the upsets and evil things happening in Russia.

Carmel was somewhat bemused about the engagement, but rather pleased in her vague way. 'She's such a sensible girl,' she said to Astrid when they were alone. 'So clever. Do you know she paid for half of her own ring? She told me. A new kind of girl, perhaps.' Carmel looked blandly into her daughter's eyes. 'A bit like your dear friend Constance Redoute. Or perhaps not?'

Constance! Through the years Astrid had lost her closeness to Constance but they still exchanged letters. A letter from Constance in her dashing script would always include an amusing account of some scrape or other. In the end it had only been the advent of war that had rescued her and Gertrude, the two now inseparable, from a life spent in and out of prison in their efforts to get the government to grant women the right to vote. Gertrude's aristocratic connections had saved her only twice. In the end she was placed in cells three times but, never courageous enough to go on hunger strike, had not had to endure the killing nightmare of the braver women. Constance, not as forthright as Gertrude, and at first less certain of the issues, had in the end declared her loyalty to her friend and been arrested for causing an affray in a political meeting. Her colourful American parentage had provided some good copy for the inevitable newspaper reports.

At the outbreak of war, with many other of the suffragist women, Gertrude and Constance suspended their campaign as an act of patriotism. They trained as nursing auxiliaries and, when America entered the war in 1917, travelled together to Paris to tend the wounded in the American hospital there. Constance's letters to Astrid were fervent and funny but in reading them, and writing back, Astrid began to realise that her once dear friend had been transformed into her acquaintance and their true friendship was history.

It was from one of Constance's letters that she learned of the death of Richard Redoute. Staring at the words scrawled on the page she felt the sadness run through her like a physical pain, from her head to her heels. She was pleased, though, to learn that Richard had not died in bed, like the old man he was. He'd been riding the old trails up by the Ute pass when his horse – a young one that he was trying out – slipped and threw him over the edge of a redstone bluff and down a deep ravine. The horse had cantered back to the castle but it had taken the General's men nearly a day to find him. *Mercifully,* wrote Constance, *my mother tells me he died when and where he fell. One cannot bear the thought that the dear old man should have lain there through the bitter night.*

Astrid wept quietly over the letter in the privacy of her bedroom, while her children slept. *The dear old man!* He was never an old man. Never. She thought of that bright dry place with its brooding mountain. The clear air. The companionable rides and the sense of absolute communication with another human being. The pulsing amazement of loving someone and being loved in return.

Sitting there in the window seat she wondered again whether, without that liberating time with Richard, she'd have woken with such courage and at such speed to the way she felt about Jack Lomas. Would she have acknowledged that powerful feeling at all? She'd probably have ended up a shrivelled old maid, drawing small pictures in books and helping her aged mother in the garden. The thought of how important Richard had been to her cheered her up. She wiped her eyes and smiled at her ghostly reflection in the window. Then she said out loud, 'Thank you and bless you, dear Richard.' Rufus stirred and whimpered then, and she put out a hand and stroked his back until he settled again.

Today, the morning had properly broken and the watery sun was lighting the elegant façade of Seland Hall. She jumped off her bicycle and wheeled it round to the side entrance reserved for the nurses. She hung up her damp cloak on its hook, and as she bent to change her boots for shoes Sister McManners – a proper nurse, not an auxiliary or a volunteer, who'd seen service with the Indian Army medical service – put her head round the door. 'I thought that must be you, Benbow. You'll have heard the news?'

Astrid blinked. 'What news?'

'Today's to be the day. All signed and sealed. The war is over.'

For a second Astrid allowed herself to think of Jack. 'Over? Can they say that? They've said it so many times.'

'It's pukka. Army tom-toms sending the message down the line.' Sister McManners reached out and shook her hand in a vice-like grip. 'They sign at eleven o'clock. It's over, Benbow. There'll be a few poor boys through here before it'll be over for them. But the killing will stop today. It's pukka.'

'Over . . .' said Astrid. 'Can you really believe it?'

'Always believe the tom-toms,' said Sister McManners. 'You can rely on them.'

Three

The Scavengers

10am

'Twins? Now that strikes me as a very interesting thing, sir.'

Fred Swailes, who'd been assigned to Captain Jack Lomas as batman – not called here 'servant' as they were in some regiments – had learned that craven deference was not quite called for with this captain. Workmanlike respect, yes. Confidentiality. Interest in the progress of the war and their own role in it. This was fine. About all these matters the two of them talked freely, in a way not common between the master and the man.

This quite suited Fred, who was not a typical batman, if any such was to be had. A 1914 volunteer, he'd been active on the front line since the first battle until late 1915 when he was badly injured in the shoulder. Patched up and sent back, this brave man became drenched in unspoken terror at having to return to the booming threat and the nightly risk of the trenches. Even the cushier task of stretcher-bearing proved difficult. After two mishaps his medical officer advised that Private Swailes would be of less risk to others behind the lines as a servant. That way he'd free up some other chap to retrieve the wounded and carry the dead or dying without dropping them from shaking hands.

Fred didn't know what to expect in his new master but this smooth brown-skinned man with slow, sometimes eccentric speech, and no airs and graces, was something of a surprise. You'd certainly not place him as a *gentleman* – that strained and excited type who had come up to the front in the early part of the war and displayed their breeding in their bravely dogged, occasionally distinguished, and sometimes flamboyant acceptance of whatever the Hun and the British army could throw at them. After the most dangerous of sorties, such admirable men would sit in their dugout or their billet, smoking their pipes, playing their cards, reading their poetry, even drinking whisky on high days, and still retain a certain eccentricity and style in these most extreme of circumstances.

But this chap fought his war by himself, set apart from his brother officers. On a loose kind of attachment to the engineers, he was making some kind of detailed inventory of German guns, armoury and shell dismemberment. Sometimes he'd take a week to disassemble a particular German machine gun, make his notes and neat drawings, and put it together again from parts he found scattered about the line. Then he would parcel it up, complete with notes, and send it back to his masters.

He usually dined in the mess with whichever officers happened to be on the part of the line on which he was working. These days he was not as much the odd man out as he'd have been at the beginning of the war. In these last days such was the shortage of blue-blooded leaders that officers often comprised something of a mixed bunch. These days sons of shopkeepers, tradesmen – even the sons of workmen – might achieve commissions in the desperately depleted officer ranks of the British army.

Even so, one of the other batmen had muttered to Fred when they arrived at this part of the front that they were letting anyone in these days if they'd let in that Captain Lomas. A gyppo plain and simple. Anyone could tell. Fred had shrugged his shoulders. 'Meks no difference to me, mate. He's a fair chap. Brave enough and clever. You should see him dodging out to get them bits of metal of his. Nothing about them ruddy guns he doesn't know. All sorts of ironware they bring to him now. Like a ruddy armoury in his billet. Feller can read a bit of metal like a book.'

Today Fred had just reached across a table in the Captain's billet when he knocked over a photograph perched on the stock of a German machine gun. It is a photograph of a woman, narrow and elegant as a greyhound, with bright, watchful eyes. A curly-haired child stands at her shoulder and two small boys link legs across her knees. 'Twins, are they?' repeated Fred. 'Are they like as two peas? Hard to tell here.'

Jack sucked on his pipe a second, then shook his bullet-like cropped head. 'Different as chalk from cheese.' He pointed with his pipe. 'Rufus, the one with the curls, he's a bright, cheerful lad. Warbles like a skylark all day. He's everybody's friend. Bit of a handful at times. T'other one, the lad with the smooth hair, he's wise and watchful as any owl. Thinks a long time before he speaks. The clever one, he is. Like his grandfather, husband to my mother-in-law, who was a great scholar. Well known for it.'

'And the little girl, sir? She's like your skylark, I think. Same curls. Same bright looks.'

Jack eyed him. 'You think so, Fred? She is a good girl, the child Rose.'

'Seems you'll be seeing them soon, if today's news holds.'

'The armistice?'

'Already signed, so they say.'

'Do they?'

'But, even so, no cease-fire till eleven o'clock. Ruddy silly if you don't mind me saying so, sir. Pity the lad that gets shot or blowed up in the last minute.'

'Aye, that would be a pity.'

'And us, sir?'

'We'll make one last walk down the last section and collect a few more bits and pieces. I want to get the last bit of that Hun machine gun.'

386

'Very well, sir.' Fred sighed. These sorties, where they filled their rucksacks with the detritus of war, played havoc with his bad arm, though he was so fond of Captain Jack he didn't complain. These days his muscles were soft and his heart was not too willing. But today he was willing, even eager. Today his heart lightened when he contemplated the fact that, perhaps within the month, he'd be playing bowls with his friend Tommy Sacks at his local bowling green in Oldham.

The fact that things were different today was evident to them both as they made their way along abandoned trenches and saps some hundreds of yards behind the front line. Today the men they passed going forward with supplies actually greeted them, instead of keeping their chins on their chests and miserably trudging on. In these last weeks, going about their work locked in the apparently purposeful banal routine of trench life, passers-by usually paid little attention to the scavenging gypsy captain and his particular Sancho Panza. There was something out of kilter with this pair. The soldiers liked their certainties clear and hard. There was safety in it.

Today was different. One corporal and private trudging forward with provisions even put down their kitbags and stopped to talk to them. The older one, still half-crouching, leaned on his rifle, his tin hat hard down on his nose. 'Beg pardon, sir, I've always wondered what'n blazes the two of you do down here, pickin' and pokin' about. I allus wondered that.'

Jack Lomas stared at the man. Fred answered for him. 'The Captain finds bits of the Hun metal and tests it. He rebuilds their guns and shells to see what we can learn. Things like that.'

The corporal chortled. 'Testin' the bugger's metal? Well, Captain! Testin' his metal? Haven't we just done that and found him wantin'?' He picked up his sack, swung it back over his shoulder and set off again. As he made to pass, Jack stepped in front of him, took his shoulder in such a powerful grip that he dropped the sack again. 'Without the courtesy of a salute, Corporal? Even on this day you'll be on a charge.'

The corporal hurriedly saluted Jack. He nodded to his private, who did the same. 'Sorry, Captain, sir. Me gettin' carried away here, sir, today of all days.'

Jack let out something that was more like a bark than a laugh. He slapped the corporal on the back and stood back to let them by. 'No worries, soldier. Not long to go now.' He watched them make their crouching way along the trench then shouted, 'Keep your heads down, lads. They're still snipin' away out there. Not a gentleman among 'em.'

Jack and Fred Smailes moved back to a stretch of earth that had been no man's land but was now well behind the front line. Most of the bodies had been moved from here but still, as one dug down to clear a section of shell or the stock of a gun, one became accustomed to turning over a skull caked in four-year-old mud or the bones of a hand clasped tight in pain or grief. Jack usually put these mementos of the dead into the bottom of his sack to hand over to the padre. He kept a box of them just outside the back of his billet. He would not have them inside. Fred was not so bothered. He imagined it must be something to do with gypsies and luck.

There were other extraordinary finds. One time Fred turned up a forage cap from the first months of the war, from those optimistic days before the tin hats, comical but very necessary, were brought in. Four years old at least. He also found a squashed, rakishly brimmed Australian hat, a German dagger and three rosaries that at first he thought were necklaces. All these went into the bottom of his kitbag beneath the Captain's precious metal detritus. These mementos were his, and would be something to savour with his cronies at the Oldham Bowling Club.

Today's progress was more leisurely and relaxed than usual. Even though they worked well behind the line they usually crouched as they went about their work. Today they stood a little straighter and did not hurry.

They moved on to a wide shallow crater where a German bunker had been wiped out more than a year before by British shells. They'd worked there before. Jack was looking for a bit of the breech mechanism from the German machine gun that had seemed to him to be of a more advanced manufacture. It was the last bit of a particularly fascinating jigsaw.

Jack set Fred digging with a shallow entrenching tool in the place where they'd discovered the main part of the breech. 'The other bit must be here somewhere,' he said, kicking a clod of mud against the hardening wall of the crater. Then he made his way to the other side, poking with his longer, narrower spade into a section of the bunker they had not yet explored.

They'd been working for ten minutes when from behind him Jack heard Fred shout. 'We got ourselves sommat here, Captain!' Then there was a low crack and a louder ear-splitting boom and all Jack could see and feel was mud and earth and harder debris falling on him, burying him to his shoulders. Somehow, in the instant of the explosion, he'd thrown one hand upwards and this saved him. With that hand he was able to row frantically against the clods of sticky soil and claw his face clear. Then he scraped his other shoulder and hand free so that with enormous effort he could use his powerful upper arms to pull himself above the shuddering surface of the dissolving crater.

He sat there for a moment and scraped more mud from his eyes and his mouth. 'Private?' he shouted hoarsely. 'Fred, boy, where are you?' He rubbed his eyes again and peered across to the other side of the crater where he'd last seen his batman. There was nothing, just the changed landscape, entirely re-formed when the shell that Fred had disturbed in his poking had exploded in its paroxysm of latent vengeance.

Jack pulled himself to his feet and made a slipping, sinking, drunken progress across the new crater and started to scrabble down into the earth at the place where he had last seen Fred Smailes. At three feet down he came across a forearm, clad in muddy khaki. On the little finger of the hand was the signet ring Fred had shown proudly to Jack when they'd known each other three days. His friends in the Oldham Bowling Club had presented it to him as a leaving present on his embarkation leave in 1914. One way or another, he'd never managed to get home after that.

Jack sits back on his heels. In the distance he picks up eerie echoes of laughter, singing and cheering. For a split second there is silence and then he hears the cheery lilt of a penny whistle playing an Irish air. Then the cheering starts again. The sky lights up with flares as men shoot into the air in celebration.

'That's it, Fred. It's all over.' He says the words out loud. 'But too late for thee, old lad.' He takes the ring from the finger. It will go in the letter to his mother. Jack knows there is only the mother. No wife or children. Then his mind goes to Astrid. He sees again her photograph held with due reverence in Fred's podgy fingers, one of which sported its bowling club ring. 'Seems like it's all over, my flower. It's over now for all of us. Over for that good man Fred Swailes too,' he whispers. 'But you know and I know there's been far too much waste in all this, too much waste altogether.'

Four

Ceasefire

10.55am

Since his conscription in 1916 Ambrose Benbow, with tens or even hundreds of thousands of his fellow private soldiers, had been moved across the muddy pathways and shellholes, the blasted woods and the ruined villages of the theatre of war: forward and back; to the left and to the right; forward again; back again.

They were moved in accordance with the well-meaning although obscure strategising of leaders who seemed to be learning the methods of this new warfare as they went along. These virtuous men hoped against hope that their fervent aspirations would be translated into strategy: that such and such a raid would 'knock out' a German battery; that the British shelling had actually broken the German wire; that the supply lines had indeed delivered the shells and bullets to win the various *coups*; that the men were sane enough, well fed enough, and wide awake enough, after months of the toiling sweated industry of war, to walk steadily forward under the German guns without faltering; furthermore that sufficient numbers of them would survive to knock the German line back a few yards. That's what they hoped.

Participation in this ebb and flow had hardened Ambrose Benbow into a less lyrical, more resigned creature than the one who'd come unwillingly to war in 1916; it had gained and lost him many friends in episodes of fleeting intimacy. It had fixed wondrously in his head bright imagined images of Gwennie Taggart, of his sister Astrid, the child Rose and young Rufus and Kenneth. These images had distilled into the purest of reasons for surviving this nightmare and returning to Bishop Auckland, whence, he vowed, he'd never stray again for the rest of his life. He now knew that there were much worse things to do than to clerk for Mr Kilburn till his hair turned grey. That gentle nail-maker had sent him several ponderous, patriotic letters, accompanied by packets of tobacco (which Ambrose didn't smoke), and toffee (which he hoarded like a miser and ate very slowly).

He would end up marrying Gwennie, of course. (Looking at her new photograph, he could tell she was becoming more elegant by the day.) The two of them would have a little house in Bishop Auckland and beget three children: a trombonist, a violinist and perhaps another flautist. When he got home from the war he'd go back down to Benbow and set up the chessboard again and show all the children how the game in the hallway worked in the proper Benbow fashion.

Ambrose had never discussed such things with the transient groups of soldiers with whom he shared his life at the front. They saw him as a quiet enough fellow, dogged and even brave when called upon. He knew how to listen to a bloke well enough, and knew more of the lives of his fellow soldiers than they knew of his. Many of them would have been surprised if they knew that he lived in a house with its own lakes, woods and coalmines. They took him for some kind of clerk, one not used, till this 'lot', to working with his hands.

The thing that most endeared him to any platoon or company in which he found himself, in this army of flux, was his reputation for playing the tiny flute that he kept wrapped in a cloth rag in the inside pocket of his tunic. The reputation for playing chirpy tunes that cheered a fellow up went before him from one group to the next. The word went out, 'You know that

Benbow bloke? He's the one who plays the penny whistle.' And they would urge him to play 'Smile, Smile, Smile', or 'Sweethearts' or 'The Long Long Trail Awinding'. He could even pick out tunes that the other men hummed to him, and play them back to them with trills and refurbishments, with twiddles and ta-rahs that gave them new life.

He was fond of recalling Gwennie's mother, on the first night they all met, saying in effect that in the worst of times music was the best of comforts. He knew that for a few seconds, in this dark place of drudgery and sacrifice, his flute gave a fleeting sense of order, even beauty, to men who could not, like their officers, retire to a smelly dugout and read poetry by the light of a candle or discuss the elegant perceptions of Plutarch with a like-minded soul.

This very morning at dawn Ambrose, with the others in his trench, had been shaken to life by his corporal, told to 'stand-to' and present himself for rifle inspection. He'd stood up, scratched himself and tied his coat tight with the rope that did a better job than his leather belt, which had been stolen. He'd jumped up and down on the duckboard, kicking at a rat that trickled with silky threat down the side of the trench. He missed the rat, stubbed his toe on the wall and sprayed himself and the man beside him with chalky soil. He put on his tin hat, removed the oiled sacking that protected his rifle and rubbed the barrel lovingly to enhance its brightness so that it gleamed in the very early morning light.

Obeying the leaden routine of stand-to, he'd set himself at his own place before the fire-step and stood easy. All along the trench men were doing the same. This morning was just routine, like any other early morning stand-to; when they peered over the top to see if the Germans were trying anything on today. Today there was a subdued buzz all along the fire-step. This often happened but now it was laced with an unease made up in equal parts of hope and the fearful instinct that it was bad luck to hope. Underneath all this cowered the desire that now, perhaps, the horror would all just stop. But how many times in these years had such false palms of hope been offered and withdrawn?

But today the buzz was stronger. Perhaps this really was it? Their optimism had faltered yesterday when their captain, who'd survived with them for five months, had chosen to leap onto the parapet at the dusk stand-to and had been shot from the sullen German line by a feisty sniper who wanted the last word. The shot went right through his neck and the last they saw of him was his supine body as he was carried by two wiry stretcher men who stumbled along the cluttered trench with their bloody burden. The captain was still conscious. He smiled weakly and raised his hand, like a benediction. The men watched numbly, their hearts sinking yet again. Another brave man goes back.

But here they were on the 11th of November. A new day, a new dawn. They'd been assigned this new officer. There were whispers that this one had just come off a jaunt where he lost all his men and won a medal. Indeed, here he was, he was bustling along the trench now, checking rifles, talking to the men.

When he glimpsed the man Ambrose had blinked and felt an old familiar tightening of his throat. There was something about the deep timbres of the voice. This new captain took his rifle from him and hefted it in his hands. 'Fine condition, private,' he said. 'You could give some other chaps a lesson here. How long have you been in the line?'

Ambrose looked up into the face of his brother, who did not by a flicker of an eyelid acknowledge their connection. He was conscious of his own dirty face and his three days' growth of beard. 'Since 1916, sir. I was called up. I come from County Durham . . . sir,' he said very deliberately.

Michael John thrust the rifle back at him. 'Keep up the good work, private,' he said. He turned to the sergeant, who barked the order for the men to stand-to on the firing step. Ambrose climbed onto the step and, keeping his head right down, peered across the mists of no man's land. His brother's voice came from behind him. 'Now, private, what d'you see?' He had a periscope in his hand.

Ambrose's voice was muffled by the scarf he always wore round his neck. 'Bit of movement to the left, sir, where the battery lies. The periscopes are waggling around like daisies. You can just see them through the mist.'

'And to the right, what do you see to the right?'

To the right there had been some kind of barricade going up for a day or so. Ambrose had been watching them, wondering, if the news of an armistice was right, why the Hun were bothering. He stretched his neck a bit to get a clearer view. This time the feisty German sniper took a crack at him. Simultaneously Michael John pulled him down from the step by the rope that did him for a belt. A bullet breezed past Ambrose's right ear. 'You bloody fool,' growled his brother. 'What d'you think you're doing, private?'

Ambrose looked up into Michael John's face and remembered the time in Benbow, tied to a tree, when he had been saved by Jacob Ellenberg and Jack Lomas. 'I was doing what you said . . . sir.'

'You're a fool. Now get back up and stand-to.' The captain turned to the sergeant. 'I always say we really reached the dregs with these conscripts, Sergeant.'

The sergeant coughed. 'I wouldn't say that, sir. These lads have given their all and the sooner it's done for them the better . . . sir.'

Captain Benbow stared at him and shrugged. 'As you say, the sooner the better.' And he turned to make his way back to his dugout and Ralph Gooding's very welcome shaving water and bacon.

At that dawn stand-to Ambrose had not known whether to be pleased or angry at being 'cut' like that by his own brother. One part of him wondered whether Michael John had actually recognised him. But of course he had. That had been the whole reason for the pantomime.

After standing down the men had pursued the usual cautious trench routines. They ate the mucked-up hash that passed for breakfast and drank tea from a tin. The sergeant bade them all look lively. They should make a morning of it if the Hun were laying low. They tended to bad feet, brushed the whitish mud from stringy puttees and the worst of the dust from their tunics and coats. One or two brave souls tried a cold shave in their scoop of washing water before they splashed it across their grimy faces. The hardy, assiduous souls who could remember real drill buffed away at their buttons with the heels of their hands. They didn't forget that any movement up or down the trench required a tin hat firmly on. The new captain stayed in his dugout. The sergeant checked the guns again and gave each man a bare mouthful of grog from a can he kept in a satchel attached to his belt.

Later in the morning when they were at rest, awaiting the inevitable but not quite believing it, someone sent the word down the trench to Private Benbow to play his bloody flute. So Ambrose started to play all the tunes he could think of from 'Alexander's Ragtime Band' to Brahms's Lullaby. Ordinarily the men would have joined in, growling along in time with him. But this time they left him to play and let the notes trickle along the trench and linger where they may.

At one point the captain came out of his dugout and stood staring round the curve of the trench. But he didn't make his way down to where Ambrose was playing. Then his sergeant came down and told Ambrose to leave off playing, as it was getting on the captain's nerves. 'Even though, to be true, private, it ain't been bad for morale this morning of all mornings.' This was clearly his own personal opinion. The men around him groaned but Ambrose wrapped his flute in its cotton sack and tucked it in the poacher's pocket in his greatcoat. The sergeant leaned against the wood-clad trench wall and shook his head. 'Even today I wouldn't come across this feller if I were you, private. This last bad do he's been through'd make any feller blench. And you and I know this war can make fellers funny. And not just toffs.'

It was then that the order came down the line for the men to stand-to yet again, just before eleven o'clock. Again they lined up by the fire-step. Ambrose, eyes forward, heard rather than saw his brother do this latest inspection. Captain Benbow spoke to other men, but said nothing to Ambrose whom he passed without a glance.

A minute before eleven Captain Benbow actually climbed up onto the parapet. Then he crouched down, looked down the trench at the faces of his men, and lastly towards his brother. 'P'raps you'd play a patriotic tune for us on that flute of yours, Private Benbow.'

Ambrose leaned his rifle against the step and got out his flute. After one false start, he tongued the first few notes of 'Drink to me only with thine eyes'.

Michael John stood up. 'This is it, gentlemen,' he shouted. 'The victory of the right . . .'

Then, not for the first time in this war, history repeated itself. A shot snapped out from the German lines and in a split second it thumped into the captain's shoulder. Even as his brother fell beside him clutching his shoulder in agony, Ambrose thought that feisty Hun sniper had certainly got his eye in now.

At that same moment, somewhere along a line a clock struck eleven. Bells rang, horns hooted. In the trench there was a stunned silence, a blankness, a difficult letting-go. Then, slowly at first, the whole trench erupted in noise and shouting and laughter as the men clapped each other on the back and shook hands.

Michael John falls right into Ambrose's arms. His head is back, his eyes are closed, but Ambrose can feel his breath on his cheek. The sergeant struggles along through the cheering men. In his hurry to get closer his big boot crunches Ambrose's flute into the mud. 'Silly bugger. I told him. Up on the parapet like that. I told him. Hungry for medals, these toffs. Careless of themselves and others.'

Ambrose's arms close round Michael John. 'I have him. I'll keep him here till the stretchers come.'

'Come away, lad. The medics'll see to him. You go and celebrate with your mates.'

Ambrose looked at him. 'Don't you see, sergeant? Maybe you can't tell but this is my brother. He's a queer old stick, but he's my brother. The war's over, so I'll stay here with my brother, if you don't mind.'

Five

La Petite Parole

1.30pm

Constance Redoute had been obliged to work hard all morning
to get away from the hospital in time to make her way, as
promised, to *La Petite Parole* for two o'clock. As she put on her
cloak and bustled away the celebratory luncheons had been
served and cleared and the cheers were still echoing through
the wards.

On the verandas and in the corridors, soldiers in their
medical fatigues ignored the discipline that normally operated
inside the hospital. They stood around and gossiped and
laughed, smoked and sang as the implications of the armistice,
finally signed, reverberated through the building.

She escaped and made her way down one of the narrow
alleyways to *La Petite Parole*. Once in her seat she ordered her
first food since she'd come on the ward at eight that morning.
She'd welcomed the escape as she felt weary, even though, like
the men whom she cared for and her colleagues, she delighted
in today's wonderful news. It had been a long thirteen months.
What at first had been a jaunt, a patriotic enterprise, another
adventure in her restless life with Gertrude Seland, had grown
upon her as a personal commitment. She'd become fascinated
by the arcane details of bodies and medicine; her own early
hypochondria transformed itself into an interest in the sickness
of other people. She supplemented her early training by reading

medical journals and talking with any doctor or qualified nurse who could bear her questions.

Though her friend Gertrude had embarked on the same work with equal patriotism and fervour, in the end she thought such pedantic devotion to medical subjects terrifyingly dull. Within a month she'd decamped to the British Embassy where her godfather, who was a big cheese there, found her a job where she could use an embassy car to deliver important messages for the gathering dignitaries in Paris. In this way she was allowed to wear a uniform, work quite hard and demonstrate her patriotism.

Gertrude had rooms in a tall house off the Boulevard St-Germain which Constance visited on her rare free days. Despite the travails of her bureaucratic, patriotic, diplomatic life Gertrude had still managed to institute a Saturday afternoon salon where gathered musicians and artists, secretaries and attachés; writers who were just beginning to drift into Paris from the front line to become themselves again, and journalists from across the world anticipating the feast of stories which would flood in with the tide of armistice.

Constance had visited Gertrude's crowded salon on the previous Saturday to find Gertrude showing off her latest acquisitions, a troupe of five acrobats who'd been performing at a small exclusive theatre just up behind the Pigalle. This troupe had made a great impression on the Paris crowd, not least because they'd just returned from a tour of makeshift theatres behind the front line where, for an hour or so at a time, they'd taken the soldiers' minds off the grim realities of trench life.

At Gertrude's request the acrobats had come to her party all ready for their performance: their faces were painted, their spangled tights were taut. The girls had wrapped lace shawls round their waists, but without petticoats these were more of an enhancement than a disguise. The three men were obviously a father and two sons. One of the girls was fair, with a spangled blonde braid down her back. The other was dark. Her hair was oiled slickly back onto her head and then tumbled down her back in curls.

Constance's gaze had passed over her at first. She was exotic, but Gertrude's rooms were always full of exotica. Then something pulled her gaze back and she stared at the painted face, into the kohl-rimmed eyes. Just at that moment the girl recognised her and a wide beam of a smile split the painted mask. She glided across, her hand out in greeting. 'Miss Redoute! I thought it was you.'

Constance was already shaking the hand when it finally dawned on her who this was. 'Oh my!' she said. 'Honesty Leeming, I do declare!'

'How are you, Miss Redoute? How often I think of that journey on the ship when we were all so jolly and everything was simple.' Honesty collapsed gracefully onto the tasselled cushion flung carelessly on the floor at Constance's feet. 'So what're you doin' here?' Her voice was tinged now with an American lilt. She settled herself comfortably on the cushion with her legs crossed and her back to the rest of the room.

'Me? Well, I'm at the American hospital tryin' to help with nursing our boys.'

'You?' Honesty's painted brows climbed into her hair. 'I been to the hospital to look for Slim, but he wasn't there. But a hospital? You?'

Constance laughed heartily. 'Does that sound so strange?'

'Why yes it does, Miss Redoute, if you don't mind me saying so. I cain't imagine you takin' care of yourself, still less other people. Leastwise not the Miss Redoute I knew in Colorado.'

'It's a long time ago, Honesty. More than ten years. None of us are the same. The world is not the same.'

Honesty's smile faded. 'Aye. A long time ago. Aunt Beatrice'd not recognise you. D'you know I went and saw her once, in this cute little ribbon shop, in a bit of New York where all the coloured people live. She was the queen of the street.'

'I imagine she would be. She was like that, Beatrice.' Constance looked past Honesty into the room. 'And you are one of these performers? An acrobat?'

'So I am. You remember how I did my cartwheels? Well, I can do a lot more now. I'm very strong. We're a gypsy troupe, all but one. That's Movena there, who comes from Russia. They came to perform in Denver and asked me to join them when Movena's sister was run over by a train. We did our stuff right across the West and then got on your poppa's ole train and went East where the money was. That's when I caught up with Aunt Beatrice and Cousin Vera. Now we're here to perform for the American boys stuck in this war. I came along 'cause I'm lookin' for Slim. The foolish man was mad to get into this war.'

'You enjoy it? The theatres? The performing?'

Honesty shrugged. 'You get tired sometimes of doin' the same thing time and again, but it's good when they applaud. And we make money. Plenty of that. It's better'n clearing fireplaces for a living.'

At that point Gertrude Seland came tittuping across. She put her hands firmly on Honesty's shoulders and looked up at Constance. 'So, Connie, you've discovered our little cart-wheeler! Well, you can't have her. She's mine.'

Very deliberately Honesty unclasped Gertrude's hands from her shoulders. 'I ain't anybody's, Gertrude,' she drawled. 'I'm not a *thing* to be passed from hand to hand. Miss Redoute and I are old . . . acquaintances. We know each other from way back.'

Gertrude stood back and dusted her hands carefully, one against the other. 'Dearie me! I do stand corrected. I'll leave you old comrades to reminisce.' She drifted across to the tall window and leaned against the wall to listen to her new protégée, a young Belgian woman, injured in the war, who was sitting on the windowsill and playing a Spanish guitar.

Honesty turned back to Constance. 'I was sorry to hear about the General, Miss Redoute. Slim wrote me that he'd had an accident and had died. Slim talked real fondly of him. He was real cut up about it.'

'So you still . . . you're still friends with Slim?'

'Oh, yes. He did real well down in his diggings and has got to be quite a rich feller. And kept it 'cause he doesn't gamble. He's still my old sweetheart, though he's never stood me still enough to get me to marry him. Right up to the time he came away to the war he'd travel right across America to see me perform. Then came the war and I think he wanted some of it. Seems like some of the hero-stuff rubbed off the General onto him. But from what I've seen here in France it's not the same kinda war, not the same at all.'

'So you've come to find him?'

Honesty frowned. 'Like a needle in a haystack. I didn't really know if he was still alive. But now I know he is. I know it here in my stomach. I'll wait here till he comes and this time I guess I'll have to stand still and ask him to marry me.'

'Good for you. He's been very patient.' Constance nodded, pleased for the girl to a degree out of all proportion with the strength of their acquaintance.

Honesty was silent for a second, then seemed to gather herself together. 'And Miss Benbow? How is she?'

Constance stared at her. 'I don't see her much these days but I do believe she is well. She is married now.' She hesitated.

'And the . . . that little girl? She still has her?'

Contance smiled. 'The child Rose? Oh, I hear that she's a wonder. Quick and clever. She's everyone's favourite. Mrs Benbow has named a rose after her that's become quite famous. The Benbow Rose, they call it. Astrid writes that your mother Keziah and your aunt Edith are also besotted. They all love Rose.'

'Keziah? Has she taken to the girl?'

'Oh yes. Astrid wrote to me once that it's as though the child Rose has three grandmothers.'

'Does Keziah know about her? The truth?'

Constance shook her head. 'Whether she knows or not I am not at all sure. But I do know no one has told her.'

Honesty closed her eyes and for a moment, in her painted state, she looked like a Russian icon. Then she opened them. 'You said Miss Benbow was married. Who's the lucky man?'

Constance frowned at her. 'Don't you know? Have you never heard from home?'

'Not since I left your poppa's house. How could I? How would they know where I was?'

Constance took a breath. 'Well, now, Honesty. Here's a surprise for you. Astrid married your brother Jack Lomas.'

At that point Honesty fell off the cushion backwards, then swung over in a back flip, laughing. 'No!' she shouted gleefully. '*No!*' The buzz in the room stopped and people shot amused glances in their direction. Honesty sat down again, and crossed her legs demurely. 'Is this the truth?'

Constance laughed. 'It's the truth. They live in a very fine style. Or they did until he went to war. They're very happy, it seems. They have twin boys. Wonderful to have two the same. And Rose is their big sister.'

Honesty chuckled. 'Well I never. I never did.'

'You should go and see them, when all this is over, Honesty.'

Honesty shook her head. 'Nah. I'm just here really to get Slim and take him home. Then I'll get him to come to Los Angeles with me. I met this American man, here in Paris, who's with the army taking photographs. He's going to make a moving picture about the circus and he wants me to be in it. Maybe Slim can be a circus cowboy. I'm not letting him go after all this.'

'And what about your troupe, the acrobats?'

Honesty shrugged. 'It's over now. This is the dog end. Apart from meeting you, all we are is blinkin' monkeys for the toffs to gawp at. I've had enough of it, I'm tellin' yer.' She stood up. 'It might be for the last time but I suppose I should get around this crowd some. They all want a bit of you.'

Constance stood up too and shook her by the hand. Then she took both Honesty's hands into hers. 'It's been real nice to talk to you, Honesty. A breath of fresh air.'

'D'you say you're at the hospital?'

'Yes.'

'One street down from the hospital there's a café called *La Petite Parole*. Do you know it?'

'I know it.'

'Will you be there on Monday at two o'clock?'

'I can be.'

'I'll come there to see you then. Two o'clock. I have sommat I want you to give Miss Benbow.'

Constance protested. 'Honesty, I don't know when or where I'll see her.'

'You'll see her before me. Please.'

'Very well. Monday at two o'clock. *La Petite Parole*.'

So here was Constance in a corner seat before the wide open doors, sitting over her *tisane*. There was a buzz of relief, of joy in the streets. Passers-by, known and unknown to her, greeted her like an old friend. One tall man with luxuriant moustaches swept his soft brown hat from his head and bowed low. She laughed and inclined her head in acknowledgement and he passed on, his long coat ballooning behind him like a sail.

When it got to twenty past two she wondered whether Honesty would really turn up. Since the events of Saturday rumours of, and the final news of the armistice had sent Paris spinning on its axis. And after all, her encounter with Honesty had occurred in the exotic blur of one of Gertrude's parties. Those events always meandered to the far edge of reality. Many promises were made which were never kept. In fact, to keep promises could be seen as quite *démodé*. It was the style of the thing.

Constance's thoughts wandered back to Gertrude. Their years in close quarters had fizzed with fun and adventure but with the coming of war this came to an end. Gertrude was not bored with Constance, but tired of the hard-working life her friend insisted on leading. The mutual passion was gone but the two of them stayed firm friends. Gertrude conceived new passions for other women but these days Constance's closest companion was Daniel Gryce, from New York, who, as a Quaker, would not fight but still came to sweep the wards in support of his wounded countrymen. Though he didn't realise it, Constance had decided to marry him after the war. Perhaps she would have Gertrude as an attendant. Perhaps Astrid, too, would do the honours.

'Miss Redoute?' Honesty's voice brought her back to the present, but she didn't recognise the Honesty she saw before her. She was exquisitely dressed in a narrow coat in fine mushroom-grey cloth, with a tiny fur collar and cuffs. An elegantly restrained toque tipped forward on her head over her severely dressed hair. Her face, scrubbed clean of the mask of stage make-up, gleamed with honey translucence in the pale November light of the Paris afternoon. She slipped into the seat opposite.

Constance, surprised into ill manners, drawled, 'Why, Honesty, you look so smart. Such a lady.'

Honesty beamed, sweeping away the patronage with good-will. 'That's the difference money makes, Miss Redoute. And the eye to know what suits you. I always thought you had that.' She lifted an eyebrow at a long-aproned waiter who brought her a small cup of coffee, a *pichet* of water and a glass.

'*Merci beaucoup*, Antoine,' she said. He beamed at her, showing a broken tooth at the front. She turned to the watching Constance. 'A long way from cleaning fires at Seland Hall, ain't it, Miss Redoute?'

Constance laughed out loud. 'A world away, Honesty. A million miles.'

Honesty sipped her coffee then poured herself some water.

'Do you know of the bad thing that happened to me there at
Seland? Did Miss Benbow tell you?'

'She said nothing to me. But I kinda guessed. Some man
there . . .?'

Honesty stared at her. 'Mebbe you didn't guess it all.
Anyway, I was thinking. If that hadn't happened d'you know
what I'd be now? A lady's maid in some big house, mebbe. Or
mebbe trading horses somewhere for Keziah my mother. Funny,
ain't it?'

'Hilarious,' said Constance, waiting for the purpose of all
this.

Honesty reached inside the long velvet reticule that hung
from her shoulder on a mink-tail strap. From it she pulled out a
heavy velvet pouch that chinked onto the faded green wood of
the table. 'That's gold,' she announced. 'There are a hundred
gold sovereigns in there. Fairly earned in the rough and tumble
of my life.'

Constance let out an unladylike whistle. She touched the
bag with a finger. 'So what's this, Honesty?'

'I want you to give it to Miss Benbow. Half of it's in thanks
for her taking care of the little girl. The other half is for the
little girl herself. She already has one sovereign. I give that to
Miss Benbow for her the day she was born. These will go with
that to make sure she can make her way with whatever life she
may want.'

'Oh, Honesty, dear, wouldn't you like to take it to her
yourself? You must wish to see the child Rose.'

Honesty sat back and shook her head. 'She is nothing to me.
But I do think of her from time to time. That's all. She has her
life and I have mine. That's our future.' Then she stood up and
moved swiftly, elegantly out of the café and Constance was left
staring at the small cup of coffee, the *pichet* of water and the
velvet bag containing a hundred gold sovereigns.

Six

A Carte de Visite

4pm

By the time the child Rose was ten years old Jacob Ellenberg reflected to Carmel that they appeared, almost by accident, to have designed for her a very unusual and particular all-round education. She did her lessons with him every afternoon. In the mornings she was with Carmel in the garden; in the evenings she was at the forge housekeeping with Edith, or playing with the dogs and the cockerels, or talking to Keziah. She had her bedtime hour with her mother Astrid, which could count as educational even if she had to share it with her little brothers who liked tumbling about rather more than listening to some old story.

By this means Rose built up a fund of knowledge through Jacob in fields of mathematics, French, the aims and methods of archaeology, her grandfather Rufus's writings on Mesopotamia and the gypsies, the history of printing and bookmaking. From Carmel she obtained her education in heredity, horticulture and garden maintenance; from Keziah she learned how to barter, how to tell a good horse from a bad horse, how horses get to be born, what to put in their feed to make them more speedy, more fertile, or more strong; how to calm down animals and men; how to cure sores and infections with material that could be picked up from the fields and the hedgerows. From Edith she learned to bake a fine fairy cake and a mouth-watering fruit scone. With Astrid she read stories and poetry, and before Ambrose went to war she learned from him how to sing English sea songs and Irish love ditties.

Her teachers treated Rose with gravity and respect, and in this way she learned of her own consequence and dignity. She learned that she could make the old ones laugh by turning a knowing phrase or making a particular kind of face. Even the grave Keziah was forced into a smile now and then. Rose had an intuition about when to stay quiet if people were busy or preoccupied. And she would stay comfortingly by if a person were a little down or sad, as she did when Astrid's mind was too much on Jack and whether or not he would return.

On the day of the Armistice Jacob had come up with a plan for a celebratory tea. It was to be in the kitchen, where they had all their teas these days, to cut down on the work for Mrs Taggart and her aunt who helped with the boys. Gwennie had sent a card by the morning post to say that she would be there for tea, as Mr Kilburn had given them a short afternoon in honour of the expected news. So, as far as was possible, the company would be complete.

Jacob had sent Rose across to Edith to help her with the batch of fairy cakes and cheese scones for the party, while he took the twins for a walk across to the garden to collect their grandmother Carmel. He had tethered them on two reins like two little horses and they all shouted *giddyap* right across the sodden meadow.

Mrs Taggart had even persuaded Melanie Tyler to put on her best frock and come and help to lay the table in the kitchen. Melanie wandered around, picking and poking at things for a while, then vanished back into the house. Minutes later there was a rattling in the back corridor and she came in wheeling a mahogany trolley laden with crockery and covered with a damask tablecloth. She looked at Mrs Taggart with clear eyes. 'John says that if this is a celebration, then we must have the best pots, Mrs Mac, even if – war conditions holding – we have to eat in the kitchen like scullions.'

Mrs Taggart looked at the Crown Derby plates glittering with gold and vermilion enamels. Then she shrugged. 'Mebbe you're right, Melanie. We do have sommat to celebrate, after all.'

With her old aunt's help Mrs Taggart moved all the serving dishes and other gear back into the scullery to make space. Then they threw the damask cloth over the long kitchen table and set it with the Crown Derby, which gleamed in the leaping flames of the kitchen fire. They scoured the back areas for benches to seat everyone. Mr Ellenberg had been clear about that. *Everyone*. It would be quite a squeeze.

Astrid had just retrieved her bicycle from the Seland stables and was walking it down the drive when she came across Lady Margaret, well wrapped up against the cold, walking beside a limping older officer in a greatcoat. Her ladyship nodded to him and he continued his slow progress. She strode across to Astrid. 'Well, my dear, this is good news for us all. Don't you think?'

Astrid nodded. 'Wonderful.'

'And your brothers are safe? What a blessing.'

'As far as I know.' She looked carefully at Lady Margaret. 'My husband, also. He seems to have come through.'

Her ladyship coloured. Her normal strategy was to pretend that Astrid had not made that painfully inappropriate alliance with Jack Lomas. Astrid took pity on her. 'And Gertrude has been doing her bit in Paris? Perhaps she'll be home soon too.'

Lady Margaret shook her head mournfully. 'I regret to say Paris is too much to her liking. She talks now of buying a house there.'

Astrid moved the bicycle forward, wanting to get away. She was anxious to get home and take some time to herself to gloat over the fact that Jack was coming back to her safe and sound. She'd thought of him from time to time during her busy day, but had had no time to dwell as lovingly on that fact as it seemed to demand.

Lady Margaret, still blocking her path, stared at her. 'I've been wanting to speak to you for some little while, my dear.'

Astrid sighed. 'Is there something I can help you with, Lady Margaret?'

'I visited your mother some while ago. A year? Two years? Time has gone so fast in this war. Some time before I persuaded you to come and join us here.'

Astrid waited.

'She was in the house, for once. In the library, in fact. It seemed she was teaching the child to read, the child you brought from America.'

Astrid's nerves sharpened. 'Rose? What are you saying, Lady Margaret?'

Lady Margaret was rummaging in her handbag. 'Ah! Here!' she said triumphantly. It was a *carte de visite*: a photograph of a child with fair curls sitting on a high stool, one foot dangling. Except for a greater solidity of figure, it could have been the child Rose. 'See this? It is an old photograph of the Princess Royal. D'you see?'

Anger was flooding through Astrid. 'What am I supposed to see, Lady Margaret?'

'The resemblance. Your found child is no American, my dear. She is the child of that maid and . . .'

Astrid took one hand from the handle of her bicycle and grabbed Lady Margaret's forearm tightly. 'Do you ever feel ashamed, Lady Margaret? Of what happened in your house that night?'

'Astrid!' Her ladyship wrenched away her arm and took a step back.

'Never?'

Two spots of red raced across Lady Margaret's cheekbones. 'I cannot think what you're saying, Astrid. It's an old custom, an honour . . .'

Astrid's laughter pealed across the long lawns of Seland Hall. 'An *honour*? Are we Viking hordes? Is this the middle ages? If we connive at this we have no honour. We should be ashamed of ourselves.'

Her ladyship grabbed back the *carte de visite* and stuffed it in her bag. 'Really, Astrid, where are your manners? Where is your loyalty?'

Astrid stared at her, unable to speak.

Her ladyship sniffed. 'I only mentioned this because I would have offered support for the child, perhaps encouraged you to get her away from here. It does not do to keep them close.'

'*Them?* What is this?'

Her ladyship shrugged. 'I was merely offering help.'

Astrid set her feet astride her bike and put one foot on the pedal, ready to go. 'Rose is my beloved daughter, Lady Margaret. She is the beloved daughter of my husband, Jack Lomas. She needs none of your, or anyone else's, help. She is our daughter. She has no other heritage.' She mounted, then set the pedals spinning and careered right round the goggle-eyed Margaret Seland. Then she threw words over her shoulder. 'You are right, Lady Margaret, it is a day to celebrate.'

On her ride home she began to think about the child Rose: how she had slipped into the Benbow household as of right. How she in herself somehow reflected the special, true bond between Carmel and Keziah. How intuitive the child was. How kind when one was down. How clever and quick and entertaining she was. That charm. For one brief moment Astrid was visited by an image of the King at Lady Seland's table: the epitome of charm and kindness. So now, a thought pursued her. How much of Rose's make-up came not just from sweet Honesty but from the father of the present king?

HONESTY'S DAUGHTER

As she pedalled away in the growing dusk Astrid pushed away these thoughts and, bit by bit, retrieved Rose for herself, as her own, her sweet, sparkling daughter.

As she turned the corner of Benbow Lane the object of her thoughts was there, sitting on the marker stone, a mackintosh over her head, her blonde curls plastered to her forehead. When Astrid dismounted Rose ran across and took the handlebars, and they walked up the lane together. 'The war's over, Mama, and we're going to have a party. Mr Ellenberg has decided. Everyone's coming. It's all set. We have the pretty golden cups all out. And I've made fairy cakes and fruit loaf with Auntie Edith. And Gwennie's here as well. Do you know she came in a taxi-cab? What a lady she is! She has read me a letter she has had from Uncle Ambrose. She thinks he's the bravest man in the army. And as well as this, Mama, Miss Melanie's there in her best frock? And she doesn't smell any more. And her hair is combed perfectly fine. And she really *really* smiled at me. She's not scary at all. And the twins have stolen the first pot of jelly and Mrs Taggart's auntie made them stand in the corner for being naughty. But they ran away when her back was turned so that was no good.'

Astrid, very tired but quite happy, put a hand on her daughter's shoulder. 'We *have* got something to celebrate, Rose, haven't we?'

'What? No more war?'

'Yes. No more war.'

Seven

The Changing Garden

4pm

Carmel's garden, although no longer the beautiful bower it had been, was still the place to which she went to find peace. Each day she sat in the glasshouse looking over her old seed and bulb catalogues, examining the qualities of specimens she could no longer obtain and admiring yet again the representation of her own Benbow Rose in the 1913 edition of a rose catalogue.

The garden was so changed now. The three grandfathers who had made their allotments in the bottom segment often brought along hefty grandchildren to do the lifting, barrowing and digging for them. When they were not doing that they played at kicking a football made from a pig's bladder against the high wall where once a great magnolia had run riot.

On some high summer days the old men's daughters and daughters-in-law would come, pulling small children by the hand or carrying them on their backs, bringing tin cans of tea, and egg and bacon pies tied up in tablecloths. Then, while Carmel kept her head down in the dusty glasshouse, there would be picnics and laughter at the far end of her garden.

Today, however, on this cold and misty November afternoon, there was blessed quiet. Carmel walked the whole garden, celebrating in splendid isolation the coming of peace. She winced as she moved for her right knee was troubling her. It was swollen and aching: a consequence of the years spent toiling up over the meadows in all weathers and kneeling down on wet soil to tend her plants.

She stopped by the allotments. Although they had broken the squared symmetry of her garden, she was forced to admire the way the old men kept them. Their sections were neatly blocked off in narrow, almost feudal strips. Today they were mostly dug over ready for the spring planting, although one strip showed the corduroy furrows of raked-up potato plants. Each section had its own bed, raised on old railway sleepers, for the growing of leeks. For the three seasons that they'd had the allotments her old men had won prizes at the depleted wartime shows for their enormous leeks.

'Garden in't half empty, innit? It being the day it is.'

She started at the sound of the deep voice and turned. 'Keziah! Yes. I was looking and thinking what a sound job Mr Portlock and his friends do here.' She fell into step with Keziah and they made their way through the grizzle to the glasshouse.

'And will you take it back off those old fellers now they say this war's over?'

Carmel looked sharply at her friend to see whether this was criticism, but Keziah's profile was impassive.

'I think so. When the sons and sons-in-law come back they can provide for the families. There should be goods in the shops then, and the men will have jobs. It will surely be a new start for everyone.'

'That's all right then,' said Keziah calmly.

'They could keep them if they wanted to,' Carmel hurried on to say. 'Or I could have the bottom field by the pit ploughed up for allotments ready for the young men when they come home.'

'Like I say, that's all right then,' Keziah repeated.

They had reached the glasshouse. Carmel looked at Keziah. Her friend never came to the garden without a purpose. 'Shall we sit inside? It's a chilly day.'

'Aye, we'll do that.' Keziah led the way and sat in her usual seat. 'Though not for long. The night'll set in soon.'

Carmel sat on the other side of the rickety table and looked up at her friend. 'It's a good day for all of us, isn't it, Keziah, the ending of all this? Your Jack is safe and he'll be back. Ambrose—'

'Should never have gone, that young one,' interrupted Kezia. 'You'd just as like send a banty chicken off to war. Not like my Jack nor your Michael John. Made for it, them two. Risk-all *gadgies*, those two. Wonder is they've got through it.'

'Well, Ambrose may be a banty chicken, Keziah, but he'll be coming back. And Michael John, he's safe, though I do doubt whether he'll be coming home.'

'Oh, that one'll be coming home,' said Keziah. 'I seen it. Mebbe then you'll manage to mother him like you never did before.'

Carmel stared at Keziah. 'I did mother him,' she said.

'Oh did you now?' said Keziah.

'So will your Jack let you mother him when he comes home?' Carmel realised she was challenging Keziah for the first time in their relationship.

Keziah shuffled around a bit in the wicker chair then stamped her boots on the tiled floor. The sound echoed through the long shadowy building. 'I've borned a thousand foals and mothered'm. And two young'ns, one of 'em half *gorgio*. I've mothered the lot of them and none of them have been found wanting.' She frowned. 'But then our Honesty's lost to me in all but one thing. And our Jack? I'm sure of most things but I've never been sure what gans on in his mind. Buying houses, making claim to soil. 'Tain't natural.' Her voice dropped. 'Motor cars! And now fighting a war for the *gorgio*. For *gorgio*'s land. There's no knowing the lad.'

Carmel shook her head. 'I know we can't agree on this, Keziah. But I was proud of your Jack when he went off like that. And a commission! He's an officer. You must be proud.'

'It's matterless to me.'

Carmel shook her head again. 'You will always be a mystery, Keziah,' she sighed.

There was a silence then. Keziah always treated any intimate allusions to herself with silence. After a few moments she reached into the leather satchel that she always carried. She brought out a paste pot with a rag tied round the top, and a green bottle that had once done service as a beer bottle. She put them on the table. 'Some stuff for you. Put the liniment on the knee. It's good stuff. I use it for the hosses, but this is a weaker mixture. And take an inch of that tincture in a cup of water every day till the lot's finished,' she said carefully.

Carmel looked at her. 'What's this?'

'It's for that offside knee of yours that's been givin' you gyp.'

Carmel put a hand on her knee. She never complained. 'How did you know?'

Keziah uttered a rare spurt of outright laughter. 'Why, lass, a one-eyed man on a galloping horse could see it, the way you walk.'

Carmel laughed. 'I thought you were weaving a bit of magic. Thank you. I will do as you say.'

'Magic?' said Keziah scornfully. 'Now that's for the ungodly.'

They sat for a while then in companionable silence. Then Carmel said, 'What is it, Keziah? There is something else, isn't there?'

'It's the child Rose.'

Carmel relaxed. They often drifted into talking about Rose and her little ways. It was as comfortable as stroking a cat.

'That bairn,' said Keziah. 'She brings sommat to mind. She's not like those two other *charvers* out of Astrid by our Jack.'

Carmel knew how much Keziah liked the twins. Apart from Freddy Leeming they were the first people, large or small, whom she allowed to invade her physical person. Young Rufus always shouted in delight when he saw her. Kenneth would come and stand by her and pleat her skirt in his hands and look up to her in amazement as though she were a mountain that moved.

Carmel took extra pleasure in the fact that these were their shared grandchildren. They were the visceral connection between her and Keziah. 'Rose?' she said now. 'I saw her at breakfast. She seemed quite cheerful then. Full of this tea party Jacob Ellenberg has dreamed up.'

Keziah frowned. 'I was trying out a yearling and my mind went out to our Jack and whether he'd get hisself shot or blowed up for the *gorgio* or sommat. Then like it or not the thought of the child Rose came into my mind. Then t'other night Freddy Leeming was snoring like the old bull he is an' he woke us up. I was just gunna kick him to stop his noise when this idea hit me. I was so surprised I forgot to kick him. But he must have felt me intention 'cause he stopped his snuffle.'

Carmel had followed this with some difficulty. 'So,' she said slowly. 'Something struck you? About Rose.'

'Carmel. You and me's been as blind as old pit ponies. It struck me then just who the bairn really was.'

'Who she was . . . is? But we know who she is. She is ours. She is Astrid's. Astrid adopted her—'

'She's Honesty's daughter,' interrupted Keziah. 'I saw it then in the night and I see it now. It figures now, how familiar she was. How easy it was to see her, to have her close by.'

'Honesty's? What are you saying?'

'Look at the bairn. Watch her walk, hear her talk. Once I knew I could see it all. I knew. I saw.' She sat back and for a moment seemed almost vacant, relieved of a burden. 'I needed to tell you this, before they all came back, before . . . well, before they all came back.'

The chair creaked as Carmel sat back in it. She stretched out her painful knee to relieve it. She peered at the shining green of her shrubs as they sang their survival in her misty, depleted garden. She breathed in the dusty residue of her peaches, now long since picked. 'There is some logic in it, I admit,' she said slowly. 'I could never understand why Astrid should pick up this child and just adopt her. She's a different person now, Astrid. She's changed. Blossomed, you might say. But the person she was before would never take up a strange child. She was never sentimental over babies.' She paused. 'Any more than I was.'

Keziah took out her pipe and set about lighting it, sending a dense spicy wave into the delicate atmosphere of the glass-house.

'But when I actually saw Rose,' said Carmel slowly, 'when she kissed me, I was comfortable. She engaged me, so I could understand she had engaged Astrid.'

'No,' grunted Keziah. 'What you did was *recognise* her. Just like now I've recognised her. But you were a hell of a lot quicker'n me.'

Carmel relaxed. Keziah was right, of course. It seemed she was always right. 'This makes no difference. We know her. She is ours. We all . . .' she hesitated '. . . love her. So there's to be no drama, surely?'

Keziah stirred her bulk. 'Th'art such a bright woman, Carmel. I recognised that in tha the minute I met tha. But here's where th'art way out of the game. No difference, you say? That bairn is the light of the lives of all that touch her. Your Astrid. Our Jack.' She puffed on her pipe a second to keep it alive. 'But what of my Honesty? What for was this whole story started?'

Carmel's heart was sinking. She was ashamed that she'd not really begun to think of Honesty. She recalled now how small and childlike Honesty had seemed on the station at Bishop Auckland, as she lifted Astrid's last bag on board. A child. She blinked. 'Did you say blind as a pit man's pony, Keziah?'

'Blind?' Keziah laughed again. 'Carmel, I'm telling yer, we are two queer old mothers. I been thinking here. As a mother

419

you're a fine gardener. As a mother, I'm a hell of a horse-dealer.'

This forced Carmel to laugh and the worry drained from her a little. 'We all love the child Rose,' she said slowly. 'She's had a good life as a child of this family. Better than Astrid or Michael John or Ambrose.'

Keziah nodded. 'That's fine. But what of Honesty? Don't my girl's name tell us what to do with all this?'

Carmel stared at her and tried to be wise but could not come up with a single thought.

'You have to talk to your Astrid,' said Keziah. 'And get her to tell you the truth. No more'n that.'

Carmel frowned at her. 'But that's not all, dear old friend,' she said slowly. 'We must find Honesty, wherever she is in that wilderness, and tell her . . .'

'That she has a daughter? The lass knows that.'

Carmel looked at her friend. Outside, the November gloom was gathering. She could hear the chirruping music of the voices of the twins. Peering through the dusty glass she saw them bursting through the wrought-iron gateway tethered on reins, followed by Jacob Ellenberg, sweating more than a little. She turned to Keziah. 'She needs to know she's not alone, and what a fine child Rose is,' she said. 'At the very least she needs to know that.'

Eight

Succour

9pm

Ambrose sat with Michael John's upper body against his, trying to protect his brother from the bumps and dips in the road as the ambulance made its way from the dressing station to the hospital. Michael John was white and probably conscious but his eyes were closed. There were four other men in the ambulance strapped into stretchers. A medical man was moving from one to the other trying to hold them still as the ambulance made its cautious way forward.

'Commers? That you, old boy?' Michael John muttered. 'Where have you been, you old bugger? I've been looking for you everywhere. Bloody fog.'

Ambrose put a hand on his brother's face. ''Tain't Commers, Mick, whoever Commers may be. It's me. Ambrose.'

Michael John shuddered and forced his eyes open to look into his brother's anxious face. 'You?' he grunted through gritted teeth. 'How d'you get here?' He frowned. 'You were playing that damned flute. How'd they let you come here?'

'They wouldn't normally, would they? I told them I was your brother and hung on. I think the medical officer must have felt a bit lenient because of the day.'

'The day?'

'They signed the armistice. It's over. The war's over.'

The ambulance jerked over another bump. Michael John winced and clutched Ambrose's arm. 'Ouch.' He started to sweat. 'What's old Fritz done now? Blown off my bloody arm?'

'Not quite. The doc splinted it. Said something's wrong with your shoulder too. He said it was all mendable. I said I'd go forward with you to the hospital.'

'Against protocol, you coming along.' Michael John clutched Ambrose's arm again as a wave of pain hit him. 'Stay with me, Amby.'

'I'm staying, Mick. The King himself couldn't move me now.'

Michael John closed his eyes. 'Talk to me, Ambrose, there's a good fellow.'

'There was this private chappie fussing like a mother hen as we took you through. Soft hands.'

A shadow of a smile passed across Michael John's white face. 'Gooding. Ralph Gooding. Good man . . .' Eyes still shut, he started to giggle in an alarming way.

'Commers,' said Ambrose desperately. 'You thought I was Commers. Who's he?'

'Dead, dead.' Michael John giggled again. 'All dead.'

'Who *was* he, then?'

Michael John's face stilled. 'He was a fool . . . He was the best of men. My good friend. I loved the old bugger.'

The ambulance hit another pothole and the man on the opposite stretcher screamed. Michael John grunted.

'And he was your friend?' asked Ambrose hastily.

'Oh yes. He was a big galoot. No better man could you see on a horse though. He could make the barest nag fly.'

The ambulance became silent except for the soothing murmur of the medical man as he swabbed the face of the panicky man opposite.

'And—' Ambrose began his questions again but Michael John interrupted him.

'Tell me about Benbow, Amby. How are things there?'

Ambrose eased his back against the iron pole behind his shoulders. 'Last time I saw it the old place was just as it always was, Mick . . .'

'If you remember, the last time I was there it was going to the dogs. It was the day the Colonel bolted with the booty.' The words were forced out through gritted teeth.

'Oh yes. A bit ago, that was. I forget. You'll be pleased to hear that between them Jacob Ellenberg and Jack Lomas cooked up some mortgages and things, put a couple of good men in to keep things on a proper keel and it's steady now. Jack bought the Lodge off Mother outright and set up there when he married Astrid. Fixed it up really well. No finer house in the county. Not that anyone knows, except Jack's business friends. The county does *not* come to call. They think our dear Astrid's let them down good an' proper, marrying a gypsy.'

'Can you blame'm? So she has,' said Michael John painfully.

Ambrose ignored him. 'Astrid came back to live at the Hall when Jack joined up, of course, which pleased Ma. The Lodge was rented out to some government wallahs coming to supervise the munitions factory. Mother seems quite content with it all.'

'Does she now? Can't imagine it would make much difference to her.'

'Well, those two were as happy as sandboys. Astrid is quite transformed. That little girl, the one she picked up in America, she's quite a character. And you probably know Astrid and Jack had two sons? Twins. Fine fellows. One of them, the older by ten minutes, has a look of you. I noticed it straight off. Everyone remarks on it.'

They had to stop talking then because the ambulance came to a stop by the railway and they were forced to wait at the head of a queue of traffic while a noisy clattering supply train trundled its weary way back to the line. The ceasefire may have been declared but the business of provisioning and servicing the front line would have to go on until the politicians had sorted the whole thing out and God knew when that would be.

As the ambulance stood waiting Michael John drifted into unconsciousness and sagged against Ambrose, his head on his brother's chest. Ambrose dropped his chin onto his brother's dark hair and felt peculiarly happy. He'd stay with Michael John. All the way. Wherever the ambulance took them. He would not leave his side.

The *estaminet* was thick with tobacco smoke and stank of wet wool and cheap red wine. Jack had a large jug of it in front of him and was drinking it steadily in the hope that a fog would rise in his mind and obliterate the feeling of being buried alive. A woman slipped into the seat opposite. He looked up to protest but on seeing her dark looks he desisted.

'Something making you sad, boy?' She used a *romani* dialect that Jack just about understood. 'Why for d'you look sad when all around you men celebrate?' She glanced round at the crowded room and the noisy revellers.

'How d'you know this about me?' He spoke the *romani* words carefully, placing his thick wineglass on the scrubbed table.

As she leaned forward to pour more wine for him from her pitcher he caught sight of her untrammelled breasts swinging under the wool of her gown. 'We always know, don't we? You're different. Don't you always know?'

He glanced around the *estaminet*, which was crowded with soldiers who'd made some effort to clean up but still carried with them the mud-urine-potato smell of the trenches. He'd turned down two invitations to dine from officers he had come across during the afternoon, who were intent on celebrating the armistice. He didn't begrudge them their celebration but he wanted to be on his own, to celebrate his own survival and dwell on the prospect of his return to Astrid. And also to drink to Fred Swailes's cheerful life and to mourn his wasteful death.

The woman was younger than he was, perhaps not much older than Honesty. 'My name is Milena. And what are you called?'

'My name is Jack.'

'The other soldiers stay away from you,' she said. She looked around again.

He followed her gaze round the buzzing crowd of men, who avoided his eyes. He was an officer. Out of place. They wished he would go with his own. He gulped down some wine. 'They think I am different,' he said.

'Why?' she said. 'Because you're *romani*?' She tossed back her hair and caught the eye of a big red-faced private at the next table.

Jack shook his head. 'Because I'm an officer. There's a line they feel they shouldn't step over with me. They don't like it because they think I should leave them in peace and take myself off to celebrate with other officers.' He drank again and looked down at the table, at the signet ring he'd forced off the bloody finger of Fred Swailes.

Then the girl stood up and spoke in English. 'I think you need no company tonight, Captain?'

He shook his head. 'I've all the company I need.'

She placed her hand over his for a second, then moved away to fill the glass of the red-haired private.

Jack picked up the ring. He'd need to find an address to send it off to. It wouldn't be hard to find someone to do with the bowling club. The captain or chairman or something. They would know the mother's address. He would write to her and tell her how brave her son was and how he died quickly and with no pain.

Then tomorrow he would go back into no man's land and complete the job of scavenging he and Fred had begun. There were reports to be written. The sooner they were written, the sooner he would get home to Astrid.

Then, as he watched, the red-haired private grabbed Milena's hand and she twisted right away from him. Jack stood up and put his hand on the man's shoulder. 'Steady on, old lad. We're celebrating a victory, not on the attack. Now you say sorry to the lady.'

The private glowered at him and dropped her hand. 'Why, sir?' he said. 'She's just a . . .'

'Say sorry,' repeated Jack quietly.

The woman stood watching, rubbing her hand.

'All right then, I'm sorry,' said the private.

Jack let him go and turned to the woman. 'Now I'll take you home,' he said to her in *romani*.

She glanced at the bar. 'I can't. All this work.'

'I'll take you home.' His voice was just as implacable as it had been with the private. 'This is no place for a good woman.'

She stared at him, shrugged, then put her heavy jug on the soldier's table.

As the two of them walked out of the *estaminet* shoulder to shoulder the red-haired private relaxed. He turned to his mates. 'What I say is good riddance to fuckin' bad gypsy rubbish.'

Milena led Jack to a house three winding streets away from the *estaminet*. Here she rented two rooms from a couple who had lost three sons in the very earliest part of the war. Her rooms were at the back so she introduced Jack to monsieur and madame as they went through.

Jack looked round. 'You have no one? No family?'

She shrugged. 'I'm not sure. The soldiers moved us back three times during the bombardments. We were on the road. So many people. My mother and my little brothers seemed to melt away.'

'So they're still alive?'

She shrugged again. 'There is no way of knowing. But when normal times return, I'll go and find our people. They will know.' She turned up a small lamp and the tiny room came to life. She indicated the one comfortable chair. 'You will sit down?' she said.

He sat down, suddenly very relaxed for the first time in many months. She was tense, looking round, thinking of what she could do for him. Then she said, 'I will leave you there. You may sleep or just relax. No one will bother you.' Then she slipped through the narrow door to the back room and closed it behind her.

He must have gone to sleep almost instantly. He slept without dreams and awoke very fresh. He stood up, straightened his jacket and very quietly opened the intervening door. She was lying on a narrow bed, her hair now in a loose plait on the pillow. Her face looked relaxed and worn. She was not like Honesty at all. He realised that she was quite a bit older than he'd thought. He took three gold sovereigns from his inside pocket and was just placing them on her night table when she opened her eyes.

'I'm going,' he whispered.

She held out her arms. 'Stay with me,' she whispered sleepily. 'A little time in no-time. At these moments we need some comfort.'

He turned up the lamp and took out his watch. It was well after three. As he sat on the bed and she put her arms round him he realised that tears were running down his cheeks. 'There was this good *gadgie*,' he said to her as they lay down together. 'He died today . . .'

She stroked his cheek and then his hair. 'Many good men have died. And women and children here in this village. Too many of them.'

Nine

Dead Birds

3.30am

Astrid woke suddenly, pricked by the sharpness of threat. The bedroom was still very black and even in November she knew it was a long way from dawn. Then she realised that Rose, who usually slept like a curled-up cat beside her, was sitting bolt upright, letting the cold night air into the warm fug of bedclothes.

'What is it?' Astrid whispered. 'What is the matter, Rose?'

'It's Daddy,' Rose said. 'I thought of Daddy.'

'Lie down and go back to sleep. You're letting the cold in.'

'I can't. I can't do that.' She started to cry.

Rufus, lying with his brother in the bed by the window, whimpered.

Astrid sat up then and put her arms round Rose. Rose struggled away and climbed out of bed. Astrid could barely make her out in the darkness, but she knew she was there, standing very still. She climbed out of bed, grabbed her dressing gown from the bedpost and bundled it around Rose. Then she took her by the shoulders and steered her into the landing and towards the back staircase. The kitchen, now more than at any time in the life of the house, was the warmest place.

Mrs Taggart had banked up the fire in the wasteful way normal in the house that owned the coalmine that supplied the fuel. Astrid stood Rose on the rug as she dug into the heart of the fire with the big poker. When the flames started to surge she sat on Mrs Taggart's big wooden rocking chair and held out her arms. 'Sit with me, Rose,' she said.

They sat there rocking gently for many minutes by the flaring fire before Rose's teeth stopped chattering and her body relaxed.

'Now,' said Astrid. 'Do you want to tell me about it or do you want to forget about it?'

'I was in this place and there were lots of guns firing,' said Rose. 'And birds were falling out of the sky.'

'Birds?'

'Birds. I saw blood on their feathers and in their eyes.' She shuddered. 'There were thousands of them.'

'It was a dream, sweetheart. Only a dream,' said Astrid.

'It was like I was there but it wasn't really me.'

Astrid moved a little to make herself more comfortable. Rose was no lightweight these days. 'Is that it?' she said.

'No. There was a crowd of men.'

'Soldiers?'

Rose stared into the flames. 'I don't think so. But they had guns like soldiers and rippling belts. And they were laughing. They had deep voices. They were all laughing.'

Images raced through Astrid's mind. A vision of war perhaps. But then she thought she recognised the scene from years ago. Men enjoying the shoot at Seland, the morning after Rose had made her microscopic entry into the world. Peculiarly, Astrid was relieved at this. At first she thought Rose was seeing some dream metaphor for the war, and that something had happened to Jack. 'It's just a mixed-up dream,' she said. 'The party and all those treats you had yesterday are making you dream. And all that talk of war and victory. All mixed up.'

Rose relaxed and snuggled her head into Astrid's neck. 'That's all right then. Tell me about Honesty, Mama. My daddy's sister. Auntie Edith was talking about Honesty when we were making the fairy cakes.'

Astrid frowned. The child was frighteningly acute. Last night, after the party, her mother had trailed her to the library and told her quite plainly that she knew about Rose. That she and Keziah had at last realised that the child had been born to Honesty. That it was the child's right to know who her parents were. 'And do you know who the father is, Astrid? Surely you know?'

Astrid had shaken her head. 'Only Honesty can say that. That's her secret.'

'And will you tell the child? Will you? About Honesty?' Her mother's voice had trembled with rare determination.

Now she said to Rose, 'Well, as you know. Honesty is your auntie, sweetheart, your daddy's sister. She was very beautiful. She was the most wonderful acrobat. She was a very special girl. Now she is a very special grown-up.'

'Where is she? Is she at the war, like Daddy?'

'You've heard all this before, Rose. She is in America.'

'Will she come to see us?'

'Would you like her to?'

Rose pulled away from her and peered at her in the flickering light of the fire. 'Yes, Mama. I think I must see her. I think she wants to see me. I know it. Just like I want to see Daddy again, back from the war.' She snuggled back down, her face hard into Astrid's neck. Astrid sat, staring at the fire over her curly head. How many people had been saying for months now that the war would end, and that everything would be different after the war. And she'd agreed, joined in the chorus of hope and optimism. But she hadn't reckoned on this particular difference, here at the heart, the centre, of her family. If she did what her mother – and Keziah – desired, then the centre would be broken and things would never be the same again.

Part Five

Rose's Version

June 1921

June 1 UK: Result of the Derby is broadcast by wireless for the first time

June 10 UK: Unemployment has reached 2.2 million

June 20 USA: Washington imposes fines on women for smoking

June 22 UK: King George V in Belfast to open the Northern Ireland Parliament. In his speech he pleads for peace and reconciliation

June 28 UK: Coal strike ends as Government agree to subsidise the coal industry

June 30 China: The inaugural meeting of the Chinese Communist Party is held in a girls' school in Shanghai. Among those attending was Mao Tse-tung, a librarian and primary school teacher

One

Setting Keziah Free

8am
It's my birthday, so this should be a memorable day for me. I'm
fourteen and what's more have had my hair cut in a bob. You
wouldn't believe how easy it is to wash and to take care of.
Unfortunately it won't lie flat and the curls spring up. Melanie
Tyler screamed when she first saw me and said she thought I'd
changed into my father.

But today will be memorable for other reasons, as will soon
be clear. My mother has explained (as if I were a much smaller
child) that today there'll be no cake made by Melanie Tyler, nor
candles lit at dusk in the dining room. That would be disrespectful. I know this. You see, my grandmother's dead and the
ceremonies that take place today will be for her, not me.

My mother asked whether I would mind this happening on
my birthday. But I'm pleased because each birthday I'll have
this special memory of my grandmother.

I'm quite used to death, of course. My uncles and my father
faced death front on in the Great War although they don't
speak of it. Lal Burnip, who helped my grandmother with the
garden, he and his two brothers were killed. I worked alongside
Lal as a little child and knew him as a friend. It was hard to
understand that he was dead. To be honest I've always found it
hard to imagine he and his brothers dead on the heroic field of
battle. They were so ordinary. I shouldn't say this but every one

433

of them wiped his nose on his sleeve. But still they died for their country and are heroes.

And a year ago my pony Sailor died when he got out of his field and crashed into the Co-op milk cart. Poor old boy was very badly hurt but not dead and I thought Keziah would mend him because that's what she always did, mend animals. She even mended people sometimes. I begged her to mend Sailor but she shook her head. Little shards of grass shook themselves out of her hair and kind of sat in the air. She always has grass about her.

That day there in the road she bent down and whispered into Sailor's ear. He stopped threshing about, closed his eyes and was still. I asked her what she'd said to him and she said she'd told him to let go, to die. So he let go and was still.

I was crying like a baby but my mother held me tight and told me that Sailor was at rest, that anyone else would've had to shoot him and at least he didn't have to be shot. That's what Keziah had done for him.

I say 'my mother' but she's not really that, but I'll tell you about that later. Today we must think of my grandmother. It's *her* day, after all. They'll say some words for her in the little church. And then they'll put her in her *vardo* with all her things and burn her to black dust. She told me about this before she died. How a person must do this to set their spirit free. Having listened to her then, I don't feel quite so miserable today. I'm surprised at myself.

Keziah had been quite poorly with this thing inside her, that stopped her eating. She wouldn't go into the hospital. She wouldn't even go over to Forge Cottage to let Aunt Edith look after her. No, as things got worse and worse and she winced with that pain inside her, she stayed in her *vardo*, receiving visitors like a queen. It was in there that she told me about the burning of the *vardo*. My other grandmother Carmel was there with us. She was always there. She came to the *vardo* every single day to talk to Keziah, to look after her. She was her guardian. Anyone who wanted to see Keziah – and there were plenty – had to ask Grandmother Carmel if they could.

And lots of people came: many of them were travelling people who are camped now in a higgledy-piggledy fashion alongside the main drive, waiting for the final act. I imagine when it's all over they'll go on to Appleby Fair to meet their friends and shake hands when they make a trade, just as Keziah has always done. She and I go to Appleby every year. Went, I mean. I loved to be there and was proud to walk the long lane with her and whichever horse she was selling. Everyone – even the gypsy kings – looked up to Keziah.

It is not just travellers who've come to see Keziah, though. There have been others: farmers and horse breeders and people who through the years have come to Keziah for cures. Also people from the village have come, some of whom used to sneak up to the *vardo* in the darkness for some kind of help or advice.

My grandmother Carmel has made sure they keep their greetings brief and leave their gifts by the door. (These too will be burned with the *vardo*.) In the end all this stopped. The last callers went away again in their fine boots, or soft shoes, or their two bare feet.

In all that time I stayed there by the *vardo* sitting on the steps, waiting to see if they needed me, those two grandmothers of mine. But I can't say they did. They are closer than a double-yolked egg, those two! For as long as I can remember, if you wanted one of them, you had to look for the other.

Or *vice versa*. That means the other way round. Mr Ellenberg taught me about *vice versa*, as well as a lot of other things. He's very old but I do like him. Old as he is, he has learned to drive my father's second motor-car so that he can come and collect me and the boys from school in Bishop Auckland.

I sometimes think I can see a kind of velvet love chain going round, joining us all together. Mr Ellenberg most especially loves my grandmother Carmel. He loves my father too, who, like Carmel, loved Keziah (although he and Keziah never made a show of it). He loves my mother Astrid who loves me and my brothers and then she loves her own mother Carmel, who says Mr Ellenberg and my father are as thick as thieves, but laughs when she says it. I suppose that kind of completes the circle.

When my father's at home from his travels and his work, his head is always close to Mr Ellenberg's. They get together over books or reports, or some design for a new machine my father's involved in. He's sold all our pits, which is just as well when you think of this strike that's happening. And he gave up making guns when he came back from the war. Just like that. 'No more guns!'

My father stayed on in France six months after my uncles came back. In the end my mother Astrid had to go to get him. All the way to France! Like I said, she loves him very strongly: her love is as certain as the sky and as strong as the wind. My father's latest thing, apart from dealing massively in scrap metal, is a washing machine that's driven – can you believe it? – by electricity.

But yesterday, for the first time ever, I heard my father shout at Mr Ellenberg. I was listening at the door so when he stormed out he sent me flying. (This listening at doors is a new thing for me. I think it's to do with my age. When I was smaller they all used to talk as though I wasn't there so it was easy to find out what was going on. But now their talk fades when I enter a room so I have eavesdrop to know what's happening.)

Anyway, Mr Ellenberg had been talking to my father about going back to Russia, his own country that he left before he came here with my grandfather Rufus. There has been this Bloody Revolution in Russia and famine because of the blockade and the mess they've made of things, and the Bolsheviks are on top now. Everybody knows that. My father shouted to him that such a journey would be lunacy. But Mr Ellenberg said he wanted to go and find his daughter.

He lost her once and now he feels strong enough to go and find her.

Talking of daughters, there was something I was going to say. I'd been feeling them buzzing all around me for weeks – my mother and father and my grandmother Carmel, as well as Keziah orchestrating things from her bunk in the *vardo*.

Then one night, just a week ago, we were all stuffed together in that tiny space. As always it smelled of horse-liniment and was dusty with shards of grass. With all those bodies packed in there you could hardly breathe. Suddenly they were all staring at me. Then in a halting voice my mother started to tell me that, in fact, Keziah was my grandmother twice over – once because of my father but also in a more true fashion because of his sister Honesty Leeming who is *really* my mother! If the *vardo* hadn't been so crowded with bodies I'd have fallen off my stool. As it was I merely sagged a bit.

My mother's eyes are full of tears so I lean across to kiss her to make her feel better. She puts her arm round me.

'But Honesty's American,' I mumble. I know all about my father's sister Honesty. She's in the moving pictures. Honesty Leeming. Her name was on the poster outside the picture-house where we went to see two of her films. She had this peek-a-boo face and had all kinds of adventures where she escaped death by a whisker. She's very beautiful.

'You were born in America,' says my *now-not-mother* Astrid. (I have to call her Mother even so. How else would I name her?) 'Honesty gave you to me to take care of, and that's what I've done.'

'She didn't want me?' I say, still trying to work it out. 'She gave me away?'

'She was a young kid,' says my father gruffly. 'Not much older than you now. Too young.' He seems very stiff. I wonder how long he's known.

I briefly wonder what it would feel like, having a baby. I've seen horses and dogs have their young. But people? My mind is blank. Then I wonder about my father, who is really my uncle. If Honesty is my mother then Jack can't be my father . . .

'Honesty does think about you, care about you,' my mother is saying. 'She sent something for you. Constance Redoute brought it here, just after the war. I kept it safe for you till I told you about this.' Then she takes out a velvet sack and pours a whole heap of gold coins into my lap. More than I've ever seen in my life. They glow even in the dim light of the *vardo*. Crikey. 'Honesty sent this for you, with her love.' My mother leans back in her seat as though she's just done a very hard job.

Then I ask them about my real father who can't be Jack Lomas, and they look at each other as though I've sworn or something. Finally my *not-father*, Jack Lomas, speaks. 'You must talk to Honesty about that.' He glances down at Keziah who is lying there with her eyes closed, listening. 'She's on her way here now.'

'It must take ages to get here from America?' I say.

'She's in Paris,' says my mother. (Should I call her Astrid now?) 'Performing on the stage there. She's staying with a friend of Constance Redoute. Gertrude Seland.'

That's the famous suffragette. She's been in the papers.

'She's on her way.' My father repeats his words. 'You'll see her soon.'

Then Keziah's voice comes from the bed, as though it wanders into the air from a very deep tunnel. She tells them all to go and leave me with her. We watch as my father – crouching because he's too tall for the van – helps Grandmother Carmel down the steps and sets her straight again with her stick. Then he puts his hands round my mother Astrid's narrow waist and jumps her down. As I close the little door I can see how he keeps one arm round her waist as they walk away. You can't tell where one ends and the other begins. Those two are happier than Mr Rochester and Jane at the end of the novel. I've always

438

known that and liked it. It's a kind of miracle, when you think of it.

'Come here, *charver*.' Keziah's deep voice comes from behind me. As I sit beside her she lifts her head up from the leather pillow. She's shrunk in the last months; her skin is stretched over her bones. But her eyes are as large and bright as ever. I put my hand over her old leathery claw.

'Do you remember old Sailor?' she says.

'Yes.'

'Well, child Rose, I want you to do the same for me.'

I wait a while before I answer. 'I don't understand.'

Her old hand turns and clasps mine like a vice. 'You remember how we sent old Sailor on his way? I want to go like that and you must help me, give me the strength. You're to whisper right close, right here in my ear.'

'What should I whisper?' I am whispering already.

'Use my name. Say *Now Keziah, set thee-self free.*'

Sailor. Now I know what she means. 'I say that? Is that all?'

'And then, afterwards, you're to go to get Freddy and your Auntie Edith. Bring them here. They'll be cut up. Daft old Edith'll bubble like a bairn. But they'll know what to do.'

I take a few deep breaths, then, 'But what about Honesty, Keziah? Can't you wait for her?' Now my face is very close to hers and I can feel rather than see the shake of her head.

'I'd only say this to thee, *charver*, but I'm weary with waiting,' she says. 'You're here. You're her daughter. The daughter of my daughter. You'll do.' She lies her head back on the old leather pillow. She looks at me, her eyes wide open. 'Now, *charver*. Do this for thee grandmother.'

I lean close until my lips touch her ear and whisper, very clearly, *Now Keziah, set thyself free*. I repeat, *Now Keziah, set thyself free*.

Her eyelids drop over her eyes and I can see the shape of her eyeball through the fine veil of her eyelid. Her body relaxes, seems to close in on itself on the bunk. Her grasp on my hand loosens and I look down at her closed face. In this moment I know that I'm entirely alone now in this space. I stand up and hit my head on the curved beam of the *vardo*. (These days I'm nearly as tall as my father.) Then, my eyes streaming with tears, I go to find Freddy and Aunt Edith. Freddy sits down hard on a chair and Aunt Edith throws her pinny over her head and starts to wail. Keziah was right about that.

I've never told anyone what I did, what Keziah asked me to do. I've watched them all go about the business of the funeral and I still haven't told anyone. It is a secret between Keziah and me. Sitting thinking about her over these last few days, I marvel at how she always does ... did ... exactly what she wanted. Somehow she made them tell me the truth so that, in the end, as her daughter's daughter, I could do that last thing for her. She got what she wanted.

And this truth is her deathbed gift to me. I can't reject it. I can't let it be a problem. It's just as though Keziah had given me my grown-up self on a plate; she has fused a part of herself into me so that now I will always know what to do.

Two

The Chain

11am

The church service is at three and everything is ready. Melanie Tyler has a wonderful spread of baking and meats, all arranged on the best china in the dining room. Grandmother Carmel's instructions, of course. But Melanie Tyler has also, without consulting anyone, spread druggets over all the carpets. She told me, 'You never know who may turn up to such a do! They'll be off the lanes and the hedges.'

Melanie Tyler's really up to the game these days. I can remember when she was ill for quite a long time, roaming the attics like the madwoman in *Jane Eyre*. But she got better on Armistice Day and has been my grandmother's right-hand woman ever since. At first Melanie worked in some kind of partnership with Mrs Taggart, but Auntie Gwennie came to take her mother down to live with her in the house in Bishop where she lives with Uncle Ambrose. These days Mrs Taggart takes care of their baby and the house in Princes Street while Gwennie manages Mr Kilburn's hardware shop. To be honest I find Aunt Gwennie a bit scary but Uncle Ambrose seems to like the way she bosses him around.

The first thing Uncle Ambrose did when he came home from the war – even before marrying Gwennie – was to set up the chess game in the hall again. He designated me a white and he showed me four moves to start it off again. After that it has

441

to be only one move as a person goes through the hall, and never if the lever is against you. (A bit like this family. Not much goes on face to face.) Of course I knew all about the chess game but still, Uncle Ambrose sat me down there and told me again how the game had gone on all of his life until he went off to war. And now, he said, we needed to start it up again.

My Uncle Mick, who was in the hall at the time, laughed out loud at him. He told me there used to be weeks when no one moved a single piece and this was all sentimental hogwash. Then Uncle Ambrose said, 'Ha! And I haven't forgotten the day you kicked the lot over, you rotter.'

Uncle Mick laughed again and told me that after he'd crashed the game, old Ambrose had put all the pieces back in their exact places: every one; that he had a memory for that kind of thing. An amazing memory when you considered it. Then Uncle Mick clapped Uncle Ambrose on the back with his good hand. (I should tell you he was shot in the shoulder during the war and that arm doesn't work too well.)

The two of them are quite good friends, although Ambrose is rarely at Benbow Hall, what with the orchestra and the nail-making works. And Gwennie and the baby. I expect he blesses the day Mrs Taggart went down to live with them.

I do have this pretty good memory. I sometimes think I can remember everything since the day I was born. That might be because my grandmother and Aunt Edith, Mrs Taggart and Melanie Tyler, when they sit together, have the habit of going over and over the various things that have happened and I listen. I have always listened. So now I don't know which is me remembering their stories and which is me really remembering the truth about what has happened to me. If I ever get to write this down as I'd like to, I have to admit there might be guesswork in it.

But there is one thing. My mother Astrid told me once that she thought I could remember things from *before* I was born!

Something I'd said to her once, it seems. I don't know how she would know that, really. She often says things to me that make me feel good. She doesn't say things like this to my brothers, so just now I'm thinking that perhaps that's because of the adoption thing. It does put a new light on everything.

In these last few days – since I've known I was Honesty's daughter – I've watched my mother Astrid closely as she deals with my brothers. But as far as I can see she's exactly the same as she's always been: with me, with them. I know all the wicked stepmother stories but she's not in the least like that. No poison apples. In fact as far as I can see she'd rather offer the poisoned apple to Rufus when he's being the devil he can be when the mood takes him.

She says Uncle Mick had a touch of the devil in him when he was young but you can't see that now. He's really quiet when he's here, which is most of the time. She says the war took care of his temper and made him half the man he was. But seeing as neither he nor Uncle Ambrose talk about the war, I don't know how she can know that. Maybe, though, that's why Uncle Mick has a soft spot for Rufus. You can see there's something between the two of them. They walk the bounds on any fine days and he's teaching Rufus to play golf. Uncle Mick is wonderful in the way he can play golf just using one arm. You should see him.

And Kenneth spends his time in the library with Mr Ellenberg. The two of them play maths games or Kenneth goes through those old books of photographs and notes of our grandfather Rufus who was a great traveller.

It's Kenneth that Uncle Ambrose takes notice of, when Aunt Gwennie lets him come down to the Hall. He's teaching Kenneth to play the flute so that he can play in the town orchestra and has already introduced him to Mr Kilburn who's the emperor of that little music world. Kenneth is very keen.

Mr Ellenberg just sits by the fire and smokes his pipe, watching the fun. He's just about my favourite person round here, after my mother and Grandmother Carmel. There has been such a flurry today about this idea of him going back to Russia. He told the rest of us at breakfast today (of all days!). My grandmother was very angry. Her lips went into this straight line and she banged the table with her porridge spoon. 'You will not get there, Jacob,' she said. 'You will die on the way.'

My father was already at the door, his napkin still clipped to his waistcoat button and his bulging briefcase in his hand. He promised Mother to do only two hours in his office in Durham today and to be back by twelve.

He turned round. 'I told you, Jacob, that's a bad notion. A mad notion, old boy,' he said. 'An't you feared of those old Bolshevik *gadgies*? An't everyone starving there now what with the blockade and the Revolution and the mess they're in?'

(I should explain here that my father is *romani* and likes to flaunt it sometimes. He may not be my father but I'm glad that, at least, we still share the same blood. My new mother Honesty is half *romani* and that makes me a quarter *romani*.)

Mr Ellenberg is patting his moustache with a napkin that, I notice, is much darned. Melanie Tyler puts out only the old linen at breakfast. Mr Ellenberg nods. 'They are letting food into the country now, Jack. Things change.' He puts down the napkin and strokes back his sparse hair. 'In the years before I came here, my boy, I was in great danger from the cruel henchmen of the Czar. Bad as things are in Russia, these are better times in my old country. As I explained to you already, Jack, it is a last chance to seek my daughter if she is still on this earth.'

My mother Astrid is not as red-faced with anger as my grandmother but she's still concerned. 'It would be very difficult for you, Jacob. Impossible. Anyway, we need you here. How could we manage without you?'

He looks round and his glance settles on my Uncle Mick who has his head down and is managing his breakfast, as always, with one hand. 'There are so many people of talent in this house now. When I came, all were children. Perhaps I was needed then.'

Mr Ellenberg and my Uncle Mick circle round each other like kitchen cats; it's clear that they are wary of each other. I remember the time after the war when Uncle Mick came back with his medals and his useless arm. Mr Ellenberg stayed away from the dining room, and the library, for days. He asked Melanie to take his meals to his room. Then one day my mother went to find him, and some kind of truce was declared.

I can't see why they dislike each other. Mr Ellenberg is the kindest of people and Uncle Mick is nice enough. If you get him in the right mood he'll tell you all about India and his adventures there. He'll even get out the map and his photo books and show you where he went. He sometimes talks of a wonderful friend of his who was very good at horseracing. And the fine times they had. It seems to me that this was a golden time for him. I overheard my mother saying once to my father that this man must have been the love of Uncle Mick's life. She was smiling but I think she meant it.

After the truce between him and Uncle Mick, Mr Ellenberg started to come to the dining room for his meals but was rather quieter than he ever had been. Then there was some kind of conference and my grandmother and my father decided that Mr Ellenberg should not work so hard. Perhaps, said my grandmother, Uncle Mick might learn the intricacies of the big ledgers and perhaps Mr Ellenberg might teach him? Since then I sometimes creep into the library and find them with their heads together. One day I even heard laughter.

Early this morning Mr Ellenberg and I were sitting in the deep seats in the library. My mother had stopped Uncle Mick in the doorway. By glancing sideways I could see them very clearly. My mother asked Uncle Mick whether he'd be at Keziah's funeral today. He waited a bit then said to her, 'Well, old girl, I suppose it's a matter of respect. Your mother-in-law, what? Should be colourful if nothing else.'

'Oh, Michael John.' She sounded cross. 'You never change.'

He took her by the forearm. 'Oh, dearest sister.' His voice was soft. 'We all change. Time changes all.'

Then she sighed. 'Oh, Mick. You must hate being here. You seem so bored. Is it so very boring for you here?'

'Boring? Boring? Is a man with one arm allowed to complain to someone who puts food in front of him, clothes on his back?'

I felt sorry for him. I glanced at Mr Ellenberg, who shook his head slightly. We sat tight and quiet. But I did feel sorry for Uncle Mick. I'm stuck here myself, but one day I'll fly the nest. My life is set before me. I'm sure of it.

Three

The Inappropriate
Survival of Dinosaurs

Noon

School? Oh yes, I go to school. I go to the girls' school in
Bishop Auckland. My brothers go to the boys' school, and I
think're doing very well. We're all clever in this family. It's
easy to be clever when you are ... well ... clever. The other
girls at school sometimes call us names because of my father
dealing with scrap and the fact that Mr Ellenberg comes to
collect us in the car. And me being as tall as a beanpole. But
apart from that, school's not so bad. I like the English teacher
who keeps giving me all kinds of books to read but most
especially the works of Charlotte Brontë and George Eliot
(who is really a woman). Then there's the history teacher
who's very keen to get me to talk about my grandfather and
his discoveries and borrows his books from my mother. And
there's the biology teacher who reminds me of Keziah, the
way she would have been thirty years ago.

Lady Seland, this ancient biddy who's some kind of relative
of my grandmother, is mother of the famous suffragette,
Gertrude Seland. (The one Honesty's been staying with in
Paris.) Anyway, this old biddy saw me one day in Newgate
Street, in my school uniform. The next day she made a special
visit here to the house, complete with grand motor-car with its

447

chauffeur. I overheard her lecture my mother and grandmother on how they'd all failed *me* regarding school! It seems they should have sent me away to school. How common and vulgar it was to send me to the local grammar school where I would rub shoulders with tradesmen's daughters! (I would hate to think what she would say about Miriam Carlton whose father is some kind of pit official.)

I was standing by the door, of course, and heard my mother tell the woman in a sharp spiky voice that *her ladyship* was very much mistaken. Rose was doing well at school and would in all probability go to university. Perhaps *her ladyship* had not noticed that we lived in a new world now, where status had to be earned by effort and talent? Birthright was meaningless in these modern days without achievement. Had not her own husband – Rose's father – made his way in the world without the aid of such overweening snobbery?

I was so proud of her. She said all the right things.

Well! Lady Seland charged out of the room so fast she nearly bowled me over in the hall. (You're right. This does happen to me quite a bit.) When I regained my balance I found her staring at me as though I were a snake, or even a lion.

Then, 'Yes! You!' she shouts. Her face is very, very red. She strides past me, pulling on her gloves. At the door she turns and stares at me. 'You, miss, should have been sent away years ago! I told your mother then and I've told her today.'

When I go into the room my mother and grandmother stop speaking.

'What was that about?' I say innocently.

They exchange a glance. 'It was about the inappropriate survival of dinosaurs,' said my grandmother dryly. 'And the end of a friendship that has gone on far too long. Margaret Seland has departed from this place. She'll not come here again.'

* * *

All this, of course, is taking me away from my main concern today. That is the fact that the woman Honesty – who is my mother – arrives this afternoon. Mr Ellenberg has gone to collect her. She'll probably be at Bishop Auckland station at this minute, getting into my father's car, heaping up her luggage, settling down in the leather which, as I know, squeaks as you settle back in it.

I've been wondering how I should greet her, when I meet her. Should I curtsy? We learned how to curtsy at school for when a Member of Parliament came to present prizes. I had to curtsy when I got mine. And I've seen people curtsying on the picture screen at the cinema when they showed the King and Queen launching this great big ship. The King just looked like a trusty old sailor but the Queen was quite beautiful. Like a stiff doll.

When I asked my father whether I should curtsy to Honesty he laughed and asked why.

'Well, she gets up there on the screen like the Queen, and people curtsy to the Queen.'

He laughed again and ruffled my hair which is not so difficult since I had my bob. 'No need for curtsying and bowing in our lives, Rose. We should curtsy to no man. Or woman.'

'But what should I say?'

'Just say hello and smile. Then wait for her to say what she will say and answer her. It always works for me, however grand the person may be, or think they are. Don't worry, *charver*. It'll be all right.'

I'm sitting on the wall by the great door all coiled up about meeting Honesty when my mother Astrid comes up and pulls me to my feet. 'Come with me, Rose. Your grandmother thinks she can do without her lunch today, but we'll take a little picnic up to the garden for her, to help her through the day. It's not easy for her, losing her old friend. I know Keziah really is your grandma, but those two . . .'

I have to nod at this. 'Like a double-yolked egg. I always think that.'

She laughs and we make our way across the meadow to my grandmother's garden. We plough through the kingcups and the nodding heads of ragged Robin lurking in the long, still-damp grass, and our new black skirts and stockings get a little wet. I have to adjust my stride as my legs, these days, are rather longer than my mother's.

Four

The Garden Again

My grandmother is sitting making notes in the glasshouse, surrounded by her papers and catalogues. The glass walls are gleaming and the fruit is growing, bursting into well-pruned bud. The floor of the houses are all clean and scrubbed and the shrubs are staked, in order, in their pots.

These days it all looks just a bit like alien territory. When my grandmother was fully in charge with her garden boys, things were a bit more dilapidated than this, even though the garden and the glasshouses bloomed and produced in a mad cycle of growth. But when he finally came back from France, my father took on two ex-soldiers as gardeners. One of them knew lots about gardens and the other was very strong and enthusiastic. These two burly men soon had the allotments taken out and cleared away the detritus and got the garden back into trim.

These gardeners have always done the things my grandmother ordered but, ever enthusiastic, would decide to do much more than that. Then, as her arthritis got worse, she left most of the work to them; she let them have their head about the form, the look and the organisation of the garden. So of course we still have all our flowers and vegetables from the garden, with lots over to give away. And we still have this wonderful place in which to sit and work and play. But it was no longer Carmel's domain. No longer *her*.

451

Even so, she still comes here every day to sit at her table and look at her catalogues and order a few plants. The men plant the specimens willingly enough but when these plants grow in the garden they're lost to her. She has little interest in them.

On this soft June day, we find her at her table, pencil in hand. 'How kind!' she says brightly, as though we are visitors. 'Sandwiches!' She doesn't invite us to sit down with her. Then, after clearing space on the table for the plate and the flask, she looks up at my mother. 'Why don't you show Rose your wonderful books, Astrid? It's all part of her heritage, after all. Do show her.'

I can feel Astrid's hand trembling on my arm as we walk away from the glasshouse. 'My mother!' she says through grinding teeth. 'My mother can send one away as though one were some stranger or servant. The most important things happen to her when one is not there.' Her voice trembles and, astonishingly, she is crying.

I pull her down to sit on one of the garden benches that Lal Burnip made from a lightning-struck elm harvested from Low Wood. I stroke her arm until the hiccoughing stops. 'She's just in a mood about Keziah. You know what we said about them being like a double-yolked egg?' I say. 'Like you and my father. You're the same. A double-yolked egg.'

She plucks a handkerchief from her sleeve, dabs her eyes and blows her nose. 'You're such a romantic, Rose.'

'But to see you two . . .' I search around in my head. 'You're just like Jane and Mr Rochester.'

She shakes her head. 'It's not as easy as it looks, dear girl.'

'He seeks you out all the time. Whenever you're in the room he has to be close.'

Now she's blushing. 'Oh, Rose, you miss nothing.'

'A blind bat could see how much he thinks about you.' I'm quite cross with her now.

'It mightn't have been like that at all.' She sits up straighter and sniffs. 'I shall tell you something. A secret. You remember that your . . . that Jack . . . didn't come home from the war at the same time as Ambrose and Michael John? How we waited those months?'

'I do.' There was a lot of tension and whispering behind doors in those months.

'Do you remember I went to France to find him?'

'You brought him back.'

'I had quite a search for him. Went from town to town. They told me he was with some *romani* people – well, a *romani* woman who was looking for her family who'd been displaced in the war. Well, by the time I got there they'd found her relatives. He had stayed on with them.' She laughs suddenly. 'He did look wild. So young. Very brown. He looked just like he did the first time I ever saw him, riding a horse bareback on the road to Benbow.'

'He would be pleased to see you. There in France.'

She frowns. 'I don't know. Surprised, yes. We talked quite a bit. And with the woman too.'

'What was she like?'

'Well. Very hard, and very kind too, in the *romani* way.'

'Were they in love?'

She swivels round now, to look at me. 'He said no. He told me of a terrible thing that happened to a friend of his just as the war ended. A nightmarish thing. He said he didn't want to come home with the nightmare in his head.'

'So what did you do?'

She is pleating her skirt on her knee. 'I just took him in my arms.'

'Oh.' I try not to sound too disappointed. 'I thought you might have fought the woman.'

She really laughs at this. 'No. No. She was a good woman. This was all about the war, Rose. Michael John lost the use of his arm and so much of his confidence. Jack, for a while, lost the sense of who he was.'

I sit there, a bit stupefied, hardly daring to move. I'm honoured at this very grown-up confidence. I think perhaps that my days of standing behind doors are numbered.

She stands up. 'Well!' Her tears have dried on her face. 'If my mother says I must show you the books to make sure you know your Benbow heritage, then I must. I'll do this before the Lomas or Leeming in you, or any other part of you, takes you away from me altogether.' It's lucky that she's smiling now because I can't think up any reassuring words for her as I'm not sure myself just what is happening to me.

In the war when my father finally went away, Astrid set herself up in the garden in the end peach-house which she used as a studio. In the summer she'd cover two of the side walls with cardboard to give some shade, and make the heat bearable. She laid long planks of wood on the potting bench to use as her work table. The light in there is wonderful. The stove in the corner keeps it warm in winter and in the summer you cool the house by opening the double doors. She has the habit of vanishing down here to work. Just like Carmel, when you think of it.

She unlocks the padlock and pushes the door open. It only strikes me now that she still keeps the peach-house locked, even when the wild children from Benbow village are not roaming the garden. And we never venture in there even though we belong to the house. She's as cool as her mother Carmel in sending you away when she doesn't want you.

Her work space is very neat. This great table. Two kitchen chairs. A spider-legged easel. A battered bureau rescued from somewhere in the house, with books piled behind dusty glass. She pulls down the front of the bureau and there, wrapped in brown paper wrapping, is the book.

'It's done now, Rose, just about finished,' she says as she unties the string. 'At least one publisher in London has said he may be interested in publishing it. But your father . . . Jack . . .

says we must print it ourselves. Ever the businessman. More profit that way.' She pulls me down beside her.

We turn the pages. The title page declaring 'Carmel's Garden' is decorated by a frieze of spring flowers. Then, page by page, the garden year unfolds, showing the cycles of digging, planting, growing, watering and harvesting that make this garden live. Each page has close-ups of flowers and plants and three or four lines of elegant, spidery writing describing the important things in this part of the year. Within the paintings the same writing identifies the plants with their country garden names. Some of the pictures even show Carmel in the distance, wearing her battered old hat, kneeling at her work. One or two of them show me, much smaller than I am now. The child-me is kneeling beside Carmel, giving her a hand. I blush at this strange outside-view of a self that I know so well from the inside.

I sit back. 'That is amazing. Wonderful! It is so clever. You are so very clever.'

'We're all clever, in our own way.' She shrugs. 'Your grandmother told me this morning that I'd better get a move on printing it, before . . . well, before it's too late.'

I know what she means and turn back through the book to hide the flood of feeling that her words have set off in me. A world without *both* Keziah and Carmel is unthinkable. For the first time in this whole week tears start to squeeze into my eyes.

She takes the book from me and places it on the big table. 'There's more, Rose. More of your heritage.' She nods at a line of perhaps a dozen brown-backed notebooks on the shelf of the bureau then selects one and places it in front of me. 'You know I keep these drawing books?'

I nod. They are usually somewhere near her and she is often scribbling in them. But no one sees into them.

'This one was from the year that Constance and Honesty and I went to America.'

I turn the pages. The great ship with funnels, seen from the dock. Constance in a high-necked gown with her massy hair swept up. Some kind of a bandsman on the ship's deck. On the sixth page I come to a picture of myself, staring out, smiling. No. Another person like myself. Her eyes are open and bright. Her hair, wild and curly, is much darker than mine and will hardly be kept in her demure cap.

'You are very like Honesty,' says my mother. 'Except that she is very dark and you are very fair.'

'Did you like her?'

She is silent for a second. 'I think I quite loved her in the end. She was so brave.'

I turn the pages. Another drawing of the great ship from somewhere on the deck. An image of Honesty brushing Constance Redoute's hair, which drops in waves down to the seat of the dressing stool. Honesty's arm reaches out in a pure arc. I stare at her and then something dawns on me. 'When you drew her doing this, brushing the hair, was she . . . was I already there?' I'm not entirely ignorant. I do know it takes nine months to have a human baby.

'Yes,' she said. 'None of us knew then, not even Honesty.'

I turn the pages and we move to more neutral ground. A great mountain. A very peculiar castle. A tall woman, very dark-skinned, with round glasses, sitting up very straight. A man with a moustache sitting up just as straight on a horse, as though he owns the world. She tells me that's Constance's father. 'He was a very fine man, Rose, one of the finest I've ever met. I was so very fond of him. I think I loved him too.'

Then I come to tiny sketches of a baby wrapped tightly in woven clothes. Her eyes are closed and her hand is reaching out to clutch the edge of the blanket. I have a very tight feeling in my chest. I know who that is.

I close the book. 'And my real father, who is he?'

She's already shaking her head. 'You must talk to Honesty about that, Rose. It's her place to tell you about that.'

'Do you know nothing of him?'

'Honesty! Talk to Honesty about those things.' She closes the book and puts it with its fellows on the shelf. 'These books here, Rose, are for you. I have put that in my will. You are to have them. Not the boys. Not Jack. They are for you.'

'*Your* will? You're not going to . . .?'

She laughs. 'Not for a million years yet. I just wanted to tell you this today.'

I help her parcel up the big book and lock the bureau so that all the books are safe. Now I see the need for the lock on the door. I look at the books through the glass and have a vision that makes me blink: of myself poring over them with other children. Just as Kenneth and I have pored over my grandfather Rufus's books with Mr Ellenberg.

Continuity. Perhaps that's all that families are. Not so much blood as continuity. Even if Mr Ellenberg does go to Russia like a lunatic and get himself killed, we are his continuity. He'll always be alive in our heads, just as old Rufus is alive in my head even though I've never met him. And even though, as I've discovered this week, he's not my blood any more than Astrid or Carmel are my blood. It's not about blood. I know their story and in my heart I know how they see their world. I am their continuity.

Five

The Arrival

We've had nearly a hundred days now without rain, and the church is hot and still. It smells of dust and sweat, cut grass, lavender and roses. My grandmother's gardeners have scythed grass from the meadows and raided her garden stores. She asked Melanie Tyler to spread the cut grass and the dried lavender and rose-petals on the deep window sills before the pointed windows and on the floor behind the altar. All this grown stuff is heaped up in aromatic tides that lift and stir every time the big door at the back is opened. I know this because every time the door is opened I turn round to see if it is Honesty.

It never is.

The pews in this little church are small. I sit between my mother Astrid and my grandmother Carmel. In the pew behind sit my little brothers with our father Jack. Uncle Mick sits next to Rufus. Behind them again sit Uncle Ambrose and Aunt Gwennie, and Mrs Taggart with the baby on her lap, and Melanie Tyler. (Melanie hurried in late, as she'd been delayed uncovering the carpets again. My grandmother was angry when she'd found Melanie was defending the carpets from the feet of travellers.)

Across the aisle the massive frames of Freddy and Auntie Edith almost fill the front pew. The pew behind them is left clear for Honesty and Mr Ellenberg.

The woman Honesty's still not here.

The murmuring people who fill the rest of the church are almost all women: mostly travellers and *romani*. Their menfolk are crowded outside, sweating in the dry heat. Their caps, swept off when we all trooped down from Benbow Hall to the church, will be firmly back on their heads to keep them cool. Keziah's coffin has been here in the church for two nights, watched over by Freddy and Edith in turns. It's a very fine coffin, made by the *romani* coach maker who built the grand coach my father has never really used. It is strange to think it will be burned to ashes.

Now the vicar moves forward and mutters something to Freddy, who looks round towards the back of the church then nods. His face is dark and dry-looking. He doesn't look like the Freddy I know.

The vicar starts the service. He's two minutes into some holy babble when the grass on the sill beside me lifts in the breeze as the door at the back clashes. The vicar puts a hand on his book and pauses. Everyone looks round, so it's easy for me to do the same. The women closest to the door gasp and murmur to each other. I catch my breath when I see the two women coming down the aisle. Like the other women in the church they are dressed in black but there the resemblance ends. The younger one – who can only be Honesty – wears a tiny black hat with a long downward sweeping feather on her very short hair. Her immaculately cut moiré coat ends at her knees, leaving the *whole* of her silk-clad calf and ankle in public view above her high-heeled suede shoes! The older one is my mother's friend Constance Redoute. Her outfit is not so daring but she too demonstrates a Parisian elegance that can only be described as alien to this place. Myself, I think it's all wonderful. I want to wear clothes like that, I want to walk like that: a confident person who knows she's watched but affects not to care.

I drag my attention back to the vicar and feel rather than see Mr Ellenberg shepherd the two women into their pew. The rest of the short service is a blur to me. I can feel her behind me. I know that she's looking at me. Suddenly Freddy, my father and my uncles are going forward to pick up the coffin. Two *romani* men walk right down from the back of the church and take up a position at the back. At a word from my father they all lift the coffin onto their shoulders and begin a steady movement down the aisle.

Only Auntie Edith is crying but I can feel the despair of my grandmother beside me like a cold blast of air. She moves out of the pew with my mother Astrid close behind her. My grandmother takes the arm of the weeping Edith and they hustle down the aisle after the coffin. I can hear other people moving behind me too, but I stay where I am, staring hard at the small peaks of lavender and rose-petals heaped up behind the altar. Gradually the little church reclaims its echoes and I know it's just about empty.

Then there is a click on heels on the floor. An exotic perfume far removed from lavender makes my nose prickle. With a rustle of silk Honesty sits down beside me. I keep staring at the altar.

'You must be sad about Keziah?' Her voice is low, musical. I want it to be ugly and croaking, but I don't know why. Her voice is as beautiful as herself. I don't want to like her but I do.

Finally, I turn to look at her. Her eyebrows are plucked into a fine dark line and she's wearing powder. She's even, if you can believe it, wearing lipstick. She looks young, girlish. She's unlike any mother I've ever seen. She's looking at me with such intensity I think she might eat me up.

I have to speak to stop myself being devoured. I look back at the altar. 'Of course I'm sad. Our Keziah was extraordinary. A magician. And she was my grandmother. I used to think she was my grandmother in one way but it turns out she's my grandmother in quite another.'

From beside me comes a long sigh. 'So you know? How long have you known?'

'Since the day Keziah died. Just before. She wanted me to know I was her daughter's daughter.'

'I'm sorry, Rose, so sorry.'

She sounds so desolate I want to cheer her up. 'No need for that.' My voice is loud. Too hearty. 'My family – the one I've grown up in – has suited me very nicely, thank you. And I've had Keziah anyway. I wouldn't have liked not to have Keziah.'

There is a long pause and she says, 'Good. I'm pleased about that. But if there's anything, anything I can do for you . . .'

It's funny. I am waiting to feel something but I don't. I don't feel that this very pretty woman beside me is my mother. I know about her and I'm curious about her. But I don't want to throw myself into her arms. I think if she put her arms round me I'd be embarrassed and that's my least favourite emotion. At least she hasn't done that.

'Just one thing,' I turn again and look at her. Then I blush when I see the tears in her eyes. 'They won't tell me one thing. About my father. I need to know about my father as well as my mother.'

She stares at me for a long time. Then, her words stumbling, her voice going from smooth to rough, she tells me this very extraordinary secret. I am embarrassed, angry, then I remember in the picture house seeing the film of the stocky, bearded sailor king making a quacking speech as he launched that great ship. He is another child of that old man that started me. He is a son. I am a daughter. I start to giggle, then laugh till my ribs hurt and my lungs ache.

Now she touches me, takes my arm. 'Rose, what is it?' She shakes me. 'Rose, stop. Take a breath or you'll choke.'

I calm down a bit. 'I'm all right,' I gasp. 'For a minute it was just so funny. Ridiculous.'

'It is. It was.' She nods. 'But look what happened. You're here. The darling of the house. That Mr Ellenberg never stopped talking about you all the way from the station. Says Astrid and our Jack think the sun shines out of you. You're Mrs Benbow's rose-child and the one at last to give peace to Keziah.' She pulls me to her and I am enfolded in black silk and drenched in Parisian perfume. 'Mebbe it was worthwhile after all.'

I pull away from her then, and make air and space between us. 'Glad you think so.'

She laughs. 'Now don't go sulky on me, now.' She's pulling on her gloves and with them her stranger's armour. 'I needn't have told you this but I thought you had a right to the truth. I wasn't going to tell you, not at all. But the old magician Keziah pulled me here so I can tell you the truth. I felt it. And now, you have the truth your own self and can judge for yourself, but if I was you I'd keep this a very deep secret. It would blight your life otherwise. Only one thing that old feller ever did for you and me. Give you life and me a child in the world, even if she really turns out to be another woman's child.'

I can feel the tension draining from me, I'm calm again. I can be polite. 'You have no other children?'

She laughs at this. 'One day, sweetheart, one day. I still have time.' Her voice has changed back again and she is a stranger.

The big door at the back clashes open and to my relief my mother is standing there illuminated by the sunlight she's just let in. She opens her arms wide. 'Rose! Honesty! Perhaps you should come. They are across at the *vardo* ready with the torches. Jack says you should come.'

Six

Honesty's Daughter

Astrid stood away from the crowd as the flames licked their way up into the still sky. At the front of the crowd she could see Jack with Honesty on one side and Carmel and Rose on the other. She slipped further and further back until she got to the wall by the forge. She sat down on the wall and rested her feet.

A few minutes later she was joined by Constance. 'I saw you escaping,' she said. 'It must be the smoke but I have an almighty headache.' They talked for a few minutes – more like warm acquaintances than friends – of Constance's belated medical studies in France and enduring problems of disposing of Richard's assets in Colorado. And the fact that her wealth had frightened off the only beau in whom she had the slightest interest, the Quaker ward cleaner from the army hospital.

Then Constance said, 'D'you know, Astrid, as I travelled here with Honesty, and then sat in that church, I was thinkin' of the very long arm of coincidence?'

'Were you, now?'

'I was thinkin' how you liked this quiet life and you always did. Wonderin' if it hadn't been for me you'd have not bothered to go to Seland House that weekend.'

'Probably not.'

'Then you wouldn't have made the bond with Honesty and neither of you would have come to America with me.'

'And I wouldn't have met Richard.'

'True. I wasn't too happy about that, was I? What an unbearable brat I must have been. Would that have made a difference, not meeting the General?'

'I sometimes think if I hadn't met Richard I wouldn't have come together with Jack. I wouldn't have had the courage. I might have had the feeling for him but would have been too shy. I would probably have ended up a dry, withered old maid instead of a mother and a painter. And perhaps a better daughter than ever I have been.'

Constance whistled. 'Is that so?'

'And Honesty would not have come to be a woman of the world. And you'd not have met Gertrude and become a suffragette and a nurse and now, it seems, a doctor. And all these things seem to me to be the essence of who you are.' She paused. 'And there would have been no Rose in my life.'

'I see that. Ain't it frightening?'

'It's wonderful, Connie. Thank God for the long arm of coincidence.'

Constance jumped off the wall and smoothed down her skirts. 'I must go and take a pill for this headache and wash some of the grime from my face. I swear it's covered with soot from the train and that weird fire.'

Astrid watched her hobble in her fine shoes down the wide field path. She called after her. 'Don't forget the funeral tea, Connie. Melanie Tyler would be really disappointed that the General's daughter missed her fine funeral tea.' She thought again about the long arm of coincidence and blessed the day when she went to the art class where she met Constance Redoute.

'I suppose you think it's all a bit gruesome.'

She looked up to see Honesty, who hitched up her short skirt even higher and perched on the wall beside her.

'I'm my father's daughter, Honesty. I respect these rituals.'

Honesty lit a cigarette, placed it in an elegant holder, and drew on it with evident enjoyment. 'You've done a great job with Rose, Astrid,' she said, using the name for the first time with comfortable familiarity. 'She's a great kid. She seems happy.'

'She makes other people happy. She's made me happy. She's taught my mother what it is to love a child. She has a certain quality.'

'Yeah. Like I say, she's a great kid.' Honesty blew on the tip of her cigarette, making it glow red. 'I told her about the night . . . when we first met? And the old man.'

'Have you? Well, if that's so she seems . . . well, she seems unfazed by it. You couldn't tell.'

'Good. I told her she should keep it a secret. That's not her real heritage. Nothing gained by . . .'

'Absolutely.'

Honesty drew on her cigarette. 'She's better off being the granddaughter of a *romani* queen than the daughter of some old king.'

'Absolutely.' Astrid paused. 'You're not thinking of . . . well . . . taking Rose with you?'

'I gave her to you. I told you she was yours. I wouldn't go back on that.'

'But Rose might decide for herself.'

Honesty shook her head. 'I don't see it.'

They both looked up as a great roar came from the crowd as another part of the *vardo* ignited and threw flames into the sky.

'Are you happy, Honesty?' said Astrid. 'I know you're famous, and good at what you do. But are you happy?'

'Are you?' said Honesty.

'I'd say I've had a happy life so far, especially because of Jack, and because of Rose herself. As I said. She made such a difference to me. For me.' She paused. 'You haven't answered my question. What about you?'

Honesty shook her head. 'My life has had some great spots, Astrid. A new film. Applause. Another investment that comes off. Building the house of my dreams. But I'm always alone.

Even with Slim there it seems I'm always on my own. When these things happen I sometimes think of the shadow life I might have had if I'd not been sent to that room that night. It makes me very angry. I have to go to my doctor and get pills to deal with the anger.'

'But your life . . . you might have had a very ordinary, perhaps a very mundane life . . .' Astrid found herself spluttering.

Honesty looked her in the eyes. 'Like yours, you mean?' Her voice faded as down the pathway from the dying fire came Rose and Michael John closely followed by Jack and the boys, and Ambrose and Carmel. Rose had sooty streaks on her face and a flake of black ash on her fair hair. Astrid reached up and removed it.

'Guess what?' Rose sat down on the wall beside Honesty and dragged Michael John to sit beside her. 'I was just standing there looking at the flames and I got an idea, right from Keziah. I swear it.'

Astrid had to smile. 'And what's that?'

'That Uncle Mick has to go to Russia with Mr Ellenberg. Being a soldier, he'll keep things in order and get them both safely there. And back. I think he needs an adventure. I told him it would be just like India only cold.'

'That's a fine idea,' said Jack, moving to sit beside Astrid. He put his arm round her.

'And what do you think?' Astrid asked Michael John.

He smiled thinly. 'I think you didn't know what you were doing when you brought the child into our house.'

This made them all laugh, even Kenneth who didn't quite know what it was all about; even Carmel who still had the trace of tears on her soot-grimed face.

Then one by one they walked on towards the house, leaving Rose on the wall with Astrid and Honesty. The three of them sat on in silence, watching the exotic cavalcade of excited, murmuring mourners pass by on their way back to the Hall and the funeral tea.

HONESTY'S DAUGHTER

When the last of them had gone Rose jumped from the wall. 'Come on,' she said. 'Aren't you starving?' She held out both hands. Honesty took one and Astrid took the other and the three of them walked together down the path to Benbow Hall.